ONE HUNDRED
AND ONE
WAYS

BANTAM BOOKS

New York Toronto London

Sydney Auckland

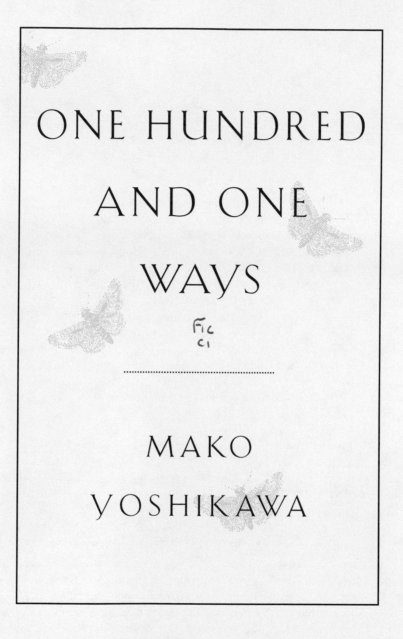

ONE HUNDRED AND ONE WAYS

....

MAKO YOSHIKAWA

ONE HUNDRED AND ONE WAYS
A Bantam Book/May 1999

Book design by Dana Leigh Treglia

Library of Congress Cataloging-in-Publication Data
Yoshikawa, Mako.
One hundred and one ways / Mako Yoshikawa.
p.   cm.
ISBN 0-553-11099-3
1. Japanese Americans—New York (State)—New York—Fiction.
I. Title.
PS3575.O645O54   1999
813'.54—dc21   98-45483
                                                        CIP

Published simultaneously in the United States and Canada

Bantam Books are published by Bantam Books, a division of Random House,
Inc. Its trademark, consisting of the words "Bantam Books" and the portrayal of a
rooster, is Registered in U.S. Patent and Trademark Office and in other countries.
Marca Registrada. Bantam Books, 1540 Broadway, New York, New York 10036.

PRINTED IN THE UNITED STATES OF AMERICA

BVG   10 9 8 7 6 5 4 3 2 1

For my mother, Hiroko Inoue Sherwin,
and my stepfather, James T. Sherwin,
who have always listened

CHAPTER ONE

SOMETIMES I CAN smell him, rain and salt and cigarettes and
something else, curiously, like cucumber, when I step out of the
shower. Out of a sense of delicacy, perhaps, he has never appeared to
me in the bathroom, but whenever I smell him I dress myself slowly,
making sure to hold in my stomach. I wring my hair and whip it back
from my face, I clean the mirror of steam and stretch and strike a few
casual poses in front of it. I lather lotion onto my body, first my legs, one
foot up on the sink at a time, then my stomach, smoothing in the cream
in small circles, and then my arms and last of all my breasts. I dress at a
leisurely pace, pulling my underpants up and sliding into them with a
swivel of the hips, snapping on a bra with all the strut and reluctance of
a striptease. I may have spent most of my life in New Jersey, but the
blood of a geisha courses through me yet.

When I first saw Phillip he was only a flicker in the corner of my
eyes, gone even before I turned. Only gradually did he become bolder,
moving out of the dusty corners to reveal his full form in quick flashes.
Now he will stay in one place for hours. If I am reading I can look up at
odd moments and he will be there, watching me. Often he will remain
with me until I finish the book.

He is fond of small spaces. Lazy as ever and cured, apparently, of his wanderlust, he likes crouching in a fetal position under my desk, and he enjoys folding his long body into an improbably tiny package so he can fit into the fireplace, along with the violet moths. Less frequently he peeks out from behind the door or he stands picturesquely shrouded by the curtains; every once in a while he lies on his side with his head propped up by an elbow. One day as I was reading, I reached for my iced tea and saw him through the clear glass of the coffee table, his face pressed right up against it and his eyes peering out at me as if I were a goldfish in an upside-down bowl. He is always naked, he hardly ever moves, and his expression never changes. Even his eyes are still.

Although I cannot control the time or the frequency of his visits, I still like him like this, silent and anonymous as my left hand. Behind the cover of my book I rub my thumb against the tips of the other fingers, feeling the shell-like hardness. I spread my hand open and look at it, palm up. In public I keep my secret clenched inside and when I lie in Eric's arms at night, I am careful to hold my fist against my breasts so that I fall asleep hugging it to myself. But when I think of Phillip, I like to feel my hand and gloat over the smoothness where the fingerprints used to be.

Maybe the lesson is that in the end, you can't buck genes. In my family, being haunted by a lost love is not even news. I come from a line of women with a tenacious grip on the man in their lives.

"Kiki, are you listening to me? Kiki."

I look down at my novel, in which I have long ago lost my place, and then back up at Eric. "I'm sorry," I tell him. "I didn't hear you. What did you say?"

His eyes grow round for a second, and I can tell he is holding his breath in as he does during sex: an unhealthy habit, which I need to tell him about at some point. Then he lets his breath out in an explosive laugh. "I don't know if I can say it again," he begins. "It was kind of a spontaneous thing."

He kneels beside me—why, with his trick knee?—so that his head is for once at a lower level than my own. His face is unexpectedly close to mine, and as he shakes his head, still laughing a little, his hair lightly brushes my shoulder.

Eric has brown silky hair and fine dark eyes, and his face, like his penis, is long and lean and intelligent. His knees are white and skinny, a disappointment, but he is handsome and elegant, and his arms and shoulders are well developed. If he stood next to Phillip, he would even seem husky.

His fingers are small and they are not much to look at when they are motionless, but when they move they twitch with an odd grace of their own. When I read, I use my fingers only to turn the page or occasionally push back my hair. When Eric reads, he takes copious notes in the margin, even on a newspaper, underlining and scribbling until his fingers are cramped, and his words outnumber those on the page. He can simultaneously crack two eggs, one in each hand, without getting his fingers messy and without spilling bits of shell into the bowl, and even in his sleep he remains active, wrapping my hair around and around his fingers until I cannot go to the bathroom in the middle of the night, because we are literally chained together.

"What if—" I begin, but I am interrupted by a tapping at the window. I turn around half expecting to see Phillip, yet it is only a fly banging against the glass. "Just a second," I say. I walk to the back of the room and open the window to let it out. The fly leaves and the heat and the smell of the city come pouring in, and I feel sticky where the outer air has touched me.

"You should cover yourself before standing in front of the window," says Eric, still on his knees beside the couch, all but clucking his tongue.

"They're all naked out there, too," I tell him reassuringly, a fact that can be verified by a glance into the windows across the street, but that does not necessarily alleviate the problem of prying eyes. Still, my rejoinder has the desired effect, for he nods, his lecture forestalled or, with any luck, forgotten completely.

Even with the air conditioner on, the heat is such that we made the decision to shuck our clothing for the day. I wear underwear only, without a bra, and he wears boxers, and for some reason (a trace of shyness, a hangover from his prim childhood?) socks. The heat is still uncomfortable, though, so much so that I cannot bear the pressure of my wristwatch, with its dainty weight of gold, and I remove it, exposing a neat line of untanned skin flanked by two rows of sweat.

As I turn away from the window, I stub my foot against the growing stack of Eric's discarded newspapers, and a couple of moths fly out, startled, from the pages of the *Wall Street Journal*. I have seen few moths in the apartment within the past year. In the coolness of the air-conditioned room lit by hazy sunshine, in spite of the life and the color that they bring, the flitting of the moths seems a slightly sinister warning, an omen invoking not the future but the past.

I love them. A year and a half ago my apartment was infested with ants, and though they were harmless scavengers while the moths nibble holes in the wool blanket on the sofa, I hated the ants and love the moths. Fragile and vulnerable, the moths make me feel as if I am living in a land of butterflies and scorpions, of love and cholera, where beauty and danger feed on each other. Eric warns me that the moths will eventually eat up all my sweaters, but I cannot bear to get rid of them. After all, there is something both noble and pathetic in the moth's love affair with light, and even if Eric refuses to admit it, the ones in my apartment are especially lovely, unusually large and flecked with bits of blue-green that turn into violet when they fly. There are moments when they actually gleam, luminescent, in the half-dark of the evening. If I squint or if I am not wearing my contact lenses they look like stunted blundering butterflies, and late at night if I wave my book at them as they flock against the wall near the light, they rise and fly away together like dust, perhaps, or dreams.

Eric has not moved from his vigil by the sofa. His knee must not be so bad today.

I am just sitting down again when the ring of the phone makes me jump. "Oh, not again," I say. The telephone is at Eric's elbow but he does not even turn to look at it, though I can tell from some shift in his posture that he has to restrain himself from doing so. Only a few months ago, he used to answer my phone freely.

I stand back up, stretch over him, and reach for the receiver. I speak into the phone, and there it is again: a whirring sound so high-pitched it makes my teeth ache. I shiver, suddenly wishing that I had kept my clothes on. I put the receiver down, sit back on the couch, and look at Eric, who is scratching the inside of his wrist with some attention. Usually full of unsolicited advice, he does not like to discuss these phone calls. When I ask, he tells me that he does not think I should call the police, despite the fact that I have been receiving these calls now for almost two months.

"Don't you think—" I begin, but looking up from his forearm, Eric interrupts.

"Will you marry me?" The words come out in a rush, so fast that at first I think I misunderstood. His face is flushed, his hair tousled, and he is clad only in boxers and socks: scant evidence here of the confident young lawyer who wooed me out of mourning. His gaze (so direct, bright and eager as a child's) unsettles me, and I drop my own onto the floor.

He has a hole in the heel of his left sock. I had not noticed it before, but with him kneeling, the bottoms of his feet sticking out behind him, no one could possibly miss it: a good portion of his heel is showing through the hole, and the whiteness of his skin makes a striking contrast to the dark blue of his sock. Yet his right sock looks brand new. Suddenly I realize that Eric must secretly favor his left leg, with its problem knee, when he walks, and I chalk up yet another question for my grandmother, one more to add to the list I have been compiling for her arrival. Did my rich and powerful grandfather, in whose presence the world cowered and bowed very low, secretly wreak havoc upon his footwear with his limp? And did she, too, want to swallow both a laugh and a lump in her throat when she saw how ridiculous was his exposed patch of heel?

"You've been on your knees—your bad knee—this whole time, waiting to propose?" I say at last.

"It's killing me," he says, not a bit sheepish, if anything proud.

"Come sit down," I say, patting the spot on the couch beside me. "I can't think, knowing you're in pain."

The bones of his knee click loudly as he straightens it, and he clambers to his feet with a measure of awkwardness. Taking a seat at a decorous distance from me, he says, "I know it hasn't been long—"

"—Just a year and a bit—"

"—but I'm sure," he says. He pauses and then he adds, in a voice so low I have to stoop to hear, "I'll always love you, you know. Scout's honor."

This whisper is so unlike his usual confident tone that I am struck with the strangeness of this scene. This is not the proposal I would have expected from him, for who would ever have guessed that Eric Lowenson would kneel in front of a woman clad only in her underwear, and pledge eternal devotion with one foot exposing a worn sock, and two fingers upheld in a childtime vow? He, the man who loves to stage meticulously planned pleasures: one evening, a fine silver bracelet presented with a flourish on the top of the Empire State Building, and another afternoon, my birthday, a bottle of wine, along with two glasses, hidden behind a bush (and, miraculously, still there) when we went rowing in Central Park. The only thing he forgot that afternoon was the corkscrew, a disastrous omission, as he cut his fingers so badly when he broke open the bottle that I ended up turning twenty-six in the emergency room.

"No ring," he says, mistaking the reason for my glance at his empty hands. "Sorry—this really was a spur-of-the-moment thing."

I shrug. "You do know, don't you, that I haven't forgotten Phillip," I say.

"I know. But you're almost there, right?" he says, and then answers his own question for me. "So it's not a big deal."

"And your family? After all, I know they're upset about me not being Jewish, and there's the Japanese thing. Plus my grandmother's coming soon, and she's—well, you know."

"Don't be silly," he says with some relief, on firmer ground here. "My family's going to have to like it, and once they meet you, they *will* like it, because they'll like you. And as for your grandmother . . ." Waving away the monumental presence of the past with one clean sweep of his hand, he continues, "She's just an old lady. She hasn't been a geisha now for what—half a century?"

I nod absentmindedly, troubled, as I so often am with Eric, by a feeling that I am in the wrong story. As if I were a glass, Eric sees in me a future that mirrors his own. It is a world in which moths eat sweaters, bills are paid on time, and things are no more than what they seem; a place in which my grandmother, stripped of her geisha past, emerges looking gray, shriveled, harmless. What Eric will give me is a reason not to wait and watch by the window; what he offers is a band of gold that anchors me to earth, a talisman to prohibit old loves, no matter how dear, from coming back from the dead.

He sees in me a future that I myself could never see. But then again, my sight never has been very good.

"Okay," I say. "Thank you. It'd be good to marry you."

For the second time today, his eyes grow round. Startled, even thrown off-balance, he struggles visibly to maintain his smile for a moment, and I think, belatedly, that I spoke too simply and too soon, a girl accepting the offer of an ice-cream cone, a stroll in the park, an umbrella held over her in the rain. Eric quickly scratches at his arm again, troubled as well, perhaps, by a sense that I am not a part of his story.

But the moment passes, and soon we are kissing on the crackling, tearing pages of his newspaper, my novel tossed to the floor.

The bedroom is almost cool, the curtains still drawn from last night. Sitting on top I climax, as usual, long before he does. He reaches out and holds my hips still; his own movements slow and he pauses, as he sometimes likes to do in the middle of his lovemaking. "Let me look at you," he murmurs, and gathering my hair at its ends, he pulls it back until my throat extends and my back arches, to a degree just shy of pain.

All I can see is the ceiling, but I feel him place his hand on my exposed throat and clasp it for a moment, as if in preparation for a murder. Then he lets his hand slide slowly down my collarbone, over my breasts, my ribs, my stomach. "I can't believe you're all mine," he says, but there is a cockiness to his touch that belies the humility of his words. He releases my hair, then, and I bend my head forward again, to find him still absorbed in the contemplation of my body. It is a gaze of satisfaction, the conqueror surveying his loot, his proudly won land.

When I was an overweight teenager and my prospects of ever finding a boyfriend were depressingly dim, I never thought I would have a man who actively wanted me, let alone enough to gloat over my body.

"I am a lucky man," he whispers. I am silent, looking down at him, but he has begun moving with a passion I could not have foreseen, and he does not seem to care.

Afterwards we return to the living room and pick up my Jane Austen and his papers. But before I can start reading, he reaches out once more and gathers me to him. "Hey," he says into my ear, "now that we're engaged, can I call you Yukiko?"

With my face buried in his shoulder, I let my smile slip away. I abandoned my given name for good when I left high school, but Eric has wanted to call me by it ever since he saw my driver's license.

I consider telling him that I gave up the name because I did not enjoy being saddled by a three-syllable clunker that everyone pronounced wrong, no matter how often I explained that the second syllable should not be stressed. I ponder saying that for all that I would like to bear the same name as my grandmother, it is bad enough to have bone structure and hair that brands me as foreign on the streets of New York, let alone a name that does, too. I think of explaining that I hate that Yukiko means Snow Child in Japanese.

But I have presented these same points to him countless times before, and they have never worked yet.

"Are you sure you don't have an Asian-woman fetish?" I say, trying to keep my tone light, but in vain.

He pushes me away so he can peer into my face. "Are you going to start that again?"

I look away, deliberating the question.

He sighs. "I'm sorry I brought it up. I just prefer Japanese names, that's all. We're not going to fight just after getting engaged, are we?"

"But you know that those men who ask me out in coffee shops, and who always try to talk to me in Japanese, and secretly yearn to see me dressed in a kimono, would just so much prefer Yukiko to Kiki. . . ."

"Stop it," he says. "I don't have an Asian-woman fetish, okay? I would never ask you to walk on my back, and I wouldn't—"

I freeze, stilled, momentarily, by the memory of a dark room with a crooked pool table, and a tall man I had fled from without a word. "What did you say?"

"I said I'm not going to ask you to—"

Quickly, before he can repeat that phrase, I stop him. "Ever heard of the expression 'one hundred and one ways'?"

He wrinkles his forehead. "It rings a bell," he says. "Why?"

I shake my head, and manage to keep my voice even. "Just something somebody told me once. I'll tell you about it sometime."

I reach out and draw him close again. My left hand is pressed against his back and as I slide my fingers across the smoothness of his skin, I imagine that I can feel the emptiness in the center of each of my fingertips. "Promise me," I say, my voice muffled against his shoulder. "Promise me you aren't attracted to me because I'm Japanese."

Again he draws back to look me in the face. His eyes, searching mine, move back and forth as Phillip's always did. He draws a deep breath in, and holds it. I count the seconds, waiting, expecting and dreading a lecture, but when he finally lets his breath out (. . . seven Mississippi . . .), his voice is quiet. "I promise," he says. "What's gotten into you?"

"Nothing," I say. "I'm fine. Should we go out to dinner tonight, to celebrate?"

He nods. "But—"

I pick up the phone and drop it in front of him. "Here, make a reservation," I say, standing up and moving away before he has a chance to refuse. "I'll be right back."

Grandmother, I will say, my tongue stumbling over the word that I learned three months ago, when my mother first told me about her visit: *Obaasama*. What did you do when faced with the assumptions of the men who desired you, the men who believed you possessed a set of keys that would unlock their bodies with a groan, one hundred and one times, one hundred and one ways?

In the bathroom I automatically flick on the light and I catch a quick glimpse of myself in the mirror before I turn the light off again; my face is pale and vague without the definition of fresh makeup. I shut and lock the door, and then I put down the lid on the toilet and sit on it to rest. The faint light coming through the shades of the small high window illuminates the toiletries lining the shelves. Eric's green toothbrush has a place of its own in a cup of its own. My brown toothbrush, which is in a smaller cup next to his, looks dwarfed and dull by comparison.

One night I sat on the edge of the tub and watched Eric as he brushed and flossed his teeth. A lot of people remark on how striking his smile is, but I think his teeth are too large and too white. He is very proud of the fact that he has never had a cavity. Standing up, I move my toothbrush to another shelf.

I lift the lid of the seat and flush the toilet, letting the good clean water explode away, and then I step out of the bathroom. The hallway to the living room is long and tunnel-like, and my feet move slowly. As I pass the open doorway to my bedroom, a movement out of the corner of my eye catches me and then I stop and stare into the room because Phillip is sitting on the windowsill, his arms hugging one leg to his chest while the other dangles down just above the floor. Apart from the threat of Eric in the next room, Phillip is in plain view from the window across the way, perhaps even from the street.

He looks more solid and vivid than he has for a long time. These past few weeks I have been able to see the light shining through him when he is positioned at certain angles, but today he is opaque, every feature distinct, even with the sun streaming behind him. As usual he is expressionless, watching me intently.

Grandmother, I will say, *Obaasama*. When my grandfather tendered you his far less reputable proposal, did you, too, feel inside you the silence of a house in mourning? Or were you able to blot out the memory of the eyes of your secret lover, and the thought of a sick and hysterical woman? Were you so happy that you walked away from your geisha home without a backward glance?

"Kiki." Eric is calling out to me but caught beneath the set gaze of Phillip's eyes, I cannot move. "Kiki, what are you doing back there?" I wrench myself away from Phillip with a suddenness that tears me.

"I'm coming," I say to Eric. As I walk past the bookshelves I run my hand along the spines of the books, and they bump against my fingers like actual bones. When I enter the living room I keep my eyes fixed upon Eric, handsome and elegant in spite of his knees, but I can feel Phillip's unblinking gaze piercing my back until I can no longer bear it; I tell Eric I have a headache so that I can escape to the bedroom and lie with my back pressed against the bed, my hair fanning outwards as my grandmother's never did, and my eyes scanning the blank ceiling in a futile effort to avoid the now empty windowsill.

There is time, in the last seconds before I fall asleep, for me to wonder once again at the oddness of Eric's proposal. How strange to run smack up against a happily-ever-after ending, when here I had been thinking that my story's just begun.

CHAPTER TWO

THE SLIT BETWEEN an Oriental girl's legs is as deliciously slanted as her eyes. Or so the saying goes, according to one man who never did find his way to my bed.

It happened seven years ago, when I was a sophomore in college, and still overwhelmed with gratitude for what a toss of the head (a shake of black hair) could do to the male students who hovered around me.

"I bet you do know one hundred and one ways, don't you," he said, putting down his drink.

"One hundred and one ways of what?" I asked, raising my voice slightly: the music from the party was audible still, though distant enough not to be deafening.

"One hundred and one ways to love a man," he said. "That's what you Japanese women—or is it Chinese?—are supposed to know."

His hand drifted down to rest on my shoulder. I felt an itch beginning where his hand rested; it spread upward to my throat, the back of my neck, my scalp. Slowly, as if without thinking, I eased my shoulder out from under his touch.

"Says who?"

"I don't know. It's the name of a book or something. Maybe it's some geesha thing."

He was tall and well built, athletic as well as smart, and cousin to one of the more famous families of the country: women sighed and re-crossed their legs as he walked by. I had been flattered by his attention, enthusiastically allowing myself to be led to this dark room, which was empty save for a crooked pool table, and two worn armchairs placed conveniently close together in a dark corner.

"Geisha," I said, correcting him automatically. "It's pronounced geisha."

"Whatever," he said, moving his face closer to mine. "Anyway, shouldn't you walk on my back or something?"

A crash of glass and a burst of laughter came through the door, followed shortly by a group of six or seven revelers. Without noticing us, the group crowded around the pool table; fishing a cue and a couple of balls from the ground, they began to argue loudly about who would be first to play.

His face was two inches away from my own. The smell of alcohol was strong on his breath.

"You are so pretty," he said. His hand was once again upon my shoulder; the itch was once again spreading. "You know what they say about girls like you?"

Blue eyes wide, he gazed at me; he did not seem to need to blink. I stared back, for the moment, spellbound: mesmerized as any student faced by a charismatic don.

"The slit between an Oriental girl's legs," he said, reciting, as if by rote, as if it were a line he had learned at school, "is . . ."

I jerked my head back, clearing it of his spell; I stood up, none too steadily, and began to walk away, picking up my pace as I went.

". . . as deliciously . . ."

That well-bred Boston voice was raised a notch now. At the pool table, heads were turning, curious glances cast our way.

". . . slanted . . ."

I was all but running at the end, but he finished his sentence in a piercing stage whisper that sliced through the music, silenced the crowd at the pool table, and followed me across the room and out the door.

For years now, though especially of late, I have been hoarding questions to ask my grandmother Yukiko. These questions start out to be about her life, and then turn out to be about my own. But then again, the differences between us have always seemed slight.

We have never met, except once or twice over the phone. Her English is poor, my Japanese worse. Yet my mother assures me that three months from now, when Yukiko comes to New York, we will be able to communicate, and I believe her. Even on the phone, in those recent conversations filled with static, stammers, and banalities about our health, there is a bond that connects my grandmother to me. It is not our physical resemblance that draws us together, nor does it matter that we share the same name. I know that our similarities run deeper than that, for I have thought long and hard about the key to our secret kinship, and it is this: what a geisha is to Japan, a Japanese woman is to America.

My grandmother worked before the war, when being a geisha meant bedroom entertainment as well as the more innocent pleasures of music and party help. These days, of course, business suits are the norm for Japanese women, and a geisha decked out in her old-style kimono rides on the novelty of being as patently a period piece as a dinosaur. But even back when my grandmother worked, a geisha trafficked in sexual nostalgia, since her makeup and especially her manner were heavily, headily redolent of another era, a time in which the division between a man and a woman was even more sharply drawn.

In Japan and even America, the word "geisha" casts a spell of enchantment, conjuring the apparition of a beautiful woman, demure, docile, highly sexed and, most of all, always available. What my grandmother was to her customers, so, too, am I to a significant number of American men, Eric among them: the repository of wiles, feminine and erotic, one hundred and one of them.

....

My detailed knowledge of my grandmother comes from my mother. After my father left us, she took over his old job of nightly storytelling, and began lulling me to sleep with stories from our past. I could not tell the difference between the stories of my grandmother and the tales of princesses and dragons and peas that my father had read to me from books, so that even now, life in Japan seems shrouded in myth and mystery, remote and impossible as the pumpkin that turned into a coach.

My mother never tried to teach me Japanese. We did not throw beans to bring luck and chase the trolls away in February, nor did we decorate bamboo with wishes scrawled on paper and cranes made of origami in July, and we did not light lanterns or leave food in the cemetery during the week in the summer that our ancestors return to earth. Instead we faithfully punctuated the end of December with a pine tree, the third weekend of November with a turkey, and the last day of October with a pumpkin candlelit from within. We ate with fork and knife; I did not know how to use chopsticks until the age of twenty-four, when Phillip showed me how.

But almost in spite of myself, those nighttime stories about my grandmother got under my skin. My mother told me the stories in her usual measured way, with little variety of expression and such leisured pacing that I often had to break in and bark at her to hurry, or I would fall asleep before she finished. Yet my barking was to no avail, since the cadences of my mother's storytelling never changed; every night I fell asleep with the singsong of her voice murmuring on, and her words and images blending with my dreams.

I am, perhaps, more Japanese than I know.

CHAPTER THREE

WHEN MY GRANDMOTHER Yukiko worked as a geisha, she kept her hair coiled in a round tea box next to her as she slept. Every night she brushed out her hair, the ends of it tickling the upper slope of her buttocks, and poured it into the box in a glossy black pretzel before she knelt to crawl into her futon.

Although a restless sleeper, she managed to wake in the mornings after her nights off with her hair more or less still in its rolls. The essence of the tea that had once been stored in the box lingered still, and faintly scented her hair with the poignant smell of smoking leaves in autumn. But after her working nights she usually woke with her hair impossibly tangled, and damp and rank with a strange man's sweat.

The box was lacquered black on the outside and red within, with a spidery pattern of pine trees along its walls. Every morning a fourteen-year-old apprentice put it away, along with the futon, which had to be folded and lifted and stowed into a closet, while Yukiko brushed out her hair again and rolled it up on her head. She used two pins carved out of ivory to hold it in place. Her hair made a heavy crown, but she always kept her head upright, her neck long, and her back effortlessly straight.

She had come a long way from when she was a child. She was born on Hokkaido, the northernmost island of Japan, where the climate, with its dark, snowbound winters and long-lit summers, came closer to that of the continent than that of the rest of Japan, and where there was only one carefully tended crop of rice per year, growing a rich green through the water that mirrored the coolie hats of the peasants and the cranes flying in the sky. In Hokkaido the West could be felt in more than the weather. At some distant point in the past, the people there had intermingled with Russians. They were therefore taller and fairer than the other Japanese, and as such much admired.

Yukiko's mother had been married at the age of fourteen. A small, plain woman who still looked like a child long after her wedding, my great-grandmother Akiko was blessed with a sunny disposition and a miraculous store of energy. As poor a sleeper as her daughter later became, she stayed up far into the night, cleaning and doing the cooking for which her work in the fields left her little time, and humming all the while. As if her nonstop activity, her bad sleeping habits, and her constant humming had drained her body of the capacity for much noise, she spoke in a lisping voice that was hardly ever more than a whisper. Demonstrative to an extent that was not often seen in their little village, she hugged her children often. They paid her back with their adoration.

Yukiko was a tomboy, spending her free hours in the trees with her three brothers rather than sewing or throwing bean sacks with the neighborhood girls. Serious and given to strange fancies, she lacked her mother's easy charm but had apparently inherited more than her share of plainness, with dark skin, gangly limbs, and mortifyingly large feet that outran, outjumped, and outclimbed those of her brothers. Her hair was gorgeous, though, even then, and her mother stroked it often, marveling aloud at its softness and weight.

From an early age Yukiko and her brothers labored with their parents in the fields. In the spring she waded into the paddies that had been flooded with water, and set the roots of the baby rice plants into the mud. She developed cricks in her neck and back from weeding all day, and ran screaming with her brothers to keep away the birds. They were helped in this last endeavor by the scarecrow they had fashioned by tying two sticks together in the shape of a cross; dressed in an old cotton kimono, it flapped to great effect when the wind blew.

The peasants worked the land for a local lord, whom they regarded with an ancestral awe that bordered on religious worship, and an inkling of scorn and condescension that they did not admit even to themselves. The scion of a minor dynasty, the lord had been born into wealth and power, but while his rule had once extended over seven villages, with the decline of the feudal system the base of his power had shrunk steadily until it consisted only of this: his handsome house and its tidy gardens, and the fields, no more than fifty acres, where the rice grew. At the height of his career he had been but an ineffectual ruler, petty and weak. Now he spent all his time watching the peasants work the land. Leaning slightly forward, his old eyes weeping in the sun and the wind, he stood all day at the edge of the fields with his hands clasped behind his back. At his feet, the birds feasted fearlessly on the grains of the rice crop.

At twelve, Yukiko was lean-hipped and unusually tall, with features that were spare and clean. She could have passed for a boy had it not been for her breasts, which were clumsy and enormous, an embarrassment far worse than her feet.

The boys in the village made loud rude comments about mosquito bites and bee stings whenever they were in Yukiko's presence. Among the girls it was fashionable to be smooth and straight, as streamlined as a boy, and so to them Yukiko was an object of pity. Her breasts distorted the lines of the cotton kimonos she wore in the summer and threatened to burst the folds open, straining to break free. Arriving before her when she walked through a door, they eclipsed her entrance. Even worse, they weighed her down so that she could no longer run with ease as her brothers did; they flopped from side to side, up and down, in great untidy arcs, and they continued to sway even after she stopped, leaning against a tree and panting.

Like mushrooms, they seemed to have sprouted overnight, but they were far more difficult to accommodate. The young Yukiko managed poorly, underestimating her own dimensions and banging into the table when she bent over with the dinner tray, and whacking walls and people when she suddenly turned, so that at night when she bathed by the light of a waxed paper lantern, she was not startled to find bruises the color of a sunset, blue and red and gold, splashed across each of her breasts.

There was a new ungainliness to all of her movements, an almost touching awkwardness that made her mother bite her lip and smile with narrowed eyes. Although the girls in her school giggled, they winced with her, too, when she miscalculated yet again, ramming her chest into the sharp edge of her desk.

But the men of the village were fascinated by Yukiko's breasts. Even the local lord, hovering with milky eyes at the fields' edge, covertly watched them as they bounced by.

That Yukiko showed signs of being a famous beauty at the age of fourteen, after years of almost remarkable plainness, was not really all that surprising, given the peculiar nature of her appeal. Even when she reached her prime, she would not conform to the standard ideals of Japanese beauty. She was too tall; her skin was not white, but olive; her face was too long and her hair, while strikingly lovely, was almost over-poweringly full. Yet she was breathtaking, perhaps all the more because of the slightly foreign flavor of her looks, at fourteen, in the year that spring failed to turn into summer, when the rains came so heavily the roads turned to mud, the walls of her family's house rotted, and the crops failed.

In that year of hardship, the peasants elected an envoy to petition the lord for extra money, but their requests were denied and the lord re-treated into his house. Yukiko's younger brother, always sickly, came down with pneumonia and almost did not recover. He crept around the house like a wraith, his kimono hanging loosely on him, dark shadows beneath his eyes. It was the thought of his well-being that kept Yukiko from damning her father forever for the decision he made concerning her fate. For he never gave her a choice about becoming a geisha. On the twentieth windy, rainy day in August, Akiko, acting on his orders, and crying all the while, brushed out Yukiko's hair, dressed her in a red kimono borrowed from a cousin, and took her to an old woman in the neighboring village, a former geisha, who bought young girls and sold them in Tokyo. Yukiko fetched a high price, enough money to keep her whole family in rice and pickled plums for two years.

On the day that Yukiko left, her father hugged her hard. "You are a good girl," he said gruffly, adding in a lower tone, "Your brother will die otherwise." It was not an apology, nor even a full acknowledgment of all that she was being asked to give up for the family, but in later years, Yukiko was to recall this last statement, and to appreciate the measure of understanding that it afforded her: a glimpse into the choices, all incomparably bleak, that her father had been forced to face. She had hated him then, and could not bring herself to return his embrace, yet she never forgot those last words.

Their feet shuffling and their faces red, her older brothers wished her well and said good-bye without meeting her eyes. She had bathed with them, and napped curled up beside them; she had raced them, climbed trees with them, and worked in the fields by their side. They had always staunchly fought for her against the bullies of the village. As she bowed back to them, she heard her younger brother wailing softly inside the house.

Akiko had to reach her arms up to draw the head of her tall daughter towards her. She promised in her lisping whisper that she would go to Tokyo within two years, before Yukiko's apprenticeship ended, to buy her and bring her back to Hokkaido. Then she wept like the child that she still almost was, while Yukiko, white-faced but dry-eyed, clung to her for the last time.

It was a long, hard trip to Tokyo. Along with the ancient geisha and another peasant's daughter, Yukiko took a train from her village to the southern coast of the island. The crossing to the mainland was rough, a ten-hour ride in a creaky boat over choppy water, and after arriving there, they rode on another train for two days until they reached Tokyo. There they clambered into a rickshaw, pulled by one man. Traveling through streets dense with people and houses, they arrived at nightfall at the geisha house, set on a street lined with red paper lanterns.

At the geisha house Yukiko served her apprenticeship without undue complaint. She scrubbed the floors, put away futons, and carried buckets of water in and out of the house. Her work as well as her beauty pleased the mistress of the house, and she was signed on as an apprentice and given the music and dance lessons that would prepare her to be a geisha. She was one of the lucky girls. Heavy and dull-witted, the other peasant from Hokkaido was kept on as a servant, and another girl was sold to a brothel, where there was the same work without the fine clothes, the training in the arts, the good food, or the rich clients.

During her apprenticeship, Yukiko's function at parties was strictly ornamental. The flirtatious repartee, so much a part of any geisha event, was left to the older women. Yukiko's face was covered with white pancake makeup and she wore an embroidered kimono that trailed behind her, and an obi that dangled gracefully down her back. She wore clogs with five-inch heels and bells that heralded her arrival, and her hair was piled elaborately high on the top of her head. She towered over most of the men, but she managed to keep her back upright, fighting the urge to slump. Although her feet were still far too large, she had almost grown into her breasts. Under the supervision of an older geisha, she was learning to carry them with grace and dignity, if not with pride.

She poured tea and saké, bought and fetched rice facial powder and the lipstick that came in big enamel-painted seashells, and she carried the geishas' kimonos and fans. She practiced dancing until her body ached. Still, there were compensations. Yukiko watched closely, and she knew that the best geishas led lives that revolved around pleasure, and that they were feted and respected by everyone, not just by the clients and the apprentices, but by the merchants and the common people of the city as well. So her first compensation was that she had a goal that made all her hard work seem worthwhile: before her mother came to reclaim her and take her back to Hokkaido, she wanted to sample this life of luxury and leisure; she yearned to become a geisha, if only for a time.

Her second compensation was her friends. Along with five other young girls, she slept in a small room with a cold bare floor. High on the walls were windows, and at night they slid open and pale faces looked down on them. It became a game the girls played, timing the appearances of those pale faces, and they were soon so skilled at it that they could have whispered and giggled together throughout the whole night, if they only had the energy to do so.

In the winters, when their communal bedroom was bitterly cold, they slept together in pairs in their futons, and on those nights they whispered and giggled even more loudly together, rendered doubly giddy by the smoothness and the warmth of another person's skin. The other girls never knew who they would share their futons with, but for Yukiko, it was always the same. She liked all of the apprentices, but her closest friend, and the only girl she ever slept with, was Kaori.

When Yukiko first arrived at the geisha house, terrified by her new settings, shaken by exhaustion from her long trip, and sick with longing for her mother, Kaori had taken care of her. Hearing Yukiko's smothered sobs beneath her covers, Kaori had without a word slipped into her futon with her, and offered her the immeasurable comfort of two short, plump arms that reached around her neck, just as her mother's had done, and a rounded white shoulder on which Yukiko could rest her aching head.

Kaori and Yukiko soon became inseparable, so much so that they began automatically responding to each other's names, for no one, not even the other apprentices at the geisha house, could accurately remember which was Kaori and which was Yukiko. This despite the fact that they looked nothing alike, a seemingly ludicrously mismatched pair when they wandered the streets together: standing more than a full head shorter than Yukiko, Kaori was a girl who dimpled when she smiled and also when she frowned. She had a body made of nothing but smooth curves. Her face, pale and round, resembled the moon.

The daughter of a young geisha who had died while giving birth, Kaori had never lived outside of the geisha house, and she was riveted by Yukiko's tales of growing up in the country. Yet although she often said how much she, too, would like to go live in Hokkaido, Kaori loved everything about the geisha house, tackling even the most backbreaking of chores with a willingness and grace that reminded Yukiko of her mother.

While it may seem that Kaori's contentment with her lot was grounded in the fact that she had never known any other way of life, it was actually part of her nature. She met all of what the world threw at her with a wide-eyed smile, a deep-seated calm, and a touch of resignation that would have passed for philosophy in another time and place. Yukiko, who would spend a large part of her life trying to hammer what destiny had given her into the shape she thought it should be, admired Kaori's stoic acceptance of the all-too-often unwanted offerings of fate, but never came close to attaining any semblance of it. Still, she did learn from Kaori to bear the hard work with a better temper, if not exactly with a good-humored shrug.

Kaori also opened Yukiko up to the pleasure of studying her own body. They may have been teenagers, in training to learn how to please and service men, but like children, they scratched hard at mosquito bites, picked at scabs, and compared calluses with grave absorption. Alone of all the apprentices, they did not only share a futon in the winter, the solace they derived from each other's bodies outweighing even the discomfort of sharing a narrow bed in the sticky heat of a Tokyo summer night.

Kaori's presence by her side eased the loneliness that Yukiko had felt since her older brothers, shamefaced and tongue-tied, had let her go without an embrace; it chipped away at the block of bitterness she had carried around inside her, ever since her father had given the order for her to be sold. With time, Kaori came to take the place of the sisters that Yukiko never had, and even, eventually, of her mother, too.

For Akiko never came. She could not write so Yukiko did not get any letters from Hokkaido, although on her seventeenth birthday she received a box filled with an assortment of cheap tea. After throwing out the tea, Yukiko began keeping her hair in the box, and did so until the day she married.

My mother is not a religious woman, but when she told me these stories about my grandmother, she was practicing what amounted to a kind of sacred ritual of her own: an act of penance for the rift that had opened up between her and her mother, the coolness and the nearly complete silence that would last for twenty-nine years. Consciously or not, my mother had made the decision that it was enough of a punishment to deprive Yukiko of her own presence, the company of her only daughter; it would be going too far to deprive her of me as well. So she told me these stories to make sure that I understood and loved my grandmother; to ensure that when we did finally meet, we would not be at a loss as to how to be friends.

Although the oldest child and the only girl, my mother slipped through the cracks of her family's loving but tight hold. She was separated from them, and most of all her mother, by a deep ideological rift. There was a deeply ingrained conservatism in Yukiko, who learned from her own life rather than from books and school; judging that a woman's power lay in swaying her husband, she set great store in a woman's charm. My mother, modern before her time and country, prizing intellectual and artistic achievement above all else, was frustrated no end by Yukiko's attitudes. She tried to be docile, but she balked at Yukiko's attempts to teach her how to enter a room with showstopping style, and titillate a crowd of men with mere words; she lost her temper trying to get it through to her mother that such lessons were appropriate for an apprentice geisha, and not for a proper young lady from a rich family. They clashed bitterly and often over this and other related issues, their daily antagonism covering and finally masking entirely their basic similarity: the single-mindedness of purpose with which they pursue what they want, and the pigheadedness that leads them to refuse, ever, to let go of their men.

Deep and old as it is, the struggle of wills between my mother and Yukiko is not the only reason I have never met my grandmother. Responsible, too, is a series of unfortunate circumstances, following each other in such well-timed sequence that it seems as if there is a conspiracy afoot to keep my grandmother and me apart.

There was, first of all, my father, and his bitterness towards Yukiko for spurning him as a suitor for her daughter's hand. When he and my mother first moved to America, he refused to let her communicate with her family. In the beginning, in the first flush of love and in the throes of righteous indignation at her parents' attitude towards her husband, my mother was complicit in this severance of family ties. But after I was born, she went behind his back, and began sending them photographs of me twice a year.

Later, when the marriage failed, my mother was too poor to pay for the visit, and too proud to ask her parents for help. More than ten years passed before she could even admit to them what they had guessed long before—my father's desertion and our subsequent poverty. And later still, when my mother got a job with decent pay, she was too busy, and probably too exhausted, to take time off for such a strenuous trip overseas.

Still, even though my father was to a certain degree responsible, even though finances and timing and the sheer logistics involved in carrying two people halfway around the world have all played a part in keeping my grandmother and me apart, it is difficult for me to avoid blaming my mother for this, the deprivation of my grandmother, as well as for so many other things.

Unlike other children at school, I did not go to my parents and crawl into bed with them when I had nightmares about nameless beasts. When the nightmares were very bad, I fled up the creaking wooden steps and through the long dark hall to my parents' bedroom, and there I curled up in a small ball against the door. They often talked for hours through the night: although the actual words were indistinguishable, the murmur of their voices came through low and sweet from the crack beneath the door.

Usually I crept back comforted to my own bed, but one night, lulled by their voices, I fell asleep on the floor. In the morning, my father nearly tripped over my body when he opened the door; he said something in Japanese and my mother began to laugh. I was four or maybe five by then, and already quite tall with unmanageably long legs, but he lifted me easily and carried me down the wooden steps, she following behind as they whispered to each other in Japanese. I kept my eyes shut, but I think that he, at least, may have known I was awake, shamming sleep for the chance to be the baby once again, held and carried and tucked into bed in the early hours of the morning.

As they put me into bed, I peeked quickly at them and she caught me looking. I instantly plunged into an explanation of what I had been doing outside my bedroom so late at night, but they stopped me before I could get far. "Go back to sleep," he said. "You need your rest," she said. His hand felt warm and heavy over my eyes; she pulled the covers over my body. She laughed again. Then they left my room and went to the kitchen to have their breakfast and tea.

In the early stages of her marriage, my mother was like that, the kind of person who laughed for no reason. She was also eager, chatty, and apple-cheeked, with a face that was usually lit up with excitement and hair that flew in a tangle all about her head.

Thinner now, her cheeks neither full nor red, her hair fashioned into a neat and becoming bob, she is barely recognizable as that young woman I have studied so carefully in photographs. The intellect that she had then is still intact, of course, but where she once possessed a keen curiosity about the far-flung corners of the world, as well as an insatiable appetite to experience them, she is now content with merely reading about them in the papers. She hardly ever laughs.

I was ten when I made the vow that I would never be like my mother. Trudging up the driveway after school, I saw her stationed at her usual spot, ensconced in that hard upright chair by the window. I waved, but she did not respond.

After kicking my shoes off in the entryway, I entered the spare bedroom and squatted on the ground beside her, maybe two feet away from the left side of her chair. It was early fall, and we sat drenched in full sunlight.

I took out my latest book report from my knapsack and placed it on my mother's lap. "I told you Mrs. Jennings would like it," I said.

Waiting for my mother to respond to the comments, I brushed the carpet in ever-widening circles with my hands. It was while I was making the sixth or seventh circle that I shivered, suddenly and quite literally chilled.

Having soaked up a day's worth of sunshine, the carpet felt pleasantly warm for the most part. But in the space immediately to the left of my mother's chair, where her shadow thrust backward, the carpet was so cool that I knew the sun had not lit upon that spot for hours.

I looked up at my mother. She sat looking ahead of her, the book report lying unregarded on her lap. Her hair was dank and matted, uncombed as well as unwashed.

"How long have you been sitting here?" I asked.

It was the note of urgency in my voice that made her turn. I watched her eyes (. . . three Mississippi, four Mississippi . . .) as they came into focus on me. "I don't know," she said.

My father had been gone for a year by then. While it has been many years now since my mother sat in that spot by the window, her romance with Mr. Lewis, our vegetable-bearing neighbor, ran aground just last fall: clearly not all that much has changed.

Grandmother, I will say. *Obaasama,* is it any wonder that the thought of my mother's prolonged pining for my father nags at me? Would it really surprise anyone that it is the image of you—the woman who parlayed a practical arrangement into the longest and most passionate of romances—that I look to as a beacon?

Whether I like it or not, the lives of my mother and my grandmother are the stars by which I chart my course.

The phone call comes almost exactly at four. Jarred awake, I scramble madly for the phone and knock it over, so that I have to use the cord to pull up the receiver, as if it were a fish. "Hello? Eric, is that you?" I ask, hoping but knowing it is not, and sure enough, all I hear is that now-familiar wail on the line. I would disconnect the phone at night were it not for the fact that every time I make a move to do so, I am visited by images of my mother falling down the stairs and breaking a wrist or worse, and her or the hospital trying to reach me in vain.

These phone calls in the middle of the night shock me to the core, leaving my hands tingling. After replacing the receiver, I bring my sheets up to my chin, and meditate on the question of calling Eric.

He worries about me because I live alone. He even made me a set of keys for his apartment, to be used whenever I am lonely or frightened, and it is too late to call him. Although situations like that occur all the time, I have never once used his keys. At this very moment, though, I could sit up, put on clothes and a light jacket, pick up my purse and the keys, and catch a cab downtown. Perhaps he would welcome me with a glad drowsy kiss; his bed would be warm with his body. It cheers me just to know that even at 4:14 on a Monday morning, there is someone, somewhere in the city, who would be happy to see me.

Like all the women in my family, I sleep so poorly that I dread going to bed, the hours spent lying awake, eyes wide open staring up at the ceiling and all around the walls. When I feel bored and playful, I use the light of my alarm clock to make hand shadows on the wall, geese or rabbits or noiseless barking dogs. When I feel glamorous, I practice artsy model poses, the wrist bent, the fingers extended, and the pinkie up.

My preoccupation with hands may have started with my mother, who loved to play Chopin on the piano. I think she loved Chopin almost as much as she loved my father. Once our house overflowed with preludes. I remember standing on tiptoe near the piano and watching her fingers, long and thin and supple, how it seemed that they sang as they glided across the keys. I started lessons at the age of five, but though my fingers were later so deft and confident on the typewriter, they were clumsy and thick on the piano, noisy and songless even after hours and hours of practice. I gave up after four years of frustrating lessons, and when my mother's fingers grew deformed, the joints grotesque and swollen with arthritis, the piano sat in proud and silent splendor for years. When eventually it fell hopelessly out of tune, there was nobody to notice or care. On the most desolate nights, when missing Phillip becomes a physical ache, I make shadows of myself playing scales on the wall.

Sometimes I get up and read until daylight, and once in a while I turn on the television set and flip through the channels; little interests me, but perhaps I am not being fair since few good shows could be on during the gray hours between night and morning. The television is perched at the foot of my bed, balanced rather precariously on the top of my dresser, and it is placed sideways so that I can see it while lying down. I rather like it there. The potential of the blank screen intrigues me, even though some nights I am sure that it will fall off the dresser and smash my toes in.

The television is from Eric, a present bought without any special reason. When I thanked him for it, he kissed me and told me it was a necessity. "I'm going to coax you into the twentieth century before it's over," he said. "By the time I get through with you, you'll be handling VCRs and CDs with ease, a bona fide nineties woman. Just wait—it'll be painless and even fun."

I wake at noon to sunshine slanting across my bed, and a singing in my body that extends all the way down to my toes. Why this shiver of happiness, this overflowing of delight, this absurd notion that my toes will burst into strains of Handel's *Messiah*? Rolling over to my side and stretching my back until it arches into a smile, I review the options, and then I remember: just three months more, and my grandmother Yukiko will be coming to America.

She will be here in mid-November, just in time for Thanksgiving. We will sit around the table together with my mother, three women from three different generations, and then, after Yukiko's first American turkey, as I stack the dishwasher and she leans her long body against the kitchen stool, I will ask her about her secret love, for she had one, too: she, too, knows what it is like to love two men at once, at least for a while. I will ask her about desire, that topic which (in spite of meandering discussions on the side effects of birth control) I could never quite broach with my mother. It will be different with Yukiko, since we will meet as women of the world. She will be amused at the extent of my experience, nothing more.

I will tell her of the space, secret and inviolate, that I once shared with Phillip. I will tell her of how I have grieved for him for over a year, and of how I live with him still, and she will nod and understand.

CHAPTER FOUR

Phillip came to New York on a two-day layover from Africa, and stayed because he fell in love with the subways.

He had ridden in most of the great subway systems of the world: Moscow, Vienna, Paris, and London, but it was the New York subways, clunky and dirty and often hopelessly inefficient, that he loved. When I pressed him to explain why, he did not even stop to think. "They remind me of dinosaurs," he said.

He had spent his childhood on a farm in Iowa. "Where there was enough corn," he told me, summoning a flat drawl from his past, "to drive a feller crazy. Certainly it drove this feller crazy. There was miles and miles of corn, a whole ocean of it, on land that was as flat as this table."

"I'd be curious to see it," I said.

He looked up at me thoughtfully. "We could take a trip there, if you really want to, but I'd be willing to bet you wouldn't like it, either. There's a lot of sky there, and not much else, and I think most city people can't take that. My mom hated it, you know. You wouldn't think anybody could get cabin fever in a place with that much sky, but she did, and so did I."

After his mother ran away, Phillip took care of his father for years.

He left town just as his father's second wedding was winding to a close. His father's new wife was a lusty Greek woman who fed the wedding guests food soaked in olive oil until their faces had a sheen to it. She loved the Iowan sky.

I used to like to imagine Phillip on the night he left home— shivering a little in the cool air, swatting at the occasional mosquito, a scrawny seventeen-year-old with a jean jacket slung over his shoulder, and one thumb held out in proudly indifferent supplication. These days, though, I try not to think about his past, mostly to avoid sinking into the black hole that the word "if" opens up: if Phillip had been born with normal sight, if he could have passed the eye test for his driver's license, if relying on the kindness of strangers and friends had not been his only way of getting around his hometown, maybe he would not have felt the need to travel all the time. Maybe he would have stayed in New York with me forever.

But then again, if those ifs had occurred, he might never have left Iowa in the first place.

Earthbound as he was, it is small wonder that he left the cornfields, where nothing stirred for miles except the breeze and, of course, the corn. I never told him, because he hated pity, how sorry I felt for him, condemned to standing on the side of the road as his classmates (on whom licenses conferred wings) flew by.

He had a gift for stillness. Although his eyes flickered from side to side with a will of their own, he could keep his body motionless for hours at a time. He did not seem to feel the need to flex a muscle periodically, or to stomp his feet to get the blood flowing, as most people do. At boring movies I would shift the weight of my body, jog my knee up and down, and scratch at nonexistent itches, while he, just as bored with the film, would not even twitch. Often he came over while I was reading and I would forget he was there, so quietly did he sit, wrapped in his own thoughts.

But at the same time he was deeply restless. By the time I met him, he had been almost ceaselessly on the move for nine years. He was happiest when he was traveling, and it was a revelation to him as well as to me that he did not have to be biking across South America to feel as if he were on the move. It was enough for him to ride on the subway, rolling the names of the stops like exotic spices on the tip of his tongue: Smith, Carroll, Bergen, Jay Street, York.

Whether through practice or just a natural sense of balance, he remained unfazed by the jerks and lurches of the trains. I glared but he still shook with laughter when I ended up on the lap of the same old man for the second time. "Go with it," he said, "sway with it. You've got to learn to move with the train."

We took long rides in which the journey rather than the destination was the point, on routes that crisscrossed the city according to a master plan that he had carefully devised. We also racked up a lot of hours in coffee shops, parks, and my apartment. I always took the sheer amount of time we spent together for granted—a presumptuous move, for when it came to Phillip, I had a lot of competition. As Russia had told me before she introduced us, he was a chick magnet, and one of the highest magnitude.

He had what I call the X-factor, the intangible element that renders its lucky possessor irresistibly, mystifyingly sexually attractive. Shy to the point of rudeness, he made no effort to charm women or even, often, to talk with them, and inured, perhaps, by a lifetime of female adulation, he barely seemed aware of the stir that he caused, and the excitement that he left simmering and unsatisfied in his wake.

Moreover, in spite of a certain lanky grace that made people turn in the streets to look at him, he was not actually good-looking. Eric, with the well-drawn planes of his face, his pale coloring and dark eyes, is far more handsome than Phillip ever was, but it was Phillip women loved, looking at him with a yearning that was not only sexual, although, of course, it predominantly was. Drawn to him as to sunlight, waitresses in coffee shops and bars, bank tellers, shop attendants, acquaintances of mine or his whom we ran into in the street, striking, glamorous Russia and old Mrs. Noffz, my confused neighbor from across the hall, all found excuses to hover around him; they glowed in his presence and sighed wistfully as they said good-bye, all the while darting speculative looks in my direction, as if wondering what made me so special, or weighing their chances against me.

Perhaps they, too, fell for his air of calm, and the hunger that lay hidden beneath it like a steel trap.

One night in October, Phillip and I were walking by an alley near my street when we heard a crash of garbage cans and a startled animal's cry. We had to move three trash bags and one plastic bin to find the cat, and even then we almost missed him because he was crouching in the shadows. He looked tough and ugly with blood caked over his left eye and across his back, and he was so dirty that I could only guess at the color of his fur. We spent a long time talking to him before he even let us near; he spat and growled but we had him trapped and he was too weak to protest for long. I could see the relief in his eyes when he finally gave in and let us approach, and though we could not avoid touching the raw wounds, he surprised me by lying limp and relaxed in my arms. Phillip carried him into my apartment, and by then I was already in love with him for trusting us.

"This is one big cat," said Phillip, panting a little from the weight.

"Well, I always wanted a horse," I said.

I poured the cat a bowl of water and opened a dusty can of tuna fish that I found in the back of a cupboard. He was ravenous but I fed him only a little, saving the rest for later.

"I wish I knew what to do," I said, gnawing on my knuckles. "Maybe we should call someone, a vet or something."

Crouched on his knees, Phillip was enthralled, staring at Horse as he washed himself. "What, are you kiddin'?" said Phillip. "This cat lucked out. I used to be a lifeguard, you know. I know CPR."

I laughed, my knuckles still close to my mouth, and watched them from behind my hair. Phillip picked the cat up and held him at arm's length, just out of reach of his claws, and looked into his eyes. "Don't worry, you're in good hands," he told him. "You're going to love it here."

Horse responded with a throaty growling sound. "You better put him down," I said, backing away cautiously, but Phillip just laughed. "Don't you recognize a purr when you hear one?"

I kept my distance. "That's a purr?"

33

"So he's a little rusty," said Phillip, sounding defensive.

Doughty old warriors both, Phillip and Horse had a natural respect and understanding for each other. Phillip caressed Horse roughly, mashing his mangled ears against his head with a brutal tenderness that made me wince but also dream, and Horse responded by purring in his rusty way, and sometimes even keeping his nails sheathed.

I cleaned Horse as best I could, and eventually his wounds healed and most of his fur grew back. While he was large and strong, he was ugly even after his fur was clean, and though he grew to care for me, he was surly and ill-tempered, and he never became truly affectionate. But I doted on him just as much as Phillip did, for when I woke up terrified by my unremembered nightmares in the middle of the night, the warm solid weight of Horse would press against my feet when I moved, and as if sensing my need, he would put up with my hand on his back, even purring until I fell asleep.

On an unusually warm night in January when the moon was full, Horse escaped down the fire escape and never came back. Phillip and I spent the night looking for him, and much of the next three days, too, but he had vanished. Even though New York City is not exactly a haven for stray cats, Phillip insisted that Horse would thrive, battered body and all. He said Horse would lord it over the other toms, stealing all their rats and their fish-heads, if not all their women. I was still worried, but I had to agree with Phillip in the end.

Horse is tough, a direct descendant of the feline hero who inspired the nine-lives myth. He is probably happier as the resurrected king of the dark and twisting alleys than he ever was in my apartment. Still, I have not stopped hoping that some night, perhaps when the sky is cast over, he might yet return. Cleaning out the cupboard last week, I came across two cans of catfood. I wiped off the dust on them and left them there, next to Horse's old monogrammed dish.

I blame his escape on the moon. I had left that window open many times before, and he had never once tried to get out.

I cried at Horse's desertion, but I did not cry when Phillip left. Maybe that is why I still see Phillip everywhere and in all things. The lopsided crescent moon looks like his crooked smile, every pen and pencil seems like one of his long skinny fingers, the slats of the toaster remind me of the scar along his stomach. When I look in the mirror, I see myself with his eyes and now, as I pull my gaze away from the ceiling and sit up, I notice that he is watching me from the northeast corner of the living room. I do not know how long he has been there. Flanked by a quartet of violet moths, he is standing on his hands. He remains as solidly balanced as if he were on his feet, and his hair defies gravity, lying flat around his ears. His face is not reddened by blood draining into his head, and his features show no trace of strain.

In the summer of his twenty-second year, while working on a construction site, Phillip stepped onto a loose beam one foggy morning, and slipped. He fell only fifteen feet, but he hit concrete, and so the local media (Nevada, or maybe Wisconsin) hailed his survival as an Act of God. His brush with a higher authority left its mark, though, and I can see his old wounds from where I sit now: the paler, shinier, and slightly raised surface of the line on his stomach, the gash on the inner side of his left forearm where the flesh was removed to patch in his torso, and the three deep scratches that run across his left rib cage. Like those saints in medieval pictures, whose bodies are naked, impressive, and riddled with arrow wounds, Phillip is beautiful because of his scars.

He observes me solemnly from his upside-down perspective, and as I gaze back I feel saddened at how much weight he has lost. Throughout the summer Phillip has been getting increasingly thinner. Motionless and bone-thin as he is now, he no longer seems human: throw a tattered kimono on him, and he would be indistinguishable from the scarecrow that my grandmother had built with her brothers when she worked in the rice fields as a child.

His weight loss is not the only change that I have noticed in him in the past few months. Some of his features have also begun to blur—a development that I can only chalk up to the passing of time. I am beginning to forget. Yet although I had expected that after my engagement to Eric, even more of Phillip would fade, instead he is looking more and more solid and real. The contours of his muscles are sharp and clear today; the planes of his face are shaded in detail. I can even make out the individual strands of the fine blond hair growing on his legs.

I study his face for signs of anger or disapproval, but he is as unreadable as ever. His unblinking gaze is hard to take, and I turn away. I wish he would talk. I loved his voice, with its ghost of a Midwestern accent, its trapped laughter, and its easy note of teasing.

Obaasama, I will say. Grandmother. You, too, know what it's like to hear a voice with your body, don't you? Like music played on a lower floor in the building, a vibration traveling through the ground and into your feet.

He said that the crunch of snow was what made it worthwhile. It was December, and we were talking about the trip he was planning to Nepal; I had told him that I like watching winter through the window, from the inside of my apartment.

"Snow in New York is beautiful," I explained. "It covers up the dirt on the streets and it makes all the traffic seem quieter. I wouldn't miss it for anything."

He laughed and shook his head at me. "In the mountains, the air is so fresh, so sharp, and so cold that your lungs ache whenever you breathe in."

"That's hardly a recommendation."

"Well, it's true, it isn't always fun. Once I was absolutely positive my toes had fallen off with frostbite." He paused. "But you've got to trust me on this. In the very early morning, the crunch of snow underfoot makes it all worthwhile." He leaned forward then, stretching his arms out to grip the edge of my side of the table. "Come with me," he said, his eyes shining with excitement. "We'll climb the mountains together, and trek across all that snow, and you can hear the snow yourself."

I smiled at him. "But I have school."

"Oh yeah," he said, releasing the table's edge and looking a little startled. And then he sat forward again. "Couldn't you leave for a little while anyway—just a week or so?"

I gazed at him across the table and idly cursed that pull of his, the X-factor he had in spades. For there it was again, like the rumblings of a train beneath our feet, passing us by all but unheeded: the undercurrents of sexual desire, which unfortunately seemed to run in only one direction. Hark, I thought. Ha.

"I can't, if you're leaving in February," I told him, looking down at my fingernails, with their chipping polish. "I honestly can't afford to miss all that school."

The light in his eyes flickered and then was gone as if it had never been.

"I would postpone the trip," he said uneasily, "except that I'm signed up to lead that group out on a hike."

"Of course," I said, looking at him with some surprise. "Obviously. No one's asking you to give up the trip."

He continued as if I had not spoken. "I do want to live in New York. It's just that I've stayed here longer than I've stayed anywhere else since I left home, and these days, it doesn't seem enough to ride around on the subways anymore. I've got to go. . . ." He stopped, drawn up short, as he frequently was, by the inadequacy of the English language. He extended an arm upward, palm turning inward, and then he clenched it, head cocked, as he thought. "Somewhere else," was all he managed. "Somewhere completely else. At least for a while."

"Somewhere completely else," I repeated. "It does sound good."

He told me then that he would come back by the spring, and that we would have the whole summer ahead of us. That it was only a short trip, just three months. And that I was busy with school, anyway.

I interrupted him just as he was beginning to speak about the trip out west that we would take during the summer. "You don't owe me an explanation, you know," I said.

He met my eyes, then, and slowly smiled. There was a skeptical tilt to his eyebrows, and I thought he was going to contradict me, but instead he reached across the table, bent my head down, and peering near-sightedly at my scalp, began sifting through my hair.

"This is it, this is my favorite," he crowed.

In his fingers was a long and shining silver strand.

"If you have to get your hair dyed, Ki, don't do this one. I'll be looking for this guy when I get back."

For a second I could not speak.

It seems entirely fitting, given how Phillip died, that when I was close enough to hear him breathe, I was sometimes beset by the symptoms of an attack of acrophobia: vertigo, light-headedness, even a touch of nausea. At such times I could only take in air in quick, shallow breaths. Mostly, though, I just tended to freeze when his body was too near, some atavistic reflex kicking in to prevent me from taking another step forward. Much as I would like to pass this strange paralysis off as yet another trait that I have in common with my mother and grandmother, a flaw, like my insomnia, which is woven into my genes and therefore beyond my control, this failing is mine alone: fear just served to galvanize Yukiko into action, while my mother is only afraid of literal heights.

"You shouldn't be doing this in public," I said at last, my voice harsh. "It's undignified. You're like one of those monkeys picking out his mate's fleas."

He clumsily tucked the loose strand back into the rest of my hair, and then he patted my head. "We'll travel together in the summer," he said again. "I promise."

After I fall asleep on some nights, I wake up to find myself standing in the cold. I want to walk on the snow to hear it crunch, but as I lift my foot, a crack spreads slowly through the white of the mountains. The rush of the snow is silent and deadly, and I wait with one foot suspended in midair.

I heard about his accident while I stood in line at the deli on Broadway and West 113th Street. It was the last Monday in February, and Phillip had been gone on his trek for three weeks. The deli was crowded and I was waiting to buy two poppy-seed bagels when the door opened and a tall figure wrapped in a scarf and a long, dark coat entered, along with a gust of chilling air.

"Kiki."

I looked up. She pulled off the scarf, which was as black as the coat and her hair. Russia likes black.

"Hi." I felt the strain on my lips as I smiled. Although Russia and I had spent a lot of time together at the start of the school year, our friendship had cooled over the past months.

She came and stood close to me. "How are you holding up?" she asked. "I was going to call you again tonight."

"Oh, fine. How are you doing?" I had spent a frustrating day in the library and I wanted to go home, but she was being so friendly I felt obliged to move away from the cash register to let the other customers go ahead.

"Oh, I'm hanging in there, I guess." She blinked a few times and bit her bottom lip. She did not look well. Her eyes were bloodshot and swollen, her nose was running slightly, and her skin was shockingly pale.

"You all right?" I said, readjusting the weight of the knapsack on my shoulders.

She glanced at me sharply, and then narrowed her eyes. "Haven't you heard?"

"About what?"

"Phillip. Haven't you heard about Phillip?" She sounded almost angry. "I left you a message on your answering machine—didn't you get it?"

I shook my head, too embarrassed to admit I had turned off the sound.

"Didn't you see the news? It was in the papers and everything."

"No." I felt a tightening inside of me.

"Kiki, he's dead." Her voice was low and steady. "There was some kind of avalanche, and a lot of people got buried in the snow. It happened two days ago, on Saturday."

Russia is very striking, with stark white skin and black hair. She is so fair that she freckles and burns easily, but of course it was winter then. At some point in the fall she had had most of her hair shaved off, and I was glad to see that it had almost completely grown back. I was envying the length of her eyelashes when she grabbed me by the shoulders. "You okay? Kiki, snap out of it." She shook me hard enough to make my head hurt.

"I'm okay." I shrugged her hands off.

"Want to get some coffee? You shouldn't be alone now."

I looked away. At the counter, a small gray-haired man was having a coughing fit. The woman at the cash register was waiting for him to pay for a pack of cigarettes, and I wondered if the man tried to quit sometimes, or whether he had given up trying long ago.

"Kiki?" Russia's voice was gentle.

"I think I need to be alone, but thanks." I handed her the bag with the two bagels. "Could you do me a favor and return these for me? I don't think I want them after all."

"Oh, sure." She took the bag from me and fiddled with it, twirling and twisting until her forefingers were wrapped in plastic. "I'm sorry, Kiki."

I told her I had to get home. I buttoned the top of my coat and pulled my gloves on, and then I waved even though she was standing less than six inches away.

She called out to me once again, but I had already opened the door by then, and her exact words were swallowed by the wind.

Obaasama, I will say. Grandmother, Phillip died eighteen months ago, but here I am now, engaged to be married. Are you impressed, as I am, at how quickly I moved on?

In those first few months following Phillip's departure, I went through the motions. I woke up late, went to class, went to aerobics, and ate store-bought food, cake and cookies and fudge. I had written a couple of letters to Phillip in the weeks he had been gone, and I continued to do so after the accident. I mailed the letters to the lodge in Nepal and later, when they turned up in my own mailbox marked "No such person at this address," I opened them up and read them as if they had been sent to me.

I continued to avoid Russia, just as I did before I saw her in the deli that day. I did not talk to anyone about Phillip because there was no one but Russia to talk to, and nothing really to say. I did not get my hair cut; it grew long and ragged and the ends became coppery and dry. I did not trim my nails, and they cracked and split with their own unwieldy

40

length. I thought of him often. I sat in a corner of the kitchen and killed hundreds of ants with my bare hands.

Then I resolved to keep busy. I bought a digital watch so I could plan and budget the hours to the minute, and I studied hard, reading Milton and furiously scrawling notes onto pads. Dressed in an old pair of jeans and a dirty sweatshirt, I waxed the floor; I scrubbed the bathtub until its ring was only a faint breath of scandal from the past. I signed up as a volunteer at a local high school and tutored basic English to pregnant teenagers. I went to classical music concerts.

In the late winter I went out in the evenings for long punishing runs in Riverside Park and came home in the dark with aching knees and eyes that teared with the cold, my sense of virtue in direct proportion to my discomfort. I stayed at the library far into the night so I could go straight to bed when I got home. In bed I read and reread novels by dead people from distant lands, masturbated over memories of ex-lovers, and had dreams in which I drank boiling hot saké and danced with my grandmother the geisha. I got a haircut. I went to movies during the day, when other people also go alone; New York theatres are filled with solitary strangers between noon and seven. I felt as if our shared silence was companionable, yet they sat far apart from me in the darkness.

Even though we only talked about my thesis, I called my mother often. I hated New York. My face looked so huge and hideous that I started swimming a mile every other day, and I increased my weekly running minimum from thirty miles to forty. I skipped meals but late at night I scooped out sugar from the bowl and crunched on the white granules. I lost all the weight I gained, and then some. I wore turtlenecks all the time because the bones stuck out sharply from the base of my neck and because I was always cold. I missed Horse. Sleepy and dazed from watching a movie one Friday afternoon, I slipped and fell to my knees on the wet sidewalk outside Lincoln Center. When I looked up from the ground, the April sunshine dazzled me so that for a moment I could not see.

Such was my life before I met Eric.

CHAPTER FIVE

On Saturday Eric wants us to go shopping for the engagement ring, but I plead the horror of midtown crowds in the heat of August, and so we decide instead to be tourists for the day. We take the subway down to 59th Street and then we catch a cab, over to Queens. It is muggy, as always, but the sun is shining and the sky is a hazy blue.

Eric wants to take my picture against the skyline, to send home to his family. He uses up a whole roll of film in the sculpture park, and scolds me for making faces, although I do my best to smile. There are fishermen standing at the edge of the water, and they watch and nod encouragement to me.

Afterwards we wander around the park, admiring the sculptures. Orange beams crisscross against each other like an enormous pile of sticks, and a huge face gazes out at Manhattan. We stop at an otherworldly contraption made of what looks like scratched silver; it has swooping curves and looks like an asymmetrical bubble.

"I wonder who made this one," I say. But Eric has been accosted by a pair of real tourists, and does not hear.

A head pokes out, then, from behind one of the curves. "David Smith," it says, and disappears.

I walk a little farther, tripping over the artist's plaque: David Smith. Around the bend, the boy peers out at me from the shadows of the sculpture.

"Can I come inside, too?" I ask.

"I'm six," he says, still blocking the entrance.

"That's a coincidence," I say. "I'm *twenty*-six."

He nods at me, then, the shared digit proving to be the password, and moves aside to let me in.

I glance back at Eric, but the tourists, it seems, want to know how to get to the Brooklyn Bridge. Eric, whose sense of direction is impeccable, has thrown himself into explaining the way, even to the extent of drawing a map on the ground with the toe of his shoe.

The interior of the sculpture is cool; it smells faintly of basement. The walls, which are smooth to the touch, muffle the sounds from the park. The boy crouches on the inside of one curve, but there is ample room for me to take another.

We embark on a conversation, one that has its own rhythm, filled more with silences than with words. He tells me that he lives out there, gesturing in the general direction of Manhattan, and I tell him I do, too. When he grows up, he says, he is going to live in this sculpture all the time. After a particularly long pause, during which he scrutinizes me carefully, he shows me his secret: the niche in which he keeps his stash of food, in anticipation of his move. Nestled in a nook of the sculpture is a candy bar, a bottle of juice, a bag of potato chips.

I tell him that he should start collecting cans, as candy and chips will eventually attract bugs. He nods. I open my purse and rummage in its deepest corners until I find the can opener. It is miniature and perfect, more like a toy than a tool, and I show him how it flips open with a flick of the wrist.

"It's from Japan," I explain. "My grandmother sent it to me when I was little, but you can have it since she's sending herself over pretty soon."

He accepts it gravely, looking down at it and flipping it open and shut with such attention that he does not look up when I thank him for the visit and get up to leave.

....

Eric is pacing impatiently back and forth by the huge stone face, but he stops when he sees me clambering out of the bubble. I am smiling as I approach him, yet there is something in the stiffness of his posture that smothers the light apology rising to my throat. He stares down at me, his sunglasses rendering his expression unreadable.

"I'm just going to pretend you didn't do that," he says finally.

He takes me by the hand and begins walking swiftly towards the park exit.

"What exactly did I do?" I ask, half-skipping to keep up.

He does not stop to answer my question. "You ran away," he says, "again. Just like you always do."

In all of the photographs, which we get back just a few hours later, my hair is in my face, and the sun in my eyes. Eric flips through the stack with mounting disbelief, for (as he says again and again) the wind wasn't even blowing. In the one photograph of us together, taken by the oldest fisherman, Eric huddles over me protectively. Buried in his shadow and masked with hair, I am unrecognizable, a shapeless, sexless figure crouching for shelter against a nonexistent wind.

In the evening, Eric and I go out to dinner and we get home early, well before ten, so I call my mother. Today is not the first time that Eric has lost his temper with me, nor is it the first time that I have called my mother after he has done so. It is not as if I would ever even think of telling her about the tiffs that Eric and I have. But even so, even if we never do talk about much of anything together, it soothes me to hear her voice (her cadences, those misplaced pauses) after Eric and I fight, just as it did on those nights I was most missing Phillip.

I can dial her number faster than any other. While I wait for her to answer, I envision her flipping on the lights as she moves through beautifully decorated rooms. With excellent taste and unlimited time and money, she could not fail to make her home a wonder. It is Western with a few choice Japanese details: the carp in the pond by the woods, the rock garden, the bonsai under the window, the demure doll dressed in a kimono on the mantelpiece. The food she eats is also a mix of cultures, the pasta dishes flavored with Oriental spices and a small bowl of rice accompanying tuna fish sandwiches. While she makes a point of eating with fork and knife and spoon, she can only cook with a pair of chopsticks in her hand.

Her feet are deformed with the swelling of her joints and her replaced hip moves with some stiffness, but my mother always manages to pick up the phone before the third ring. When she uses the phone, she does not sit down; the cord hangs slack and it curls in the middle by her knees. It cannot be comfortable for her to stand so, and I feel guilty whenever our conversations go on longer than five minutes.

I could make a fair guess at the exact distance between my mother's feet as she stands by the phone. I know how still she will be as she listens to me, and I can almost always predict what she will say and how she will phrase it. Yet when Eric, soon after I met him, asked me to describe her, I hesitated, daunted by the task of summing up my mother.

"She's been disappointed a number of times in her life," I said finally, "and it shows. She was a different person when she was young."

Then I described for him the concrete nature of her possessions, her daily habits and her physical appearance: the lush, healthy plants she waters at six every morning, the Persian rugs and the somber dark furniture, the newspapers and the magazines she reads meticulously and religiously, the fastidious way she compartmentalizes and cuts up her food, the tailored cut of her clothes and the hair that always falls impeccably into place, the paleness of her skin and the ravages of her disease. Eric seemed satisfied with my account of her, but I knew the extent of its inadequacy.

He met her soon afterwards, when she came to New York to get her thumb straightened. She has met other lovers of mine, but I was surprisingly nervous when she and I walked into the cafe and saw him waiting at a table.

"Mom, this is Eric. Eric, this is my mother, Akiko T-Takehashi," I said, stumbling on the familiar name.

Did I really believe he would address her as a Ms. or even a Mrs.? If so, I was being foolish, for of course he called her by her first name, and with such naturalness that she relaxed visibly under the intimacy of it.

"Nice to meet you, Akiko," he said. He even stood up, pulled out a chair, and called over the waiter, all in one smooth gesture.

He then sat back down and looked at her, then at me, and then at her again.

"So?" I said after a while. "Do we look alike?"

He smiled. "Yes." He turned to my mother. "Now I know where Kiki gets her good looks from."

It was a hopelessly cheesy line, but Eric has the sweetness to carry it off. She smiled and maybe even reddened.

We met only for an hour, as she had her appointment at the hospital. Mostly they talked about politics, leaving me out. When our tea came, Eric watched closely as I put the sugar into my mother's tea and stirred it in, while she reached around me and poured milk into my cup and then into hers. "You two work well together," he said.

They squabbled with good humor over the check when it came, with Eric gracefully conceding defeat at the end.

Later that afternoon, when Eric was on his way back to the office and I was walking with her to the hospital, she said, "You shouldn't be so critical of him." I began to protest—when had I ever complained about him to her?—but she had not finished. "He's a good person for you, especially now," she continued. "He'll hold you together."

And later still, when my mother was riding her train back to New Jersey, and Eric and I were having dinner together: "Nice lady, your mother," he said.

I nodded and chewed.

"She's so frail, though," he continued, and then he paused. "I didn't expect that."

"But I told you about her arthritis a zillion times."

"I didn't mean physically. It's more that you always make her sound like such a tough cookie, with her wartime childhood and her emigration for love and her bad marriage, and now her arthritis and her solitary life. I suppose she must be strong to have lived through all that, but she seems so vulnerable."

"Most men think that about her," I told him. "She plays up to that, I think."

He raised his eyebrows and tapped his fork against his plate. "She's not reliant on men, at least not on me. She relies on *you*."

"Don't be silly," I said, the quickness of my own retort startling me a little.

"I don't think I'm being silly. She depends on you—I can see it in the way she listens to you. She listened politely when I spoke, but it's your words that she really cares about. It makes sense. After all," he said, lifting his fork to his mouth, "aren't you all that she has?"

The phone rings and rings, seven, eight, nine times. My chest begins to hurt. Why would my mother be out on a Saturday night? Tormented by visions of her falling, overwhelmed by premonitions of death, I run over to Eric, who is reading his newspapers in the bedroom, to tell him that I am going to New Jersey to check up on my mother. He looks up, astonished, and it takes him half an hour to coax me out of my fears. He spreads open his paper to regale me with accounts of the latest wonder playing at the art cinema house, and then with considerable eloquence expounds upon the fallibility of the phone system, until finally I smile.

"You are such a parent," he scolds, and while I return his laugh, it takes me a full five seconds to understand the joke.

The train ride to my mother's house would only have taken an hour. I thank him, though, and get up to return to the living room, but he takes me in his arms and squeezes me tight, and does not release me until I assure him twice that I am fine. I wander back to my favorite place on the sofa, and sit down in the dead center of the circle created by the glow of the lamp.

Phillip is dozing in the darkest corner of the room. Turning my back to him, I force myself to recall the boy who wanted to spend his life hidden in the quiet metal bubble.

....

Obaasama, I will say. Grandmother, surely it's not just me; surely it's not just that boy who knows how sweet it is, how necessary and even natural it is to want to take shelter, whether or not there are winds?

And in the silence that passes between my question and her response, perhaps she, too, will think of my mother, and those swollen hands.

CHAPTER SIX

MY MOTHER WAS born a bastard in Japan. As a little girl saying good-night to her parents, she sat with her legs folded under her and bowed until her nose scraped the ground. No one ever kissed her. Under the guidance of a maid, she practiced pouring and serving tea in small cups without handles. With a paintbrush, she wrote letters in a language I do not understand, and when she read, her eyes went from the top of the page down to the bottom, and from right to left.

She wore long, tight robes that hugged her knees and whispered softly against the floor. She dined on fish and rice until the advent of the war, and then she ate weeds and grasshoppers to supplement meagre portions of rationed food. It was not until after the war, when she was nine years old, that she set eyes on white people, pale giants with eyes that came in vivid shades. When she first saw them, she thought they were a race of chewers, closer to cows than to people in their digestive habits, and it was not until three weeks had passed that a friend at school enlightened her on the wonders of gum.

I cling to the thought of the differences in our childhoods because it serves as a partial explanation of why my mother and I no longer talk. There are the stories about my grandmother, of course, but they function almost as space fillers, clouding the silence around our own private lives. When I told her that Phillip died, I did so a month after the fact.

Once we did not talk because we did not need to talk. We had an innate and implicit knowledge of each other's thoughts and feelings, an understanding so deep it might have begun in her womb. Now we do not talk because there would be too much to say, and no common ground on which to begin. Sometimes I cannot believe that we are so estranged; the rift between us seems logically impossible. She is the woman who bore me inside her stomach for nine months. Her breasts fed me and my urine stained her fingers. She nursed me through scarlet fever and the chicken pox and pneumonia, and she taught me how to speak. She bought me my first book. She stayed to raise me after my father left, and she bore the burden of my tantrums. Most of the meals in my lifetime were prepared by her and later with her, and we ate them sitting side by side. Even throughout the time that I most hated her, I sat through dinner with her, and when it was over, we washed and dried the dishes in a rhythm rendered perfect by the years. In the gray winter evenings, we warmed ourselves in front of the same fire as we read, and in the summer we rocked on the porch and drank iced tea in the cool of the afternoon breeze.

I do not know what she regrets most. Every once in a while, when I catch her in an unfamiliar light or an unexpected pose, I can almost see her as others must: middle-aged and content, serenely resigned to herself and her situation, a strong and independent woman who embraces her solitude. Yet at other times, most often late at night, there is a wistfulness in the way her hand continues to turn the pages of the newspaper while her eyes look into the fire. Dreaming over the newspapers, she seems a completely different person: forlorn, perhaps bitter, almost certainly sad.

She spends most Saturday nights at home, reading. She subscribes to far more newspapers and magazines than I could even recognize by name, and she reads all of them. In her house the recycling bins overflow with paper. When Eric and she met, they talked only briefly, but even so he was astounded at the breadth and the depth of her knowledge about the world.

Whereas I am lucky to find my stapler when I need it, my mother's desk is scrupulously organized and always neat, and the contents of her top drawer have been the same for as long as I can remember. There she keeps my navy blue American passport and her red Japanese one, with the characters embossed in gold across the front. My mother's devotion to American political events does not extend to a desire for a vote. She has lived in this country now for twenty-nine years, and she has gone back to Japan only once; changing her citizenship would be a mere formality, but out of indifference or perhaps a perverse feeling of patriotism, she has remained Japanese.

In the top drawer of her desk she also keeps matches and candles. Years ago, some time after my father left, I asked her what they were doing in there among our passports. Her answer was delivered in typically telegraphic fashion: "Earthquakes." I laughed a little uncertainly at the thought of an earthquake in central New Jersey, but she had turned away. I stood up and was almost out the door when she spoke again. "Bombs," she said, tight-lipped. "Earthquakes and bombs." That was all. After a pause I walked out of the room. We did not discuss the candles again, but I knew then that there is no escape from the terrors of our childhood, that they become our adult nightmares and haunt all our days.

Grandmother, I will say, *Obaasama*. How is it that you gave birth to a woman like my mother, so cool and self-contained, and she gave birth to me?

The violet moths have multiplied; I count them and there are eight. I move out of the circle of light cast by the lamp, and with my head averted, I walk past Phillip, curled in fetal position now on the floor beneath the windows. I pour myself a glass of iced tea, and go to my desk and rustle through the papers until I find the two pictures.

The first photograph is of myself when I am three. I am sitting on white sand in front of a very blue ocean, and by some accident of the camera, I am caught in a pose more than half flirtatious, a small hand lifted in a provocative gesture to hair disheveled in the wind. Although my lips curve with only the faintest trace of a smile, my eyes are laughing. I was a happy child then, and it showed. I sometimes think I can almost remember this moment, the sun shining down, and me on the brink of laughter because of something that my father said. But I do not really possess such a memory. Rather I look at this picture so often that I have imagined myself into it, like the stories about Japan I heard over and over until they became first a myth and then a dimly remembered part of my own past. I love this picture, with my body size just right and my face looking remarkably like it does now—thin, with the features in even harmony; I look cheerful and normal and effortlessly beautiful. With this photo in hand, I can almost pretend that all the intervening years of fat and misery and ugliness had never been.

The next photograph has sharper detail and the paper is of a superior quality. It is in black and white, and it is a very obviously posed shot. The picture is of three children. They are slender and they seem almost deliberately doll-like, with delicate hands and wrists peeking out through the wide sleeves of their kimonos. Their faces seem scrubbed clean of smiles, though the younger boy looks as if he is just barely suppressing one. The girl has long dark hair that drops straight down, like water falling from a great height. She stands apart from her brothers. Her face is round and she is frowning slightly; while the others are merely solemn, she is grim. With her hands folded primly in front of her, my mother looks so stiff and serious that few would guess she is only ten years old.

My mother was born in the spring but she was named for a different season altogether—Akiko, or Autumn Child, after Yukiko's mother, the sunny-tempered, energetic woman who hummed as she worked through the night. In naming her child after an unknown grandmother, Yukiko began a tradition that my mother followed. While I was born on a warm day in May, my name is written in Japanese with the character for snow, in honor of the blizzard that raged on the night that Yukiko was born.

From a very early age, my mother displayed a wholly unexpected gift for music. Just as Yukiko's beauty seemed to spring out of nowhere, so, too, did my mother's talent appear without precedent: her grand-mother's humming was never in key, and her parents were similarly tuneless. Her nurse sang lullabies to her, though, and family lore has it that my mother sang with her from the crib, her coos and gurgles and babybabble striking every note like the hits of an expert marksman: bull's-eye. Yet it was not until the age of four, when she was placed in front of a keyboard, that my mother's musicality found its true outlet, and she became irrevocably smitten. Her love affair with the piano lasted for decades, although eventually it, too, came to an end.

She was born with her grandmother's marvelous store of energy, her father's ambition and brains, and her mother's single-minded approach to the passions in her life—a disastrous combination for a girl growing up in the Japan of the forties and fifties. Through luck and sheer will, Yukiko, who came from a family so poor that they had to sell her to sur-vive, got everything she wanted: the man she loved; a home of her own; children or, more specifically, sons; marriage. Born into wealth and privilege, smart, talented, and doggedly hardworking, my mother was defeated at every turn.

She was eight when the bombing in Tokyo became so dangerous that her family packed up their things and moved out to the country. Only her father, busy as always with work, stayed in Tokyo, taking the train into the country on the occasional weekend to see his wife and children.

To Akiko it seemed a glorious vacation. Food was scarce and she missed the calming presence of her father, but the lush fields, the mountains, and the wide spaces of the countryside made an impression on her, a born-and-bred city girl, that she was never to forget. She ran and played until her knees and shins, like her mother's at her age, became check-ered with scabs, cuts, and bruises. At school, the village children mocked her for her Tokyo dialect, but she had her brothers, and she felt con-firmed in her view that this was paradise on the day her cousin arrived.

Kenji was a fabulous child, clever and energetic, and able, too, to make boats that skimmed the surface of the lake from sticks, string, and scraps of cloth. He knew half a dozen card tricks, and he was tolerant of his little cousin, in large part because he, with his Korean blood, was also shunned by the village children.

Kenji was the son of Akiko's father's sister, Mieko, who had had the unspeakable temerity to marry a Korean against her parents' wishes, to give birth to a child and then to die, with the bond between her and her family still severed. While Mieko's parents would eventually have forgiven her for the marriage, they could not forgive her early death, which left the child permanently out of their reach: Kenji's father hated them for their snobbery, and refused to let them associate with the boy.

Mieko died on Kenji's fifth birthday. Seeking, perhaps, to make up to his son for this early trauma, Kenji's father spoiled and indulged him, often leaving him to rule over and abuse the maids and nannies, who dared not quarrel with the young master.

But Kenji was unusually kind to Akiko, even though a certain amount of bullying was probably inevitable. Given that kindness, as well as the fact that he was easily the smartest boy in school, a genuine whiz in science and math, it is not surprising that she came down with a severe case of hero worship. An only child, he reciprocated by sharing with her his darkest secret: his chronic bed-wetting, which all the ingenious punishments devised by his father could not cure.

Akiko enjoyed an easy, uncomplicated relationship with her father, and felt sad that work kept him so busy that even in Tokyo, he was rarely at home. While she was closer to her mother, her relationship with her was far more difficult, for even at the age of eight, Akiko was beginning to strain under the enormous burden of the expectations placed upon her as a girl, and no one was more responsible for this weight than her mother. It was Yukiko who insisted on practicing the tea-ceremony lessons, when Akiko would so much rather be playing outside with her brothers; it was Yukiko who dressed Akiko in those expensive kimonos that caught and tripped her when she tried to run.

Akiko's brothers were fiercely defensive of her when it came to outsiders, folding in to present a united front to any tormentors. Even Tadashi, who was almost four years younger, worked hard to shield her, as if guessing in her stubbornness the outlines of her fate. Still, despite their protectiveness, despite the fact that they liked and respected her, Tadashi and Isamu were an almost inseparable duo, which made Akiko the odd man out.

So it was in the absence of any other real companionship that Kenji and Akiko became a twosome. He liked to play, most of all, on the railroad tracks, which they followed a little farther every day until they came to a gorge, over which trains traveled on the narrowest possible strip of a bridge. Climbing on the strip on her hands and knees, which was all that she could manage, Akiko peered through the slats of the tracks and saw the stark edge of a cliff, falling many kilometers downwards, and at the bottom a river, which was so far below that only if it was absolutely quiet, and only if she really concentrated, could she hear the rushing of the water.

Drawing back to the safety of the ground, she looked down again and felt her stomach somersault, and experienced a perhaps hereditary urge to fall. She did not realize she was gradually leaning into the abyss until Kenji, with a curse, caught her by her kimono sleeve just as her foothold slipped, and she began to pitch forward. "Stupid," he yelled, his face red with anger. "What are you doing—trying to kill yourself and get me in trouble?"

They did not know the train schedule, and had not been successful in figuring out even its roughest guidelines. At times the trains came in rapid succession, with one appearing from behind the hill even as another disappeared around the bend, and then Kenji and my mother would exhaust themselves by running and screaming beside each train, chasing it as far as they could. At other times, none came for hours, and birds would roost on the tracks while rabbits ran across them, and then the two children would be bored. He told her stories, then, to while away the time: mostly tales of what he would do with his life, the inventions he would make and the countries he would visit, and the tree house he would build and live in with Akiko at his side.

After they discovered the gorge, his greatest delight was to run up and down the bridge, on a few memorable occasions chased by oncoming trains. When the wind blew, the tracks creaked and swayed, yet

Kenji never paused. Dazzled by hero worship, dying to follow but afraid of the yearning to jump that came over her like a spell when she looked down, Akiko crouched on the ground by the tracks, and prayed for Kenji's life.

Kenji went back to Tokyo in the spring, yanked away from this pastoral romance by his father, who had begun to fret in the absence of his only child. It was a selfish move on Kenji's father's part, for food was even more scarce in Tokyo than in the country. My mother later heard that Kenji's stomach had swelled up as if he were with child, while the rest of him grew thin and wasted away—a second false pregnancy in the saga of my family.

Talking to me about him more than a quarter of a century later, my mother said with a sigh that while she cried hard when he left, she was young and callous, and so had forgotten him before she returned to Tokyo. Yet really she only mislaid the memory of him, for when they encountered each other years later, she knew him as soon as she saw him.

I heard the teakettle's whistle faintly through the door as I fumbled in my knapsack for the keys. It was a cold day in March; I was nine years old and I had just stepped off the school bus. In the front entrance, I stood still and listened for my mother, but the whistle drowned out all other sound. "Mama?" I started to walk towards the kitchen. "Mama?" The whistle seemed to get shriller, and I moved faster until I was running.

Although the kitchen is not far from the front entrance, it seemed a longer way than usual on that day. Yet when I finally got to the kitchen door, I could only stand there because there was nothing else for me to do. I do not remember if I was breathing hard. The kettle was out of control, whistling furiously and spitting steam from its spout, but my mother was sitting calmly at the table; she was drinking tea and flipping through the day's paper, and she looked as she always did: neat and smart in her well-tailored clothes, every hair impeccably in place.

While it was gray outside, the kitchen was warm, and the lamps gave off a golden light. Copper pots gleamed on the wall, and the plants glowed with health. The shrillness of the whistle made me grit my teeth.

"Yukiko," she said, and she raised her teacup to her lips and drank. "Yukiko, you're home."

It was hard to hear her over the whistle of the kettle. I nodded mutely back: Yes, I'm home.

"I have some bad news."

With another nod I showed her I was listening.

"It's about your father."

I waited.

"Your father has gone away. He won't be living with us anymore."

I walked across the room, turned the stove off, and faced her. We stood maybe five feet apart in the large, airy kitchen. She took a long, slow sip from her cup without taking her eyes off me. Her hand did not shake.

I turned around and was about to walk away, but she stopped me.

"Yukiko . . ."

"Yes?"

"It was his decision."

I remember wondering why she had bothered to articulate the obvious. "I know," I said.

At the age of sixteen I fell in love with Hamlet, the Prince of Denmark. On a school trip I had seen him on stage in New York City, but I was not interested in the actor, lithe and graceful though he was; I was in love with Hamlet himself. Although his treatment of Ophelia left something to be desired, I pined to spend my life with a man like that, mad and brilliant and witty. In contrast, the boys at school seemed tame and bland.

When my mother was sixteen, she wanted to be a doctor more than anything else in the world. She had a passion as well as a natural aptitude for math and science, and her favorite activity was to pore over textbooks until well into the night.

Aghast at the studious habits of her only daughter, my grandmother Yukiko waged a none-too-subtle campaign against them. She spoke ominously of the damage that long hours spent hunched over tiny print would do to eyesight and posture, and she nagged at Akiko about her music, asking why she spent only two hours a day at the piano, when she used to spend four. Complaining that she could not find her way alone through the meandering streets of Tokyo, Yukiko made Akiko go for long walks with her, and when they passed by fine stores, she dragged her into them, and tried to tempt her fancy with fine clothes, and trinkets for her hair.

Worst of all, at least according to Akiko, were the lessons in conduct. When Akiko became a teenager, Yukiko set about teaching her once again how to walk, dress, and talk, as if she had not already learned these skills as a young child. Akiko was reinstructed in how to get from one side of the room to the other (one foot placed directly in front of the other, and the toes turned ever so slightly inward); she was shown once again how to put on a kimono (low in the back, so that the skin can be seen below the hair); she was retrained in how to engage men in conversation, with bantering and also flattery.

In her own way, of course, Yukiko was trying to be a good mother, as Akiko knew even then. But she was so determined to procure a wealthy husband for her daughter that she could not bear to hear Akiko say that what she really wanted to do was study, and her quick temper flared up when Akiko refused to wear the clothes and baubles that she bought for her.

It was with little hope, therefore, that Akiko went to her parents and bowed low to them, her nose resting on the ground. "In the matter of my going to medical school, what do Father and Mother say?" she asked.

My grandfather inclined his great head and thought. "If you go to medical school," he said at last, "no one will marry you."

My mother kept her eyes on her hands, which were shaking slightly inside their long empty sleeves. She thought of how close she and her mother had been, and still were; she thought of all the hours they spent walking and shopping together, and chatting, too. No one knew her better than her mother.

"And what does Mother think?" she asked.

Yukiko did not bow her head, heavy with the weight of her hair, to think. "Your father is right," she said. "For a woman, marriage is the most important thing."

Akiko did not ask them again. She stayed home and continued to read medical books late at night, after she finished practicing the tea ceremony.

At some point in my teenage years, a neighbor of ours donated a box of trashy romances to me, and I read them all. Invariably these books featured a heroine with a small, heart-shaped face, a pair of huge, wistful eyes, and a body with curves that she strove in vain to conceal. Forced by her wretched life to take a humiliatingly subservient job, she would somehow meet up with a dark, aristocratic man who slept around a lot. At first he wolfishly hungered after our heroine, but her baggy clothes could not hide her virtue any more than her breasts, and after becoming first convinced and then enamored of her goodness, our dashing scoundrel of a hero would forsake his wolfish ways, and beg her to be his bride. The books were old and early on I spilled some ice cream on them: it is for this reason, perhaps, that I associate the idea of fairy-tale romance with the smell of mildew and rotten milk.

When I was eighteen, I was a freshman at Princeton, and terribly homesick. I was also thin for the first time in six years. At the end of the first term, my roommate dragged me to a party given by the debating club. I felt so uncomfortable there among all the drunk students that I ended up losing my virginity to the club treasurer, a lanky senior who went on to Washington and later became an important White House aide. We went out for two weeks and feverishly vowed eternal love to each other, but when he called me over the winter vacation, I felt no desire to be friends or even to talk.

When my mother was twenty-one, she walked into a small apartment in a trendy students' district in Tokyo, and saw a young man standing amidst the crowd. He was by the window, deep in impassioned argument and with his back turned towards her, but she noticed him immediately. It was something in the way he stood, the tension in his shoulder blades that stretched the shirt taut across his back, or the length of his neck rising naked and exposed above his collar. She was distracted, consumed by an almost physical sense of loss, which came welling up inside her throat and tasted unexpectedly like lime. Her best friend, Rié, who was chatting in an endless stream into her ear, had to ask her twice if she wanted something to drink.

When he turned around, he saw her staring. His eyes passed over her, sweeping by as he took in the rest of the room, and then they flicked back, and then again. She saw his eyes narrow and then widen with disbelief, and then he walked over to the host, who was sitting on a couch not far from him, and she saw their quick whispered consultation, their eyes glancing over at her, and the host's repeated nods of confirmation. The young man straightened his narrow back, squared his shoulders, and moved towards her.

His voice was deep, a stranger's pitch. "I believe I am your cousin," he said, using the honorific. "Your cousin Kenji."

Thirteen years had passed since they had run across the train tracks during an idyll in the middle of the war. In spite of the malnutrition he had suffered, he had grown well, and now stood half a head taller than most of the men in the room. Where his face had once been rounded and smooth, it was now gaunt and angular, and the new geometric theme continued with his head, which was almost triangular. His nose was tall, as the Japanese say, always with admiration. His Adam's apple was prominent in his long neck, and his chin had a new, aggressive thrust to it. His hair, which had once been straight and fine, had thickened and coarsened so that it now stood up on its own like a brush.

Neither he nor Akiko noticed Rié, who had come back bearing two glasses of water, and who for once was speechless, dumbstruck at the intensity of their gaze.

My mother looked into Kenji's eyes—so earnest now, and darker as well—and innocently smiled. "You haven't changed a bit," she said.

Two months later, she went out on a date that had been set up by her parents. The matchmaker introduced her to Tatsu just outside the restaurant, and then quietly disappeared.

Running her eyes quickly over the man picked to be her future husband, Akiko smiled in spite of herself, liking what she saw—a slim young man with bright eyes, and an overbite that gave his smile a disarming vulnerability. Her favorable impression of him held up through the course of the three-hour meal, for the matchmaker had done her job well: Akiko and Tatsu had so much in common that there was not a chance they would run out of things to say.

He had performed poorly in his studies at the University, but he was a music lover, and inquired with real interest and intelligence about her playing. While they had not met before, they traveled in the same large social circle, and they discovered with some hilarity that they shared the same opinions of all the people they both knew. By the end of the evening, they felt so comfortable together that they were able to joke about the awkwardness of this prearranged date, and the profound skepticism that they each had felt at the thought of their matchmaker—an old woman so nearsighted she could not reliably tell men and women apart—finding them someone to marry.

There was much about the date that was delightful, but what impressed Akiko most of all was Tatsu's sweetness, a desire to please and be pleased that she felt most keenly at the end of the meal, when they were pushing away their plates and getting ready to leave.

"What do you think?" he said, just as she was about to stand. "It could work out, you and me."

Halted in her movements, Akiko looked across the table at him, and knew he was right. Not just because she, having been briefed by the matchmaker, knew his particulars (his kindness to his elders, his gentleness to women, and the high-paying job he held in the company owned by his father), but also because the three hours they had spent chatting over dinner had given her a glimpse into the life that her parents—or more precisely, her mother—wished her to have. It was a life with few worries and even fewer surprises. There would be large family gatherings at fancy restaurants; two, three, or even four children running around at her feet, and that strangely disarming overbite beaming down at her at all times.

Seeing the hopeful expression that lit up Tatsu's face, my mother sighed, and stifled a momentary pang of regret. It was not that she had the perplexing sense of standing at a crossroads, for the course of her life had already been set. Nor was it that she regretted having promised herself to her cousin Kenji just four days earlier: she did not wish even for a second that she could spend her life with Tatsu instead.

What Akiko felt sorry about was that she had not backed out of this date, as she had originally intended. She should have announced to her parents that she had already decided she was not going to marry the man they had selected for her through the long, expensive, and elaborate matchmaking process. She should have resisted her curiosity; she should have turned down what seemed to her a perfect lark—the chance to take a peek at someone else's life; the opportunity, even, to live inside someone else's skin, if only for a night.

"I'm sorry," she said, and then she hesitated, not knowing how to continue. "I am so very sorry."

From the way my mother recounts this story (and I have heard it from her dozens of times), I know this was a hard moment for her: watching the brightness in Tatsu's eyes dim, and that caricature of a smile falter.

Without Kenji's success in his field, Akiko's old case of hero worship might not have made the transition to adult love, for she was like her mother in that she needed a man she could respect. As it was, the transition was amazingly smooth, and swift to boot: she knew in a week, a full month and a half before he did, that she would marry him.

Kenji was a physicist. His professors and fellow students whispered that he was brilliant, the best in his generation, a genius.

Confident and almost too proud, he knew of these rumors, and spun them into webs that eventually snared him as well as my mother.

"Honorable Parents, please may I marry this man," she said. She bowed, her heart thumping against the tatami floor as she waited for their response, her nose pressed against the ground.

"No," said Yukiko, preempting her husband. "Tatsu liked you, and thought you liked him. He's a nice young man, and second cousin to the Prince—"

My mother sat up, her face red from the blood that had rushed to her head as she held her bow, and glared at Yukiko. Five years had passed since her parents had denied her medical school, and she was stronger now and more truculent, with a will to match her mother's. "Is it because Kenji's my cousin, or because he's poor, or because he's Korean?" she demanded.

"None of those reasons," replied Yukiko, yelling back. "It's because you would be ruining your life with him. I know what he's like, and—"

"You're lying," said my mother, and then she screamed, "You're lying! You've forgotten that you were once just a fancy whore, and I never, ever want to be like you."

Bursting into tears, she ran out of their room; as soon as she reached her own, she began to pack.

She never looked back—or so, at least, she told me, many years later. But I have always figured that statement for a lie, if one made with only the kindest intentions: to keep me from feeling that she ever had cause to regret the marriage that led to my birth. For how could she possibly have avoided looking back? Sure, she likes America, with its roomy, well-built houses, its broad streets, and its well-tended green lawns that remind her of the Japanese countryside. I will even concede to her the point that New Jersey was a far better place than Tokyo to raise me, a girl. Still, even so, I find it impossible to believe that in all the years that followed that breach with her parents, she never once mused wistfully on the life that she let some other woman take.

Abused and then abandoned by Kenji, left with a child on her hands, poor, alone, stranded in a foreign country and cut off by her own pride from her family, she must have looked back, at least once, on that moment she ran out of her parents' room, and wished that instead she had stayed.

Yukiko's rejection of my father, which lies at the root of the years of coolness between her and my mother, will be the subject of the first set of questions that I ask her.

Obaasama, I will say (respectfully marveling), how did you know about Kenji? How did you see through the promising student to guess at the spoiled child who lay underneath, the strain of madness, and the abusive temper that no one had ever controlled?

Did you ever wish (I will say, bolder now, daringly moving on to far more rocky terrain) that you hadn't been able to predict how my mother's marriage with him would fare? Or even that you had kept your fears to yourself, and supported her in her wish to marry him instead? Did you ever regret that you—wishing your daughter only the best, the brightest, and the happiest of all possible futures—tried to make her repeat your successes, rather than let her create her own; did you secretly weep with remorse, as my mother did, over the rift that lay between you for almost thirty years?

CHAPTER SEVEN

OLD MRS. NOFFZ catches me, as she almost always does, even though I all but sprint on tiptoe the two-yard stretch from the elevator to my front door. The problem is that I am too slow and too loud with my keys.

Mrs. Noffz lives alone with a moody parrot across the hall in 16D, an apartment that is the mirror image of my own, and she spends her days lying in wait, listening for the sound of my locks being unbolted.

She makes an unlikely stalker. With wide eyes, an O of a mouth, and a pink-tipped little nose, she bears an uncanny resemblance to the children in a Dr. Seuss book. Even her hair, white and sparse though it is, looks childlike, tied in a single braid that follows the slope of her neck to reach the top of her back. Tonight she is standing under an umbrella, and she is wearing red Wellingtons under her nightgown. Smiling vacuously and continuously, shrunken but upright, she calls out to me from her doorway. "Good evening."

"Hi," I say, holding the door open just enough to be polite.

"It is hot out, isn't it." Mrs. Noffz's clothes are shabby and her hair is in constant disarray, but she takes great pains with her speech, enunciating every syllable with care.

"Yes, it is. Well, I should be going now. My mail, you know," I say, nodding at the bills in my hand.

"I think Mabel is feeling the heat quite a bit. She has buried herself in her feathers and she refuses to speak to me."

"That's too bad," I say, pulling the door shut another inch.

"Last night it was so windy. We hoped it would rain then, but not a drop came down."

I nod.

"Well, I don't want to take up too much of your time."

"That's okay," I say. "Good night, Mrs. Noffz."

"Good-bye, sleep well," she says, and under the protection of her umbrella she smiles at me as I hurriedly pull the door shut.

Eric thinks that my grandmother is going to be like old Mrs. Noffz—a little embarrassing, a lot annoying, but wholly endearing and sweet when considered in the abstract, as a photo in the album, or a name on a tombstone. Remembering his great-aunt Julia, who grew so enormously stout that her coffin had to be custom-made, he smiles fondly now. "Dear old thing," he murmurs (waxing British, not coincidentally, as he waxes sentimental), forgetting, or choosing to forget, how her belches and gas spoiled their unfortunately intimate family reunions.

He does not know, for I have kept it from him, that my grandmother is the last person to elicit the kind of fond, indulgent smile (perilously close to laughter at her expense) that the memory of dear old Great-Aunt Julia seems to provoke. I have long been cherishing the thought of Eric's surprise when he finally meets her. Even though she will not be unusually tall by Western standards, even though her beauty has been dimmed by the ravages of age, he cannot fail to be stunned by her presence.

The most recent photograph I have of her is from three years ago, taken by my mother on the day after my grandfather's funeral. Looking straight into the camera, she is poised and impossibly elegant in a plain dark suit; her face, with its careful makeup, shows little sign of grief. She towers a full head above her two daughters-in-law, meek Aunt Tomoko and brassy Aunt Tomoko, and she is a shade taller than her sons, who take after their father in terms of height as well as temperament. It seems odd, contrary to nature, even, to see her silvery head rising above the dark ones of her children. But then again, my grandmother has lived in defiance of most social rules, clawing her way up from her humble beginnings to a cool, aristocratic demeanor and deportment that would rival any woman's in Japan, so why should she not live in defiance of the process of evolution as well?

She has been listless, lately, so much thinner and less haughty since her husband's death that her two daughters-in-law wrote independently to my mother—Yukiko's one blood daughter, and her oldest child—for help. Shuttling back and forth between her sons' households, for all the world like some latter-day Lear, does not suit Yukiko. Her sons and their Tomokos welcome her into their homes dutifully, but she, with a virulence that surprises no one, hates that life.

Both Tomokos, the meek as well as the brassy, dislike her, of course. While their worries about her may very well be sincere, they must be relieved that she will soon be out of their houses, far away in another country. Yukiko, with her imperious ways, is a nightmare of a mother-in-law, never hesitating to abuse my poor aunts in public. What makes it worse for the Tomokos is that they get scant support from their families. Their easygoing husbands, long used to the quick temper and sharp tongue that masks their mother's fundamental warmth of heart, offer sympathy but no help, laughing off the news of her latest tirade. My cousins like her because they know she is their friend, though a grand-mother she is not, at least in the sense that her lap (bony and hard) does not make a comfortable refuge; nor does she knit, or bake, or even smile with crow's feet by her eyes. But she likes to talk with her grandsons, as she will with me, her only granddaughter.

Gleeful as I am at the prospect of Eric meeting my grandmother, the prospect of her meeting him worries me a little. Chary with her ap-proval and capricious in her tastes, she might decide to take a dislike to Eric, just as she has to my unfortunate aunts. Still, the chances of this happening are remote, for Eric is too handsome, too polite, too obviously successful and, finally, too male to excite the scorn that fell on the heads of the well-intentioned but completely and infuriatingly girlish Aunt Tomokos.

I will know right away, of course, in the first few moments after they meet, whether my grandmother likes Eric. Well? I will say, smiling with pride as I lean against the doorframe, my shoulder still warm from where he brushed against me as he left the room. What do you think, *Obaasama*? He's okay, isn't he, this man that I have promised to marry.

Phillip had been gone for five months by the time I met Eric, in July of last year. Usually I love summer, but that year I hated the sight of couples strolling in the park, and the sound of people laughing as they roamed the streets at dusk.

I had been studying inside my apartment all week, and I was nervous about going out; if the ticket had not already been purchased, I would not have gone. I dallied so long that I was late leaving the house. Yet I was lucky with the subways, and when I stepped inside the hall, flushed from the brisk walk through the crowds, it was to find that the lights were still on; that the patrons of the arts, in varying degrees of fine attire, were still standing around and chatting as they fanned themselves with programs.

While I took a program, I waved away the usher's offer of assistance; my mother had given me the season tickets in March, and by July I knew my seat as well as the people I sat with, the perfumed lady with the dimpled elbows to my left, and the snoring fat man on my right.

I took off my jacket and placed it on the seat to my right, and sank gratefully into my chair. A dark-haired, clean-cut man standing two aisles ahead of me caught my eye; he was talking to an Asian couple, but kept glancing at me all the while. I pegged him immediately as a man with an Asian-woman fetish, and sure enough, after a low word to his friends, he began edging towards the aisle, excuse-meing to the three old ladies on the end. He came up my row slowly, a smile on his face, his eyes fixed on me, and his step the stealthy, dogged tread of the hunter.

New York is filled with men like that. They have introduced themselves to me in coffee shops, libraries, bookstores, and even over the phone, where a mere mention of my name once triggered a flood of conversational Japanese, delivered in a flawless accent, as well as a discount on the software I was ordering. If our conversation goes as far as career talk, I make sure to tell them I am studying English *literature,* with all the emphasis on the second term, but no matter what I say or what big words I use, they all too often ride over my hints and ask me how long I have been in this country, or they compliment me on my English skills. I always snub them, some less rudely than others.

"Do you mind?" asked the young man, waving at my coat and bag. "Could I sit down?"

"No," I said, but in spite of all my righteous anger, I softened my response with a smile, for his tone was impeccably polite, and close up, he was very good-looking indeed.

His smile abruptly vanished from his face, and he looked, just for a second, like a pouty child. "What do you mean, no? That's my seat."

I wanted to flee, but I would have had to brush by his knees or vault over the seats in front of me to do so. So instead I picked up my jacket and purse and placed them on my lap. Mercifully the lights soon began to dim.

It was not until after the tuning of the orchestra, the arrival of the conductor, and the start of the concerto that I mustered the courage to speak. "I'm sorry," I said, leaning towards him a fraction of an inch, and keeping my voice to a whisper.

"Don't mention it," he answered politely, but I could hear, almost imperceptibly, the smothered laugh in his words.

"I thought—well, I thought you—"

"I know what you thought," he interrupted. "It's not surprising—you must get that all the time."

The woman to my left turned, her dimpled elbow brushing against my arm. "Shh," she said sharply. "Have some respect for the music."

"Excuse us," said the young man, once again exhibiting beautiful manners. As the woman sat back, somewhat mollified, the perfume proved too much, and I sneezed. I bit my bottom lip, fighting another sneeze as well as a wave of hysteria, and then I felt the man next to me begin to shake. Under cover of the Chopin concerto, as the woman beside me glared, we laughed together in the dark, conspiratorially, like children.

His friends, the Chinese couple, came up to claim him during the intermission. The last piece on the program was the Pastoral Symphony, and as I heard its opening measures, I felt a pang for the snoring fat man, the usual occupant of the seat to my right: although most composers put him to sleep right away, he loved Beethoven dearly and he would have enjoyed the symphony much more than me or the young man who kept half-turning to look at me in the darkness.

Mostly I was thinking about one of the novels I was reading, but I remember the rousing finale, how the conductor bowed, everybody clapped, and the lights went on. I had not enjoyed the concert particularly, but perhaps I was more stirred by the music than I realized, because when the stranger sitting next to me confidently, almost carelessly, leaned over and said, "Would you like to have dinner with me?" I smiled and nodded yes as if I always went out with strange men at night in the city. As we stood up, I wondered if the people sitting behind us thought that this stranger and I were a couple of long standing, perhaps even married, and were so familiar and comfortable with each other that we did not need to speak for hours at a time. Now I know that most people trust Eric immediately and instinctively. His instant charm is probably his most critical professional asset.

"Eric Lowenson," he said, reaching out his hand in a mock-formal gesture. "I'm Kiki, Kiki Takehashi, nice to meet you," I said as I shook his hand; usually I am shy during introductions, but I felt at ease with him.

There was a crowd at the door and a marked shortage of cabs on the street, as a light but steady rain was falling. No one seemed prepared for the rain, for the skies had been clear throughout the day and in the evening before the concert, but Eric surprised me by pulling out an umbrella, a large navy one, which he held carefully over my head even though the rain was so light. As I discovered later, Eric almost always carries around an umbrella, clear skies and favorable forecasts notwithstanding. At first I believed this habit bespoke volumes: wariness, worry, and a fastidious, almost feline distaste for water and mess—all the hallmarks of a momma's boy, and everything that Phillip was not. Yet as Eric and I walked through more and more showers, increasingly I began to see that the umbrella he always carries is not really so at odds with the one lock of hair that insists on falling rakishly over his eyes, giving him the smoldering potential of a teen idol. He does not actually care about getting wet, although he does not care for it, either. He is in fact much more likely to use his umbrella to cover others, and though even now, when he whips one out from some hidden pocket, I tease him about how his umbrella is a (tried and true) means of getting close to women, it is used, often as not, to keep his male buddies at the office dry, as well as dozens and dozens of female ones.

He steered me through the crowds on the sidewalk, clearing a little space so that I walked without hindrance. Gray smoke swirled and curled out of a grate on the street, and the rain at once blurred and heightened the lights of the city. We walked a few blocks until we found a tiny French restaurant that he had heard about and wanted to try. It was such a small and unassuming place that I did not think it would cost much, but the prices were startling and the portions, when they came, were minute. The waiters were quiet and benevolent. Eric told me that the wine we were drinking was first-class, and that the food was fair, although the fish was a bit overcooked.

Over dinner I gave him the usual simplified summary of my dissertation, and he described his work. Soon the food was gone, his fish expertly deboned, and his glass emptied of wine. Neither of us wanted coffee. He signaled and the waiter brought him the check, which I reached for but he picked up first. "I'm paying," he said. "I asked."

"But I took your seat," I said, "and I wasn't going to let you sit down."

"Ah," he said, handing his credit card to the waiter, "but you did let me in the end."

"That hardly warrants such a nice dinner," I said, laughing.

He grew still as he watched me, a slightly puzzled look on his face.

The waiter stepped in, then, with the receipt. Eric glanced at it, calculated the tip with record speed, and signed it with a flourish. Only then did he look again at me. His brow was still faintly wrinkled in thought, but he did not ask a question or voice confusion. Instead he paid me a compliment, speaking to me in the tender tones of a lover, or a parent.

"I really like it when you smile," he said.

As we stopped to pick up our coats, I saw a china fixture on the counter, a sculpture made up of two levels of plates, one balanced on top of the other like the skeletal frame of a building under construction. Each plate was filled with mints. Standing there and looking down at them, I thought how Phillip would have loved this: we went to one Chinese restaurant all the time because it had a whole bucket of mints on the counter, and we took turns covering each other so that we could fill all our pockets with them. But because a young lawyer in a suit and tie stood behind me this time, I picked up just two mints and daintily nibbled on one as I pulled on my coat. Then, without moving my lips, I sucked on the other until it was gone.

It was past twelve. He did not suggest another meeting until he had found me a taxi and put me inside it. When he bent down to talk to me through the open door, he did not hesitantly say, "Would you be interested . . . ?" or "Could I call you?"; he seemed to assume that I would be, and that he could. "You're in the phone book?" was all he asked, and I said yes, or maybe I just nodded my head. He spelled out my last name to check that he had it right, and I nodded again, impressed with the ease with which he reeled it off. Then he shut the door; I waved good-bye through the window, and the cab pulled away into the light summer rain.

As I sat in the taxi and watched the city lights go flashing by, I was reminded of the way I felt when I was a child, and my father tucked me into the front seat of the car before driving me to school in the morning. Sometimes in the winter, the windows of our car were all white with frost. "Let's see," my father would say on those days, examining the depth of the ice. "Give me thirty of those rivers today. And don't cheat."

I never did cheat, mouthing out the numbers slowly (. . . fi-ive Mis-sis-sip-pi . . .), as if I could in this way slow down the ticking of the seconds on my watch: it was a rare day I finished before he did. The glare of the sunshine hurt my eyes; I hated school, where the children mocked me with rhymes about Chinese eyes, and I was always grumpy early in the morning. But as my father scraped the frost off the windows, he sang silly songs and wiggled his tongue at me through the clean patches, so that I laughed and forgot to dread school, at least for a while.

That night in July, Eric made me feel safe in a way that I had not felt since the loss of my father, so many years ago.

The following morning, Eric called to ask me out to a movie over the weekend. I hesitated, but then I thought again of my father, and the umbrella held over me in the rain. I thought of my mother, and the years that she lost grieving for him.

"Sure," I told him. "Thanks, that sounds like fun."

After all, *Obaasama*, I will say (shrugging as I explain), what more did I have to lose?

Phillip first appeared in late March, and by July he was a part of my apartment. He was almost a household fixture, not a piece of furniture to sit on or eat off or rest books upon, nor even a lamp that you would want to be near, but rather something to look at from afar, like a sculpture or a souvenir. Except that unlike a statue, of course, he refused to stay stationary, the suddenness of his appearances and disappearances always keeping me slightly off-balance.

Given that this incarnation of Phillip was and always has been as silent and immobile as stone, it now seems faintly ridiculous and more than a little eccentric that I used to talk to him, trying to keep up my side of the seemingly unending conversation that had once been ours. Although it was rare indeed that I felt up to making a joke in those days, on one or two occasions I even tried to coax a smile from him, mock-cheerfully calling out to him when I returned home from the grocery store, playing at regular-coupledom ("Honey, I'm home . . . got you some of those doughnuts you like—you know you are just wasting away. . . .").

I abruptly ended these attempts to chat with him after a few months. These days, I try as much as possible never to talk to him, or even to wave or nod, for as I know from experience, it is none too pleasant, waiting in vain for his response.

But back then, before I knew any better, when I still hoped that Phillip was listening, and someday might even reply, I made sure to keep him apprised of all the (very few) events of note in my life. So I told him about Eric, breaking the news offhandedly ("I met this guy, see. . . ."), and before the first few dates, I tried to emphasize to him the casualness of each event: "It's just a movie"—or dinner or a picnic or a walk— "and then I'm coming home."

He was always there to watch me leave. While he did not smile, he did not look sad, either. Yet one night, as I pulled open the door, I looked back and saw his body stretched and flattened against the wall. Visions of martyrs flashed through my head, and I had to fight down a sudden urge to yank him off his cross, and pelt him with rotten tomatoes. I regretted the urge almost as soon as I felt it, though, and so instead of flying at him with my nails extended, I tendered him yet another explanation. "Just because you're dead, doesn't mean I have to be," I whispered, before hurrying out the door.

Later that night, after an outdoor concert, Eric invited me to his apartment, and I accepted. He lives way downtown, in a modern apartment building made of glass and steel. We took a cab to get there and I had no idea where we were, but of course that did not matter because Eric was with me. In his presence, strange and hostile neighborhoods begin to look friendly and familiar, waiters snap to attention, and harried shop people suddenly have time to spare. Even on the busiest streets at the busiest times, unoccupied taxis spring out of the traffic whenever he lifts his arm. I have rarely seen him lost in any sense of the word.

That night he led me through the double doors and waved at the doorman, and he hit the elevator buttons so fast I did not know we were going to the eleventh floor until we got there. Our footsteps muffled by the carpeting, we walked in silence down the long hallway from the elevator to his door. There are many doors along the corridor of Eric's apartment building, and they all look the same, off-white with the shiny brass knob and the numbers in matching gold above. I may have been more nervous than I realized, because I found something frightening in the thought that any one of those doors could be his.

His door was a little different, though, since it came at the very end of all the rows of other doors, and was sheltered and private, on an angle from the rest. Neither of us had said anything since we had stepped out of the cab, and we entered his apartment still without speaking.

He turned on a few lights, but the room remained pleasantly dim. His apartment is so well insulated that it is always very quiet, and the thick carpeting further deadens the noise. High though my apartment is, city noises break into my bedroom late at night, and after I spend a lot of time at Eric's place, I find myself missing the sounds of traffic, loud music muted by distance, even the occasional car alarm going off.

I sat down on one end of the black leather sofa. He pulled out a chair from the dining table and turned it around before he sat down, so that he straddled the back between his legs. I crossed my ankles. He was watching me quietly, perhaps expectantly. I looked down at my hands as they twisted around each other on my lap. We sat together like this for a long time, maybe a minute, and then he broke the silence. "You're the damnedest woman." He spoke seriously, and though the term did not sound too flattering, the tone of his voice made it seem a compliment.

"What's that supposed to mean?"

"You're strange," he said. "Different."

"How so?"

"Well, a.) because you don't talk much."

I was a guest and had no desire to prove him wrong. I smiled and waited quietly for him to continue.

"And b.) because any other woman would be curious about my apartment."

"I'm curious about your apartment," I said.

"Then why haven't you looked around?"

"Good idea," I said. "I will."

With my hands clasped behind my back, I walked around and examined his living room. There was one healthy-looking plant on the windowsill, but everything else was gray or black or white. The room was fashionably bare of furniture, and it was absolutely spotless.

"It's so clean," I said. "Is it always like this?"

"Yes. I like things to be neat."

Electronic equipment lined the walls of the room. There was a very chic black television, a VCR, a large stereo and strange-looking speakers. There was even a movie camera tucked away in the corner. I peered into the lens of the camera and saw myself distorted, my nose swollen and my eyes and mouth tiny and obscure. "Wow," I said.

He stood up and pushed the chair in. "Yeah," he said. "It's a fun toy."

"What do you tape?" I asked, and then I caught myself and laughed. "Never mind—you don't have to answer that if you don't want to."

"I'll answer it," he said. "The firm recommends that trial lawyers see themselves on tape, so mostly I just watch myself giving speeches. Not exactly X-rated."

"No," I agreed, and then I stopped because I had seen his bookshelves, and in the murky light, they looked very full.

But when my eyes got used to the lack of light, I found that I was able to scan the shelves in less than five seconds because there was not much to see after all: well-bound and identical-looking books like rows and rows of encyclopedia sets, beautiful and clean and doubtlessly very expensive. There was nothing scruffy and paperback to mar the uniformity of these books; perhaps he kept his pleasure reading by his bed. Phillip did not finish his last year of high school and he had always done poorly in English, but he had had a few dog-eared copies of novels, many of them by Peter Matthiessen, that he had taken with him on all his travels, and in New York he had accumulated an enormous pile of biographies and political histories that he bought in the Strand and other secondhand bookstores. Eric went to Yale as an undergraduate and then immediately to Harvard Law School, but he was not a reader. I sat back with my legs stretched out in front of me and my fingers half-buried in the richness of the carpet. I needed a rest.

I looked up at Eric. His ankles crossed and his arms folded, he leaned against the wall and watched me. He threw a stark shadow against the wall, and his lips wore a faint, fixed smile. We looked at each other for a while in that position. I was trying to think how I could leave gracefully, and he was just smiling quietly, and then he slowly walked over and knelt down on the ground beside me.

He put his hand under my chin and tilted my face upwards. He had not seriously kissed me before, but he was clearly about to do so now. He smelled nice, like a lotion, and I could feel the heat of his breath upon me.

"Aren't you nervous?" I asked quickly, just before his face came into contact with mine.

For a split second he paused, and then he shook his head. "No," he said, and then he kissed me.

It was an aggressive male kiss, with lots of strong tongue reaching towards my throat, and I judged it a failure. It was not really his fault. He had to bend down quite a bit to reach my lips, and my head was tilted at an awkward position: it was almost inevitable that our teeth would clash. First kisses are usually not much good, but I was disappointed anyway. I was suddenly conscious of how inelegant I looked sprawled on the floor with my legs sticking out in front of me; my skirt was bunched up by my thighs, and my feet splayed awkwardly outwards. I tucked my knees under me and tugged at the ends of the skirt. It fell around me in a circle, leaving me framed like a frog on a lily pad.

He was panting a little and I furtively wiped at the corner of my mouth, where his tongue had been too avid. He kissed me again more slowly, and this time the feel of him traveled down my spine to warm my body. Then he took me by the hand and led me into the bedroom, austere and modern like the rest of his apartment. The stream of light from the hallway showed me that there were no books on the nightstand next to his alarm clock—all I could see was a package of condoms. I laughed to myself at that because I had condoms in my purse as well. In fact I was well prepared for the night: before leaving the house, I had packed my purse with a small travel kit for my contact lenses, my toothbrush, and all of my makeup.

Eric moved towards the bed and I shut the door behind us. He called out softly to me and I groped my way towards him, my hands outstretched in front of me so that I would not trip and fall in the dark. It was a windy night but at his window the blinds did not rattle, and his radiator worked far more efficiently and quietly than mine did at home.

The sex was excellent.

Afterwards, while he slept, I crept around the room to gather my clothes together. Naked on my hands and knees, I felt for my bra beneath the bed. In spite of the heater and the plush carpeting, I was chilled.

He woke up when I sat down on the bed to put my shoes on. Still half-asleep, he reached out and put a hand on my knee.

"What're you doing?" he asked.

"I have to get home."

He was hoarse with sleep. "Can't you spend the night?"

"No."

"Why not?"

"I don't want to."

"Are you serious? Come on, you don't really mean that." His words were cut off at the end by a huge yawn.

"I have some things to do tomorrow."

"Like what?" He propped himself up on an elbow, and squinted in an effort to see me. "Kiki, tomorrow is Sunday. There is absolutely no reason for you to go home. I'll make you pancakes in the morning and we'll read the *Times* together."

"I don't like pancakes."

He laughed. "You sound like a little girl. I'll buy you bagels instead—is that better?" He pulled me down on top of him, and began to unbutton my shirt. "You've got to stay. I insist."

I did not get home until late afternoon of the following day. My body still bore Eric's imprint, as if he had been a careless criminal leaving clues to his identity all over the scene of the crime. It was not an unpleasant feeling, and I caught myself humming Beethoven as I put the kettle on.

Sipping on my tea, I looked around the kitchen. It was not in good condition, for after Phillip left, I had avoided it as much as I could. For so long, the entire space, all sixty-odd square feet of it, had seemed crammed to overflowing with his presence—the actual, living Phillip, not the pale shadow of him that hid mouselike in the closets and corners of my apartment.

It was in the kitchen, more than any other place, that Phillip shed the cool that he wore like a cloak. The very act of preparing food together, an act that he took very seriously, though with varying degrees of success, unleashed memories of both his mother and his travels in him, and brought him close to something approaching a state of pure bliss. When he was in the kitchen, he was a terror and a delight—vibrant, noisy and, above all, clumsy, dropping dishes and knocking over glasses of water and wine as he waved his arms around, searching for the words and gestures to convey all the wonders of Europe. He was a fearless cook, trying soufflés as well as fancy Thai dishes, and he attempted to make bread probably every other week, thus ensuring that both of us were regularly doused with flour. When we washed dishes together, as my mother and I had always done when I was at home, he sang while I beat out the rhythm on the sink, soapy water sloshing in four-four time onto the floor. On a couple of nights, when the hour was very late, we hauled ourselves on top of the counter and danced to the accompaniment of our voices.

Standing in the kitchen on that Sunday afternoon in August, with Eric's fingerprints all over my body, I barely recognized anything around me. It was as if I had been away at Eric's apartment for weeks instead of a night. The gleaming Formica of the counter defied dust and dirt, but the old, dried-out onions had sprouted spring-green stalks, the potatoes had white knobs sticking out all over them, and light orange hairs and the green top were growing back on a shriveled carrot I had left out on a plate. A single ant, one of the last of the tribe haunting my kitchen during the winter, appeared out of nowhere and marched across the white expanse of the kitchen counter.

Even food that had never been alive had miraculously found a life force. Blue-green mold brightened the bread by the toaster, and when I took the milk out to add into my tea, I found that it had changed into a curd with a strong sharp smell. The food had relapsed into the habit of life, just as nails and hair grow to crazy lengths on a body in the grave.

For more than three years, ever since the fire, my grandmother has been stupefied with grief. On some mornings, she—a woman who, blessed with the constitution of a peasant, has not been really sick in all of her seventy-four years—all but refuses to get out of bed. During the day, her stare is often glassy; her expression, blank.

Obaasama, I will say (for the sake of politeness, knowing her answer before my own question), do you know what it feels like to forget that you are dead?

Then, after she shakes her head, I will describe for her that tingling sensation, so like pins and needles in the feet.

CHAPTER EIGHT

It just so happened that she was looking out the window when Sekiguchi approached the geisha house for the first time. Although the path was placed on level ground, he walked on it with the flat, uncontrolled gait of someone coming down a steep hill. Yet he moved quickly, so that the dust flew around his ankles in a cloud. His head was absurdly large, his body squat. As he came closer, she saw that his features were oddly blurred, his right eye drooping and his mouth twisting down, as if someone had thrown a bucket of water on him, and his face had melted.

The owner of once morbidly unwieldy breasts, Yukiko did not smile, instead keeping her eyes fixed solemnly upon him until he disappeared through the entranceway of the geisha house.

My grandmother was eighteen, and already completely accustomed to the feeling of the high, tightly bound obi of a full-fledged geisha. If she was not already versed in the one hundred and one ways to love a man, she was at least well on her way. She had lost her virginity two years earlier, during a middling large earthquake, and the two events were linked irrevocably in her mind: the muggy morning, the noontime cool winds, and her sense in the split second before the quake struck that the earth gave a downbeat, like the intake of a breath before speech. He had been a heavy man with soft, pampered hands, who paid a lot for the privilege of deflowering her. He hurt her, poking and prodding so roughly that she almost cried out, and although she knew the other women would be disappointed in her, she tried to push him away, her fingers fluttering in vain against him. By the glow of the fire she saw his face flush a dark red, as if he were suddenly drunk, and when the earth moved, she confused it with his shudders.

When it was over she wanted to laugh, it had been so quick.

Her work, consisting as it did of looking pretty, going to parties, and lying under a man, was not difficult. She enjoyed her status and sometimes, even, her job, and was especially grateful when she considered the arduous work she did in the rice fields as a child.

Her activities in the bedroom were not only limited to business, for she had a steady boyfriend, a man younger than most of her clients, and far poorer, too. Yukiko had met Jun at the local fish market, where he worked, the smooth long muscles of his thighs and arms shown off to full advantage as he bent down to lift and carry crates of fresh shrimp and eels.

Theirs was an easygoing relationship, blissfully free of what she considered was the inevitable condescension that came hand in hand with paying for her time. Jun was reserved about his feelings for her, but she, for one, was sure this was love. She was especially appreciative that he expected so little from her. When she was with him, she relaxed, so much so that she could feel her prized posture slowly beginning to slump, and her normally careful speech gradually starting to slur. After a few hours by his side, she could barely force her muscles to raise her to her feet.

Yukiko thought Jun well worth the conniving and duplicity required to carry on an extracurricular affair, one that did not feed the already full coffers of the geisha house. Kaori, her futon-chum of her apprentice years, was less sure, but feeling that the geisha house owed it to Yukiko, she helped to arrange their secret trysts.

Yukiko was the most successful geisha of the house. She had a steady pool of clients who came back again and again, and she took in a lot of yen in tips. Yet even when she talked back to the men and flirted, as all the geishas were trained to do, there was an air of remoteness about her. Proud and tall, she intimidated some of the clients, and alienated others.

When in bed with them, she was helpful but distant, musing on earthquakes, and the pungent odor of fish.

A week after she had watched him make his flat-footed way to the geisha house, Yukiko met Sekiguchi at a party that he hosted. She concluded that he looked worse, on closer inspection, than he had through the window. His skin was pitted to the point that it no longer seemed like skin, but rather the surface of some alien land: ravaged, ruined, lunar. His right eye, pulled down in a steep droop, was glazed over; when he talked with people, he had to turn his head so that he could peer at them out of his left. He was clearly a familiar sight to his friends, but his face and his sidelong glance unnerved the other geishas, their gazes flickering away from his face and then back again.

He said little during the party, but whenever he spoke, the men fell respectfully silent, to an extent perhaps beyond the courtesy accorded to the man footing the bill.

Yukiko was repelled by his appearance, and determined not to show it. She marched up to him as well as she could on her knees, the saké decanter in her hand. "Let me pour for you," she said.

They stared at each other. She kept her eyes steady in spite of the face, which was far worse than she had thought, and she saw him slowly smile, and knew he liked her for her boldness.

His skin aged him, and she was startled when he told her that he was only twenty, an astoundingly young age to host a geisha party, and a mere two years older than she.

The geisha house was serviced by a redoubtable network of gossip. The geishas had spies and informers everywhere—servants of the rich, mostly, but also the destitute members of the upper and middle classes, who were reduced to selling whatever they could (kimonos, books, the secrets and scandals of their friends) in an effort to stave off ruin for another day.

By these means Yukiko heard tell of Sekiguchi's success. Young though he was, his financial acumen was already widely known; his capacity for hard work, legendary. He had a talent for leadership, which gave rise to rumors of a political career in the offing.

She also heard of his past. He had been a handsome, robust boy, although shy and quiet, until the age of four, when he had been struck by a nearly fatal case of smallpox. By the time he recovered, almost a full year later, he was a different child. Handsome and robust no longer, he seemed to have shed his shyness as well, and he began speaking out, in the process revealing an incisive intelligence that not even his mother had suspected. Had it not been for the smallpox, speculated the gossips, his life might well have been an unexceptional one.

She learned, too, that he was married. His wife was sickly and, after two years of marriage, still childless.

After the party, Sekiguchi began visiting her regularly. He did no more than drink tea—an expensive drink, for he of course had to pay for her time. She sat on her knees with her feet tucked under her, chatting to him for an hour, and through years of practice she was still able to stand up at the end to bid him good-bye, despite the tingling of her feet. He sat cross-legged, listening to her talk, and sipped at his tea.

Yukiko was preoccupied during the first couple of visits, and had to strive not to let Sekiguchi know it. After nineteen months of rushed encounters in unlikely rooms, her lover, Jun, had come to the decision that he resented the work that she did. First he pouted, refusing to tell her what was wrong, and then he sulked, his well-cut mouth turning down at its ends. When the thought that she spent her nights luring other men finally became too much for him, he ceased talking to her altogether, staring moodily into space whenever she spoke. Jun and Yukiko had never talked much to each other, judging it wiser to spend their all-too-brief sessions in intercourse of another sort, but this was a silence of a wholly different degree and ilk. During their assignations (for there was no question that they would stop meeting to have sex), hers was the only voice that was ever used.

In the beginning, with Jun acting up in this way, she was relieved, albeit a little surprised, that Sekiguchi did not attempt to make love to her. When she talked it over with Kaori, as she did with every predicament of her life, she wondered aloud if he had no desire for her at all, but came out of loneliness, as some of the older clients did. Not until his fifth visit in as many weeks did she admit that Kaori had been right to scoff at her suggestion: it was neither shyness, nor impotence, nor respect for his absent wife that made him hesitate to touch her. Sekiguchi spent his sessions watching her almost calculatingly, and she was at first infuriated, and then amused, when she decided that he, with his face that frightened children, was attempting to determine whether she was love-worthy. He had gall, but she rather liked that in a man. Besides, there was a certain sexiness to the way he carried himself, as if his matter-of-fact assumption of authority could command desire as well as obedience.

Sekiguchi was in fact attractive to women, and would be so for the whole of his life. With the exception of Kaori, all the geishas and apprentices of the house at first openly pitied Yukiko for his interest, for she was notoriously fussy, and her new admirer was not only ugly but unkempt as well, with dirt under his nails and his hair perpetually overgrown. Kaori, who alone knew how little Yukiko cared about Jun's lack of cleanliness, and who was also aware of how sullen he had lately become, watched Yukiko's increasingly careful preparations for Sekiguchi's visits with concern rather than pity. But as his visits continued, the other geishas also began to fall under the spell of his authority, and then they all fell to worrying about Yukiko.

Love was, of course, an occupational hazard in their trade, and as the mistress of the house was wont to remind them, married clients posed the greatest threat of all. Only two alternatives were available to the geisha stupid enough to fall for a married man. If he offered to keep her, buying her out of the geisha house and setting her up in a home of her own, she would lead a precarious existence at best, vulnerable to the vagaries of his affection. The security of marriage would be denied her, as divorce was virtually unheard of in those days, and she would have to live with the fear that at any point he might decide to give her up for his wife. The geisha house, where shelter, daily meals, and the warmth of female companionship were guaranteed even for a woman long past her prime, offered a far better future.

In the other scenario, which was far more likely, the married man would simply tire of the geisha and move on to another woman, or perhaps back to his wife. The wisdom here was that if a man could cheat on his wife, he would cheat on his mistress as well. The tears of the geisha would mean little to him, as he had already paid for his time.

As the mistress of the house continually warned them, either alternative was grim, spelling doom for the geisha, heartache and much unease.

At about this time Yukiko began to be troubled by falling dreams. She knew from her friends that such dreams were common. Every woman in the house, it seemed, suffered from the disorienting experience of falling, seemingly out of control, in her sleep, and then jerking herself awake. But Yukiko's case was an extreme one. She had those dreams three, four times a night, every night, for almost a month running. In the mornings she was cranky and sluggish, and in the evenings, when she went to work, she had to wear two coats of paint to mask her puffy face.

Her puffiness notwithstanding, the sleeplessness improved Yukiko's looks, conferring upon her a languidness and sensuality that her somewhat forbidding beauty had always lacked. Her lips were fuller and her eyelids heavier, and her movements had slowed, so that when she reached down to smooth her kimono over her hips, it seemed an invitation. She was more popular with clients than she ever had been before.

It was an unusually cool October. Sekiguchi's face was lightly flushed when he came in at his usual hour on Saturday, and she thought as they greeted each other that his color was due to the north wind.

"I am going away," he announced without preamble. "My wife is finally pregnant."

She did not immediately register the meaning of his words, so abrupt had they been. Then she felt herself slipping, the sensation she had experienced repeatedly in her dreams. Struggling for level ground, she forced herself to scan his face clinically for signs of the handsome boy that rumor said he had been. She found nothing.

She lifted her hand to her hair, for a moment veiling her face with her sleeve, and then she moved her hand back to her lap. "Congratulations," she said. "I hope all goes well."

His head tilting, he peered closer at her. Her voice had been cool and steady, her eyes clear and her face smooth, but Sekiguchi's mouth contorted as if he wanted to speak, and she realized with horror and a burst of anger that he was gazing at her with pity.

Yet when he reached out to embrace her good-bye, she did not resist. As he held her, she thought of Jun, with his smooth long muscles and his lovely, petulant mouth, who had finally acquiesced—just last week—to her decision that they part. She shivered, but with such tight self-control that Sekiguchi thought it was his breath on her that stirred the flyaway hairs near her ears.

When he came back a mere two months later, she was waiting for him. Forewarned by the gossip line, she knew of the pregnancy that had one day simply melted away, the stomach that had flattened, and the retreat from all society made by the wife.

She thought at first that he looked much the same, except that his flat-footed gait may have been a shade more noticeable than usual as he stepped into the room. He slid the paper door shut behind him and returned Yukiko's bow, his good eye brightening as it lit upon her face. It was not until he hitched up the ends of his kimono and sat down on the floor that she noticed, with a peculiar tightening of her chest, how he had changed. His mouth and his weak eye drooped even more than they used to, giving him the comically morose look of a bulldog, and there was a dullness even to his left eye now. For the first time, she could spot lines etched into his forehead.

He asked her about her life during the past two months, and the parties and the activities of the geishas. Sekiguchi's requests for the gossip of the house always made her want to laugh, but it touched her, too, for few of the other clients evinced any interest in her except as it concerned them. So she always readily acceded to his desire and regaled him with stories, as she did then: of Michi-chan, the youngest, newest apprentice and the darling of the house, who pined after her parents, her grandmother, her dog and her cat, and of how they all came to visit last weekend, turning the almost staid establishment into a veritable menagerie; of Sachiko, flat-nosed and merry and addicted to the gay whirl of parties, whom a rich young man courted in vain; and of Reiko, the ethereal Kyoto beauty who had fallen in love with a rotund shopkeeper, and of their plans for a wedding in the spring. Yukiko's face always softened when she spoke of her friends.

In the course of her storytelling, Sekiguchi laughed twice, a fact she regarded with some triumph. Afterwards there was a pause, which she finally, and as delicately as possible, filled.

"And how has Sekiguchi-san been?"

He looked through her for a moment, and she thought that at last he was going to speak of the weeks of waiting, the disappointment, and the wife who now hovered on the edge of madness, but instead he shrugged and gallantly, almost boyishly bowed.

"I missed you," he said.

A month and a half, punctuated by his weekly visits, passed, and then it was winter, and the rooms of the geisha house were filled with the charcoal smell and smoky warmth that came from fires built in holes in the ground.

There had been an earthquake earlier in the day. She may have been distracted by the memory of its rhythms, for she was in the middle of a story, spicy and scandalous, but she kept losing her place in it, stumbling over the words again and again. Finally she stopped. She stared at Sekiguchi, at his one sharp eye, which gazed back at her patiently; the wry mouth; the round head. Her heart, pounding through five layers of cotton, silk, and heavy brocade, made the outer robe of her kimono flutter.

"I can't think," she said at last.

She watched his hand, crooked and scarred, as it stretched towards her face. His touch on her was soft as a whisper. She swallowed audibly, thinking she should say or do something, but her geisha training had deserted her, and she sat as passively as the wives whom those of her profession sometimes envied, and more often scorned.

She did not even help him with the intricate ritual of undressing her, an act that even her well-trained maid could not accomplish alone. Somehow he managed, though he wrestled for minutes with the daunting bow at her back. All that Yukiko did was to take out the two pins on the top of her head, so that her hair came cascading down in all its tea-scented richness over her shoulders.

It took him much less time to undress himself. Naked but demure with her hair concealing her breasts, she watched with curiosity as his body emerged. It was unexpectedly wiry and it looked strong despite its squatness, but the skin was so badly eroded, without a smooth stretch in sight, that she flinched, and then she blushed with shame at her rudeness. He shook his head at her and smiled, his mouth twisting and his bad eye disappearing into a squint, and with a new feeling of shyness she reached out towards him.

As he climbed on top of her, her breath caught and she felt again as if she were falling in a dream. She fought against the sensation, but this time she lost.

CHAPTER NINE

I ENTER THE bedroom, turn off the light, and find my way to the bed. Eric is still in the bathroom. I swivel my body around, so that my feet lie on the pillow, and carefully cover myself with the sheet.

Eric comes into the room and slips into bed beside me. Then he reaches out and clasps the shaved smoothness of my calves and the boniness of my ankles. "What the—" he begins.

"Surprise!" I say, pulling up the sheet from the bottom.

Eric is silent, stunned, I think optimistically, by my cleverness. My eyes are still unused to the dark, and so I sit up and grope for his face. With my fingers, I read the smile like Braille on his lips.

"That's very cute," he says.

I slip a finger into his mouth and his tongue, soft and warm, enfolds it.

Lying beneath Eric while waiting for him to finish, I touch the muscles beneath his shoulder blades. His back is smooth. Broad up at top, it narrows down in a funnel shape, and his spine is especially hard and bony towards the bottom. Like a newborn animal, the swell of his buttocks is soft and lightly furred.

I am thinking of nothing but his back when he begins to spasm in pleasure. I shift myself under him, and when I turn my head slightly to the right, there on the windowsill is Phillip, his body darkly silhouetted against the night sky. I cry out a little at the shock of seeing him there, but Eric is caught up in sensation and does not notice.

In most ghost stories, of course, the sight of the spectre inspires horror in the living, fear that the dead one has come back to hound them into the grave. Yet never before until now, in the middle of Eric's orgasm, have I felt fear at the apparition of Phillip. It is a shot of pure terror, an emotion that easily overrides in intensity the pang of guilt I usually feel when I see him, so pale and quiet, and so vulnerable in his nakedness. I bite down hard on my bottom lip, to prevent a scream from escaping.

This is what it feels like to be haunted.

Then the sight of him makes me climax again, even though I thought I would not.

When it is all over, I want to crawl into a corner and hide, as Phillip himself always seems to want to these days, and it occurs to me that this is precisely what I fear most about his ghost: that he is here to prevent me from ever leaving the shadows of my apartment again.

Eric likes to stay inside me afterwards. In the beginning I did not like him to do so, but I have grown used to it by now, and I no longer really mind. Today, however, I push at him gently, to make him move away. He lies panting like a dog on top of me, and his suddenly relaxed body is much heavier than it was before. I can feel the racing of his heart against my chest.

Engrossed as he was, it did not seem as if he could have been aware of me at all, yet he surprises me, as he sometimes still does. He lifts his head up and peers at me. "You okay?"

"Yes, why?"

"I thought you seemed a little out of it towards the end. You know, just before you came again."

I crane my neck slowly towards the right to glance once more at Phillip, his figure and face cast in shadow. A wind blows, the moonlight catches him, I blink and when I look again, he is gone. There remains only the movement of the curtains in the breeze. Wearily I rub my eyes.

"I'm fine," I say, carefully moving out from under him.

Minutes pass, but Eric does not seem tired. He lies on his back, looking intently at some unknown point high above him. I place my head next to his on his shoulder, and look upwards with him. The wind whispers, and on the ceiling grotesque shadows mock the movements of the curtains. Through the window a wisp of a cloud is visible, glowing with moonshine or maybe only the artificial brightness of the city. I wonder what Eric is looking at, whether he sees something different from what I am seeing. I stroke his chest slowly while he lies almost frozen in his stillness. I believe him to be lost in thought and memory, as I am, but when I look again he is fast asleep.

He stirs. From past lovers I know that men usually look younger and softer when they sleep. Eric, who sleeps more soundly than most, occasionally whimpers or makes gurgling noises, just like a baby. Perhaps it is the contrast with his daytime self that makes him seem especially vulnerable at moments like these. When he is awake, he is always protectively putting his arm around me; when he is asleep, that same arm seems to reach towards me with need. His body curls trustingly around me now, and his fingers have already started entwining themselves into my hair.

Yet just as I am settling down beside him, he surprises me for the second time of the night. "Who—" he says, raising his head, and turning towards the window.

"What is it?" I ask, placing a hand on his chest.

"I thought I saw something," he says. "Actually, someone. It wasn't anything. Go back to sleep." His head is back on the pillow, and his speech is already blurred with sleep.

"Okay," I say, but I sit up and look around the room. Even the shadows are still.

"Strange about this apartment," he mutters. "I keep thinking I see things here. I'm probably just overworked, but what a joke if it really was haunted—"

Suddenly I cannot bear to hear anymore. "Shh," I tell him. "You've been dreaming." Turning my back to him, I lie bone-tired but sleepless, my eyes open and staring as I lie wrapped in Eric's arms.

By December, when the air is sharp and bright, my grandmother and I will be old friends. I will lend her my warmest scarf and we will stroll together, arm in arm like schoolgirls, the breadth of Central Park.

Obaasama, I will say (stumbling no longer, the word like butter as it rolls off my tongue), how have you survived, without learning to forget?

CHAPTER TEN

On Tuesday I wake up to the sight of Phillip. He looks uncomfortable, his head drooping over his knees as he sits leaning back against the wall, and his body seems gaunt and weak. My bed is large and luxurious, and smells faintly of Eric still; next to me is a soft impression of his body in the wrinkles of the sheet.

The heat and the light of the sun stream in through the window and make the air in the room hazy, but my mind feels clean and sharp. I get out of bed quietly, put on a robe, and tiptoe out of the room. I cannot allow myself to look too long at Phillip, for this afternoon Eric and I are going browsing for rings.

It is already past eleven, so I take a shower and get dressed right away. My makeup takes longer, far longer, even, than it usually does. When my grandmother Yukiko worked as a geisha and made herself up every evening, the elaborate process of painting her face white and remaking her features into the masklike ones of a doll took more than an hour. Today, after half an hour, tissue paper stained with lipstick litters the sink; my cheeks hurt from the number of times I put on blush and rubbed it off; and I have developed the beginnings of a severe headache from the strength of the perfume emanating from my wrists and neck.

In the end it is the lateness of the hour rather than any sense of completion that makes me stop. I back out of the bathroom reluctantly, keeping my eyes on the mirror as I go.

In the living room, Phillip leans against the coffee table. I can see every rib of his body, and the bones at the top of his shoulders jut upwards. His chin is pointed, his cheeks are hollow, and his eyes sunken. When one of the six violet moths flying about him lands on his eyebrow, he does not even twitch.

For the longest time, forever, it seemed, I could not go near Phillip past a particular point because a kind of vertigo would set in. So there is a certain justice to the fact that when he appears to me now, I feel acutely claustrophobic, as if my apartment, with its tall windows, skylights, and high ceilings, were instead airless, suffocating, and dark. For so it would seem, were I to be holed up here with Phillip for eternity. It is a scenario worthy of Edgar Allan Poe—a claustrophobe, surely, if there ever was one, with his nightmarish fantasies of tipsy men sealed up behind brick walls, beating hearts under floorboards, and desirable sisters nailed inside coffins.

As I am double-locking my door, 16D swings open and old Mrs. Noffz peers out. She is wearing an orange hood that looks as if it may have been torn off a child's raincoat. Her umbrella is closed, and she leans upon it as if it were a cane.

"Hello there," she says.

I am late and she is an unwelcome intrusion upon my thoughts, but I make a halfhearted attempt to be civil. "Hi." I walk to the elevator and press the button. I stand half-turned away from her as I wait.

"Terribly hot morning," she says. Squinting slightly, she gazes out from under the brim of her hood and looks up at the ceiling, right at the spot where the paint is chipping. "It's going to be a scorcher."

"I guess so," I say, and then I press the button again.

"Mabel is not fond of summers in New York," she says. "It is too humid for her." Although her voice lingers with care on the word "humid," it comes out strange, without the *h*.

"Yes," I say, "humid." I accent the beginning of the word slightly.

"Humid," she says, cheerfully repeating the word as if this were an English lesson.

She is still pronouncing it wrong, but it is too warm to press the point. Instead I turn on her. "Why are you wearing a hood?" I ask innocently. The question backfires on me, though, as I feel ashamed of myself almost before it is out of my mouth.

"I beg your pardon?"

"Nothing," I tell her. "Never mind."

"No, please, what did you say?"

"Your hood," I say, gesturing at her head. "Why are you wearing a hood?"

"Oh." With some confusion she takes off the hood and pats down her hair, but her face looks happy and calm as always, and then I look away from her because the elevator has finally arrived.

I step through the doors. "I've got to go," I tell her. "I'm very late."

"I had forgotten," she says, just as the elevator is sliding shut.

"What?" I say, jamming the doors back open.

"I had forgotten I was wearing the hood," she says. "Good-bye, so nice chatting with you." She smiles and waves at me from her door as the elevator shuts, this time for good.

Although a lazy breeze is blowing, the air is so hot and thick I can move only slowly. After only a few steps, I can feel my eyeliner begin to melt. Carefully I dab at the spot just beneath my eyes.

The subway station is even hotter. I buy two tokens, put one in and go through the turnstile. Eric's office is close, a mere seven stops on the speedy number one line, but I am still cross at having forgotten to bring something to read. In the subways I usually try to arm myself with a book, finding it cover from the panhandlers, the crowds, and the men. Phillip, who loved to ride in the last car and watch the track falling after us, got me out of the habit of doing so; it is only since he left that I find myself needing, once again, the distraction and protection of print.

Now I concentrate on the ads for foot- and skin-doctors, for watches and roach motels. I try to tease out the meaning of the Spanish comic strip on AIDS, which runs in serial form on all the trains, and I piece together one more episode in the continuing saga of voluptuous Marisol, who is HIV-positive but cannot bring herself to tell her ex-lover. It is hard to keep up with the story line, since the characters die with such frequency. What with this comic strip, and injunctions such as "No se apoye contra la puerta," and ads for "ricas" and "la Ciudad de Nueva York," I have been picking up a lot of Spanish from the trains.

Between 72nd and 66th Streets, the express passes us by, and I watch the people in the other train reading, talking, laughing, blowing their noses, begging. One woman, black and tall, catches my eye and gazes curiously back. All this and more for a buck and a quarter, as Phillip used to say. Even without him beside me, I can still faintly feel the lure of the subways.

Directly across from me in the car, there is a large brown cat sitting on a woman's lap. Despite the noise and all the strangers surrounding him, the cat sits calmly, occasionally licking at his left paw. I must have made an involuntary sound, because the woman, who is big, plump, and brown-haired, just like her pet, looks up and smiles. "He's sick," she explains. "I'm taking him to the vet."

"He's so quiet," I say. "He sits so quietly on your lap."

She nods, but her attention is already turned back to the cat. He is very handsome, with yellow eyes (Horse's were greener, but Phillip's had flecks of yellow), and long-haired enough that tufts of hair stick out from between his toes (Phillip laughing, lying on the ground with Horse's paws on his face). He yawns, showing off his red mouth and sharp teeth.

(Phillip asleep on the floor, his thin body twisted just slightly so that his hand can reach Horse, who is lying curled by his thigh.)

The woman nods pleasantly to me as she gets off the car at 66th Street, the cat slung over her shoulder like an old sweater, his unblinking eyes watching me as he rides off in style to the vet.

....

Eric's law firm is located in the heart of New York, on 51st Street and the Avenue of the Americas. It is big enough to take up almost a whole square block, and high enough to be an important part of the skyline. After the sticky heat of the city, the dustless cool beyond the revolving doors comes as a shock. The interior is all serene green marble, slippery beneath my heels, and when one set of the elevator doors opens, I am met by a tide of people streaming out for lunch break. The few people entering the elevator with me are sweaty and red-faced from the outside heat, while those on their way out look brisk and cool, their hair still tidy and the women's makeup still fresh. With the exception of two security guards and a mailman, the people are well dressed and well groomed, the men especially smart in their suits. I tug at the skirt of my dress to cover my knees.

I have been to the office many times before, but usually I come in the evenings, after work. I am unaccustomed to seeing so many people in the halls, the younger ones harried and laden with heavy files, the older, prosperous-looking ones pacing themselves with portly dignity. By the time I turn the corner, I am well aware of the eyes. Everybody is watching me. Heads turn to examine my figure and scrutinize my face. While the secretaries' fingers still move over their keyboards, they are no longer looking at their computer screens when I walk by, and documents go unattended by the attorneys. I move in the wake of staring silence.

With my front teeth I tear out the skin on the inside of my mouth and chew on the soft bits of flesh, a nervous habit that I thought I had kicked years ago. I catch myself slouching as if I were an overweight teenager again, and though I make a conscious effort to straighten my posture, my body keeps slumping forward on its own.

His door, when I finally find it, is open, but Eric himself is nowhere in sight. I wander back out, turn the corner, and there is Eric standing with his back towards me, in the alcove by the coffee machines.

He is there with a woman, and for a few moments I loiter in the corner, taking stock before I approach.

They stand together just a shade closer than is normal. He talks to her in a low voice, using one hand to hold his coffee and the other to gesture, while she leans against the wall and listens attentively, occasionally nodding, her eyes never wandering from his face. She is very thin, with that natural bony fragility that suggests that she never has to diet, or exercise, or worry. Her hair is very black and very straight, cut with geometric, almost architectural precision, in what Russia calls an "Asian-American 'do." She has a delicate face, with high cheekbones and arching eyebrows; she wears no makeup except for a little darkness about her eyes and the faintest trace of lipstick, and she carries herself with ease. Watching her from the shadows, I feel outdone by her possession, and overdone as well, exposed as a cheap painted geisha.

I dally at the corner, eyeing them, surprised at how possessive I feel. I have a strong desire to take him by the arm and kiss him on the mouth, and I have to remind myself why I am here.

"Eric," I call out, and he turns so quickly his coffee sloshes over his sleeve. He curses, farce intruding on our little encounter.

"I'm sorry," I tell him, clamping down on my glee. "I didn't mean to startle you."

"Hi," he says, reaching for a napkin, and taking a quick detour to give my nose a peck.

The woman and I nod at each other, but do not speak. Even after I turn back to Eric, I can feel her eyes appraising me. Momentarily distracted from his (futile) attempts to wipe the stain from his shirtsleeve, Eric looks at me, then at her, and uncharacteristically flushes. "Terry, this is my girlfriend—that is, my fiancée, Kiki Takehashi," he says, pulling me forward. "And Kiki, this is Terry, Theresa Chan. One of my closest friends at the office."

"Oh," I say, adding hastily, "of course." Surreptitiously I wipe my hand, and then I stick it out and we shake. "Nice to meet you." Her hand is cool and a little limp.

She watches me with her head thrown slightly back. Her eyes are thin and dark, far darker than my own. "Well, I've heard a lot about *you*," she says, as if guessing the source of my confusion. Her voice is warm and low, though marred by a trace of a head cold.

"Kiki and I are going ring shopping," says Eric, a little too loudly, his hand suddenly at my back.

I smile, she smiles, and he smiles, but no one says anything. Not only is she thinner than I am, she is taller, too. Her fingers run through her hair and then they stroke at her throat, which is long and white. Drawn by their movement, I idly watch her fingers, and I try not to look shocked when I notice how jagged her nails are; they are so chewed up I can see dried bits of blood. The thought tugs at me that there is something I should remember, some connection I am failing to make, but I dismiss it quickly.

One of the secretaries pokes her head around. "Terry," she calls out, "phone call for you."

"Excuse me." She begins to walk away, and then briefly turns. "Oh, and nice meeting you, Kiki," she says, but she is looking at Eric rather than me, and her eyes are wide.

Her calves are long and slightly rounded at the top, encased in flesh-colored stockings with a run creeping out of the heel of her left shoe. Together Eric and I watch her go, and then, with his hand at my back, Eric steers me back out into the hall.

When we leave the building, the heat is like a wall pressing down upon us. It is too hot, even, to hold hands, so instead we hold fingers, two each. He has been my lover for more than a year, and we are on our way to shop for a ring that will tie us together, presumably for life; we are walking together side by side, our fingers intertwined. Yet as if he were my grandmother, an almost mythic figure I have never met but long imagined, the questions I ask him are silent. Would you love me if I were a strapping German, a Frenchwoman with plucked eyebrows or even, God forbid, a Jew? Could you love me if I were a good white girl, one who would make your parents beam?

I have not betrayed my thoughts with so much as a glance or a slowing in pace, but he answers my unspoken thoughts aloud. "You're going to start with that Asian-fetish thing again, aren't you," he asks calmly, sounding resigned. "It's Theresa, right?"

"I didn't say anything," I remind him.

"But you're thinking it," he says. "Kiki, once and for all, I don't have an Asian-woman fetish."

I nod, still troubled by the memory of those arching eyebrows.

"You're still not convinced, are you," he says, sighing. "You have such a bee in your bonnet on this subject. Look—you may have gotten it a lot from other men, but that's not why I'm with you." He squeezes my two fingers. "If anything, what I have is a Kiki Takehashi fetish, okay?"

"That's nice," I say, smiling in spite of myself. "Thank you."

"Okay," he says, surprised but also relieved at my quick capitulation. "Okay, that's settled. By the way, did everybody look at you in the halls just now?"

I turn to stare at him. "How did you know?"

"They've been bugging me about my personal life, and I let it slip that you were coming by today. I'm afraid the news got around awfully fast. It must have made you feel uncomfortable."

"I wondered if I was becoming paranoid."

He laughs. "Dreamy, yes. Paranoid, never." Our steps slow, then, because we are standing outside the portals of Tiffany's.

"Ready?" he asks, and smiles when I nod. "Don't expect great service," he warns as he waves me into the revolving doors ahead of him. "Remember, these guys can smell that we're just browsing."

We enter the air-conditioned sanctuary of Tiffany's with some relief, though I always consider it one of the least friendly places in the world, with its rows and rows of glass cases shielding expensive baubles and trinkets, the security guards watching you from select corners, and most of all the men, dressed all alike in dark suits, austere and bored behind the counters. As Eric had warned, the salesmen can smell that we are just browsing, and are not too keen to help. Still, one eventually steps forward, and with considerable prompting from Eric, I manage to explain that I want a small ring that will not snag on all my sweaters, though pretty, of course, and with a distinctive setting.

I pick out a ring, and the salesman hands it to me. As I turn it over, my scarred fingertips are momentarily exposed, and I catch the salesman looking at them, one indiscreet millisecond too long. I draw my fingers into a fist and say to Eric no, maybe not this one after all, and I am thankful when he, after due consideration, agrees: this one is far too small.

Eric then begins to thaw out the salesman in earnest, as only he can. Making a transition that I cannot follow, he brings up the subject of British royalty, and our salesman is soon showing signs of animation. I, too, should try to draw people out, but I cannot even tell these salesmen, dressed so impeccably in their dark suits, apart. If our salesman suddenly pulled out a gun, shot Eric dead, and ran away, I would not be able to identify him in a lineup. "He was wearing a black suit," I would say over and over at the police station, and the men there—also all dressed similarly, though in their case in blue—would sigh and shake their heads at me, the poorest of all poor witnesses.

A pretty young woman at another counter glances at Eric, once, twice, and then again, before moving on her way. It is not only his looks, so fine and dark, that make women turn. Almost anybody would be able to see that Eric is a decent, likable man, a promising young professional, and an extremely good catch, and that anybody would be right. I squint, trying to see him through the eyes of the young woman, and then through those of the salesman, whose shirtfront is swelling visibly under all the attention.

To strangers Eric seems charming, certainly, but a little intimidating as well, for he has a natural authority that makes people scurry to do his bidding. He is terrifying when he gets mad, and I am lucky that we have never fought seriously, for I am no match for his rage. It is not only what he says, but rather his tone or perhaps even the way he stands. A few months ago, after I had confided to him that a computer dealer had refused to take back a malfunctioning printer, he accompanied me back to the store and had the whole place turned inside out within fifteen minutes: the manager as well as all of the available salespeople were running around trying to help us while the original dealer, a shifty and rather cocky weasel type, was reduced to the status of an abject pet dog.

For a second I think I almost succeed in viewing him through a stranger's eyes, and then I give up trying. I have gotten so used to thinking of Eric as my lover that I have lost my perspective on him. When I shut my eyes and envision him, I see his face in extreme close-up, as if we were holding each other in bed, and I can only picture select parts of him at a time: dark brown eyes, the straightness of his nose, the stubble on his cheeks, the lock of hair that falls across his forehead, the contours of his shoulder as I rest my chin against his chest. Naked and horizontal, he seems so muscular that I am almost confused by how normal he looks clothed. He has presence as well as a handsome pair of broad shoulders, and the two assets combine to make him seem much bigger than he actually is. In reality he stands a good three inches under six feet, only a few inches taller than I am, but in my mind I always see him towering over me like a giant. I cannot judge Eric as a vertical human being.

He is now talking with our salesman about cuff links. I stifle a yawn as my attention wanders, to the salesman across the way who avoids my eyes, to the dizzying pattern of dots on the carpet, and finally to a small svelte woman standing close beside us. Her clothes are flowing and white, and her hair is a striking silver over an unaged face, but contained in the bag over her shoulder is what looks like a bushel of cucumbers. Too small to bear the weight of them easily, she stops often in her scrutiny of jewels to readjust the bag on her shoulder.

Leaning against the counter, I idly muse on the oddness of her carrying so many cucumbers. If she were carting around a bushel of lemons, I would nod sagely, thinking how nice to make lemonade on such a hot day. If she had a bagful of apples, I would shrug and look away, picturing apple pie. Even a pile of onions would not seem too amiss, since the woman looks as if she might enjoy a bowl of elegant French onion soup. But why would anyone, let alone a woman of style shopping at Tiffany's, need a bagful of cucumbers, which are only good fresh? Such a ridiculous vegetable, a joke in itself, really, like eggplants, but with the added indignity of a phallic resemblance.

Yet it is this smell of this joke of a vegetable, coupled with the faintest trace of cigarette smoke lingering about our salesman, that undoes me. The smell hits me with an almost physical blow, sending me reeling back to those moments when I step out of the shower, and I know from the scent of rain, brine, cigarettes, and cucumber that Phillip has been there.

Three salesmen hover around the woman, although she does not seem in any rush to buy: to them, too, the scent of the cucumbers is overwhelming, so much so they cannot smell that she is browsing. The cucumbers smell like summer, like cool green, like seeds. The smell is making me ravenous, not for salads but for ice water in tall glasses, long afternoons of lovemaking, Phillip lying beside me in the grass.

I have been reading too much Proust, I tell myself sternly. Threatened by the onslaught of the past for the second time in the day, I force myself to concentrate on the woman's bag. It is embroidered brocade, pretty in an old-lady kind of way, an unexpected possession—though not, of course, in the same league as its contents—for this woman of high fashion.

"Kiki." Eric is calling out to me. "Kiki?" he says again, his voice growing sharper with a touch of impatience.

I shake my head, keeping my eyes fixed on the handle of the bag, which is brown and leather. The smell of the cucumbers is making me sway a little, but within the haze of memories and wishes that it brings, there is room for one moment of startling clarity.

Never again in my life will there be anyone like Phillip. He was to me what Sekiguchi was to Yukiko, what Kenji was to my mother, and if there is anything I have learned from my mother's bedtime stories, it is that the women in my family never let go. Never again will there be anyone like him, and I have nothing to show for my time with him but a naked ghost who lives in my apartment and is slowly wasting away.

The outlines of the bag blur, and suddenly I am crying.

The sobs come out in the great heaving gasps of a child, but before I can turn around to hide my face, Eric is there, pressing me to his chest, his arms around me and his shoulders shielding me from the world. He reacts faster than anyone else, but after a few long moments, I peek my head around his shoulder to find the whole store transformed as well. A chair, proffered by a security guard, has appeared out of nowhere. Our salesman is offering me a clean, well-pressed handkerchief ("He was carrying a handkerchief," I would say triumphantly to the policemen, and their eyes would light up at such a clue, for how many people carry handkerchiefs in this day of disposable goods?); another black-suited man is waiting to hand me a glass of water. Even the small stylish lady, so stately in spite of her diminutive height and her cucumbers, has turned towards me with a low murmur of sympathy.

Waving away the chair, the handkerchief, and the water, trying to smile at these people through my tears, I cling to Eric, my only sure refuge, for the past is a whirlpool and the thought of the future, which has long been lit up by the image of my grandmother, is all of a sudden dim. I have been like a stubborn child, who knows better than to believe in Santa Claus but still persists, anxiously awaiting my grandmother and her bagful of answers. In November, my mother and I will go to the airport to greet an old woman, healthy still but too tired to speak after her epic life and her husband's death, who has come to America to die.

It is some time before I can stop the tears. My nose is red and running, and my makeup, so carefully applied, is running down my cheeks and Eric's (already coffee-stained) white shirt in striking streaks of black.

After I make some ineffectual dabs at my face, we make our exit quickly from the store. It's the sun, we explain as we pass by the concerned faces of our new friends; it's cramps, a headache, fatigue, pain.

Eric leads me without asking to our favorite noodle shop in the neighborhood. We walk the five blocks in silence, our four fingers once again interlocked. But as soon as we step into the restaurant, he begins to question me with rising exasperation and deepening voice: did I love Phillip; do I love him; and when would I be ready to move on. Yes, yes, and I don't know but I'm trying, I say, repeatedly and consistently, yet none of my answers satisfy him, so he (a trial lawyer, after all) goes through the same round of questions again and then again, varying his phrasing slightly each time, hoping, perhaps, to trip me up or catch me in an inconsistency.

Then he abruptly shifts tack.

"You never slept with him, right?"

"Who, Phillip?"

He nods.

I take a deep breath in, and let it out slowly. "That's right."

Our food arrives. We move our elbows and napkins to make way for the bowls, and sit quietly while the waiter tops off our water.

"You know, Kiki," he says, "we were shopping for an *engagement* ring."

"I know," I say, looking down at my hands. "I acted terribly."

"I've been patient for a very long time."

"I know," I say again. "You've been terrific."

"What we need to do now," he says, his voice flat and robotic, and authoritative as only Eric's can be, "is to spend some time apart."

My left elbow, a mere quarter-inch from the soy sauce container, jerks, only narrowly missing staining Eric's shirt with yet another substance. "What did you say?"

"You heard me."

"How long?" I say, a note of panic in those two words.

"I don't know," he says. "We both need to rethink this relationship pretty seriously."

A long pause. We take our chopsticks out of their paper sheaths and break them apart, but neither of us begins eating.

"Eric, I am really sorry," I say, faltering. "I've been so unfair to you—"

With his lips pressed tightly together, Eric cuts me off with a nod. He leaves me with a question, one so unanswerable it finds its way into my collection. "You've idealized him, you know," he says. "How can I possibly compete with a ghost?"

When we finally do start eating, the noodles are smooth, thin, and delicious, but they do not slide down my throat with ease, and I wonder (for my mind has clearly been addled by the sun), if I were to choke on this lunch and die, whether Eric could pick our Chinese cook out of the lineup of men with receding hairlines, black hair, and slanted dark eyes.

CHAPTER ELEVEN

THREE YEARS AGO, when my mother returned to Japan, she saw to her astonishment a row of photographs of me lining a wall in my grandmother's study, the only room in the house that had been wholly untouched by the fire. There were my baby pictures, from three days old to three years old; there were photographs of me taking my first shaky steps towards the outstretched hands of my mother, looking at picture books with my father, diligently hunching over to write my first words. There I was as a scrawny, gap-toothed child, mugging happily for the camera. I look less happy in the snapshots taken after my father left, and heavier, too, so much so that my resemblance to my grandmother all but disappears under the extra flesh. Not until I hit my late teens did I shed those pounds. Seen in a row, the photographs of my teen years seem like a lesson in perspective, a yo-yo in motion as viewed from below: getting bigger and bigger and then smaller and smaller.

My grandmother has many grandsons, for with pleasing symmetry, her two daughters-in-law, both named Tomoko, were each blessed with three boys. My mother was astonished at the sight of all those pictures of me because she herself always felt slighted as the only daughter, the first child who turned out to be that most grievous disappointment, a girl. So she was baffled and, I think, not a little jealous that only my photographs, and not those of my cousins, were in evidence in Yukiko's study.

She was astonished again when I, told of this unlikely tribute to me, only nodded, for she does not understand the depth of the sympathy that exists between my grandmother and me. I have long taken comfort from this connection, only occasionally, in my very darkest moments, giving in to the fear that seized me when I sobbed for Phillip in the protection of Eric's arms: that my grandmother will be too weary to tell me the tales that she told my mother, and that my mother passed on to me; that she will be too tired to listen to my story, the words that provide the text to the photographs lining her wall.

If that does turn out to be the case, if my grandmother and I are in fact too late to enjoy the bond that links us together, across a chasm composed of two languages, two cultures, two generations, and two very different lives, I will have to struggle not to hold my mother accountable. When my grandfather died, I assumed that I would go to Japan for the funeral, but my mother told me that she was going alone. If she had explained that it was only because she was nervous about her long-delayed reunion with her own mother, I would have understood. But what she said was that the first reports of my grandmother's health were bleak, and that the responsibilities of playing host to an unknown, American granddaughter, on top of the shock of losing a husband and the pressures of managing a very public funeral, would be too much for Yukiko to bear.

Phillip used to say that I should just buy a cheap ticket and go by myself. He never could understand that when I do meet my grandmother, I will need my mother there, if only for the first five minutes. Still, what he said left a mark. If my grandmother is so exhausted that she will no longer wish to talk, I will have to live with the possibility that it is not only my mother's fault that I never had the opportunity to become acquainted with the woman who shares my name.

Really, though, these worries about my grandmother are groundless. "She could outlive us all," my mother said upon returning from Japan, echoing the cheering prognosis of the family doctor, as well as his chilling caveat—"If she wants." I give little weight to those last three words, for a period of depression is only to be expected. How else could my grandmother feel, in the aftermath of her husband's death and the burning of her home? Once she gets to America, away from the city where she once lived with him, away from a life spent shuttling back and forth between the homes of her daughters-in-law, she will become the old Yukiko again, active and sharp.

Still, in light of the likelihood of her initial fatigue, it would be better not to overtax her, at least at first. Questions about her refusal to consider my father as a likely husband for my mother are too heavy and too complicated by far—not a good beginning to the endless, delicious conversation that is due my grandmother and me.

Far better to start with a softball. On the day of my grandmother's arrival, I will make one of my pathetic fires in the fireplace, and my mother will make a pot of tea. We will first partake in inconsequential but truly pleasant pleasantries: small talk about the trip, my grandmother's health, my unknown cousins and uncles and aunts. Only afterwards, when the tea has been drunk and the fire has lived out its short life, will I begin with the first of the questions I have been hoarding for a lifetime.

Grandmother, I will say (leaning forward confidentially, close but not too close, my voice low, and my tone light to match the mood of that first encounter), *Obaasama*. How could I ever have doubted you?

With his back turned towards me and his body shielded by shadows, Phillip sits with me as I wait for Eric to call. His knees are pressed against the wall of the fireplace and his head is tilted forward at an unnatural angle, so that his forehead touches the bricks as well. Even in the near darkness of the fireplace, the thinness of his body is apparent. The backbone is a long, sharp line of knobs, and the ribs are prominent, the shoulder blades like folded wings. The sight of his back is harder to take than that of his face, unnerving though his eyes are.

Yesterday evening I called my mother. When I finally reached her last weekend, after the scare that I had when she was not at home on Saturday night, she was cool and dismissive, as always, of my fears. I, too, aim for reserve when I speak to her, and so while I mentioned that Eric and I went browsing for a ring, I said nothing about what had happened when we did so.

Yet it may have been wiser to say something to her, because in the two days that have passed since our trip to Tiffany's, Eric has returned my phone calls but once, and then in order to cancel for a picnic in the park this weekend; when I suggested that we reschedule, he said he wasn't sure and all but hung up on me. The phone has not rung all day.

Eric is most likely to phone after six, when he gets home from work, so even though I prefer to run in the cool of the evening on hot summer days, at three I put on shorts and a T-shirt, and carefully double-knot the laces on my sneakers. I bounce on my heels to test the strength of my left tendon, which had been injured in a bicycle accident years ago, and had never fully healed; the old ache is only a faint twinge.

I do not want to leave the house. Smarting still from Eric's rebuke, and worrying more with every minute about the silence of the phone, I wish to sink into the sofa and curl into a ball.

As I pick up my keys, I just barely manage to stop myself from leaning over to check that the telephone ringer is on and the answering machine is working. Clearly nothing could have changed since half an hour ago, when I last checked.

Phillip still has not moved. With a few moths hovering about his head, he huddles, Cinderella-like, bereft and alone among the soot of the fireplace. The closet door is still open, and without stopping to think, I reach inside, grab a shoe, and hurl it at him.

"Goddamn you," I hiss. "Do you know that you're ruining my life?"

The shoe, an old loafer, hurtles through the air with satisfying speed, but falls considerably wide of its mark. Still, Phillip is at least looking up at me now, and his back is straight. Although I glare at him for a few moments, there is, of course, no way that I can best him in a staring match, and I soon turn away.

I manage not to look back at him as I head for the door.

Old Mrs. Noffz keeps me company while I wait for the elevator. With interest she watches me do stretching exercises against the wall.

"This heat is so dreadful," she says.

I do not answer for a while, and when I finally do, my voice is short and hard. "I guess so."

Perhaps discouraged, she stops talking, but she stands smiling amiably in her doorway, keeping me company until the elevator arrives. "Good-bye," she says. "Have a nice afternoon."

I nod in response, staring straight ahead of me as the doors close.

She, too, loved Phillip. "Such a well-spoken young man," she often said, which always struck me as a singularly inappropriate description for Phillip, with his quiet ways and his lazy drawl.

Then, after he left for Nepal, she kept asking, "Where's your nice young friend?"

One day I lost patience with the question. "He won't be coming back," I said, and although I did not realize it, I must have raised my voice, for the phrase bounced back to me from the hallway and the stairs, and I was breathing hard.

She shrank back in the doorway, her face in half-darkness so that I could no longer read its expression. "I'm sorry," she said, suddenly and briefly lucid.

He used to chat with her for long periods, letting the elevator leave without him again and again. Once she even invited him inside her house, which she has never done for me. She gave him a cup of hot chocolate in an almost clean cup, and introduced him to her parrot, Mabel, whom I had previously suspected was a fiction.

On her mantelpiece she had an old photograph of two young women, wearing matching wide-brimmed hats and with their arms slung over each other's shoulders; when Phillip asked about it, she told him it was a picture of herself and her friend Mabel, whose name the parrot took. After that, he said, their conversation fell apart in spite of his best efforts, with her harping on the same meteorological points she always brought up.

By contrast Mrs. Noffz has never liked Eric much, though she chats with him about the weather just as she does with anyone else she can waylay in the halls.

....

The sun is no longer at its peak when I get outside, but the air seems saturated with the accumulated heat of the day. The humidity clings to my skin and makes me feel unclean. I turn left, away from Broadway. At the corner I run north towards West 106th Street, where the green statue man sits mounted on his green statue horse, and there I hop down the steps, two at a time. At the crosswalk I wait for a walk signal with a woman and her poodle.

The trees look older now, more dignified than they did in April, when they were new to their majesty. Now they are as resplendent as mature kings. New Jersey is a hazy mirage across the river. I wait for the cars to pass at 95th, and run past the well-tended gardens at 90th and 89th; a block farther down I climb out of the park and pant my way up the stairs towards the big, almost-white dome, which I circle, once. On the platform near the dome stands a frozen group of martial-arts students, perhaps twenty of them bent uniformly forward in a motionless position of menace. I jog by the two old black men who seem permanently ensconced on the bench at 86th, and who always direct some kind of comment at me; today it is "Nice legs, sweetheart." I look away from them as I run past. I count the blocks and do math problems in my head to keep myself from getting bored—twenty blocks is a mile and I want to do five miles so when I get to 83rd I am a quarter through, eight more blocks and I will have finished a third of my run.

My tendon is beginning to throb, though, and the pain intensifies until reluctantly, just before 79th Street, I slow to a halt. A few months ago, when the pain was so bad that I hobbled just like my mother, I went to see my old childhood doctor at home. He asked me questions and he felt my bones and looked at X rays, and then he shook his head at me. "If you keep running when your tendon is this bad, you're not going to be able to walk in a few years, let alone run." I slid off the examination table and smoothed my skirt down. "Thank you," I said. "I mean it," he told me. I could tell that he knew I was not taking him seriously. "You keep this up and you'll be as crippled as your mother," he said. As I walked out of the room, he shook his head again. "You runners are such fanatics."

He was wrong, for by almost any standard I am too erratic to be termed a real runner. Still, I have been running for years, and I have managed to cultivate a considerable tolerance to pain. There is no doubt that I could keep running even now, but the doctor's warning seems to have frightened me in spite of myself.

An oversized rat crosses the path in front of me: I cannot tell whether it presages good luck or bad. As I hobble back towards my apartment, a blond little boy looks up from his truck, and when I smile at him, he gazes at me with the lovesick eyes of a puppy and clambers after me, his truck forgotten. "Tommy, come back here," says a large black woman in a very bored voice and he stops, still staring at me, but held tight by her call. Children follow me around even when all I do is look at them; Phillip used to say I had Pied Piper blood coursing through my veins.

I pass a girl, maybe in her mid-teens. She is dressed all in black, in spite of the heat, and her bare arms and legs, scrawny and long, look stark and pale in contrast to her clothes. Ten years ago, Russia might have looked something like this girl.

Russia and I naturally gravitated towards each other because we were among the youngest graduate students in the English program, and because we were different from the others: I by virtue of my skin and the slant of my eyes, she out of choice, by virtue of her half-shaved head, her dyed black hair, her long black dresses, and the five small rings she wore on her left earlobe, as well as the golden one dangling from her left nipple. Her skin is very pale, tinged, as she used to say, with the slightly bluish tone of skim milk.

"Look" was all she said when she pulled her shirt up, so high that she exposed the two sharp points where her collarbone strains hardest against her skin.

I barely knew her then. We sat next to each other in our Post-Colonial Theory seminar, and during the break that came in the middle of class, we had gotten into the habit of sharing our snacks, walking to the water fountain, or going to the bathroom together, as we had done that day. I barely knew her, but I knew enough of her not to be surprised that she would bare herself to show me her newly pierced nipple, right in the middle of a large, echoing bathroom in a Columbia University building, which professors, administrators, and other graduate students were liable to walk into at any moment.

Her belly pushed forward a little in what was purely the result of the laziness of her spine, for her torso is thin and long, almost—but definitely not quite—too skinny to be beautiful. She has the curveless waist and hips of a boy.

She was not wearing a bra that day. Her nipples were small and very dark against her skin, and they turned up towards me as if they were asking for something mutely, as if they were meant to receive food rather than give it. They brought to mind the upturned beaks of hungry birds.

I studied her with some attention. Her eyes, peeking over the shirt crumpled up around her neck, watched me just as carefully and seriously, a small smile hovering all the while on her lips.

"Did it hurt?" I asked, and then, unable any longer to resist the mute plea of those upturned nipples, I reached out a finger and brushed softly against the small golden hoop that cast its shadow on her breast. Her nipple grew even smaller and darker under my touch.

She nodded. "But the pain was worth it, in the end."

While we became good friends after that, inseparable, really, I betrayed her in the end. Although I lose friends the way that other women lose hairpins, Russia's case was different. After I became close to Phillip, I stopped returning her calls, not because I liked her any less, but because I felt ashamed in her presence. I had robbed her and she had known it, but she had forgiven me without a word, and without expecting anything in return. I could not bear her generosity, and even less the fact that she never once reminded me that it was she who had introduced me to Phillip.

As I limp towards a bench and ease myself down onto it, two Asian women around my age stop talking to look at me. They had been speaking in what sounded like Japanese. They covertly glance at me with tacit recognition and as usual, I turn away without acknowledging our kinship. Like my college roommates and my adult lovers, my childhood friends were white. Still, it usually seemed that no matter how hard I tried to disassociate myself from other Asians, we were all inevitably linked together in everybody else's mind.

When I was too young to attend school, it seemed as if I was always alone and never lonely. I had a childhood filled to overflowing with the company of my parents.

In my earliest memories, the sky is blue and the sun is a golden ball. My father is beside me, and the air is filled with the smell of freshly mown grass.

Thirteen years ago, four years after my father had left home, I was a newly minted teenager, and angry all the time. I acted out this rage in spectacular performances for which my mother was the sole audience member: I bottled them up for her throughout the day, releasing them only when she returned home for work. In a frenzy I cried and screamed and cursed at her. One time I smashed a plate and it shattered perilously near her bare feet. While cleaning up the shards of glass, she cut herself on a splintered piece, and her hand bled.

She made no physical effort to stop my tantrums, and only once did she even speak to me during those moments. Still in her raincoat and with her briefcase in her hand, she was watching me from the door of my bedroom as I beat my fists and kicked my feet against the bed.

"You're just like your father," she said: a lie by omission, for in my rage I was like her, too.

Her words shocked me into silence at least for a second. I soon began screaming again, but my heart was no longer in it, and later, after I had calmed down, I went to the bathroom and carefully studied myself in the mirror. Even back then, I kept a photograph of my grandmother, the first Yukiko, whom my mother said I took after, in a special box in my desk. I had seen how my hair and my body and the ovaline outline of my face resembled hers. My eyes were my mother's. I looked into the mirror, then, and thought about how all of my other features had to have their source in my father, whose face I had already forgotten. The nose, the slope of the cheekbones, the arch of the eyebrows, and the height and the breadth of the forehead might be his as well as mine.

I did not want to be like him, any more than I wanted to be like my mother. From that moment on, I tried to swallow my tears and my anger, and I became better and better at controlling myself, until eventually I was as quiet at home as at school.

Apart from my crush on Hamlet, the Prince of Denmark, in high school I nursed a more carnal passion for a football player two years older than I was. He was stupid and crude, given to loud burps in the cafeteria and coarse jokes about different parts of the female anatomy, but I hungered after the width of his shoulders and the length of his thighs. I was well aware, though, that my lust was doomed to be unrequited: even in comparison to other adolescents, a group not generally famed for its beauty, I was among the most repellent.

I was an overweight teenager and unattractive even beyond the question of weight; only as my face matured did my features regain the harmony they had known when I was young. I was skinny throughout my childhood even though I ate an extraordinary amount, and I can pinpoint the exact moment that I discovered my eating habits had caught up with me. Fourteen years old, I was easing myself into a hot bubble bath when I suddenly became aware that the water, displaced by my weight, was spilling over the tub's edge and making bubbly puddles on the rug and the floor: Eureka. I looked down at myself and saw that my calves were thick and unlovely, and that the hugeness of my breasts, stomach, and thighs was terrifying. I got out of the bath. With suds dropping off me, I stood on the toilet seat and faced the wall, and then I craned my head over my shoulder so that I could get a view of my rear. I wanted to scream. Seemingly overnight, my body had become an unfamiliar thing, fleshy and laden with strange curves.

My mother noticed soon afterwards. This was a triumph of sorts, for she did not notice much in those years. I saw her eyes studying my body when she thought I was not looking, and one night at dinner she did not move when I asked her to pass me the mashed potatoes. "You shouldn't eat so much," she said. I looked up, momentarily startled: we hardly ever spoke during dinner. I then reached over her plate and picked up the bowl. I loaded my plate with an enormous serving and ate it all, glaring at her defiantly, although I began to feel sick and full after the second bite. She pressed her lips tightly together and turned away, and once again silence reigned over dinner.

I do not even like mashed potatoes.

While I tried to cut down, I found myself eating more and more instead. I bought bags of cookies and ate them secretively at night; always I slept on sheets strewn with crumbs. After midnight, when the cookies were all gone, I sneaked into the kitchen and ate what I could find by the light inside the refrigerator. My cheeks became puffy with an unhealthy sallow tinge, the line between my chin and neck all but vanished, my stomach was perpetually distended, and my thighs were so large I gave up jeans and wore only loose-fitting skirts. I moved ponderously.

I hated myself in high school, and so I resolved to become a new person when I got to college. It was there that I became Kiki. I filched the name from the captain of the cheerleading squad, a redhead who probably had the best figure in my entire high school, and it seemed to work a certain magic on me. Since there were far more than three Asians at Princeton, I started to feel less conspicuously different, and while the other freshman girls were becoming heavier with fleshy curves of their own, I kept on losing weight, as naturally and easily as a snake shucking off its skin.

I lusted after the tapering legs of tennis players, and by the end of my four years at Princeton, I had gone out with almost every single one on the team. Politely I encouraged the young men who surreptitiously pawed at me at dinner, and I was always ready to leave rowdy parties for the comparative quiet of a dimly lit bedroom.

I have always been bemused by the irony there, that it was not until I abandoned my grandmother's name that I began to look like her; that it was not until I became Kiki that I was able to adopt out of choice the life that she was forced into leading.

....

My transition to a new way of life after college was abrupt and pain-less. I simply stopped going out, and I did not miss it. I did not like the postcard-perfect town of Princeton, and after graduation, with most of the students gone, it seemed even stuffier and more staid than usual. But I form deep attachments to places and I have a hard time leaving any-where, even a town I despised as much as Princeton, so I got a job shuffling paper in one of the administrative offices, and deferred my admission to Columbia for a year. At the end of my year of shuffling, I vacationed alone at the New Jersey shore for a few weeks. There I slept with a lifeguard, also a Princeton graduate, and the last of my college flings.

I arrived in New York three years ago, and in spite of the crime, the filth, the poverty, and the pollution I fell in love with it. In the suburban comfort that characterizes Princeton as well as my hometown of Garrison, I always felt vulnerable and exposed, but in New York I am cloaked in an anonymity that makes me feel secure even in the midst of a million human beings. The anonymity confers freedom. Other than Mrs. Noffz and the doormen, I know no one in my apartment building, and I therefore owe nothing to my neighbors, not even a civil response to their chatter as I ride down the elevator with them. The city itself is filled with strangers who leave me alone, and ask nothing more than the same treatment in return. The people here are so indifferent to my pres-ence, and indeed all presences, that by a paradoxical turn they make this city the most accepting place in the world. In this respect all New Yorkers are equal. I fit in here more than anywhere else because I am as faceless as the best of them.

When I got to Columbia I was surprised at how much effort it took to make friends. It may have been only the difference between living in a dormitory and living in an apartment by myself, but it was easy to fall into the simple rhythm of going to class and talking only at the most ca-sual level to people there, fulfilling the most minimal requirements of social contact, and then going home alone. Many of the other graduate students already had a social life within the city; some were living with boyfriends or girlfriends, and one or two were married. I could have started conversations with students at the Law School Library, or joined the organizations that other graduate students joined; I suppose I could even have sat outside on the big steps outside Low Library during the warmer days and chatted with the sunbathers there. But I did not get around to doing any of those things, because once I met Phillip, I did not care to meet anyone new.

By the time my grandmother arrives, of course, Phillip will not even be a shadow in my apartment, and my blissful future with Eric will be assured.

So there I was, I will say, telling her the story of this day. So there I was, sitting on a bench in the middle of a painfully hot summer afternoon, stalling on going home because I had hurled an old loafer at a ghost.

By then, two months hence, we should be able to laugh at the absurdity of this scene, at least a little. Yet my grandmother (understanding all the sides of this many-sided situation) will sympathize, too, nodding when I explain to her that what made it hard was that Phillip was different from anyone else I have ever known.

Obaasama, I will say, you do see my dilemma, don't you? How I wanted to rush home to see whether Eric had called, but how I was also glued to the bench, terrified of the possibility that Phillip might not be there when I returned?

CHAPTER TWELVE

I MET PHILLIP in a bar. I dislike bars, and if Russia had not shown up that night to make sure that I came, I would not have gone. We talked in my bathroom as we often did, with me perched on the edge of the tub while she reapplied her makeup.

"You've got to come," she said. "Please. When have I ever asked you to do anything? Never, right? So just do this one thing for me."

"What are you so nervous about?" I asked, smiling at her habit of answering her own questions. "Is it this guy?"

"Well, I guess I am a tad antsy about Phillip. I really kind of like him and I don't want to mess it up. He's a bit shy."

"What's so special about him?" I was amused and curious, since Russia seldom gets excited about men.

"He's got sexy eyes," she said, and paused.

"Go ahead," I said, laughing. "Describe them—you're obviously dying to."

"They're kind of strange," she said. "They move back and forth—actually, there's something wrong with him. He's got terrible vision, so bad that he can't drive. I don't know how he managed to do so much by himself, when he can see so little. But his eyes are beautiful, regardless," she said, thoughtfully twirling the makeup brush in her hand. "They're blue with little bits of yellow inside them. Sometimes they look green."

"Nice," I said.

"Wait, there's more. He originally lived on a farm in Iowa, but he dropped out of high school and hitchhiked down to Mexico and worked there for six months, and then in Africa for about a year, and then in Australia, and then I don't know where else. He's been all over the world. Doesn't that sound wonderful?"

"I suppose so."

"Now he's bartending at a place on Columbus. You know, he's by far the most promising man I've met in New York."

"Wouldn't you rather be alone with him, then?"

"No," she said. "No, we're not ready for that yet. You've got to come, Kiki—we need a third person. After all, what else are you going to do? I'm not going to let you sit home alone another night."

"But don't you think I'll get in the way?"

"How can you say that?" She made a face at me in the mirror. "You're the best friend I've got in this godforsaken town."

"Thanks," I said. "Likewise. But if I'm there you two won't be able to really talk together. I mean, out of politeness he'll have to talk to me at least some of the time."

"No, I'm not worried about that. You're not really his type. And he's not yours."

"Oh."

"Anyway, to prepare against that eventuality, I laid it on a bit thick about your genius abilities in English. He's intimidated by intellectuals, and I kind of made it seem as if you're the Einstein of British literature. Which you are, of course." Her reflection grinned wickedly at me. "To be honest, he'll probably be too scared to speak to you."

"Great," I said. "Sounds like I'm in for a really good time."

"I even bought new lipstick for tonight. Look, it's a great shade: Frais d'Or." She pronounced the name with a heavily exaggerated accent, and she uncapped the lipstick with a flourish.

"Does that mean you're going to sleep with him?"

"I'm certainly going to try. As usual my nerve will probably fail me at the last moment, but I brought condoms just in case. Rumor does have it that even though he looks so innocent and boyish, he actually gets around quite a bit." Pensively she dabbed at her lips with some toilet paper, and then she turned around to look at me. "At least you guys have that in common."

Russia swears a lot and she has an impressive repertoire of very risqué stories, but she was shocked when I told her that I had had sex with almost twenty men. She herself has had just three boyfriends, and she slept with only two of them.

Russia glanced at herself one more time in the mirror. She was stunning.

"Come on," she said. "Let's go get 'em."

As we were walking out the door, I hesitated. "By the way," I said, "just out of curiosity—what is my type?"

Russia pursed glossy lips and thought for a second, a modern prophetess in action. "Someone steady, probably a little older. Maybe a lawyer?"

The bar was noisy and smoky, and filled with Columbia people. In the confusion and the darkness, I could not at first distinguish anything or anybody, but Russia immediately began to pick out friends and acquaintances from the crowd. She even waved at a few of them, and they waved back. I saw a figure detach itself from one of the barstools, and so my eyes first focused on Phillip.

I did not feel struck by a bolt of lightning when I saw him. He swore later that when we met a kind of subterranean recognition flickered in my eyes, but I know he did not greatly impress me when we were first introduced. I like big men, and Phillip was thin and not terribly tall. He was wearing an outfit made up largely of denim, and I thought he seemed the way a Midwesterner should seem. He carried with him a feeling of open spaces, perhaps because he had a way of gazing far, with eyes slightly narrowed, or perhaps because he moved with grace and ease, unimpeded by the constraints of a room.

When I was close enough to shake hands, I was taken aback by his eyes, in spite of Russia's warning. As soon as they focused on me, they began to jump back and forth from one end to another, flickering as quickly as a candle. I could not make out their color in the dim light of the bar.

We ordered drinks, pulled up stools, and sat around the counter. Phillip had found us a quiet corner, with enough space so that we could face each other. Russia sat cross-legged, perched unstably on her stool.

I had to curb an urge to fidget. When I felt nervous during parties at college, the surest remedy was to fix upon one man, listen to him, flatter him, flirt with him, and eventually retire with him to his room or mine, or failing that a dark corner where the noise of the party would not overly intrude. But I could not do that with Phillip and Russia there.

"Kiki. Yo, Kiki, are you with us?"

"Sorry," I said. "What was the question?"

Russia clucked her tongue. "It wasn't a question. You know, you are hopelessly out of it." She said it so affectionately I had to smile. She turned to Phillip. "Kiki lives in a world of her own."

I glanced over at Phillip. He was absorbed in the bubbles of his drink.

"I was talking about a certain bad time in my life," she said, going back to her story. "I was flat broke, and the town was in a recession. I tried to get a job flipping burgers at Wendy's, but twenty-two other people applied, and they ended up hiring some brain surgeon, I think because he could be called upon to administer the Heimlich maneuver if a customer choked on a fry. Oh, and he also had an advanced degree in meat cooking from the Cordon Bleu."

I rolled my eyes at her exaggeration, but she continued undaunted.

"I took to haunting the local mortuary, hoping that that would make me the first to hear of any sudden job openings. My desperate situation had forced me to be creative. And you know what they say," she said, casting a sidelong glance at me. "Necessity *is* the mother of invention."

"And propinquity is the mother of love," I said, rousing myself.

"Love covers a multitude of sins," she shot back.

"The sins of our fathers have long shadows," I said, beaming.

"Nice circling back to the parent thing," she said admiringly, a good loser.

"Thanks," I said.

She turned to Phillip. "Sorry—I know it's awful and pretentious, but we *are* graduate students."

If he was disgusted or confused or bored, he was too polite to show it. "Go on with your story about the mortuary," he said.

"Oh right," she said. "It paid off big-time, because the mortuary ended up hiring me. Well, okay, the hospital did, but I heard about the job through the mortuary. It was my job to take dead people's eyes from the hospital to the lab, so they could be packaged and shipped off to people needing a new pair," she said, putting up one knee and resting her chin on it. "My boss was this really scary woman. She was all hunched over, with a hump like Igor's"—here she demonstrated the hump by fearfully contracting her shoulder—"and she had a nose like a witch and a pair of gimlet eyes."

I laughed a little at this point, and she did, too.

"Really," she told me. "It might sound hard to believe, but she really was like that." She paused to take a long drink from her beer. "Anyway, this woman used to actually chortle with joy whenever there was a snowstorm or a blizzard at night, because there'd be a lot of fresh young eyes to be had the morning after, you know, from all the accidents on the road."

"Ugh," I said, and Russia nodded.

"Well," she continued, "one day I made the mistake of telling her that I have perfect vision, and after that I didn't have a moment's peace on the job. Whenever I turned around I would catch her watching me, sizing me up as if I were some kind of lamb she wanted to slaughter."

Again I started to laugh, but Russia ignored me and went on straight-faced.

"I used to have nightmares about her sabotaging the traffic lights and the stop signs around my neighborhood so she could get hold of my twenty-twenty vision. And then,"—she said, pausing theatrically— "one night, when Chernobyl—that's my dog—had a stomachache and was making so much noise I couldn't sleep, I looked out the window and there she was, sprinkling something that looked like magic powder all over my street."

"My God," said Phillip.

"You said it," said Russia. She drank from her bottle again. "Pretty upsetting, isn't it. Well, you can bet that I didn't drive on my street anymore after that. And I quit my job the next day, too."

"Did your dog get over his stomachache?" Phillip asked.

"Yup," she said. "But a year later he got hit by a truck and died."

"I guess my eyes would be safe, at least," he said. "I'm hardly twenty-twenty."

Russia paused, but only for a second. "Are you kidding?" she said lightly. "She would kill for a pair of eyes like yours. Blue and yellow eyes are in high demand."

He smiled back at her, and even in the dim light of the bar I could see Russia's pale skin flush. "That's some story," he said. "I mean about the woman, not the dog."

"And the amazing thing is that it all really happened," she said.

As she talked, Russia rested one hand loosely around her beer and used the other to support her chin. She does not rely on her hands to speak. Her fingers are slender with short unvarnished nails. Although some days she dresses so wildly that even jaded New Yorkers turn to look at her on the street, her hands always remain the same, plain and unadorned like those of a girl.

I may have been fidgeting, because Russia turned towards me. "What are you looking at? Did you see someone you know?"

"Nothing so exciting," I confessed. "I was just thinking of going to the bathroom."

"Well," she said in a sprightly tone, her arched brows an invitation, "no time like the present."

"Carpe diem," I said. "Seize the day."

"A stitch in time saves nine," she said, and then shrugged. "Okay, so that kind of works."

"Make hay while the sun shines," I said triumphantly.

Phillip cleared his throat, and we turned to look at him. "Haste makes waste," he said.

Russia and I laughed.

"On that note—" I said, sliding off my chair.

"Oh—" Russia drew me close to her and whispered in my ear. "Check for spare rolls of toilet paper, okay?"

"All right," I said. As I walked off, she apologized offhandedly to Phillip. "Girl talk, sorry about that."

When I returned, Phillip was busy ordering drinks. Russia turned towards me.

"So?"

"At least five spare rolls," I reported.

"I don't want Phillip to know. He's a good Catholic boy, and he might disapprove." She let a few minutes pass, and then she slung her big leather bag over her shoulder. "I've got to pee," she announced, and stood up and walked away.

Left alone, Phillip and I had nothing to say to each other. After throwing him a small, quick smile, I looked away. I am always ill at ease in a bar, but even under better circumstances, I would have been hard pressed for a suitable topic of conversation. What did I have in common with a good Catholic boy from the Midwest, a high school dropout who had been all over the world?

But I did think that at least I should try to help advance Russia's cause. "She's very funny, isn't she," I said, nodding at her vacant seat.

"She is," he said. "And she has a heart of gold."

I was a little taken aback by the broad sweep of his assessment, but for the sake of good manners, I acknowledged it with a vaguely affirmative mumble.

Having fulfilled my social obligations, I had a sip of my Coke and then I looked away again, out at the other people in the bar. He startled me again by saying my name.

"Yes?" I said.

He was a couple of feet away from me, and he neither leaned forward nor talked very loud; I could barely hear him over the bar din. "Don't I know you?" Without pausing, he answered himself. "I know you."

I shook my head. "No," I said. "I mean, I know you're Phillip, but that's about it."

"Ah," he said, sitting back so that his voice became even fainter, and his face almost lost in the shadows. "I could have sworn that you recognized me when we met."

"Really?"

"I thought something flickered in your eyes, a kind of—well, a kind of subterranean recognition."

"Oh," I said. "What an interesting expression." As soon as I said that, I felt like kicking myself for sounding so condescending. Ineptly I tried to make amends. "I mean, I would have liked to have experienced a subterranean recognition when we met, but I don't think I did."

"We played hopscotch together."

"I don't think so," I said, bewildered. "I've never even been in the Midwest."

He looked across at me without changing expression. "No, we played hopscotch together in the park. Don't you remember?"

I began to shake my head and then I stopped. "Riverside Park?"

He nodded.

"In late August?"

"Yeah."

"You're the guy—"

"—hopscotching across the street."

"You waved at me."

"I did."

I sank lower into my stool. "How embarrassing."

"Why?"

"Well, didn't I look pretty silly? A grown woman in heels and a skirt playing hopscotch all by myself?"

He was silent for a moment, gravely considering. "Yes."

"Thanks a lot."

"But I started hopscotching with you."

"That made it worse."

"I don't understand that."

"It was a private moment. I thought I was alone. I wanted to be alone."

He sighed. He shifted in his seat, and his face reemerged from the shadows. His eyes, still for once, gazed directly at me, and they were blue. Mine are black. "You were alone. So was I." He shrugged. "That's why I waved at you from the other side of the street."

Once again he had startled me. I could not hold his gaze and I looked away. Then my eyes slid back to meet his. "Got it," I said. Then Phillip and I smiled at each other for the first time.

Her leather bag swollen with toilet paper, Russia came back from the bathroom to find us talking like old friends. "What's going on?" she asked, a little nervously.

"Oh, well—" and we tried to explain, we wanted to include her in our conversation, yet no matter how we tried, she sat there confused and alone, her eyes returning not to Phillip but to me, her smile pasted on like the strawberry color of her lips.

It was not Russia's fault. Nobody could understand the two of us because we spoke a private language of our own making. Our conversation seemed endless, and it would have been so if he had lived. The talk came tumbling out of us when we were together, yet just as easily we could sit in silence; our friendship ran deep and constant, water beneath a bridge of words.

Even now, when I close my eyes, it is as if he had taken up permanent residence in the secret place inside my eyelids.

I have a healthy bank-account balance, and a promising academic career that I have worked hard to achieve. I love and need the solidity of my home and my possessions, the illusion of stability that they confer upon the infinitude of space.

He had dropped out of high school, and he was a self-proclaimed vagabond who never had a fixed address; often in his travels, he did not even have a temporary bed, but slept under the largest available tree or in the shelter offered by rocks. He usually had no money, and sometimes not even the vaguest idea for a potential source of income, and he had not one profession but a hundred. His ambitions and his plans extended only to the next place he wished to see. He seemed to float in space, unencumbered and undefined, aimless but perhaps no less lost than I am.

He was mugged in Rome, threatened by a gang with guns in Ecuador, and for reasons he never could fully determine, he was held for two nights in a jail in Turkey. Not long after we met, he swore to me that he was finally tired of traveling, and that New York City was where he would settle down. But I never really believed him. He had climbed mountains and hiked through jungles; he had waded through the most dangerous rivers of the world. He died alone on a treacherous mountain path in Nepal, and—who knows?—perhaps that was a destiny that he courted.

Even at my wildest at Princeton, I remained a good student first and foremost, setting myself a rigorous regimen of work and exercise and following it scrupulously, punishing myself with double the workload when I failed to live up to the plan. I aspire to the mainstream, and it is with a sense of desperation that I cling to the straight and narrow.

But in spite of all our differences, Phillip and I had this in common: we both knew what it is like to have parents who no longer speak to each other. Before I met him, I only knew people who had perfect childhoods. They had all been raised in dream homes replete with loving parents, grandparents, siblings, and dogs, and had turned out supremely well adjusted as a result. Eric, the former boy wonder of Long Island, typifies this phenomenon, but even Russia, who seemed so unconventional when I first met her, has two very sweet and somewhat elderly parents living in a big run-down house in Connecticut, and an adorable younger brother who deserves every bit of the attention that she lavishes so generously upon him. Until I met Phillip, I secretly nursed a suspicion that all the marriage statistics lied, and that in actuality I was one of the very few to come from a broken family in America.

He had had a lot of lovers in his life, and Russia may have had reason to be shocked when I told her how many men I have slept with. Eighteen lovers for a twenty-six-year-old woman might not seem unreasonably high even in the era of AIDS, yet it may be so considering that I was a virgin until I got to college. I have, in fact, been sexually active only for the past eight years, and then with a vengeance. Sometimes I think it a miracle that I have not yet caught AIDS, but then I remind myself that all of my lovers have been such nice clean boys, upper-middle-class Ivy League types from dream homes, and that when it comes to venereal diseases, God is even more chary of his miracles than usual.

Phillip and I had five months together as best friends, and all the time that we spent together (clothed, casual, chatty) set up a physical barrier between us that we were never able to overcome completely, except at the very end. Even now, though, I am not absolutely sure that becoming friends was a mistake. If I had slept with him on the night I met him, instead of talking with him into the early hours of the morning, it is quite possible we would never have seen each other again.

Although I thought what we had was so different and special, when I leave the confines of my apartment and walk around outside, I know it was not. The great romances of literature and history do not arouse my envy, and I am left cold at the thought of a passion that could electrify the stage. But the sight of an old couple helping each other down the stairs makes me feel so wistful that even though I know I should look away, I cannot. I wish I could have had that with Phillip, and yet even as I wish it, I know I am being corny and unrealistic and stupid, because of course the cards were stacked against that from the start. For while almost by definition every true lover feels that his or her love is extraordinary, only a very small handful of lucky ones can actually prevail over the extraordinary to achieve a garden-variety domestic happiness.

I push myself off the bench, hobble a few blocks more, and then trudge up the stairs at 103rd Street to exit the park. One day, after climbing up these steps, Phillip and I turned around to look back at the way we had come. It was early November, and the leaves lay in piles around the trees. The park sloped down green and grassy to the boulevard, where Rollerbladers made moving points of neon color, and then there was the highway with all the traffic, and beyond that the Hudson River, shiny and blue; farther past that was New Jersey, rendered picturesque by distance, and finally there was the infiniteness of the sky, with the sun sinking, but still yellow. We were quiet for a time, the wind riffling through our hair, and then Phillip turned to me and put an arm around my shoulder. He spoke in pig Latin; we often did so when we were alone in public together.

"Someday, Ki," he said, gesturing grandly towards the west, "someday all this will be yours."

I laughed, my face turned up to him. For a few seconds, he looked at me without speaking, and then he laughed as well, the sunlight glowing warm upon him.

"Actually, I'm just kidding." He gazed out at the horizon again. "It's yours already."

Obaasama, I will say. You who have been displayed, sold, coveted, haggled over, purchased, traded, kept, and owned. You whom countless men have paid for and sampled. You who have survived earthquakes, a world war, a fire. Grandmother, can you teach me how to carry on once love becomes a ghost?

The shadows are beginning to lengthen.

When I open the door and stumble into my apartment, Phillip is the first thing I see. He reclines on top of the bookshelves, flat on his back, so that only his profile is visible. I greet him in silence, as usual, but with relief as well, thinking I should have known better: he is no mouse, to scamper away because of one poorly aimed shoe.

I check the answering machine. The red light shines forth without blinking; Eric still has not called, and I cannot find it in myself to cry.

CHAPTER THIRTEEN

THE RING OF the phone shatters my sleep, its sound oddly echoing my dreams. "Phillip?" I say hoarsely into the receiver, but my dreams have been about Eric and a nameless dark woman, and I do not receive a reply.

Hiding behind the bamboo that grew thickly on the sides of the road, my grandmother Yukiko staked out Sekiguchi's imposing house for four days before she saw her.

Yukiko's house was smaller and she, at least, thought it prettier, shaded by a grove of cherry trees in a quieter part of town. She had one child, aged two, who played at home under the watchful eyes of a nurse, a girl who was born in the spring but was named for the fall: my mother. The ashes of another girl, dead of pneumonia at the age of two months, lay buried in an urn that was near, but not inside, Sekiguchi's family tomb in the temple grounds just outside of Tokyo. Now Yukiko was round yet again.

Every morning for the last four days, before she set out to lurk in the shadows of her favorite clump of bamboo, Yukiko had dressed carefully in her darkest kimono. She had long ago given up tying her obi

in the butterfly fashion of the geisha, and opted now for a more decorous bow, as befitting a woman who was pregnant for the third time,
a woman no longer available for hire. She carried a parasol partly as
protection from the mild March sun, but mostly as another mode of
concealment.

She had reached a watershed in her relationship with her lover.
Sekiguchi had bought her a house and had taken her from her geisha
life, yet she knew from her old contacts at the geisha house that he had
visited another establishment. He had been looking rather than sam-
pling, ostensibly for the purpose of hosting another party, but she
thought it odd that he had not mentioned it, and immediately surmised
that he was toying with the idea of a second mistress.

He doted on their daughter, but Yukiko knew he hankered after a
son to carry on the line. She ran her fingers lightly over the smooth
slope of her stomach, and fiercely willed that the child be a boy.

She saw her in the late afternoon, when the shadows were length-
ening and the air was growing cool, just as she was contemplating going
home to ready herself for Sekiguchi's arrival: he was coming over for
dinner and also for the night. The large front doors, unused during the
day, when Sekiguchi was at his bank, had opened to a flurry of activity,
and Yukiko's throat went tight with anticipation.

Ever since her hysterical pregnancy, Eiko had lived in virtual seclu-
sion. Sekiguchi still never talked of her, and Yukiko always, though
often just barely, managed to resist the urge to ask. Forewarned by the
gossip line, Yukiko thought she knew what to expect from this childless
woman, her rival, who was (she sometimes thought with forgivable
complacency) maybe barren and even frigid. She had heard countless
accounts of Eiko's nervous giggles, her shrill demands, and the good
looks worn away by illnesses both real and imagined. But when Eiko
Sekiguchi, borne aloft on a litter, came out of the house, Yukiko was astonished at how pretty she was.

Eiko was in fact dying, although it was a process that would take another two years, and as the servants bore her closer to the bamboo,
Yukiko noted the telltale traces: the almost skeletal fragility, the cheeks

that were a little too flushed under the white makeup, the troublesome cough. But these traces did not detract from her beauty, which was exquisite. Small, pale, and perfectly formed, Sekiguchi's wife embodied the Japanese ideal, in stark, humbling contrast to Yukiko, with her outlandish height, her olive coloring, and her mammoth breasts and feet.

Unconsciously Yukiko had edged forward, so that she was almost standing on the road. Her parasol, forgotten, had floated down to rest upon her shoulder, exposing her to the direct light. She was, in fact, gaping, and so it was not surprising that Eiko noticed her. What was surprising was Eiko's reaction. Her eyes lit upon Yukiko's face, indifferently drifted away, and then quickly darted back and remained fixed there, and Yukiko knew that somehow she had been recognized.

In Tokyo in the late 1930s, keeping a mistress was an honorable practice. Everyone knew that Kurokawa, the minister of finance, kept different houses for his two geisha women as well as for his wife; he was respected for the fact that he had had fourteen children, nine of them still alive. To be a spurned wife was neither shameful nor uncommon; to be a rich man's mistress in a house of her own was a step up the social ladder from working at the geisha house. Yet for Eiko there were all the nights she did not even see her husband, the knowledge of the rejection, which lay like a permanent weight on her shoulders, and the thought that he might be waiting for her to die. For Yukiko there was fear, which she could confess only to her old friend, Kaori, for my grandmother was characterized above all by her pride. A constant voice in her head, her fear whispered that she was growing old, that she would lose Sekiguchi's love and the house that she had given up her geisha life for, that he would ultimately spurn her if she did not bear him a son. Every morning she woke to the sound of this voice, she struggled in vain to evade it through the day, and at night she could not sleep because of its nagging.

But at the same time Yukiko was also tormented by the thought that even if Eiko were dead, Sekiguchi would not marry her, with her past, which maybe was not sordid but was certainly not aristocratic and impeccable, as Eiko's was.

The motion of the litter rocked Eiko gently from side to side. The men carried her on their shoulders, which was still not high enough to escape the stench of the sewage that ran in an open stream along both sides of the path, a stench that Yukiko, well into her fourth day of spying, had long ceased to notice. The two women gazed at each other, Eiko's head swiveling to keep Yukiko's face in sight as the servants carrying her turned upon the road. Eiko began to cough again, and she buried her face in the sleeve of her kimono while her whole body shook. She emerged looking wan and tired, but she smiled wryly in Yukiko's direction. Yukiko bowed then, bending her rounded body as far as she could, and after the shortest of pauses, Eiko followed suit, slowly inclining her head.

They watched each other for as long as they could, Yukiko a tall figure standing at attention in front of the bamboo, Eiko's white face hovering above the dark heads of the servants who bore her, an oval that gradually grew smaller until it was lost in the dust and the crowds. Then Yukiko sighed, closed her parasol, and went home to greet and love Eiko's husband.

I was standing by the pumpkins when I saw them. They were headed uptown, and together they were so tall and fair it seemed as if they belonged to another species.

I recognized his walk first, his sauntering grace and the laziness that made him loath to waste motion. They walked side by side, smoothly in step, with long, slow strides that overtook the other people on the street. It was late January, and freezing. With long underwear, a turtleneck, a sweater, and an ankle-length coat on, I was so bundled up I waddled, and still I was hunched with the cold. Clad in jeans, sweaters, and leather jackets, they moved easily, their arms swinging by their sides. She was thin and tall, only an inch or so shorter than he, with shining golden hair that fell to her shoulders, and more than one passerby turned to watch them go.

From the shadows beneath the awning I watched them come closer, my mouth dry, and then she grabbed Phillip by the hand and dragged him into the store I was in, and I lost my head and dropped my basket, my books and plums rattling in their cage, and ducked behind the tomatoes.

She led him straight to the eggplants and put him to work. Under her direction he sorted through them, picking up one at a time, slowly turning it over in his hand, and then tossing it aside. After watching him for a while, she nodded approvingly and began to scramble through the pile herself, picking up two at once, discarding some with decision and putting aside a small pile of possibilities for future inspection.

They were happily absorbed in their eggplants when suddenly he turned around, and as she looked at him inquiringly, he darted a sharp glance around the shop. I ducked just in time, my heart pounding. Had he sensed my breathing, sniffed me out, heard my racing pulse from a distance of almost ten feet? Could he, half-blind, see me cowering beside the onions? After a few moments, he turned back to his search, and I cautiously raised my head again. I could see their breaths as they chatted, and I imagined my own breath rising in white puffs above the tomatoes, like Indian smoke signals, betraying me. I tried to aim my breath downwards, letting it out in slow, careful exhalations.

They took so long over the eggplants that a man waiting for a few moments behind them finally coughed and pushed his way gently but firmly past them. He picked up the one at the top of the pile and headed towards the counter, pausing only to say in a clear, cutting voice that rang even in my ears: "It's just an eggplant, you know, it's not a car." Nonplused, Phillip and the woman stared at him while I snickered, but then Phillip shrugged and the woman laughed and shook out her hair, and they both bent their heads down and resumed their careful search.

My feet were going numb when at last with a cry of triumph she brandished it aloft, the end of the quest, a prince among eggplants, the paragon of vegetables: plump and shiny, an even dark purple, neither too big nor too small, and cast in the quintessential bulbous shape. They gathered together, arms touching, while she cooed, oohed and aahed over it, and finally gazed down in silence like a fond and doting parent. He smiled and said something; she gave a shout of laughter, turned towards him, placed one black-gloved hand on his shoulder, and kissed him on the cheek.

My elbow jerked involuntarily and a tomato rolled off the top of the pyramid and hit the ground with a soft plop. Though he could not possibly have heard, Phillip half-turned his head towards me, but the woman was speaking to him now, and he soon turned away.

I watched them as they paid for the eggplant, left the store, and began walking again, faster and much more purposefully, downtown, in the direction of Phillip's apartment. In a daze I stood up, my knees aching from the strain. I walked over and retrieved my basket, waited in line, bought the plums, and went home. I worked on a paper on Joy Kogawa throughout the afternoon, but in the evening I had to trash all that I had written.

The next day he came over to laze around my apartment with me in the evening.

"Why so distant?" he finally asked.

"I have to get this paper done."

"Crikey," he said. "Didn't you say it's due next week? I've never known you to start a paper so early. It was you, wasn't it, at the market."

"What are you talking about?" I said, elaborately casual, absorbed in the papers strewn across my desk.

"It's not what you think."

"Oh," I said, determined not to ask. Then the silence of him waiting became too long. "Where does she buy her shoes? She wears wonderful shoes." Another pause, and I added, "She's gorgeous. What's she doing with the likes of you?"

"You're being silly," he said, and though my eyes were still on my papers I could hear the smile in his voice. When I did not reply or turn around, he continued, "She wasn't doing anything with the likes of me."

I drew a balloon and a school of goldfish, just to keep my pen scratching on the paper.

"I don't know where she buys her shoes," he finally said. "Somewhere expensive. Nothing happened, Ki. She's just a friend."

Turning around, I met his straightforward gaze and that crooked smile, and found I could not move, remembering her as she turned to kiss him, her cheeks flushed and her eyes shining, a plump polished eggplant lying forgotten in her hand. If nothing had happened, it was not for lack of her trying.

"I thought you enjoyed one-night stands," I said. "I thought you always—"

"Stop judging me," he said, with more than a hint of sharpness. "You have no right."

I did not reply, my eyes scanning the room for Horse.

"I've changed," he said simply, his tone more level. "I haven't gone out with any women for a long time, since I—well, since I moved to New York."

I was about to remind him that he had only been in New York for five months, but he had not finished speaking.

"And so what if I did sleep around in the past? You did, too, and you enjoyed it just as much as I did."

On the brink of contradicting him, I hesitated, remembering all the tennis players, and before that the debate-team secretary who went to the Capitol with my virginity tucked under his belt.

"Okay," I said, sighing. "All right. It was fun at the time. Kind of, or maybe just sometimes, but then I started to hate myself for it."

He nodded.

"Hey," I said, "while we're on the subject—how'd you know I was at the market?"

He grinned. "I thought I saw you reflected in one of the mirrors. They're all over the store, you know. But mostly it was a lucky guess, and a good bluff."

"Ah," I said, turning back to my desk with a sudden longing for Kogawa's novel, and the words that were like polished stones. I was looking down at what I had written, trying hard not to think about why he had not slept around since moving to New York, when he came up behind me and placed a hand on my shoulder. He moved so silently I jumped at his touch.

The fingers of his other hand moved over my head, in the gesture I knew so well. "There," he said triumphantly, bringing a white strand in front of my face to show me. "That's my favorite one."

I looked down at my desk again, and after a while he dropped the white hair, letting it fall back into place among the black. He drew back a little, unnerved as I was, perhaps, by how close our faces were.

"I have changed," he said again, whispering now. "You've got to believe me."

Why? Because our friendship would suffer if I didn't? Because I would respect you less, or because I would fear you more? I wanted to ask these questions and more, but I was too afraid. His words, uttered so quietly, confused me in a way I still do not like to remember, and in spite of the almost imperceptible note of pleading in his voice, I could not trust myself to speak. Instead I bent my head down and brushed my cheek against his hand as it rested on my shoulder, a touch so featherlight I was not sure he felt it. But before he moved away from me, his fingers cupped my face for a few moments, in a gesture that was a benediction.

CHAPTER FOURTEEN

W HEN I TELL my grandmother about Phillip, one of the incidents I will be sure to include is the night he began the practice of
brushing my hair, for in a rather pleasing mirror effect, that story begins
with me telling Phillip about how she used to keep her hair coiled in a
box as she slept. I interrupted my own account by abruptly sitting up.

"I'm going to get a hairbrush," I told him. "I'll be right back."

I went to the bedroom and rummaged through the clutter on the
dressing table. Just as I found the brush, I heard Phillip speak behind me.
"I'll do that for you," he said. I turned around and saw him leaning
against the doorframe, Horse coiling around his ankles.

He walked over, sat me down on the chair, and uncurled my fingers
from the brush.

"It's really tangled," I warned. We had spent the day in the park,
playing Frisbee, and my hair was windswept and badly snarled.

"Trust me," he said, gathering my hair into a double handful at the
nape of my neck.

I examined myself critically in the mirror, noting how my face had
changed within the past year, shucking off much of the softness of the
cheeks and the chin. Though still unlined, my face had attained some of

the rigidity of age. If I bent my head down to look at my scalp, I could usually catch a glimpse of at least two strands of white, glinting in an annoyingly conspicuous way against the black of my hair. "I'm going to get my hair dyed."

He put down the brush and held up a white hair like an antenna over my head. With me sitting in front of him and him stretching the strand as far as it would go, it reached up to his nose. "You don't need to dye your hair. You probably only have ten white hairs, all told. And besides, I like them—especially this one."

He began brushing. He did so by holding a small section near the roots in one hand and brushing it out with the other, so that my hair was not painfully pulled. Was it his weak eyesight that made his powers of concentration seem doubly intense? He peered closely at everything—a subway map, a book, the fur and face of Horse. I had no right to feel flattered.

He whistled softly as he worked, a tuneless sound, but soothing.

"You're better than my hairdresser at this," I said suspiciously. "How'd you learn?"

"A woman," he said, studiously bending his head over mine.

Knowing I should not ask, I asked. "Who?"

"A teacher at my high school," he said, smiling, but his cheeks were flushed.

"I knew I shouldn't have asked."

"She was an English teacher, actually."

"Of course. I'm a member of a corrupt breed."

"She had long brown hair, almost this thick," he said, touching the outlines of mine. "It was a bitch to comb, probably because it was curly."

"That was good of you to take over, then," I said dryly.

He shook his head at my reflection. "She was thirty and hot as hell, and I was seventeen. I was so thrilled and grateful I would've washed her car and painted her house, inside and out, if she'd let me."

The static ripped through my hair with the brush, and mingled with the sound of his whistling. His hand moved slowly, rhythmically, up and down, up and down. My eyelids were beginning to droop, but not from drowsiness. Thoughts of the seventeen-year-old Phillip and the thirty-year-old English teacher, her hair streaming down her naked back, kept creeping into my mind. I shook my head (a movement that elicited a low admonition from Phillip) and began to talk.

"Even when I was little," I said, "my hair was long. My mom used to brush out all the knots every night, and then again in the morning. It hurt a lot when she did it."

Picking up on the implied compliment, he smiled at me in the mirror, that quick brightness lighting up his face.

I paused, examining his reflection closely, as if seeing him at a re-move offered a new angle or a different perspective. With those hollow cheeks and the eyes that moved of their own accord, it was a face too broken to be conventionally handsome, yet in repose, as it was then, Phillip's face sometimes had the serenity of a stone saint in a churchyard.

"God, did I hate brushing time," I continued. "Sometimes I hid, and my mom had to drag me kicking and screaming from beneath the bed, or from behind the shower curtain."

"You hellcat," he said. "Spitfire. Wild girl."

"Maybe I was. Until—"

"Aren't you still?" he interrupted, sounding disappointed. I tried to catch his eye in the mirror, but his face was hidden behind my head.

"To get back to my story," I said, "I always squirmed and squirmed when she brushed my hair, until one day she yelled, 'I quit,' and put down the brush forever."

"That doesn't sound like your mom," he said, poking his head up. "From what you tell me, she doesn't sound like the yelling type."

I made a face at his reflection. "Whose story is this?" I asked. "But you're right. She didn't yell, but she did quit."

Phillip, smirking, let the back handful of hair go and started working on the right side.

"She told me I had to take care of my own hair. I was only about eight at the time, and really she should've just cut it short. My hair went uncombed for days, maybe weeks. I'd wash my hair and not bother to brush it, and go to school like that. This big, ugly tangle grew like a tumor on the left side of my head, and soon it was too late—I couldn't get a brush through it at all. And then"—I stopped, letting the suspense build—"then one day I got bubble gum stuck in it."

Phillip laughed. "How'd you do that?"

"I don't know. Maybe when I was trying to spit it out, I hit my own hair. Or maybe I stuck it on the table for safekeeping and then forgot and rested my head on the spot. I tend to think, though, that it was like the time I stapled my finger to see what would happen. I probably did it deliberately.

"When I tried to get the gum out with my fingers, I of course spread it all around, and more and more of my hair kept getting caught in it. It was really kind of scary, this big purple blob dangling just in the corner of my vision. And, boy, did it stink—you know that heavy, sickly grape smell?

"I suppose what my mom should have done is coax the gum out with conditioner. But she didn't. She just cut off my hair."

"Yowza," he said, holding one lock in his fingers, and letting it slide through them slowly. "What drastic measures."

"It was the one and only time I ever had short hair in my life. And it was really short. My dad said I looked like I was in the army. In the pictures I look awful, but I didn't notice at the time. By then it was summer, and it was hot."

Standing behind me, he held my head between his hands, and looked at me seriously in the mirror. "I'll brush your hair whenever you want," he promised. "And if you get gum stuck in your hair again, I'll soak it in conditioner and untangle it strand by strand, if I have to, so that not one bit of it ever has to be cut."

I gazed back at him, and our eyes locked.

"I'm done," he added, handing me back the brush.

My hair was so smooth it was silken. I was about to thank him when he stopped me.

"Now it's my turn," he said. "Have you got scissors?"

"Yes. I didn't know you cut your own hair."

"I don't," he said, following me into the bathroom. "You're going to cut it."

I got the big scissors out of the medicine cabinet and went back to the bedroom, with him tagging close behind. He sat down on the chair I had just been in, and I brushed his hair back while we discussed different possible hairstyles.

He took off his shirt before I began cutting, his hands reaching behind to pull it over his head, and when I began to cut I felt dizzy with the closeness of his bare skin and the faint salty smell that rose from his neck.

Although I had seen him without his shirt on before, we were alone in my bedroom, and the hour was late. I tried not to breathe too hard on his skin as I leaned closer to cut the fine hairs at the base of his neck. I had not yet lost my fingerprints then, and the sight of his body made me conscious of the wholeness of my own. He was well muscled but painfully thin. He had a long gash on the inside of his left forearm. There were three scratches on his left rib cage and he had a jagged and tortuous scar, very apparently stitched up, which ran down his stomach and disappeared into his jeans.

He had told me just a few days earlier of the accident on the construction site that led to these scars, the rush of air that had seemed to come almost simultaneously with the slipping of his foot, and also of how close he had come to dying.

I wanted to run my fingers through the fine hairs at the base of his neck. With my tongue I wanted to trace that jagged and tortuous line from the top of his stomach down to its end, and I wanted to lay my ear on his chest and listen to his heart beat. I wanted to hold him, and more.

We did not talk while I cut. Though he was pleased with the final result, I thought it a trifle uneven.

The knock on the door came two weeks later. It was late, perhaps around two, and when I peered through the peephole I could dimly make out Phillip's hair, just this side of blond, and his black jacket. He came by so often that all the doormen of my building let him through without buzzing me, but he always called first, even if it was only from the pay phone on the corner of my street, and so I was feeling bewildered as I undid the locks and opened the door.

"They took my camera," he said, sounding tired.

The book I was holding fell with a flutter of pages, hitting the ground with a leaden thud.

His face had taken the brunt of the beating, although he had been punched in the stomach a few times as well. There was a pink bruise on his right cheekbone, and his lip was split open, his left eye all but swollen shut. A gash slicing through the center of his eyebrow would leave a permanent line where the hair did not grow—another scar to add to his collection.

His hair was sleek with water, and his jacket was damp. It had been raining so quietly I had not heard the drops hit the skylight.

I put an arm around him and led him to the couch. I eased him down onto it, and then sat down next to him. Not knowing where to start, I brushed away the water that had fallen from his hair to his shoulders. "Should I call the hospital?" I asked.

"It's not that serious, and anyway, I can't afford it," he said. His eyes, which had been zigzagging crazily when he first walked in, slowed and steadied as they looked into mine. "I—will you take care of me?"

When I had scarlet fever at the age of seven, I surfaced once from my delirium to see my mother sitting at my bedside, with tears rolling down her cheeks. It was a sight that had bewildered me at the time.

"Don't worry, you're in good hands," I told him. "I used to be a life-guard, you know—oh, don't you know? I was, and I know CPR." I thumped on his chest a few times to demonstrate.

He chuckled, or rather wheezed, in shallow gasps, and then his face twisted. "Ow," he said. "Ow, ow, ow. Don't make me laugh."

"Boy, if you look like this," I said, trying to keep my voice steady, "wish I could get a look at th'other guy."

This time he only smiled, but the caked blood on his lips cracked as he stretched them, and he gingerly touched his mouth with his fingers.

I made him an icepack for his left eye, and wincing when he did, I rubbed alcohol onto his cuts and scratches. At his request, I brought out some wine—his, left in my apartment—which he drank straight from the bottle, and as his wincing continued in the disinfectant process, I joined him.

"There were four of them," he said, sounding drowsy as the drink began to take effect. "With knives. I shouldn't have fought back but I've had that camera for eleven years, and it's gone everywhere with me. I was heading to the subway when it happened, the Astor Place stop, you know, the one with pictures of beavers on the tiles. . . .

"I was scared shitless."

"I know," I said.

He stopped talking, then, and reached out and intercepted my hand, which was traveling with a dab of ointment towards his scraped cheekbone. He flipped my arm over, bent his head down, and peered nearsightedly at the pale inside of my forearm, studying it as if he had never seen one before. He traced a finger along the length of it, starting from my wrist, following the trajectory of my veins to move higher and higher. My head was spinning a little from the wine, but just as he was reaching the crease of my elbow, I yanked my arm back.

"That tickles," I said, looking away as I rubbed the ointment off my fingers.

He spent that night at my house. It was like a children's sleepover party, with him camped out on one couch and I on the other, within whispering distance. He fell asleep almost immediately, but I lingered for what felt like a long time, listening to the sounds of the distant Broadway traffic and the lightest patter of rain, watching him as he lay there, his body curled towards me, his face smoothed of expression, and his head cradled on one arm.

Shifting uneasily on the couch, I woke later in the night to see a tall figure standing by the windows, silhouetted in the moonlight.

"Phillip?" I murmured, terrifyingly uncertain.

The dark shape turned, moved, and soon was standing over me. I do not know what I was expecting, but I was ridiculously relieved to see that it was him. Like a little girl I held out my arms, and without a moment's hesitation, he bent down and crawled into them, stretching out beside me. He was still for perhaps ten minutes, long enough that in spite of the sweaters, the jeans, and the socks that we were wearing, the warmth of his body carried through to mine. His breathing became deep and even, but as I slowly raised myself to a sitting position, he stirred.

"Stay with me," he whispered, so low that I had to stoop to hear.

I hesitated, and then stammered. "I don't . . ."

"Stay with me," he said again. "Please."

So I stayed. With Horse the cat watching us benignly from the top of the coffee table, I lay back down next to Phillip—an awkward business, as the couch was narrow, and his body tender. I tried to be careful but I must not have been trying hard enough, for I heard a sharp intake of breath as I was easing my head onto his shoulder. I drew back, muttering about aspirin and bandages, but he pulled me back down. "Hush," he said, his eyes glinting in the moonlight, and he wrapped his arms and legs around me so tightly I could not breathe, let alone cry, and had to come up sputtering for air.

None of this was what I expected, and as I drifted off to sleep again, I reminded myself that none of it was happening, for the night had been a rainy one, and the scene was tinged with the black-and-silver quality of all of my dreams.

I woke in the morning to a gray light, the sound of rain, and the knowledge that I was alone. The couch that Phillip had been lying on was empty. My clothes were rumpled, my back was sore, and my face was mashed against the edge of the sofa. But at least, I told myself, at least I had not drooled. I was just beginning to pick myself up when I heard a footfall behind me, and I turned to see Phillip come through the hallway with Horse in his arms.

"I fed Horse," he said. "And made you breakfast. Hungry?"

"You're still here," I said, almost singing out the words, and then I hastily cleared my throat and tried to wipe the grin off my face. "I mean, I thought you'd be long gone."

He smiled and shook his head. "That's because you still don't trust me," he said, scolding patiently. "When will you learn to remember that we're friends?"

I smiled stiffly back, nodded, and went to the kitchen to eat the breakfast that he had made, but though he was more or less competent in the kitchen, the eggs and even the cereal tasted like sawdust, and I pleaded sleepiness and sent him home as soon as possible. The book I had been reading the night before still lay on the ground, and I picked it up, dusted it off, and attempted in vain to smooth out its bent pages. Finally I gave up and placed it on top of the tall stack of academic books on my desk. Turning my back to them, I went to take a bath with a Sue Grafton mystery I had been saving for just such an emergency. Yet the words of the book slipped by me, no matter how often I reread them, so that eventually I had to put it aside. After that I sat with Horse and listened to the rain striking the roof, my body curled on the couch and my head resting on my arm, for Phillip's words had been a rejection.

Grandmother, I will whisper, interrupting my own rambling narrative, I was wrong to think he did not want me. But tell me, please, whether I should have known.

In missing all the signals, was I being stupid, or just afraid?

CHAPTER FIFTEEN

FOUR AND A half months after I met Phillip, three weeks before he left for Nepal, I stepped out of my Southern Writers class at Columbia to find him leaning against the wall, chewing on a toothpick. "How'd you know I was here?" I asked, smiling for no clear reason. "I mean, you are waiting for me, right?"

He grinned. "I called up the graduate department and told them it was urgent. And yes, I am waiting for you."

"You lied to the graduate department?" I said. "What'm I going to say to those nice secretaries?"

"It is urgent. I urgently needed to have lunch with you," he said, but then he paused and suddenly there it was, surfacing from beneath his cool, that diffidence that bordered on fear. "That is, if you want to, of course."

"You kidding? I'd love it," I said, taking his arm. "Let's go."

We went to the diner down the street from Columbia, and slid into our favorite booth by the window. I reached for the menu, but he was observing me with curiosity. "You're glowing like a firecracker," he said.

"I am not," I told him. "And besides, firecrackers don't glow."

"That's true," he said. "But you're glowing like one anyway."

I put my hands to my cheeks, knowing already that they would feel unusually warm. "Must be the wind," I said, and bent my head down to look at the menu.

I had just finished reading the Daily Specials out loud to Phillip when Russia walked in the door. Reading distant signs and menus printed on far walls for Phillip became such a habit with me that I once caught myself doing so for Eric, who laughed and said it was my repressed maternal instinct surging to the fore. I never did tell Eric about Phillip's eyesight.

Russia reached down to give each of us a kiss, first Phillip and then me. "Haven't seen you for a while," she said lightly to Phillip. "And you—" she said, peering closer at me. "You're looking radiant, like a firecracker or something."

Phillip smiled.

"Did you guys plan that?" I asked. Russia raised her eyebrows, and I shook my head. "Never mind," I told her. "Wanna eat with us?"

She paused for only a second. "I was going to get a muffin to go, but okay, for a few minutes, if you're going to twist my arm," she said, and squeezed in next to me as I moved over to make room.

After the waitress took our orders and left a basket of bread in exchange, Russia turned to me and said, "My brother just got his first girlfriend."

"But he's so young," I said.

"Twelve and a half next month," she said. "It does seem young, doesn't it. But Mom says she's a very sweet girl, and Joey says that all of his friends are dating."

"As long as she's sweet," I said, "more power to him."

"Amen," said Russia, but then added, "Speaking from experience, though, I gotta say there's a lot to be said for living alone." She picked out a large piece of bread from the basket, and began buttering it generously. "Think about it: the luxury of being able to fart in peace." She looked up from her bread, and shook her knife at us for emphasis. "If I die single, I want you guys to have my mother engrave that on my tombstone. 'Russia Hannah Putnam-Jones, 1964 to 1989: She Farted in Peace.'"

Phillip and I dutifully chuckled, but I knew, and I suspect Phillip did as well, that her words were meant to reassure us. Yet they served only to remind me of how lonely she had been and still was, and how long and how badly she had wanted someone. Her hopes for Phillip had been high.

"Speaking of romance," she said, "just last week I was sure that one of my students was going to hit on me."

I could tell from her voice that she had entered story mode. "Jailbait?" I asked, teasing.

"Well, if he was, I wasn't bitin'," she said. "He's a tall, thin guy, kind of ugly and really shy, and I sort of thought he was gay, at least at first. But by the end of September, ol' Johnnie's taken up staring at me all through class, sittin' in the front row and keepin' his eyes just riveted on me. Then he takes up visiting my office hours, stammering and blushing and talking about nothing at all. He always stands too close, and though you could never consider him threatening, really, I'm starting to get a little unnerved at the way he's always peering down at my body."

Taking a big bite of bread, she chewed contemplatively for a few seconds. Swallowing with some difficulty, she continued, "So last week Johnnie comes to see me at the tail end of my office hours; no one else is in the conference room and it's getting dark outside . . . a perfect romantic moment, right? And I'm trying to think what to do, how to tell him kindly but firmly that it's unethical for me to date a student, and I'm even planning what to do if he tries to kiss me, how I'd step to the side so that he'd fall over my chair. I figured I could take him, because he's tall but skinny, and *so* unconfident.

"He talks about his latest paper, blah blah, which was a terrible one, by the way, and even though I ask him questions and he answers them, I can tell his mind's not on it, and finally I can tell he's made up his mind to speak up for himself. And he says, his face bright red, his voice almost a whisper, 'There's a Gay and Lesbian Dance this Thursday night, and I was wondering if, if'—and here he clears his throat and lifts his head, looks me right in the eye, and says, 'I was wondering if I could borrow your black imitation-Chanel suit.'"

As we laughed, Russia dreamily smiled. "I told him it was no imitation, honey, but the real thing, picked up secondhand somewhere. The next day I lent it to him with my blessing, and do you know he looked better in it than I do? I told him so, and he was so happy and grateful that he kissed me after all, decorously on the cheek, of course, and you know, I didn't mind it one bit.

"He may not know how to write," she said slowly, glancing mischievously at me and then at Phillip, and then back at me again, "but at least *he* has the courage to act on his convictions, bless his little fashion-minded heart."

Less than a week later, I bumped into Russia again as I was leaving the stacks at Butler Library. Barely returning my hello, she leaned against the counter and waited as I checked out my books.

She walked out with me towards the stairs, her heels clicking against the marble, and when we were standing at the top of them, she turned to me and said, "You guys aren't sleeping together, are you."

Her statement (for it was a statement and not a question) was abrupt and sounded even irritable, but I smiled with affection at Russia, who looks so mean with her shaved head and her nine body rings and her uniform black outfits, and yet is so tenderhearted that she cannot bring herself to kill a cockroach, for fear that it might be Gregor Samsa. She always was a good friend to me.

"No, we're not," I told her.

"How long has it been—four months, five?" She shook her head in disbelief. "Do you know that you guys seem like an old married couple? Have you been seeing each other every day, or what?"

"Pretty much," I said, feeling only a little shy. "And we always talk on the phone, whether we see each other or not."

"I knew it," she said. "I could tell just from the way you read off the menu to him. And when your tea came, and he stirred in the milk for you without you even asking for it. That's the way my parents are, and they've been married thirty-five *years*."

"I didn't notice about the tea," I confessed.

"See?" She nodded wisely. "That's because you're already so used to him that he's become a part of you."

"He's hardly that," I protested, but she did not seem to hear.

"Actually," she said, biting her underlip and frowning, "I almost envy you."

"You shouldn't," I said quickly.

"Not because I want Phillip. Obviously that wouldn't have worked, and it doesn't bother me anymore."

I nodded, feeling relieved.

"But you guys are so close. You almost don't seem to need anyone else when you're together."

"It sometimes feels like that," I admitted.

"Kiki," she said, "don't you want him?"

"I don't know," I said, almost whispering, definitely lying.

"Does he want you?" she asked.

Her gaze, like her question, was so direct I had to look away.

"I bet he does," she said thoughtfully. "You know, I didn't guess that you two would hit it off so well. But I really shouldn't have been surprised—you both live in your own private worlds, Phillip with his subways and his wanderlust, and you with your books. Somehow the two of you together makes sense, in an odd kind of way."

I flinched at her words, which were laced, after all, with the faintest trace of bitterness.

"It'd be a shame for you two not to try, anyway," she went on. "After all, how many times do relationships really work out? Once in a lifetime, if you're very, very lucky."

"Why only once?" I asked, slipping on the simple phrase, my tongue grown thick.

"Well, think about it. It's not possible to have had a perfect relationship in the past, because otherwise you'd still be with that person. Ergo no one has a good track record when it comes to relationships. At the most, if you're very lucky, it's worked out for you with your current partner."

In spite of myself I had to smile. I was thinking of my grandmother when I said the next words. "What if you have a perfect relationship and the person dies?"

She paused, thinking. "That's a good question," she said. "But I'd say that it's too easy to idealize someone who's died. You can't know what would have happened to that relationship, so in the long run, if you love someone and he or she dies, it's probably best not to think about them too much."

There was a pause. "Anyway," I said, "right now, Phillip and I are just friends."

"Why is that?" she asked curiously. "Why aren't you guys together?"

It was a question I had asked myself, too, more than once.

"It's not as if either of you's scared of sex," she continued.

"No, but neither of us has had anything close to a lasting relationship, you know," I said, striving to keep my tone light. "I've lost touch with all my lovers, and he . . ." I shrugged, and began turning away from her, towards the stairs.

"But surely—"

I shut my eyes for a long second. "Russia," I said as gently as possible, "I should go."

She was instantly contrite. "I'm sorry," she said. "I have gone on and on, haven't I. But you know I just want you to be happy."

"I know you do," I told her. "And I appreciate it."

I turned to go, but she put a hand on my arm to stop me.

"It's okay," I said. "Really. We're better like this. I do have so much reading to do, after all." I nodded at the pile of books in my arms, which was almost unbearably heavy by this point of the conversation.

Her eyes, which are a mild shade of brown, were warm and steady as she watched me.

"And besides," I said, struggling to smile, "besides, you know how Phillip is—a chick magnet, remember?"

I turned away, but she called out after me. "You're being stupid. Just because a lot of women like him, doesn't mean that he's going to like them all, too."

I glanced back. Russia had an ironic smile on her face, and I wondered briefly whether she had been in love with him, and maybe still was.

"Thanks," I told her. "I'll try to remember that."

Then I walked down the stairs, my shoes slipping over the marble, with Russia watching over me with love and pity, like a guardian angel.

....

On the day before he left New York, I went to meet Phillip at his home. His apartment was at the end of a dark, damp hallway, which smelled of cleaning fluids overlaying something unpleasant, and where cockroaches scuttled across stickers advertising exterminators in Spanish.

When he opened the door I felt my stomach turn, as on a swiftly dropping elevator.

"I don't understand," I said. "Where is everything?"

For a person who spent his life on the road, backpacking or living out of what he could balance on a mountain bike, Phillip had accumulated an unexpectedly large number of possessions in the few months he spent in New York. Spare and small, his apartment had life because of the books roosting on its shelves. Now only the furniture, a few cardboard boxes neatly stacked in a corner, and a gray, professional-looking backpack by the door remained. Without the books, the room and even the furniture suddenly seemed homely, divested of personality and romance, meekly awaiting a new tenant.

The coat closet, its door half-open, was empty but for a few mismatched hangers, bent metal as well as plastic of all different colors. Even the walls were bare. Only yellowing bits of tape hung down from where there had once been three posters: the one of the old Penn Station, with its big clock and cathedral ceilings, and the pictures from the two World's Fairs of New York. Phillip's taste for the monuments of another era had always surprised me, his nostalgia seeming strangely incompatible with his need for movement.

"I'm giving up the apartment," he said. His voice echoed in the empty room.

"Why? Aren't you—aren't you coming back?"

"I bought a round-trip ticket," he said mildly. "I'm due back in three months. As you know."

"I just assumed you'd be keeping your apartment."

He shook his head. "It's not worth it. I'm giving away all my stuff, too, to the Salvation Army. The top box on that pile there has all the things that I thought you might like—you should go through it."

"Is it really dusty in here? Because I suddenly feel like sneezing," I said.

"I just swept," he said. "The dust probably hasn't settled yet."

"Oh great," I said. "Allergies on top of an incipient cold." I rummaged in my bag, pulled out a ragged tissue, and blew my nose. "Where will you stay when you come back?"

"Well, ideally with you. But if you shut the door in my face, I'll go to the Y or a hostel, I guess." His lips twisted in that grin. "Or maybe I'll get lucky, and some old girlfriend will take me in."

Was it that reference to old girlfriends, or something else altogether? Whatever the cause, I turned up a sniffling nose at the invitation to go through his box of things. It was probably filled with books and also photographs, dimly lit pictures of subway stations, eerily effective albeit hastily shot. For reasons we could never fully determine, but that seemed to involve issues of national security, photographing the subways is against the law, and so Phillip took those pictures undercover in more ways than one. He usually limited himself to pictures of the tunnels, like the serenely arched one at West 168th Street, rarely attempting the trains because he was sure his camera would fail to capture the sense of speed, the rush of air, and the immensity of the noise.

The only keepsake I ever had of Phillip was a cactus, a funny, stunted little thing he brought to my house one day, and which I optimistically believed would live forever. Unfortunately or maybe appropriately, just after he left, it ended up under one of the leaks that my apartment is occasionally prone to, and suffered a temporary drowning from which it never recovered, and eventually died.

We went to an Indian restaurant for dinner and then he walked me home on Riverside Drive, along the edge of the park.

It was early February, and we were in the heart of the first good snowfall of the new year. Already a good inch layered the ground, and the city seemed hushed, with its usual noises, colors, and smells muted.

"Told you we could see the snow right here," I said.

"It's not the same."

"I know, I know," I said crossly. "The crunch of snow and all that. But this is still something."

We trudged on in silence for a long while, the wind whipping at our faces. Then, without conferring about it, we both came to a halt at 103rd Street, a spot where the two of us often met, and one of my favorite places in the world.

I looked out over the park, but the snow fell so thickly I could see only about fifteen feet ahead. The trees were black silhouettes, their branches stark and barren. I turned to face him. The night was so dark I could barely make out his face: it could have been anyone's.

"Are you done being crabby yet?" he asked, and I heard the sweet, familiar note of teasing in his voice, and its haunting by a Midwestern drawl.

For a second I wished for violence and blood—not rape or murder but a mugging, perhaps, a breaking of a rib or limb, that would necessitate a long stay in the hospital, side by side in twin white beds.

Phillip touched my shoulder, a pressure I felt just faintly through my coat. "You're shivering," he said. "Let's get you home."

A few minutes later, we stood outside my apartment building.

"I won't invite you up," I said. "What with your flight tomorrow, and all."

His mouth twisted, but in the darkness I could not see whether it was a smile or a frown. "Well then," he said, "I guess I'll see you soon." He stooped to give me one of his usual clumsy kisses, his breath momentarily warming my face and his lips landing squarely on my left eyebrow. I clutched the lapels of his coat to me for a second, which turned into three seconds and then into five, until I finally let go. "See ya," I said.

"I'll be back, you know," he said. "I promise. Cross my heart and hope to die."

Toward the end of *Little Women,* Jo and Mr. Bhaer go for a walk in the rain and the mud. Their love for each other is unacknowledged, and he is leaving for Germany for good the next day: the tension is high. Their walk is a long one, but eventually it nears its end, as all walks do, at which point Jo begins to sniffle. He asks her what the matter is, and she, awkward and outspoken, does not come up with some pat lie about sinuses or allergies or contact lenses, but instead blurts out that she is sad because he is leaving. He responds effusively and love triumphs, social ineptitude and honesty finding their just reward.

I did not cry, but I reached out for Phillip again. This time I hugged him so hard he laughed. "Uncle," he said. "I can't breathe." I laughed as well, the tears obediently remaining at the corners of my eyes, and the puffs of my breathing intermingled with his. I hesitated and then, as the laughter died away, I lifted my face to his. He blinked as though in surprise, but he responded, slowly, tentatively lowering his lips to mine.

We kissed on the mouth deeply and luxuriously, but only once. My heart was beating so fast my chest hurt. Then he yanked open my coat, pulling the buttons apart, and began to kiss me quickly, his hands, usually so still, moving restlessly inside my coat, and his lips covering every inch of my face. That veneer of laziness and calm—his cool—had fallen away like a second skin. His breathing was harsh and uneven, and his face almost unrecognizable as it grew grim with lust.

I had known that Phillip had passion and hid it; I had longed for it, dreamed of it, waited for it and, finally, invited it, yet when it showed itself I could not move, paralyzed by fear. My throat was clogged and I could not speak. Yet at the same time, in another part of my body, I was also beginning to sweat.

I had gone straight from *Little Women* into one of those trashy romances I used to devour, replete with dramatic snow and a tall man who fumbled roughly with my buttons. Phillip, who had been working on opening my cardigan and shirt, had changed his line of attack to move in from the bottom, untucking my clothes from inside my jeans and reaching up towards my breast. Blocked by his body, the wind whistled harmlessly past me. When he reached inside my bra and touched my left nipple, his fingers were shockingly cold.

It was as if a string connected my nipple to that warm place between my thighs, and every time he squeezed my nipple he tugged on the string. Yet the pressure of his fingers was growing stronger, and it was beginning to hurt. I was just going to clench my teeth and bear it, for the tugs on the string became sharper with the pain, but he twisted my nipple, then, and involuntarily I winced, making a small sound of protest, and a faint movement of withdrawal.

He pulled away so abruptly I nearly stumbled, and on my neck and chest, now exposed, the icy air hit me like a slap. He stared at me and the look of hunger slid off his face, starting from the eyes and moving down to the mouth, which became a thin line, barely opening as he muttered, "Sorry, Ki," and then he wheeled around and was gone.

In all the times I had rehearsed our good-byes, I had never imagined one like that: he turning away in injured pride, disappearing quickly into the snow, while I stood shivering and miserable on the street corner, cursing myself for not having spoken.

When I finish telling my grandmother about Phillip my voice will be hoarse, for the story is a long one, and once I begin I will have to continue until I am done. At the end all I will have for her is a half-question, a plea, I suppose, for a miraculous second chance, for an explanation of the workings of fate, or maybe just for sympathy.

Obaasama, I will say, all Phillip and I needed was time.

CHAPTER SIXTEEN

IN THE THREE days that have passed since I disgraced myself while shopping with Eric, the phone has rung only once. I picked it up on its first ring, a smile on my face and a salutation to Eric on the tip of my tongue, and felt worse than usual when I heard the humming that marks my anonymous caller. Phillip has not shown himself except for the briefest of cameo appearances at noon.

It is close to two in the morning now. I lean out the open window, and (for the first time in a day of loitering by the phone, a thick sheaf of my dissertation lying disregarded on my lap) I let the soft touch of the outside air brush against my face. Drawn by the memory of yesterday's jaunt through the park, I leave my apartment, take the elevator down, and walk out into the street.

I walk along Broadway for a while. A few other people are walking around, seemingly as aimless as I am. They are dressed in clothes randomly matched: one woman sporting sneakers, a miniskirt, and what looks like a pyjama top, her friend all in sweats, a boy in a pinstriped jacket and Bermuda shorts, an old beggar wearing bell-bottoms. It may not be 1990 anymore. It could be twenty years ago, when bell-bottoms were all the rage, or it could be five or ten years into the future, when the pendulum of fashion has swung back again. It could be nineteen months ago, when Phillip was still alive and I had not even dreamed of the possibility of an Eric Lowenson in my life. In my neighborhood, Broadway at two in the morning would be the same during any of those years: the streetlamps lit and most of the storefronts closed and the trash blowing in the wind, the traffic lights enforcing a titular authority over the empty, quiet streets.

I head west. Riverside Drive is almost completely deserted; I can just make out the dim outlines of a policeman walking his beat about three blocks north of me. I go south after I see him, and when I get to the statue at 106th Street, I climb down the stairs and cross towards the park, just as I did yesterday. It is so dark that the sky is black, and when the wind hits me, I tremble a little with the coolness of the air.

Although it is only a question of light, the streets I jogged through just a day earlier now seem strange and alien. They remind me of the time I was coming home early from a class party given by a professor who lived in Brooklyn, just a week before Phillip and I began our epic journeys on the subway. I was alone and tired, and at the subway station I got on the train going the wrong direction. I rode a long way without realizing my mistake, and by the time I did, I was at a stop called Rockaway Beach, miles and miles from Manhattan. I stepped off the familiar IND train and found myself outside on an empty platform, in a place marked by the feel of wide-open spaces and saturated with the smell of the sea. The land was flat and I could see far. The very stars seemed changed.

Now I walk on the sidewalk close to the ledge overlooking the park, which is visible only as a darker darkness. The lamps along Riverside Drive give forth a dim yellow glow and I move forward contentedly, with sure steps, in a New York without people. The good feeling lasts all the way until the crosswalk at 96th Street, where I stop even though there is no traffic at this hour, even though the light is green. Sounds of a fight are drifting over from Broadway: men yelling in deep angry voices, a car honking and then screeching, the crash of breaking glass, and the high and thin screams of a woman or a boy. I turn around and begin to walk quickly northward, back the way I came. I try to look confident and purposeful, as if I were hurrying to meet my biggest male friend just around the corner, but I am thinking that if I were raped and killed and dumped into the river, days would pass before anyone—even Eric—realized I was gone.

Eric has warned me over and over against taking walks late at night in the park, and I hate myself now for not having listened. The leaves of the trees move even when the wind is not blowing; the sight of a garbage can placed in the middle of the sidewalk makes me want to scream. My breath is rasping and I am almost running when I come to the enclosed part of 102nd Street, where the trees darken the sidewalk, and then I feel something choke my throat because there, almost directly in front of me, stands a large man at a phone booth in the shadows. He is not particularly tall but he looks hugely broad, and by the dim light from the faraway streetlamps I can just barely tell that he is wearing thick boots. The end of his cigarette creates a small moving point of flame. He does not make a sound, listening to a speaker or maybe just a dial tone. I am trapped; even if I were to walk towards the lamplit street, I cannot avoid passing by him.

I am concentrating so hard on keeping my steps silent that his voice makes me jump. "Wanna fuck?" My mouth dry and my heart pounding, I turn around slowly to face him, and then I feel like laughing with hysterical relief, because the man's back is turned towards me: he is talking into the telephone.

When I get home, I am still so shaken that as I unbolt the door to my apartment, I find myself wishing that old Mrs. Noffz would open the door and chat with me about the weather. I even turn around and wait for a few seconds but of course 16D remains shut; it is after three in the morning and she must have gone to bed hours ago.

I look eagerly for Phillip in the fireplace, yet at first glance the apartment appears empty. With teeth chattering and my body shivering uncontrollably, I check the more secret places he likes to hide: the insides of all the cupboards, the crack between the wall and the bookshelf, the space behind each of the doors. Clearly Phillip does not want to be found. I flick on lights as I proceed, until the apartment is ablaze. When I finally give up the search and stretch out on the sofa, I become aware of the tension in my neck and shoulders.

I want to call Eric. I want to hear the concern in his voice, and the scolding that would follow the concern. If I called him now, despite the lateness of the hour we would almost certainly get together; within less than an hour I could be enfolded within the warm and safe circle of his arms. I look down at the smooth fingertips of my left hand, a constant reminder of what life was like before I met Eric, and what it could be like again.

Obaasama, I will say (tenderly, in gratitude for her silent sympathy), you who so recently lost a husband. Grandmother, I am going to tell you how I lost my fingerprints, but you already know, don't you, the story I am about to tell.

For a month after Phillip left, I filled the days by killing ants. With eyes alert to even the smallest movement and hands poised for action, I squatted on the cold kitchen tiles for hours on end. I ate cookies and sometimes whole meals as I hunted, incidentally providing bait in the form of crumbs. Purely by accident I had stumbled upon the ideal way to kill time; there was a seemingly endless supply of ants in my kitchen that year, and they were terribly hard to kill. Their bodies were like rubber, and they had a strong and unquenchable predilection for life. Even after I rolled their bodies into malformed balls, they sprang right back into shape, untangling their limbs and crawling on, so that to kill them I had to crush their bodies again and again.

My life was a struggle with time. I suppose I was at war out of self-defense, because even now I cannot see what I sought to gain, or why I fought at all. When I woke up in the middle of the morning and could not get back to sleep no matter how I tried, I cursed myself because my wakefulness meant that I had the whole day in front of me to kill. I felt triumphant when I slept in past two. I tried to nap in the evening, and every night as I returned to bed, I congratulated myself for having won a battle, as that is what it meant to survive another day. Yet in spite of my daily victories, my eventual defeat was already foretold. While my own supply of strength was finite and easily exhausted, time was a tireless and consequently undefeatable opponent who never ran out of ammunition; another completely fresh day of equal length arose immediately and invariably to replace the one I had just vanquished. It was therefore only a matter of time before I lost to time.

Now I envision it as an opponent; then I could only picture time as itself. Time seemed neither a father nor a destroyer nor a healer, and it did not seem like a bus we get onto and then step out of: try as I might, I could not visualize it in any of those reassuringly solid forms. Time was only the seconds and minutes that stretched with deliberation into hours, and then with painstaking slowness into days and finally years. It was the movement of my watch, shifting and changing and coming back to its starting point, as regular as clockwork should in fact be, and it was the sole measure of my life.

I look back now and say that time was a merciful river as well as an unbeatable foe, that in spite of myself it carried me farther and farther away from Phillip, and closer and closer to a point that I later identified as Eric. Yet then time was nothing but the passing of it.

I lost my fingerprints in the middle of March. Rain came down in an indecisive patter, and the streets of the city were flooded in gray slush. From a store window a mannequin in a skimpy cocktail dress mocked me with a pouty smile. I had been defeated in my attempt to find a birthday present for my mother in one department store, and now I was headed for another. "Something for the house," my mother had said when I asked her what she wanted, but so far I had not been able to find anything even remotely suitable.

I munched on candy as I walked, replacing one mouthful with another even before I had swallowed the last, and pulling out such big handfuls that I dropped a few every time; behind me Broadway was littered with the bright colors of jelly beans. In spite of the wind and the rain, maybe ten or fifteen people were gathered on every corner of the intersection at Seventh Avenue and 36th Street. Policemen were waving back the traffic and trying to calm the angry drivers. Two ambulances and four police cars were parked haphazardly in the center of the street, and the sounds and lights of their sirens filled the air. I stood behind the people at the southeast corner and craned my neck to see above the heads of those who got there ahead of me; although I am not short, there were so many people I could see only bits and pieces of the stretcher at a time. First I saw a pair of grayish sneakers under yellow pants, and then as the men carried the stretcher towards the ambulance, the torso slowly swung into view. The woman was huge. Her breasts and stomach and thighs loomed upwards, and the men were staggering under her weight.

A middle-aged woman laden with Macy's bags stopped next to me. Even when she stood on tiptoe, she was far too small to see over the heads, and because the crowd had swelled considerably since the time I had arrived, she could not push through the people to get to the front.

"What happened?" she asked breathlessly.

I shrugged and shook my head. The man standing next to her on the other side turned. "She jumped," he said. "She jumped in front of a Greyhound bus. But I don't think it killed her."

"Oh," said the woman. She was quiet for a while, and then suddenly, without warning, she began to cry. Startled, the man started to say something, but his voice trailed away uncertainly.

One of her bags fell out from beneath her arms and landed in a puddle. Her tears made her makeup run down in black streaks on her face. She looked far older, and I saw that I had misjudged her age, that she was really an old woman. The farther I moved away, the more her wails became interchangeable with the sirens and the sound of the wind.

At least forty-seven vehicles got stuck in traffic as a result of the accident. I know because I counted as I trudged through the slush to get to Lord & Taylor.

It was dark by the time I gave up on finding a present. As I entered the subway at Times Square and funneled into the turnstiles with the rest of the crowd, I heard the sound of the train coming, but lacked the energy to run for it. Exhausted, I walked slowly, watching the ground and carefully stepping around the congealed vomit by the exit. Hordes of people ran by me to catch the train; it was five o'clock by then, and the height of rush hour.

Left behind by the rushing crowd, I was alone when I saw the skinny black man huddled in two blankets just outside the entrance to the Seventh Avenue line. The urine smell that hung in the air was especially strong where he stood.

"Spare some change?" he wheedled, his hands cupped in front of him.

Without looking at him I shook my head. "Sorry."

I walked past. "Sorry?" The man had yelled the word behind me, and I looked back. He was staring at me with his hands clenched into fists. "Sorry! Lady, sorry ain't gonna buy me food to live. You ain't sorry, suck my dick, you ain't sorry." He gathered the shabby blankets around his shoulders as if he were a dethroned king. "Who the hell do you think you are, anyway? Fuckin' chink," he said, and he stalked away.

My face burned and the purse over my shoulder felt heavy, my wallet a leaden weight. I turned away and tried to lose myself in the stream of people flowing towards the subway.

It was long past six when I got home. In the apartment the damp crept in through invisible cracks in the wall, and drops of water fell from the leak in the roof. Half in dread and half in sympathy, the windows rattled each time the wind blew. I went to the kitchen and had a few quick bites of butterscotch cake; I took off my coat and boots and went to the bathroom and replaced the wet socks on my feet with a dry pair. I then walked back to the kitchen to make myself some tea. While I waited for the water to boil, I had more of the cake, as usual eating the dry cake part first, and saving the sticky sweetness of the frosting for the end.

Still chewing, I got down on my hands and knees and scoured the ground for some ants to kill. Only one brave wayfarer roamed the wide and lonely expanse of the kitchen tiles. After mutilating it unrecognizably, I stood up and ate more cake. For once I was not in the mood to hunt. That was, in fact, the last ant I killed that year. By the summer they had disappeared on their own, perhaps moving outdoors to enjoy the weather.

With cake swelling my cheeks, crumbs powdering my lips, and a large dab of frosting on a finger, I looked down and discovered that my knuckles were buried in fat. I wriggled my fingers and they were un-wieldy with their own weight, while my old silver ring was uncomfort-ably tight. I was so surprised I forgot to swallow, and a bit of chewed cake fell out of my mouth and onto the stove.

The kettle was whistling by then, so I removed it from the stove and turned the heat off. After that I stood and watched the coil of the stove fade from red to orange. The color inched its way out, spiraling away from the center. Soon almost all the orange was gone, but the stove remained hot; when a last drop of rainwater slid from my hair onto the coil, it sizzled and vanished into the air. The black coil seemed a larger version of the swirls that made up my fingerprints.

I lightly rested the fingertips of my left hand upon the spiral. As if there had been a short circuit in the signals flowing from my mind to my body, my arm jerked back of its own accord. I forced my fingers back into position and began to count out loud, my voice sounding hollow in the empty kitchen.

"One Mississippi, two Mississippi, three Mississippi . . ."

My hand began to shake and twitch. I managed to keep it in place by gripping the wrist down with my other hand.

". . . four Mississippi, five Mississippi, six Mississippi . . ."

My arm and then my whole body was trembling, even though I was trying as hard as I could to keep still. My voice was both higher and louder, and I was beginning to speed up the count. I took a deep breath and continued more slowly.

". . . seven Mississippi, eight Mississippi, nine Mississippi . . ."

I doubled over so suddenly that I was frightened, and an inhuman sound came out of nowhere to disrupt my counting. A part of my hair brushed against the metal and a sharp, disturbing smell pervaded the kitchen.

". . . ten Mississippi."

Slowly I took my hand off the coil. Small pieces of my skin and flesh remained stuck to the metal, and my fingers were raw and badly blistered. The burnt flesh gave forth an odd odor, quite distinct from that of singed hair. It was a smell I had never encountered before, strong and sickening and completely unlike the aroma of steak or chicken. A lock of my hair was much shorter than it had been, the end of each strand shriveled and weighted down with tiny ashes.

With my right hand, I pried open the box of cake and cut out a large portion with my fingers. I looked at the portion for a second or two, and then I quickly put it into my mouth.

CHAPTER SEVENTEEN

Two days later, my blistered fingers covered with gauze, I took the subway to Penn Station and caught a train out to Garrison. My mother had come to pick me up at the station, and when I saw her standing by the car, something stirred beneath the numbness I had been feeling since Russia broke the news of Phillip's death to me at the deli. My mother looked frail and very thin.

Near us a family was engaged in a boisterous reunion. With glad shouts of "Granny!" they were hugging and kissing an old woman who had stepped off the same train. Adding to the confusion were two little dogs yapping excitedly at ankle level. I had not seen my mother since early January, yet we greeted each other from opposite ends of the car.

"Hello," she said, smiling. "Was it a good trip?"

"It was okay," I said.

I did not feel well in the car as we drove home. When we sat down to drink tea in the kitchen, she noticed my bandaged hand.

"What happened?" she asked.

"Forget it." I could not look at her. "I burnt myself—you know how clumsy I am."

"Let me see."

Her eyes widened when she saw my fingers, the flesh shredded and the pus seeping out from the open folds of skin. "We've got to get you to the emergency room. Get your coat on."

She called the hospital to tell them we were coming, and then we went outside again. She concentrated on the road as she drove, and I watched the familiar streets speed by through the car window. The people looked as familiar as the streets. I thought the children were the same ones I had gone to school with, lost in time, and only when they turned and I saw their faces did I know they were not.

My mother was silent until we were pulling into the parking lot at the hospital.

"It must really hurt," she said.

"Actually, it's not so bad."

I was telling the truth. When I looked down at my fingers, I felt a little nauseated at the sight of all that blood and pus, but I did not feel much pain. It was as if the hand belonged to someone else.

Later in the day, as we read by the fire, I splayed out my left hand and examined the fingers, each tip coated with funny-smelling chemicals and neatly bandaged. Because the doctor was concerned about the spread of infection, I had a bottle of antibiotic pills as well. As I reached out to pick up my book from the table, I saw that my mother was watching me over the top of her magazine. After taking off the reading glasses that she had begun wearing just that year, she wiped them carefully with her handkerchief. She held them up to the light and studied them as she spoke.

"You must miss Phillip a great deal."

I nodded.

"Try to keep busy," she said. "The time will go by faster. You'll feel better by the summer."

I nodded again, too tired to speak, although it did cross my mind to remark on the curious fact that it was my mother, the queen of long-term mourning, who was telling me that I would feel better within just half a year.

She was smiling shyly, but when she spoke again I could hear the concern in her voice. "To help you keep busy," she said, "I got you a present."

"But tomorrow's *your* birthday," I said. "And all I got you were chocolates—"

"Never mind," she said, and handed me the envelope.

I opened the envelope to find tickets for a season at Carnegie Hall.

"I wish I could go with you," she said. "But it tires me out so much to travel these days."

I thanked her, pushing myself to sound enthusiastic. She smiled again, put her glasses back on, and picked up her magazine and went back to reading, but at the end of the night, on her way up to her room, she momentarily rested one of her crippled hands upon my shoulder. I did not thank her so she did not know how much it meant, I think, how good it felt to lean against someone else's strength, even for a fleeting moment.

When my grandmother pauses between her stories, stooping to drink from her tea, I will reach out to hold her by the hand. You do know, I will say, you do know how grateful I am that you're here?

In Phillip's absence my eating habits had changed, but so gradually that at first I had not noticed. It began innocently enough, out of a desire to keep things the way they were before he left. I would buy a pound of jelly beans because that was how much Phillip and I bought when we wanted a snack; I made three cups of buttered popcorn after dinner because that was the amount we always made. Since I was used to ordering sun-dried tomatoes and three different cheeses at the deli, I continued to do so, and of course four bagels with cream cheese and lox were a sacred Sunday morning tradition. The more I ate the more I wanted, and late at night I began going out to the Korean markets, which were always open, so that I could buy and eat whole bags of cookies.

Phillip's body had been covered by snow. It smothered his nose and mouth and stopped his breath; its weight crushed his flesh and broke his bones, and eventually it froze his internal organs. I ate Phillip's food for him. I ate because while he was dead I lived, and because the rhythmic chewing motion kept me from thinking at least for a while.

My body did not seem like my own, but a shameful and heavy burden I had to bear: a punishment for unacknowledged sins. I left the apartment unwillingly because of people's eyes. I grew my hair long and kept it in front so that it covered my breasts and my stomach down to my belly button. I wore the clothes I had not worn since I was a teenager, shapeless sweaters huge enough to drown in.

Throughout the weekend that I was at home, my mother did not once mention the weight I had gained. At the time I was grateful for her tact, yet looking back I think it more likely that she simply did not notice. Although I thought then that it was a mistake when the scale at my mother's house showed that I had gained only eight pounds, now I have to concede that I had made the only mistake, and that the change in my body was all in my mind.

In the mirror I expected to see Yukiko, not my glamorous, self-assured grandmother but the overweight teenager who, in an ironic twist, shared her name, a girl slouching with self-consciousness at her lack of grace and beauty. When I went to the bathroom and saw instead the calm loveliness of my face, unmarred by the monstrous body that I thought lay hidden inside my clothes, I was sure that the mirror was playing tricks. For when fate, acting on a sudden caprice, decrees that someone as young as Phillip should die, who or what can you trust?

I did not cry after Phillip left, but in April, two months after I heard about his death, three months after Horse had succumbed to the siren call of the full moon and fled through the fire escape, I woke up in the middle of the night, moved my legs carefully so that I would not accidentally kick our cat, and began to cry without realizing that I did so. Troubled with nightmares and bewildered by sleep, I sat up and began feeling around the end of the bed. While my hands searched the tufts of my comforter, I whispered for him, certain that my hands would come across his warm furry body at any moment.

"Horse? Horse, here kitty kitty." I have a queen-size bed and I went over every inch of it at least three times. I continued calling out for him as I wiped my eyes with the sleeve of my nightshirt and got out of bed. The floor was cold against my bare feet.

"Horse, Horse, Horse," I said. I lurched through the hallway, tripping over the carpet. I could have switched on any or all of the lights, but instead I relied on the dim hall lamp alone. In the living room I checked for Horse in his basket, and then in his favorite hideout between the radiator and the bookshelf. I blew my nose on a napkin I had left on the coffee table. I did not stop crying, and I kept on calling out his name. In the kitchen I walked right over the space where I used to keep his catfood dish, yet I did not remember that Horse was gone until I saw the bars of the fire escape through the curtains of the window.

Repeating his name, I collapsed on the kitchen floor, and it was a long time before I could drag myself back to bed. I did not scream or kick or even sob very loudly; I simply cried steadily all through the night. It was as if my body could no longer contain the weight of the tears I had held back for years. They were seemingly endless and terribly bitter, each drop fresh with the memory of all the individual sorrows, so that when I cried I did not mourn only for Horse, but also for Phillip, my father's love, and my mother's hands.

In June, one month before I met Eric, a short man with burning eyes stopped me on the subway. Peering out beneath a ridiculous straw hat, his face seemed completely unfamiliar, and it took me some time to remember him as a Princeton classmate of mine. All I could recall of him was that he was something of a math star, and that he had hated rooming with a football player I had dated for a while. It was fortunate that he reintroduced himself, because on my own I would never have remembered his name.

We chatted about the usual things, college and careers and other classmates; he seemed to have achieved a modicum of success. Finally the conversation came to a close.

"Well," he said, and then he paused, his head to one side. I was about to tell him I had to go when he suddenly shook his head. "You've changed so much."

I shrugged. "We've all changed, haven't we?"

Frowning, he shook his head again. "Not all that much," he said. "But you seem like a different person altogether. You laughed at everything all the time in college, as if nothing in the world mattered. I despised you for being so shallow. I had a real crush on you, but I despised you at the same time."

He was ugly but he was ugly in an interesting way, and I liked him for his bluntness. I was also physically stirred by the thought of him nursing a secret passion for me, perhaps touching himself as he contemplated my image in the dark. When I invited him to my apartment for a drink he accepted, and after giving him three bottles of Phillip's old beer so he could relax and get his courage up, I went to bed with him.

It was the only sex I had had for some months. He surprised me by giving me a fair amount of pleasure in bed and yet afterwards, when I lay in his arms, I felt lonelier than I had before. I knew then how much I had changed. Instead of lying and avoiding his phone calls, I told him to his face that I did not want to be with him again. His hat in hand, he gravely thanked me before going home.

Seventeen months have passed since I burned the fingers of my left hand on the stove. The blisters healed long ago but the skin is different: harder and tougher, taut and almost glossy, the miniature ridges flattened and each tiny valley filled, without any more twisting pathways. My fingers are a blank. Where there once was a finely whorled pattern indicating a singular and fixed identity, there is only the unmarked smoothness of a clean sheet of paper. Now I would do the same to my memory if I could.

Russia had told me on the night I first met him that Phillip was not my type. She may have been right. He led the life of an ascetic in his tiny apartment on 99th Street, one of a long series of temporary homes. His room was clean but there was always a smell of mold and mustiness lingering in the air, and the walls were peeling and usually slightly damp. Yet I could have been happy with him there; the problem was that he never invited me to share it.

He was inherently elusive. Once he had wanted to be a priest.

When I asked him why he had abandoned his childhood dream, he laughed and said the flesh was weak. I winced at the sound of that laugh. Traveling all the time, he was fickle with women and places alike, and even now I remain uncertain that our friendship was special at all. I may have been just one of a long series of temporary friends, and he may have been just a crush, an intense but insubstantial passion, doomed to be short-lived and dissatisfying as the other lovers in my past. If I had slept with him a few times, maybe he would have gone the way of all those college tennis players or the lanky debater I lost my virginity to, or even my oldest love, Hamlet, the Prince of Denmark: dimly remembered sources of feeling, reasons for laughter rather than nostalgia. As I lie sprawled on the sofa, the front of my hair still wet with sweat from the scare I had had in the park, I tell myself that the only difference between Phillip and all my ex-lovers is that with Phillip, I never had a chance to find out how far reality fell short of the fantasy.

Eric and I are compatible. I have had many lovers but almost no boyfriends, and certainly none like him. Although our professional lives move at a different pace, together we share an easy rhythm. We both love our work and we both bring it home with us; we do not disturb each other as we work and we support each other. From the beginning few compromises were needed in our domestic life.

For the last five months Eric and I have been all but living together. Our clothes hang in each other's closets, and underwear of all kinds mingle in each other's drawers and hampers. In our bathrooms our toothbrushes touch. I do love him; more than that, I need him.

Obaasama, I will say. Grandmother, isn't this what love with Sekiguchi was like for you—sneaking up so quietly that for months you did not notice anything had changed? And if you staked your happiness on a second, quieter romance, who am I to run away when a love like that comes barreling through my door?

If my grandmother were here now, she could help sort out all these problems. No one is better qualified, for not only does she know what it is like to leave one love behind for another, but in the wake of Seki-guchi's death, she also knows what it is like to want to hold on forever.

When I push myself up onto my elbows, I see Phillip sitting on the sofa across from me. He is almost within arm's reach, closer than he has been for a long time. A half-filled cup of tea I had forgotten to finish this afternoon rests in front of him on the coffee table, and his long legs are crossed. A modest hand casually drapes over his genitals. Were it not for his nakedness and the fact that the light shines through him in patches, we could easily be taken for two people genteelly enjoying a late-night cup of tea.

"You're not real," I tell him. My voice is loud and harsh in the still-ness of the room. "You're a figment. A phantom born of loneliness and despair."

He does not move. As always, his thoughts are veiled by the immo-bility of his face. He watches me attentively, as if waiting for me to tell the end of a story.

I wish he would move. His lips are sealed together and his eyes seem cold in their unwavering intentness. I cannot endure his stare for long, and I look down at my toes instead. We sit in silence for a long spell.

"I can't depend on you," I say at last. In spite of myself it is an apology.

I turn my attention inward, away from the physical presence in front of me, and I can hear my heart as I move to pick up the phone.

Eric's answering machine answers. I begin speaking at the end of his message, after the beep.

"Hi, Eric, it's me. . . . I want to see you. Please call me—I don't want to beg but—well, I guess I'm begging."

I hang up the phone. My hands are clammy and the fingertips are cold. Phillip is gone when I look up, but for many minutes afterwards, I sit and watch the indentation his weight left on the cushion, wondering whether he left a trail of footprints behind him on a mountain path in Nepal, or whether they, too, were buried and lost in the snow.

Grandmother, I will say, Phillip is dead, you see. Phillip died, and I do not want to spend my life living with his ghost.

Obaasama, I will say (begging for reassurance), did I do the right thing? After all that you have gone through, what would you have done in my position? In fact, I will say (looking directly at her, still so lovely in spite of her years, in spite of the new lines, formed after Sekiguchi's death, that are like knife cuts in her face), what would *you* do if love comes knocking on your door yet again?

But the last is not a question that I will ever ask, for even as I think it, I can hear my grandmother laughing, and I see in my mind a door opening a crack only to swing swiftly shut.

CHAPTER EIGHTEEN

B<small>Y THE TIME</small> history, in the form of a cruel war, caught up with my grandmother Yukiko, she was married.

With every bomb that fell, and there were many, more and more buildings were destroyed, and more and more people fled to the country. Streets that had been thronged were almost empty, and shops that had once displayed clothes and jewelry were abandoned to the bombs. The rain fell inside burnt-out houses.

Often the air-raid siren let off its high wail, and then Yukiko rounded up her three children and ran out to the bomb shelter that she and her husband had dug in the garden. There they huddled, smelling the damp earth and each other, until the bomb fell or the threat passed, and another siren went off to tell them it was safe to come out. One bomb had killed a teacher at their school; another a neighborhood girl who was, at three years old, the same age as my uncle Tadashi at the time. Still, the children were usually more bored than scared in the shelter, for there was nothing to do but try to catch glimpses of the bombs, which were as loud and spectacular as fireworks, and to listen to Yukiko's stories.

While they fidgeted, yawned, and whined about hunger in the dark, she told them of her childhood in the north, and even a few choice details of her life as a geisha. They did not understand all her stories as children or even, for that matter, when they became adults, and they did not miss all those underground storytelling sessions when they moved to the countryside to flee the bombs.

As Tokyo had changed, so, too, had Yukiko. No longer beset by poverty or the disquieting growth spurts of adolescence, freed from the onerous obligations of her geisha career, and finally secure in her right to Sekiguchi's full love and attention, she had bloomed, becoming the high-spirited woman that nature had intended her to be. In the countryside she played with her children, making a game out of catching the grasshoppers that they later fried and ate with a few precious grains of rice, and she laughed them out of their complaints about the meanness of the village children. On two memorable occasions, she hitched up the skirt of her kimono and shimmied up a tree, proving that beneath the exterior of a grand lady, she was still the tomboy who could outrun, outjump, and outclimb her brothers.

Yet only her children, her husband, and her servants saw this side of her. While her neighbors and the wives of Sekiguchi's friends in Tokyo were always painstakingly polite to her, in subtle ways they also made it clear that they despised her for her former career, and that they could not forgive her for usurping the place of Sekiguchi's young first wife, who had been universally loved for her sweetness. They had tried Yukiko for the crime of fawning her way into Sekiguchi's bed and home, and they had found her guilty; they believed she had married him as a calculated move, for his money and position. They scorned her for her love of luxury and her collection of kimonos, and for the care she took to enhance her beauty. There were rumors, even, that Yukiko had had Eiko poisoned. Few were willing to countenance that she had actually killed Sekiguchi's child bride, but most were in agreement that the upstart geisha had contributed much in the way of heartache to her untimely death: on the day that she had spied on Eiko being borne high aloft a litter, Yukiko had been seen, not just by Eiko but by at least one other person of the town. The considerable lore surrounding Yukiko thus included the story that she had gone to flaunt her good health, her expensive kimono, and her pregnancy in Eiko's face.

There was yet one more reason that Tokyo's high society looked askance at her: she was envied and, therefore, disliked for the indulgence accorded to her by her husband. For even aside from its provenance, theirs was an unusual marriage.

As a geisha, she had been trained to banter and also to speak intelligently with men, and she continued to do so even after she became a wife. When business associates came to visit Sekiguchi, Yukiko did not simply greet them and serve tea, but sat in on their discussions and sometimes even participated, much to the discomfiture of the guests. Disconcertingly blunt though her remarks often were, Sekiguchi granted them the same grave attention he gave to the comments of his friends, who had no choice but to follow his lead. As if that were not bad enough in the eyes of Tokyo high society, she also traveled with Sekiguchi on all his business trips, to Europe, China, northern Africa, and even Canada, although they never quite made it to the States. While Sekiguchi sat through long hours of business meetings, she roamed foreign cities on her own. She had in common with Phillip a love of maps. She used to spend whole days poring over them, so that she could leaf through an atlas and point immediately to the dozen countries she had visited, and trace the exact routes she traveled with her finger.

Accused, on one hand, of cold-bloodedly finagling her way into a loveless marriage, and envied, on the other, for the success of that very same union, Yukiko called upon the reserve that had stood her in good stead as a geisha, and grew ever more aloof in public. If she ever felt lonely in her at least partly self-imposed isolation from Tokyo society, her children, at least, never knew it. Still, it could not have helped that now that she had a position to maintain, she found herself barred from the company of all her geisha friends.

By 1943, two years into the war, she had been living with Sekiguchi for eight years, and married to him for three. But when she was feeling dreamy after wandering through the city with her daughter, she would set off for home only to discover that her feet had led her unerringly through the maze of streets to her old neighborhood, the site of the geisha house.

In becoming the wife of the rich and influential Sekiguchi, Yukiko had given up her right to go back to that home. Deep in the swirl of preparations for the wedding, she had at first not given this matter enough thought: not until she was actually taking leave of her oldest friend did she stop to take stock of the full price of her marriage.

My grandmother said good-bye to Kaori just outside the restaurant in which they had eaten lunch together for years. The day was blindingly bright, with but a few clouds in the sky, yet while they stood chatting, a burst of light rain came down and forced them to take cover under the noodle shop's awning.

In Japan, sun showers are associated with magic, foxes that take on the shape of seductive women (with only their long noses and, from behind, a flash of a red brush under their kimonos' hemlines to give them away), and the sense that the unexpected will happen; more prosaically, they are also associated with the spring and summer months. Yukiko and Kaori had spent their lunch hour skirting around the real topic at hand—the wedding that would take place tomorrow, and their own impending separation—and now, huddling together against the wall of the restaurant, they plunged into an animated discussion of the improbability of a sun shower in November.

"It bodes well for your wedding," said Kaori at last, a trifle shyly.

Yukiko looked down at the woman, plump and sweet-faced, who had climbed into her futon on her first night at the geisha house, and she knew, suddenly, that long after she had reduced her first love Jun to an idyll in her mind (the most distant memory of breath-stealing kisses and steamy afternoons), the absence of Kaori would continue to gnaw at her, try as she might to put the thought of her old pal aside.

They had once been so inseparable that no one could tell them apart. Kaori had seen her through all her bouts of homesickness, as well as the literally but not figuratively earthshaking loss of her virginity; as they became accustomed to, and disgusted with, the need to flatter, tease, and beguile their clients, they had learned together how reinvigorating it was to laugh themselves sick over the mixture of conceit and insecurities that they found in most of these men. Anything but an un-critically supportive friend, Kaori had scolded Yukiko for falling for Jun, but then, at considerable risk to her own standing at the geisha house, she had helped her meet with him. Kaori had been there to counsel patience when Yukiko thought that she had lost in gambling on Sekiguchi, since he was going back to his wife; she had been there, too, to celebrate when he returned.

"You haven't had an easy time of it, have you?" asked Yukiko. "Being my friend, that is."

For a few moments, Kaori gazed up at her in silence, and the beat of the rain was all that Yukiko could hear. Then Kaori dimpled, her lips wryly twisting. "Sometimes," she said, drawling, "you can be so stupid."

Yukiko had not cried when she bowed her farewells to her brothers, nor when her father had tried to apologize, in his own way, for sacrificing her to save the family; she had not shed a tear even when her mother clasped her around the neck for the last time, sobbing all the while. So it was only to be expected that she would remain dry-eyed when Kaori raised her rounded arms to give her a quick, hard hug good-bye.

Yet when a gust of wind blew the rain towards them, drenching them both and sending them into a fit of giggles that was tinged with just a touch of hysteria, it was impossible to say whether the drops (winking, shining as they caught and held the light) on their faces came from the sky or their eyes.

The daughter of a peasant and his childlike wife, Yukiko felt a perhaps pardonable pride when she looked at her healthy children and her important husband. She held her head high when she walked about town, and she dressed with the elegance and flair of a native of high society. She was, if anything, almost too stylish to qualify for the status of aristocrat, her natural sense of fashion placing her outside of the class of those mostly shapeless women, who wore their high-quality, ill-fitting clothes like a badge of honor. Yukiko's collection of kimonos was extensive, and they were all not only expensive but well suited for her.

Even more than wearing them, she liked to stroll among them in the garden, where they were hung after being washed twice a year. With their sleeves swinging back and forth in the breeze, the kimonos brought back to her the scarecrow that she and her brothers had made from sticks and a rag salvaged from the town dump. Her children played tag in their midst while they dried.

Yukiko's beauty was justifiably famous, though she still fretted about the size of her breasts and feet, and she shone at the few parties to which she was invited. In the streets, people murmured and turned to watch her as she passed. None of her children had inherited her looks. As babies and as children they were pleasing enough to look at but ultimately ordinary, and they would continue to be so as adults.

She enjoyed an easy, uncomplicated relationship with her youngest son, as, to be fair, everyone did, for Tadashi was a merry child, perpetually laughing and without a weighty thought in his head. She was harder on her older son, exerting considerable pressure on him to do well at school, but Isamu, who was both competent and docile, managed to cope with her demands. So it was only my mother who clashed with Yukiko, and she did so ferociously and often.

But none of her children really knew what to make of Yukiko. Whereas they adored and even worshipped their father, they were embarrassed by Yukiko's almost foreign glamour, and spent much of their childhood wishing that she looked and acted like other mothers. Still, it was she who raised them. She woke them in the mornings, fed them all their meals, greeted them when they returned from school in the afternoons, and usually listened when they talked about their lives. She scolded them when they came in drenched and shivering after staying out too long in the rain. She was capable of extravagant acts of playfulness, as in the tree-climbing episodes, but guided, perhaps, by the memory of her own mother, who though tender and warm had still let her go, she always kept a certain distance from her children.

Deep down she knew she was too cold to them. It was for this reason that she (dogged by the hereditary insomnia that torments all the female members of my family) stayed up late at night and wrote. Those terrifying hours in the bomb shelter, during which she had pulled out her childhood like a bauble in order to entertain her daughter and her sons, had wakened in her intimations of mortality as well as a yearning to acquaint her children with her life. So she began to set her life down on paper for them, scratching away each night with her fountain pen, and when her notebooks started to pile up, she took down from the highest cupboard of her bedroom a tea box, which was lacquered black on the outside and red within—the only possession she had kept from her most distant past. She stacked the books inside it, noting with satisfaction that they fit as neatly as her hair once did.

When Tadashi's hair began to fall out, a year after the family evacuated to the countryside where fried grasshoppers were the feast of choice, it was my mother, Akiko, who first noticed. He was playing on the parallel bars at a nearby playground, and trying in vain to coax his older sister, whose fear of heights extended to gym sets as well as bridges, to join him. "Watch," said Tadashi, "it's a cinch." He swung himself back and hung upside down, his shorts slipping down to expose his belly button and his striped underwear.

Akiko stared.

"It's much easier than it looks," the now red-faced Tadashi explained kindly, still upside down.

Her mouth open, Akiko could only point at her brother's head.

When she showed the egg-shaped bald spot on Tadashi's head to their mother, Yukiko only sighed, for she had long suspected that her children, living as they did on a diet of grasshoppers and rice and powdered potatoes, were poised on the brink of malnutrition. Their diarrhea was all but constant. Lost in thought, she barely remembered to pat Tadashi's head to reassure him.

She went to her chest, chose her most gorgeous kimono, and folded it into a neat square packet of blue and gold, musing all the while on a day no more than fourteen years ago, when her own mother had dressed her in a red kimono borrowed from a cousin. After telling Isamu to stay at home and watch over Tadashi, Yukiko took Akiko firmly by the hand and walked outside. It was October, Yukiko's favorite time of the year. The trees were red and yellow, and the evening was cool and breezy.

They knocked at a farmer's house that was even shabbier and smaller than their own. The farmer's wife was spiteful and barely civil, hating Yukiko for her citified ways, her air of elegance, and even her height. Offering the kimono and begging for food, Yukiko bowed low and used the honorific. Akiko, who was sitting beside her, bowed as well, so that their dark heads rested like twin polished stones on the ground.

In one of the more ironic incidents of Japanese history, the Emperor spoke over the radio to Japan for the first time, but was not understood. He had long been regarded as a god, with pictures of him hung on the walls of every classroom and in shrines in public homes, and he spoke in a dialect of his own. Until he came on the air to announce Japan's surrender in an almost foreign tongue, no one had been sure that he was human.

The war was over, and soon Yukiko had moved herself and their children back to Tokyo. Japan had changed beyond measure and also beyond repair, but Yukiko and Sekiguchi, at least, managed to slip back into something that came very close to their old life. They found a new and more beautiful house, replaced the kimonos that Yukiko had sold, and once again fed their children full meals and fine delicacies. Most importantly, death was no longer a threat that hovered constantly in the sky.

Still, Yukiko continued to stay up late at night, writing.

CHAPTER NINETEEN

Tʜᴇ ᴅɪᴠɪᴅᴇ ʙᴇᴛᴡᴇᴇɴ Yukiko and my mother may have begun at the moment of my mother's birth, when the unmarried Yukiko, in despair over what she considered her slipping place in Sekiguchi's affections, looked up, flushed and sweaty after her labor, saw that she had given birth to a daughter, and turned away with a sinking heart from the child. An hour later, she was calling for the baby, and she cosseted her for years in an attempt to rid herself of her guilt over that initial rejection. My mother in fact only learned of that first loveless hour when she read Yukiko's diaries, but still her fierce independence from Yukiko may have had its origin in that short period, for who knows how deeply a baby's first moments of life shape and mark her?

During our nighttime storytelling sessions, my mother always lapsed into a certain dismissive tone when she spoke of Yukiko and her fantastic, fortunate life, which became, after the hiatus of the wartime years, once again one of extreme ease and luxury. Even after they healed the breach, writing letters to each other that started the steady rise of warmth between them, this measure of scorn remained. When they met at my grandfather's funeral, after a separation of twenty-nine years, they did not hug or kiss.

....

After running away from home, Akiko stayed for a few weeks with her younger brother, who was in college at the time, and ensconced in comfortable accommodations of his own. Isamu's sympathy for my mother's cause was to remain constant through the years, even though he himself later submitted to Yukiko's bidding, and married the woman she found for him. His marriage evolved quickly into a felicitous coupling, proving either that parents do know best, and matchmakers are well worth their keep, or that luck plays an unprecedented part in affairs of the heart.

My mother left her family, her home, and the country she had been born in for the man she loved. But she herself did not view it as a sacrifice. She had not been happy as a Japanese daughter, and perhaps she was right to suspect that she would have been even less happy as a Japanese wife.

She borrowed money from Isamu for the plane tickets, and taught Japanese for two years in Boston, while Kenji earned his Ph.D. in physics. He won a hefty science fellowship, and they soon saved enough to pay back Isamu with interest. Later, after Kenji found a job in a laboratory in northern New Jersey, they had enough to make a down payment on a house located in the small town of Garrison.

After my father began working, my mother enrolled in science classes at the local college. For three years she studied every day, slowly mastering the English language so she could understand the textbooks filled with technical terms, and in 1963 she received a bachelor of science degree with high honors from the college. Perhaps her elation at her triumph made her careless. She knew she was pregnant within three weeks after graduation, and though she managed to get in two semesters of medical school that year, she took an indefinite leave of absence after I was born. I was a sickly baby, and my mother gave up studying in order to take care of me.

By the time I was old enough and well enough to manage on my own, she had to deal with Kenji, who had become irrational and unkind with drink. He told her that she was too stupid to be a doctor, and that with the added expense of a child, they could no longer afford medical school. I sometimes wonder how much my mother regretted her decision to keep her first child. A year and a half after my birth, she aborted the fetus when she discovered she was pregnant again, but I could not be flushed away so easily.

My father was a brilliant and charming man given to excesses of alcohol. After the evenings on which he did not come home for dinner, I sometimes woke up in the darkest part of the night and heard his voice, pitched unnaturally loud and high, and then the sound of blows and running feet. On the mornings following those nights, my mother had bruises on her neck and arms; occasionally she had a black eye and once she was missing a noticeable amount of hair. She never said anything about those marks, and I never could bear to ask.

There were long stretches when my father remained at home and all was well; he was so funny and strange that I laughed until I screamed, and even my mother permitted herself cautious smiles. But in my memories he is mostly an absent presence. I did not see him on most mornings because I left early to catch the school bus, and he usually slept in until the last possible moment before going to work. Now I cannot clearly recall his face. When I try to envisage it, I see the unused plate and silverware at the dinner table. Every evening I set the table for three people, but almost always my mother and I ate alone, silently passing the food back and forth between us over his empty plate.

I do not know where my father is now. My mother and I packed all of his clothes and books into a trunk and two suitcases and shipped them to an address in West Virginia, but he has probably moved on from there.

My mother then sold the house, which was too large and drafty, and filled with too many memories, and we moved into an apartment building on a temporary basis. While she looked for another place, a small house in another clearing of the woods, we moved from one set of rooms to another. I badly wanted a home of our own, but she was strangely fussy and found something to criticize in every one of the houses that we saw. Her search went on for years.

The spring during which my father left us was one of the worst that Garrison had ever seen. March was freezing cold, and April even worse. To cut down on electricity bills, we kept the heater turned off, and I became used to sleeping in my coat. My mother pared away at her shopping lists until she was buying only the most essential items: spaghetti, sauce that came in a jar, milk. We sold my three-speed bicycle for $45, which is what it was worth. My mother insisted on that price even when Mrs. Wright, an officiously kind neighbor, wanted to give us $75. It was hard to give up that bicycle. My mother did not hold me when I cried, yet she did not scold me, either, when I slapped little Peggy Wright for leaving her new bike out in the rain.

My mother was in her late thirties, alone in a country run by tall white men, and she was saddled with a child of nine. She had a house, some savings, no income and no professional skills, yet acting out of a predictable pride, she refused to write her parents about my father's departure. Still, after less than a year, fat envelopes, filled with yen, began arriving from overseas on the first of every month: money that went far in those lean times. (*Obaasama,* I will say, you wise woman, you sly puss, what gave it away? Was it a mother's instinct, or clever deduction? Was it the fact that my mother had to keep up with the biannual tradition of sending photographs of me: did you realize that your worst fears had been confirmed when you saw that I was alone in all of the photographs now, my father gone and my mother always on the other side of the lens?)

By May of the year after that, after twenty-two months of waiting by the window and four months of scouring the classifieds, my mother had found a job. Long before she came into her inheritance, she was making money as a translator for a Wall Street firm. Every weekday morning for ten years, she caught the 7:25 express to Penn Station and was at her office by 8:15. I did not see her very often during those years. She got home in time to eat dinner with me, and then she usually dozed off over her work. After four months, she became the personal secretary to the Japanese vice-president, and after three years of poor pay and long hours, she climbed up into a rather high administrative position. At the end, she was making quite a bit of money, but she did not like the work. "Learn," she told me. "Read books, study hard."

My mother had been a plain child, but she grew prettier over the years, and she was a slender, elegant woman at thirty-nine, when she found herself single once again. It was widely believed that she was legally separated from her husband, and she had only one daughter. She met a lot of men at work, and while many of them wanted her, and at least a few would probably have been happy to marry her, she never dated any of those men for longer than a month.

In the summer of last year, she gained a new admirer. I always liked Mr. Lewis, a widower and one of the more recent additions to our neighborhood. Gray-haired and soft-spoken, small of stature but solidly built, he is a lawyer by training and a farmer by inclination, spending most of his free time in his vegetable garden. Even in the winter he is always working outside, clearing dead brush away or covering weak plants from frost.

I used to make it a point to go see him whenever I was visiting my mother. "Hey Mr. Lewis," I would call out, hopping off my bike. "Hey Kiki," he'd reply, taking off his gardener's gloves, encrusted with dirt, to warmly shake hands. While he was always careful to ask me about school and life in the big city, I could tell that the only answers he really cared about were the ones concerning my mother. "Is she in?" he'd ask, looking wistfully over at our house. "How's her health these days?"

"She's in," I would tell him. "And her health's okay. Why don't you go over and say hello?"

But he was too shy, or maybe he just moved slowly. Instead of knocking or calling, he took to wooing my mother with vegetables, a motif found side by side with thwarted passion in the story of my life. The gifts were made anonymously, at the crack of dawn, so that for most of last year, whenever my mother opened the door to pick up the newspapers in the morning, she never knew what she would see: a Valentine of blooming radishes; half a dozen new potatoes nestled in a basket; three ears of sweet corn, loosely tied together with string, lying like a bouquet at her feet. He also brought her cauliflower, broccoli, tomatoes, onions and, yes, cucumbers and eggplants, too, the sincerity of his ardor conferring dignity upon even these most ridiculous of all vegetables.

"He has such a crush on you, Ma," I said, coming in windswept from my bike ride, early last fall.

"Who does?" she asked, looking up from a steaming wok.

"Mr. Lewis," I said. "You know, our neighbor."

"Oh," she said, and did she blush a little, or was that the heat from the stove? "Oh, him."

"Why don't you go over and say hello?" I said to her, using the same line I had tried on him. "Throw him a bone," I added, wheedling. "Say thank you for the vegetables."

She was quiet for a while, pensive over the vegetables—his vegetables—that were cooking in the wok. "It's not as if he ever left a card or even a note, you know," she said, her voice trailing off. "But you think I should?"

"Definitely," I said. "It'd be rude not to. Shocking, in fact."

Considering that this conversation took place after almost three months of free high-quality produce, I probably would have been justified in taking her by her brittle-boned shoulders and shaking her into reason, as I wanted to ("You two are over fifty, you know—it's not like you can afford to waste time, acting like moony teens. . . ."). With this kind of drawn-out prelude to dating, it seemed clear that theirs was destined to be the slowest-moving courtship of all time. But as it turned out, the romance was over almost as soon as it began, as quickly and suddenly as it flared into life.

Hidden in the shadows and wrapped in a heavy wool blanket, my mother sat on the porch swing and lay in wait for Mr. Lewis for two mornings. When he finally showed, a head of crisp lettuce straddled by his hand like a bowling ball, she sat forward and called out to him, rising and offering her apologies when she saw how he started and flushed.

She invited him in for breakfast, and after that, for the next twenty-two days, there was no stopping them. They went to movies and bookstores together, and cafes and bars. In the evenings, after she cooked dinner for him, his own vegetables served up with ginger and a twist of soy sauce, she sang for him, Japanese folk songs and snatches of opera, too. They argued politics, played gin rummy, and read the papers side by side.

Best of all, going out with Ned Lewis brought out at least glimmers of another side to my mother: that sense of adventure that had seemingly been lost for good with the slow disintegration of her marriage.

Hobbled by arthritis though she is, she and Mr. Lewis took not only long walks but, incredibly, short bicycle rides together as well, she balanced on the seat behind him, her arms wrapped around his back, and her hair streaming out behind her like a flag. At her instigation, they drove fifteen miles out to the nearest lake, rented a sailboat that neither of them knew how to operate, and had a picnic on the water, the dock a mere twenty feet away.

It was Mr. Lewis who filled me in on the details of those twenty-two days. While my mother did mention to me that she and Mr. Lewis had been to the movies, when I called just a few days later and asked how he was doing, she responded with just a hint of tartness. "I don't know. You'd have to ask him."

So that weekend I took the train out to New Jersey, and pedaled off on my bike almost as soon as I got home. Mr. Lewis was sitting on his porch drinking coffee when I rode up his driveway.

"So what happened?" I asked, trying to catch my breath.

He looked over at me and ruefully smiled. When I pressed him, though, he gave me a capsule summary of all the things that they had done.

"So what happened?" I asked again, once he had finished. "It sounds as if it was going so well. What went wrong?"

But no matter how much I begged, he refused to say, telling me only that I should really be talking to my mother. Finally, just as I was giving up, he took pity on me, and spoke.

"Actually, I'm not really sure what went wrong," he said.

Ned Lewis is a reticent man, chary with his facial expressions as well as with his words. Yet when he spoke then, his face contorted just for an instant, and I wondered if I was wrong in guessing that the gesture connoted not just bafflement, but a fair share of pain, too.

After riding the short distance back home in record time, I dropped the bike onto the grass and ran inside. A few minutes of dead time, during which I poked my head into different rooms, looking for my mother, took away some of my momentum, but when I found her reading in the study, I managed to resummon enough anger to storm inside the room.

"Are you going to tell me what went wrong between you and Mr. Lewis?"

She looked up from her book.

"It was going so well," I said, and then, when she did not answer, "Well, wasn't it?"

Her eyes darted restlessly around the room, as if searching for an escape hatch. "Do we have to talk about this?" she said, almost pleading.

I continued, undaunted. "You liked him, right? You could have loved him. You could have had a *life* with him."

"Look," she said. Her voice sounded scratchy, as if she were coming down with a cold. "I'm fifty-four years old. I was with your father for fifteen years. And I met him when I was eight."

Taken aback, I paused, for elliptical and number-heavy as those statements were, they constituted far more of an explanation than I had expected. "But what about Mr. Lewis?" I said, rallying. "He's obviously crazy about you. Doesn't that count for anything? You should go talk to him again."

She shook her head, and stretched her arms out in front of her. "What's the point?" she said at last. She was looking down at her hands, which are so swollen at this point that she probably could not take off her wedding ring if she wanted to, and of course she does not.

"What do you mean, what's the point? And why can't you tell me what happened?" I said more quietly, already losing steam, pitying her in spite of myself.

I posed all these questions for no other reason than that they gave me the opportunity to berate my mother with some righteousness: I knew she was not going to respond to them. Besides, I already knew the answers, for it is not for nothing that I know my mother as well as I know myself.

Rigid in her ways, addicted to her solitude, and devoted beyond reason to the image of her lost husband, she panicked in the course of her sudden romance with Ned Lewis, and froze. She must have known, deep down, that no one on earth could possibly live up to the image she cherished of Kenji, the way he once was: young, smart, exhilarated by his own prospects, cocky to the point of arrogance but kind to her as no one else had ever been before, the same boy who had raced across train tracks to amuse the lonely little girl that she had been. She never speaks of my father, and no pictures of him adorn the house, yet even now, their marriage is legally undissolved.

I still make sure to see Mr. Lewis whenever I am in town. But our conversations are brief these days, for all we ever talk about is school and life in the big city, and the state of his vegetable garden.

She loved my father and she dreamed of medicine, but my mother's only successful love affair was with the piano. When she played, she could let herself go, and although she favored Chopin and Bach rather than the more turbulent Beethoven, although, too, the music was always beautiful, the piano provided an outlet for passions rarely expressed in public. Often her face flushed as she played; she bit her bottom lip, and it seemed as if she banged out the chords with more vigor than was necessary. After my father left, she played a lot more than she ever had before.

She was forty-one when her body showed the first signs of arthritis. Through the following five years, I heard a new mistake every time she played. Her hands fumbled and missed notes in the middle of the simplest of pieces, and I could hear her patiently counting in Japanese as she practiced measures with stiff fingers that had once glided across the keys. Sometimes as she sat at the piano, the sound of playing stopped entirely, and I could hear her strained breathing. One day she closed the lid to the piano, and never played Chopin again.

Arthritis is a disease that affects the joints of the body. They become inflamed, swollen, and twisted, and the pain is the burning kind. The cause of the disease is unknown, and as of yet there is no cure. The symptoms are different for every patient. For my mother, whose arthritis is of the rheumatoid variety, it began with the feet. First both big toes started to hurt, and then with a symmetry almost harmonious, the ache spread outwards to the rest. She thought her feet needed exercise, but after a long walk, the pain was worse. A month later her fingers were also hurting. A month after that, she went to the doctor. "I'm very sorry," he said when he gave her the diagnosis. At the time she did not see the need for his pity.

Throughout the years she has taken large quantities of different medications. The results have varied. Most had no effect, a few exacerbated the pain, and some eased it, but not one could stop it altogether. For some time she was injected with gold, and as at least some of that substance probably courses through her veins still, her body might after all be worth something, an unplumbed gold mine.

One drug caused her hair to fall out. We were living in a tiny set of rented rooms at the time, and every night I had to wait for her to get out of the bathtub before I could brush my teeth. If I came in before she had finished cleaning up, the tub would be carpeted in black. In the mornings her pillow was likewise covered, so that sometimes I had to look twice to see whether it was her or only her hair that still lay in bed. When she walked, the strands drifted down after her like strangely colored snow. Once as I looked out my bedroom window, I saw her fleeing from her hair. She had just parked the car in the empty street, and though her feet must have hurt her, she was running towards the apartment building. Periodically she looked back as she ran, gazing with fear at the pieces of herself she left behind.

She did not become completely bald because she was able to determine relatively early that the medication that made her lose hair did nothing to ease her pain. For about half a year she wore a wig, an ugly black thing that spent its nights draped over a faceless plastic head, and then her hair began to grow again. Where it had once been black and thick and straight as my own, it grew back thin and fluffy, and a shade lighter than it had been. Worst of all, it had lost most of its former luster. I suspected her of lying when she said she preferred her new hair because it was more Western, but perhaps my own vanity was clouding my judgment.

Leaving long scars on her body to mark where they have dug into her skin, the doctors have been taking her apart and replacing her bit by bit. The joints in her left shoulder, her right hip, and both her knees are metal now; she is half flesh and half steel, a forerunner of an age in which the human body will become godlike through the magic of machinery. But whereas those future generations will run faster than a train and perhaps even fly with a mere flap of superhuman arms, all of the steel inside my mother does not enable her to walk without pain. Doglike, she carries heavy objects with her teeth.

I go to the hospital to take her home after each of her operations. When I went in to see her after her hip replacement, she was lying down, and did not hear me come in. Her whole body jerked with an instinctive movement of shame as soon as she saw me, her torso twitching forward, one hand pulling her nightgown over stick-thin legs, while the other reached up to hide her chest and throat. She quickly recovered herself and made as if she were only smoothing down the covers, but for her sake as well as my own, I looked away from her body and her eyes, puffy and darkened with fatigue; I did not allow myself to stare at her like that, an exposed human being after all.

When the arthritis first struck my mother, I thought it was a judgment, divine retribution for the way she had rejected her mother, perhaps, or for her failure to keep her husband from drink. But after a couple of years passed, I grew to understand that she alone was to blame for her affliction. Just as my own misery had once ballooned inside me and made me fat, so, too, did the bitterness of her frustrated love poison and maim her body. It was the weight of unshed tears that clogged and swelled her joints, and it was the heat of her own rage that made them burn with pain. Her body is forever racked with the screams she stifled when my father beat her.

In spite of the bins that overflow with the latest publications, my mother has no contact with the present world. To her the newspapers are nothing but a catalogue of remote disasters; since she refuses to vote, the political events she follows so ardently have as much relevance and reality as a fairy tale. I do not want to be like her any more than I want to be like my father. I do not want to lead an existence made up only of the cold comforts of an exquisite home and the printed word; I do not want to spend my life clinging stubbornly to wispy memories of a happiness that may never have been.

I do not want to be like my mother, and I cannot be like my grandmother, who married the man she loved the best. Phillip is once again watching me from his favorite corner in the fireplace, but when Eric calls, if Eric calls, I will make him so happy he will never want to leave.

....

I met my uncle Tadashi eight years ago, when he was in America on business: a small man whose face was all over laugh wrinkles, and who did magic tricks for me until I forgot that we did not speak the same language. It was he who called us, a little more than three years ago, at the start of what I had thought was going to be a nostalgically idyllic time—my last summer at home, to be celebrated by doing nothing but reading novels on the porch. But what my uncle Tadashi called to say was that Sekiguchi had died in a fire, and that the funeral was in five days. My mother booked a flight, packed, and flew out within twenty-eight hours, and while I stayed home, living on tuna fish and marshmallows and reading to all hours of the night, she went back to visit the country and family she had not seen for twenty-nine years.

Driving through Tokyo in a cab, her luggage loaded with impromptu presents for her nieces and nephews, my mother, always sensitive to beauty and the lack of it, shuddered. The pollution could kill a baby, the traffic moved at the stately pace of glaciers, and the buildings were clustered so tightly together that the windows were a largely empty gesture. Still, not much had actually changed since she had left Tokyo all those years before. My mother's reaction was in fact due to the way she remembered the city. In the course of her long hiatus, her image of Tokyo had misted over with nostalgia. In her memory she had reverted to the city of her childhood, where the houses were low and made of wood darkened by age, and the streets bustled with people and ricksha instead of cars—a city that had succumbed almost without struggle to the bombs and resulting fires of the war.

After this massive destruction, Tokyo had rebuilt itself almost overnight, it seemed, regenerating itself with what materials could be scavenged: scraps of plywood, plaster, and tin. Not surprisingly, this slapdash rebuilding came with a price, which was found not only in the shoddiness of the new buildings, but also, and perhaps more irreparably, in the overall layout of the city. Postwar Tokyo had been planned without foresight, and it showed. Streets meandered like bad conversation, trailing off into a question mark and then silence, so that even native Tokyoites could not find their way, and there were no strategically placed squares of green, no trees to shade its avenues, and no major parks except for the largely private one adjoining the Emperor's estate.

Frozen in traffic with her face pressed against the window, her neck twisting as she gazed up at the latest earthquake-proof skyscraper, my mother thought that what astonished her was that no one seemed to notice, let alone grieve, that one city had been buried as another one had grown. Then, as the traffic thawed a drop's worth, she chided herself for her quick scorn, for twenty-nine years ago, she, too, had not noticed, numbed by constant exposure and distracted by the more consuming demands of her everyday life.

But she noticed now, and grieved.

The funeral was a protracted affair, taking place over three days and involving hundreds of people, for Sekiguchi's life had touched many. But only my grandmother, my mother, and her two brothers participated in the last rites.

My grandfather's body was brought out to them in a pan maybe the length of an adult's arm: before discreetly withdrawing, the polite young attendant warned them not to touch it, for it was still burning hot from the oven. The ashes were pale gray and slightly shiny, the bones a dirty white. My mother was handed long chopsticks, longer than Chinese ones, longer, even, than the cooking chopsticks she used to stir vegetables in the wok. She used them to fish out a bone from the ashes; though the length of a shin, it felt surprisingly light, almost hollow. Yet the chopsticks were unwieldy and she was clumsy because of her arthritis, and so her grasp on the bone was not quite firm. She dropped it and it fell back into the pan, scattering the ashes in a small cloud of dust. My mother let out a small American "Oh," but Tadashi, irrepressible as ever, chuckled, and even Isamu gently smiled.

My mother picked a daintier bone the second time. It was probably a finger, and as she dropped it ceremoniously into the urn, this time without mishap, she thought not of her father's scarred, thick hands, but of her mother's long fingers, and their cool touch on her head.

....

When the funeral was over, Yukiko and my mother talked, not of the terrible fight they had when they last saw each other, nor of the silence that had thickened between them during the long interval that had followed it, nor, even, of Sekiguchi's elaborate, well-attended funeral, which had almost done justice to his life. They talked instead of the times they had shared long ago: the stories told in the bomb shelter, the days spent playing in the countryside during the war, and the time that Yukiko hitched up the skirt of her kimono to climb up a tree and have tea with her daughter.

The war loomed large in their memories of the past, but they talked of peacetime, too: of the time that my mother chopped off her hair so that she could play as unhampered as her brothers, and of how Yukiko cried and scolded when she saw the long black locks coating the bathroom floor; of Akiko's piano playing, and the one time that she, a practiced performer, got stage fright and misplayed during a recital, and how the audience thought it was the piano rather than the popular young pianist who erred. They spoke of the days they had spent wandering the streets of Tokyo together, absorbing the sights and sounds.

As yet unable to grasp the full import of Sekiguchi's death, energized by the excitement of his funeral, and intoxicated by this reunion with her long-absent daughter, Yukiko grew younger again as she relived her past. This rejuvenatory process, which took place in department stores, on the crowded Tokyo streets, and of course over tea, went on for six days. At the end of it, Yukiko gave Akiko six notebooks, smelling strongly of smoke and bound together by string.

"What are these?" asked Akiko.

"Something I owe to you," replied Yukiko, her eyes darting away from her daughter's.

They had not hugged or kissed when they met, but when they said their farewells, Akiko embraced her mother, and Yukiko slowly raised her bone-thin hands and touched her face in response.

....

My mother came home from Tokyo laden with packages. Japanese-style, our relatives had loaded her down with gifts—the delicacies she had been craving for years, dishes, gadgets, a fancy camera for me as well as for her.

But her most jealously guarded package, the one she carried on her lap from Tokyo all the way to our house, was Yukiko's diaries, all six of the salvaged volumes, and after she read them our storytelling sessions resumed, this time over meals, in the car, and through long afternoons over tea.

The letter came two months after my mother's return. In it Yukiko announced baldly and simply that my mother had come into some money under the terms of Sekiguchi's will. Half of the estate had gone to Yukiko, but the rest of the assets were to be split evenly between my mother and her two brothers. Although at the time the yen was not as powerful as it would later become, a sixth of her father's fortune still made my mother a terribly wealthy woman.

My mother had fought with her parents and had run away from home with a man they had forbidden her to marry, and she had let almost three decades lapse before she went back to her family. Her father had died without seeing her again. She had been sure she would be cut from the will, and even with those envelopes filled with yen that arrived every month, I had never seen a reason to contradict her certainty on this score.

My grandmother is the most direct of letter writers, spare to the point of rudeness. Before she learned of the existence of the diaries, my mother had speculated that Yukiko was shy about her penmanship; afterwards, she came to believe that her mother had made the conscious decision to save her literary energies and eloquence for an account of her life. Yet whatever the reason for Yukiko's epistolary brevity, when she included in a letter even a single line that was not strictly business, it was an occasion worthy of comment, and so we exchanged a glance when the letter ended with a postscript: "Do you remember how you once wanted to be a doctor?"

My mother's hand rested on the table, over a corner of the letter. I wanted to reach out and slip my hand inside her own, but I was too afraid. The room was still and I heard the sounds of a lone car from the street, and the pine tree brushing against the window. For a few more moments we sat together, the letter and her hand lying between us on the table, and then I spoke.

"It's great news," I said. "Now you can do whatever you want."

My mother's English is very good: it is not often that it fails, but it failed her then. "What—this last question means?" she asked.

"It's like the journals—it's an apology. She's saying they're sorry they didn't give you the chance before."

"You really think so?" she said.

I nodded.

She looked past me, towards the wall again, and cleared her throat. "Well then," she said, with a return to her old briskness, "we can't disappoint her, can we?"

She had inherited so much money that neither of us would ever need to earn a salary again, and the third thing she did with her inheritance was to buy me my wonderfully spacious apartment, set on a tree-lined street. She also started giving me an envelope filled with money on the first of every month, a practice that she has kept up now through the mail despite my protests about my more than adequate fellowship, despite the fact that the money I save on rent means that I now have piled up more money than I can easily spend, even despite (for my grandmother's and mother's strange faith in the postal system is one legacy I did not inherit) my repeated warnings about the dangers of mailing cash.

The second thing she did with her inheritance was to buy our old house back. Although it had been occupied by a series of tenants, no one had wanted to keep it, and my mother was therefore able to buy it back cheaply. So in August, after fifteen years of living in places permeated with the smells of cleaning wax, raw wood, and strangers, we went home again, to the house where my parents had brought me as a baby.

But the first thing my mother did was to quit her job on Wall Street. She stayed home, poring over the tiny print of medical journals; she went to the bookstore and bought thick heavy books on biology, and she struggled over old physics problems. The day after New Year's, she registered for three pre-med classes at the same local college she had attended before, yet after her first day at school, she came home and told me that she was not going back.

"I've missed out on too much," she said. "I'll never catch up."

I felt as if I were about to cry, but she had eased herself onto the ground, and she was lifting a corner of the carpet to examine the floor underneath. I could not see her face.

"I'm going to redecorate the house instead," she told me. "What do you think about hardwood floors?"

It must have hurt her, crouching on the ground on her swollen hands and misshapen knees, but her smile as she glanced up at me was determinedly bright.

With its silvery sheen, my grandmother's hair is still pretty, but it is far less full than it used to be, and more brittle, too. It only reaches down to her shoulders now, and in the daytime she wears it gathered at the nape of her neck in a simple bun.

At night before she sleeps, I will go to her room and loosen her hair and comb it out, as her maid always did. I will work slowly and carefully, making sure the comb does not take with it any more of the precious remaining strands than is inevitable, and when I am done, I will fluff out her hair around her face so that it frames it. We will look into the mirror then, and there we will see me standing behind her in an upside-down family tree, and the woman who serves as the link between us will be an absence that both of us note.

Grandmother, I will say (busying my hands with her locks once again, and keeping my eyes fixed upon the back of her head), *Obaasama.* What price a woman's life, if all it consists of is loving one man forever?

CHAPTER TWENTY

It may be that Sekiguchi left her alone too long during the war, and after it, too. For when Yukiko returned to Tokyo at the end of it, eager to resume a life with him after their long separation, it was to find him increasingly preoccupied with his business and affairs of state.

I tender this explanation because after the war, there were signs that my grandmother Yukiko began to pine for her first love, Jun. Ten at the time, Yukiko's only daughter was old enough to notice and remember the signs, although it would take her a few more years until she could add them together and come up with the figure of another man. In the afternoons she heard sobbing, muffled but distinct, coming from her mother's bedroom door, and occasionally odd snatches of love songs, sung in that off-key voice that made Akiko, whose pitch was perfect, wince. There was also Yukiko's impatient wait for the mail, and the bad temper and sulks that followed the day-after-day arrival of nothing except business letters for her husband.

But first came the day that Akiko, walking through the streets of Tokyo, heard a man hail her mother.

"Yukiko, Yukiko," he called out, his voice strangely quavering.

Turning, Yukiko and Akiko found themselves confronting an unexpected tableau: two women wearing the elaborate kimonos and makeup of geishas, and sprawled out on the ground between them a man. He was dressed in the overalls of a working-class man; his collar was set on a crazy angle and vomit stained his shirtfront. His face was marked with the telltale flush of saké.

"I miss you, Yukiko, I love you how I love you," he said, and then to Akiko's horror, he began to cry, repeating all the while his litany.

One of the geishas knelt down to tend to the man, attempting to soothe him with words and her touch. Yukiko started forward as if she, too, would kneel by his side, but the other woman barred her way, standing guard over the man with her feet planted wide and her hand held out in front of her, as fearless as a traffic cop who would stop an on-coming fifty-ton lorry with a gesture.

Yukiko looked at her, and froze. "Kaori," she said.

The woman gazed back at her calmly. "You're the one who chose to go. You can't come back now," she said. Then she added, her voice lower, "It's for your own good."

All Yukiko had to do was walk around that palm facing her. Yet the woman who had mounted guard over the man was not only as fearless as a traffic cop, but apparently as effective as one as well: Yukiko did not approach, rooted in place with her hand still clutching that of her daughter. Without taking her eyes away from Kaori, she gestured vaguely towards the crying man. "What are you doing to him? What are you doing *with* him?"

Her tone was fierce, and when Akiko turned to look up at her, she saw that a vein stood out in the center of her forehead.

"Nothing," said Kaori. She dropped her arm, letting it fall limply to her side, and shrugged. "I've just been looking out for him, that's all. As you can see, he's fallen apart pretty badly in these last few years."

Yukiko nodded. The three of them—Kaori with her feet planted wide, and Yukiko and her daughter—remained still for a few long moments in a tableau of their own. It was Kaori who broke the spell at last. "You should go. Remember the child," she said gently, still speaking to Yukiko, but smiling down at her daughter.

Drawn by the man's sobs and ranting, a small crowd had gathered by then. Yukiko, after all, had a position to maintain. With a nod to Kaori and one last glance at the man, she turned and fled, walking so swiftly that Akiko had to half-skip and half-run all the way home.

Inside the entrance of her fine grand home, Yukiko kicked off her shoes and ran inside, leaving Akiko alone at the door. Still in her coat, she flew into the living room, where she threw herself into an armchair and began to sob.

After five minutes she looked up, tear-stained and red-eyed, to the sight of her daughter staring into her face.

"What are you looking at?" she screamed. Then Akiko's world went red in one sudden flash, and she felt a burning pain and, though she did not know it, the sense of vertigo that had come over her mother when she embraced Sekiguchi for the first time.

Then she was sitting on the ground, holding her cheek. Yukiko had hit her.

Hovering on the border of sleep, Akiko opened her eyes in the night to find her mother standing over her. Gradually she became aware of the touch of her mother's long cool fingers on her face: a mute apology that she, the girl who was to become my mother, met and accepted with equal reserve.

"Who was that woman?" she asked drowsily.

"The woman was my old friend Kaori," said Yukiko, her voice for once soft. "And the man," she continued slowly, "the man is nobody, or at least nobody you have to worry about. Now go back to sleep."

Yukiko pined for a few months, only gradually settling back into her marriage. First she stopped waiting for the mail, then she stopped the singing, and then, finally, the sobbing was heard no more. Sekiguchi was as thoughtful a husband as he could be, given his devotion to his career, and he spent every single free moment he had with his wife and children. When he was home, Yukiko glowed.

My mother is the only source for this story. When she was given her mother's diaries some four or five decades after this event, she read them carefully, searching for a write-up of—or even just a reference to—this unexpected encounter, a hint to throw light on how Yukiko felt, meeting up with these ghosts from her geisha past. Given that there was not a line in the diaries to indicate that this scene even took place, I am sorely tempted to believe that my mother dreamed it all up. Yet it is all too possible that Yukiko was being discreet, mindful of the prying eyes of her maids and even her children; even more likely is the possibility that the journal documenting her affair with him was yet another of the casualties of the fire.

I try as much as possible to avoid thinking about this man, this strange character who could only have been her first love, Jun. But he, like Phillip, haunts me. Lurking only in the edges of Yukiko's story, his is a figure that casts a long shadow, dimming and diminishing the brilliant success that is her life. Unlike Phillip, who carries with him the tantalizing, agonizing thought of all that might have been, this man makes a tedious spectre, for he appears side by side with the bleak possibility that all is not perfect in the best of all possible loves; that in the happiest of all marriages, regret is still a fact, sacrifice still a necessity.

He also strikes a discordant note, as off-key as Yukiko's singing, even beyond the question of dreary warnings. This man, sprawled out on the road, blubbering drunkenly, his face red, his shirtfront stained with vomit and his collar askew, his image all but eclipsed by the moon-faced Kaori, guarding him as if she were a traffic cop: he has no place in the picture that I have assembled from all the stories that my mother has told me about Yukiko. Surely it is not only because my father's fairy tales and my mother's family stories have become confused in my mind that Yukiko's life seems a romance for the ages, filled with enchantment and true love. The sense of longing that the reappearance of Jun provoked unsettles me because no matter how I look at Yukiko's story (and I have turned it over and over in my mind for years now, examining it from every possible angle, in every possible light), what I am sure of is that she loved Sekiguchi.

Yet she must still have nursed a secret passion for her first love, as I am otherwise unable to explain the off-key love songs, the muffled sobbing behind closed doors, and the slap that left the imprint of Yukiko's hand upon my mother's cheek. And so it is that I am forced to entertain the possibility that Sekiguchi left her alone too long during the war, and after it, too.

Grandmother, I will say. Dear *Obaasama,* my fairy-tale princess, spinning a life filled with misfortunes into pure gold. If you, ensconced in your castle with your prince, felt a momentary pang for the wild sweetness of the goatherd's son, his rough skin and his bare feet, and the hours he had to while by your side—if you pined for a time to live in another kind of story, you do know, don't you, that no one could blame you?

I least of all, for all that I dream of a fortress so strong it can lock out the past.

CHAPTER TWENTY-ONE

ERIC DOES NOT phone during the night, but I wake up early on Thursday morning, feeling unusually refreshed. After I get dressed, I go out to the supermarket, stopping to browse at the local secondhand bookstore on the way back. As I reenter the lobby of my apartment building, I nod to Julio, my favorite doorman.

"I have a surprise for you," he says, winking.

"How fun," I say. "What is it?"

"Come with me." Mysteriously he beckons me towards one of the storage rooms at the side of the lobby. "Wait here," he says, walking through the door. Almost immediately he comes out with two fistfuls of balloons, yellow and blue and green and red. He shoves them at me.

"These are for you," he says.

"For me?" I say, puzzled.

"Wait, there's more." With an enormous grin on his face, Julio walks back into the room and reemerges with another fistful, and then he goes back in and comes out with two more. Weighted down with iced tea and toilet paper and four used books, I cannot hold all of the balloons, and they drift to the ceiling, where they scatter, the strings dangling down just within reach. The lobby is teeming with them.

"They just came in," says Julio. "Somebody likes you an awful lot, eh?"

"I guess so," I say, smiling.

Finally Julio hands me a card. I thank him and read it as I wait for the elevator. Written in an unfamiliar hand (Eric's secretary? the receptionist at the balloon store?), the note capitalizes the first letter of every word, so that the message reads like the title of a song: "I Hope We Can Always Be Together. Love From Eric."

I can only get about fifteen balloons into the elevator with me at once, so I leave the rest floating in the lobby while I take the first load up. As I fumble with my locks in the hallway, old Mrs. Noffz opens her door and peers out at me and my balloons. "My oh my," she says. "How pretty."

"I think so, too," I say, opening the door and releasing them into the living room.

"They're like flowers," she says.

"They're a present," I tell her as I close the door and call the elevator, which slides right open. "This is only the first part of it. I'll be back with more in just a second."

She is waiting for me in her doorway when I come back with the next load. "I do like the blue ones, don't you?" she says.

I am busy struggling to disentangle the strings from my wrist, where I had loosely tied them for safety. "Yes," I remember to say after a while.

As I shut my door and walk back towards the elevator, she calls out once more. "However, the green is also nice."

"I think so, too," I say again. I get into the elevator, and wave at her as the door begins to shut. "One more trip should do it."

The third and last load is the biggest of all; I manage to get in more than twenty balloons by making myself tiny in a corner of the elevator. When I step out surrounded by the colorful crowd, Mrs. Noffz is still standing at her door.

"Gracious," she says, and then she uses a phrase very similar to the one that Julio used. "Somebody must love you quite a bit."

Suddenly stricken with guilt, I whirl around to look at her, yet there is no trace of envy or bitterness on her face. On the contrary, she is smiling as sweetly as she does when she speaks of the heat or the humidity or the possibility of rain.

"I have such a lot," I say. "Would you like some? After all, what am I going to do with so many?" I divide the load I am carrying into half and walk over to her door and hold them out to her. "Here."

She looks up at the balloons admiringly, but does not make a move to take them.

"The sun is too bright for Mabel today," she says.

"Is that right," I say. "Mrs. Noffz, wouldn't you like some balloons?"

Her hand does not budge from the doorknob. "We were sure it would rain this morning, but the clouds have all gone away."

Reluctantly I begin to withdraw my arm. I am absurdly disappointed. "Are you sure you don't want any?"

"I do like the blue ones," she says.

"Would you like just a blue one?" I quickly separate a blue balloon from the rest and offer it to her.

"But the green is also nice."

"How about a blue and a green?" With some difficulty I remove a green one, and hold it out with the blue. "I think they make a nice combination."

Together we look up and contemplate the two balloons.

"They are pretty," she says at last. "I think Mabel would enjoy them."

Her hand is wrinkled and bony, and it trembles slightly as she moves it away from the doorknob.

"Mabel and I are praying for rain."

"So am I," I say, passing her the balloons.

"See you later, Mrs. Noffz," I add softly as I pull the door shut, yet for once she does not answer, lost to my presence as she gazes placidly upwards, the strings clutched tightly in her hand.

I bring all the balloons into my bedroom and let them go; they rise to the ceiling and settle there, bobbing sociably against each other. There are fifty of them, and they make the room look like a garden. In the warm stillness of the late morning, a single breeze blowing in through the open window stirs the balloons into a minor frenzy. The strings beneath them become entangled as they chase each other across the ceiling, and I fall asleep wondering if this is the way that balloons make love.

My dreams are simple and pleasant, and I wake to the sound of a patter on the skylights. After what seems like weeks of drought, the rain comes down briskly, but the sun is still shining; the room is bright enough to read in. Outside the window, the drops shatter the light like glass, refracting it in a hundred different directions. I slowly turn my head away from the view outside, steeling myself to face the sight of Phillip.

He stands near the edge of the bed, surrounded by balloons. Shards of ice and drops of water drip from his hair and trickle down his body. Naked and exposed, he has never stood so close to me in broad daylight, and I examine his penis with some attention. It is limp without being shriveled, and it does not seem much smaller than it would be during an erection. Without desire I reach out and grasp it. It is smooth and wet and freezing cold to the touch, and heavy enough to weigh my hand down. It does not swell and grow, but I would be content to hold it like this forever.

Still holding on to it, I look up at his face. It is as expressionless as ever, the muscles rigid and inflexible, and yet perhaps because of his proximity, perhaps in one of the flashes of insight that often precede a full waking up from sleep, for the first time I am able to see the tenderness in his eyes. So often before have I tried to figure out the feelings that lay behind that impassive face, but if I had only looked at him, really looked without letting my own guilt get in the way, then I would have known why Phillip came back to me. He did not come back out of jealousy, paying visits to make sure that I would spend years pining for him in front of a window, as my mother had pined for my father; nor did he return out of malice, hoping to ruin my life with Eric. Phillip came back to me simply because he had promised he would, and because he loved me, just as I had always loved him.

I tighten my hold on his penis, squeezing until my muscles tense.

"Don't go," I say. "Please don't go."

Slowly he shakes his head at me. He bends over and with some effort he uncurls my fingers from his penis, and then he straightens his body.

He stands tall and ready, like a soldier. A battalion of balloons ranges itself into a spot above and before him and then, as if at an invisible signal, they fall upon him. There are so many of them that the force of their combined flight creates a gust of wind that ruffles both his hair and mine. In a silent, deadly rush, they push his body onto the floor, and at the same time they cushion his fall so that he hits the ground without a sound. Other balloons hover near me and when I sit up to see what is happening, they pin my arms to the bed so that I cannot move. His limbs are kicking and thrashing, his face can no longer be seen, and his head keeps turning back and forth as he tries to get air. For a few minutes, the room is filled with the sound of his breathing. Finally, after one last twitch, he lies still.

The balloons disperse slowly, floating upwards to their former positions. His body is relaxed and limp, and his feet splay outwards. One of his hands seems to reach out for me, yet I know that that is only wishful thinking: Phillip, with his scars, his twisted grin, his passion for the subways, and his eyes that moved with a life of their own, is dead.

Ceremoniously the balloons organize themselves into a circle above him. There are so many that they make three layers, and the strings dangle down to form a thick curtain. His face is calm and once again smoothed of all expression, with not a trace left of his former agony, and his eyelids hide his look of love.

The hum of the distant Broadway traffic grows more and more powerful, until the engine and the subway sounds are throbbing like a dirge through the window. Parting the curtain of balloon strings, I stretch out my arm to touch him, but his body leaves the floor and drifts away, the ring of balloon strings following it protectively, until it lies just beyond the reach of my hand. The traffic dies down to its usual barely perceptible murmur. His body hovers at the foot of my bed for a second or two longer, and then with a flash of light and a sound like the rushing of birds' wings during a flock's startled flight, Phillip is gone.

The hour is a little past noon. After a while I become aware that I am rocking back and forth on my heels, like a midget I once saw on a park bench. I stop myself from rocking when I realize what I am doing, and lie stomach down on the bed to look at the floor, where the dust was stirred during the scuffle. I watch the dust drift slowly back to the ground, each piece swirling in the air, some of them getting caught in the light so that for one brief moment of stardom, they are as luminescent as the gold on mothwings. When all the dust is settled, I sit up and smooth my clothes out. Then I go to the bathroom and comb my hair, passing time until Eric's arrival.

Obaasama, I will say, dear Grandmother. How did you feel after Sekiguchi's funeral? Did you, too, feel diminished but also lighter, a jar hollowed of half its contents?

I am drinking iced tea in the living room half an hour later when the phone rings. It is Eric.

"Hi," I say. "Thanks for the balloons."

"They're nice, aren't they." He pauses, and I can hear the sound of people talking behind him. "I'm sorry I didn't call you back sooner."

"That's okay," I say, and then the words come out in a rush. "I'm sorry, too—you've been so patient and I've acted so badly—"

"Stop it," he interrupts, the evenness of his tone condemning my outburst. "You weren't at fault."

"That's not true, but thanks." He does not say anything, so I clear my throat and fill in the silence. "So," I say. "So how have you been?"

"Fine. Well, at least work has been fine."

"I'm glad," I say.

"Kiki," he begins, and then he hesitates. "Kiki, I don't want to talk over the phone. I want to see you now."

"Wait—aren't you at the office?"

"I left work early. I'm actually in that cafe on 105th Street. I was going to drop by and surprise you, but at the last minute I thought I'd better call first."

"You're just a few blocks away?"

"Yes."

"Come on over," I tell him. "I'd love to see you."

In rhythm we take turns saying good-bye, and then in unison we hang up the phone.

CHAPTER TWENTY-TWO

WHEN WE FIRST see each other, Eric and I do not speak. In his elegant corporate attire, with that unruly lock of hair falling over his forehead, he stands just inside the door, his hands shoved deep in the pockets of his pants. He glances at me and then he gazes down at his polished black shoes. He rubs the floor with one foot until it squeaks. We are both watching the ground when he begins to talk.

"Look," he says, his voice loud and arrogant, "I need to know once and for all. Are you sure about this?"

"Yes."

Looking up from the floor, he directs his words squarely at a point on the wall behind me. "Kiki, I know it was tough for you after Phillip died, but I don't want to hear about it anymore. I think I've been sympathetic and patient long enough. There comes a time when you've got to forget and move on, and now is that time."

He looks away, back at the floor, as if he grudged me even that much kindness. I am about to protest the harsh tone of his voice when he coughs and rubs his hand across his forehead. He turns so I can no longer see his face, but he is a little too slow: it must be my day for seeing through people because for the first time, I can see that there is doubt lurking within those fine dark eyes, and nervousness held in check by the hard line of his mouth. Eric is scared.

Something tugs at me, then, an almost physical need to go to him and stroke his head and hold him against my chest. It is a tenderness that rises from deep within me, from a recess so hidden I was never before aware of its existence. Yet I resist its urge and remain still, watching him as he looks down at his feet.

I never could determine why, exactly, I loved Phillip, nor could I pinpoint what it was that drew me to him. But when Eric came along to romance me out of mourning, so soon after all that I had had with Phillip, I had to ask myself why I would want to be with him. And I came to the conclusion that I would grow to love Eric for the way he first took me by the hand and led me to his bed, for the breadth of his shoulders, the comforting circle of his arms, the umbrella he held over me when it rained: I would fall in love with him for his strength and confidence. Yet I was wrong.

Obaasama, I will say, you whose husband founded and ruled a banking empire, becoming a man so powerful that the Emperor himself inclined his head to him. Grandmother, is this a secret that you and I share: that the most admired of men are the neediest of all?

If a person is male, white, heterosexual, and even good-looking, if he is earmarked for success by virtue of birthright, upbringing, talents, and his own predisposition, if he has been praised, admired, and cheered from all sides throughout his lifetime, if he has in fact achieved success and success only, then I would guess that he must be one of the world's more vulnerable people, as well as the luckiest. It must be a little scary to have gotten everything one ever wanted, or could want. If a person has always been that lucky, then he does not know how much misfortune he can take, and how far he can fall without dying.

Given that after Phillip died, I was so numb I could not muster the energy to desire on my own, perhaps it was only inevitable that what I responded to was the depth of Eric's need for me. It was his weaknesses that drew me to him: the bluster behind his bravado, the skinny white knees and the hole in his sock, the fingers that clutch at my hair as he sleeps. In the end, I fell for Eric because he needed me enough for the both of us.

No longer able to resist that urge which rises from deep within my body, I move or rather sway towards Eric slowly, almost involuntarily. But even as I approach him, I am thinking that with Phillip (the apex to our triangle, the guest of honor at our party) well and truly gone, my relationship with Eric will be a completely different affair. Through no fault of his, we are going to have to start over.

He has been waiting, studying his shoe.

"Okay," I say.

"Well?" he asks. "What's the verdict?"

He looks and sounds cool and businesslike, as if he really was just waiting for a verdict in a remote court case, but I will not be fooled by his mask again.

"I'm over Phillip. He's dead." Then I laugh at how silly that sounds. "I guess it's about time I figured that one out."

He looks at me for a moment in silence.

"And you want to be with me?"

"Did I forget to mention that?"

He holds back, perhaps still shy. "Are you sure?"

"Oh Eric," I say, and that is all I can manage, but somehow my feelings must come out in my voice, because his eyes widen and he slowly begins to smile.

He holds out his arms; I walk into them and then he holds me, tight.

Throughout the afternoon and the evening and well into the night, Eric and I made love beneath the slanting shadows of the swaying balloons. In between the sex we lay on our backs with our hands behind our heads, talking and laughing as we watched the balloons scud across an imaginary cloudless sky, our feet bumping and rubbing against each other. When it became too dark to see more than the outlines of the balloons, we whispered together as we lay entwined around each other, our limbs anonymous in the soft glow of the New York light.

In the living room the moths were giddier than usual, drunkenly soaring in gorgeous arcs and loops. There were dozens and dozens of them. They seemed to be celebrating, and when I walked among them I felt as if I were standing in happy clouds of violet. If life with Eric is balloons in the bedroom and dancing moths in the living room and sex all the time, then my future with him bodes well indeed.

It is five in the morning now; the room is filled with shadows, and the balloons are starting to sink. Colorless and shapeless in the pale light, they seem to loom over us. A loose string dangles down, and when the last night breeze blows, it brushes against Eric's forehead. His face twitches, and I pull the string away from him.

One evening, as we stepped out of a restaurant downtown, a Mexican boy came up to us and tried to sell us rosebuds. It was past midnight and the air was chilly; the streetlights were very bright. Eric wanted to buy me one but I told him how I dislike getting flowers, how depressed I feel when the petals fall off and the leaves shrivel and curl up into brown balls that litter the floor, how even flowers pressed in books eventually and inevitably disintegrate into dust. The boy was persuasive and terribly funny, though, so after much friendly bargaining I ended up buying four awfully overpriced rosebuds for Eric, and all three of us—Eric, me, and most of all the boy—walked away pleased with the transaction. But all this time, Eric has remembered that I do not like getting flowers. Instead he buys me candies from India and pastries from Greece, and big presents like gold earrings and the television, and now the balloons.

While the sky is blue and getting bluer, the sun has yet to rise. In the murky light of the bedroom, I cannot make out the details of the fingers on my left hand, but when I rub them together, I can feel the hard surface where the skin has grown over the blisters. I look at Eric lying next to me, sleeping so deeply that for once he is beyond making little noises, and like my mother and her mother before her, I bow my head to express gratitude. In his sleep he stirs as if he understood, and he rolls over towards me. Like a wave, his arm hangs suspended in midair before it crashes down over my body. It is too heavy, and suddenly the bed seems overcrowded and stiflingly hot. I want to push him away and run outside, and then just as quickly, the moment is over. "Eric," I whisper, the word like a charm. Silently I thank him once again and wrap his arm tighter around me, and then I close my eyes.

....

After only three or four hours of sleep, Eric gets up at six so he can go home and change before heading off to work again. For once I wake up with him; we remain glued together all the way to the front door and then out to the hall. Dressed in a floral print nightgown and her red Wellingtons, Mrs. Noffz opens the door and benevolently watches us as we kiss outside in the hallway. When the elevator comes, Eric gets into it and still we do not miss a beat, our lips remaining stuck together until the doors almost close on our noses.

He calls me three times from the office just to say hello.

In the evening, he comes over straight from work; I meet him with a big hug at the door, and we go right back to bed. Three hours later, we are so hungry that we reluctantly get dressed to leave the apartment. I am wonderfully sore from all the sex. We go to an Ethiopian restaurant that Phillip and I had discovered; I feel proud of myself because the memory does not cause me even a pang.

After we get home, we sit on the sofa in the living room until midnight. His kisses are sweet and I savor their taste on my lips. The room is completely dark; even the moths are sleeping.

I go to the bathroom and brush my teeth; he is so tired that he goes directly to bed. He is more asleep than awake when I get under the covers, and his voice is a murmur nearly lost in the quiet. "You know," he says, "you seemed like such a little girl when you cried so hard at the jewelry store."

"I guess I was acting like one," I say, my voice low.

Without replying, he slips an arm over me, just below my throat. Its weight is warm and comfortable, yet I can tell that unless he remembers to take it off before he falls asleep, I will wake up with a stiff neck tomorrow.

"Eric?"

His breathing has already become deep and regular, and it takes him a long while to answer. "Yeah?"

"Oh, never mind," I say, for what does a stiff neck really matter in the face of his love?

His arm enfolds me closely, and in less than a minute, I, too, am almost asleep. This time it is he who wakes me.

"Kiki."

"Hmm?"

"I really missed you."

I hesitate only a fraction of a second. "I missed you, too."

He kisses me on the shoulder and then he falls asleep with his body curled around me like the shell around a snail, his fingers woven into my hair.

CHAPTER TWENTY-THREE

This honeymoon period, sweet and all-consuming as it is, has to bend itself around the obligations of the outer world, so the next day Eric and I resolve that we can see each other only if we work as well. Still, it is not until after yet another blissful interlude in the bedroom that Eric can concentrate on his papers, and I can pay attention to a book. I think I am just maybe becoming convinced by Eve Sedgwick when the phone rings.

"Hello?" I say, unsuspecting, lulled by the happiness of the last couple of days, but then the skin on my arms starts to prickle, because again I can hear the faint wail on the line and now it is finally, unmistakably identifiable: it is the sound of someone tunelessly humming. I listen for a while, hypnotized by it in spite of myself, before replacing the receiver on the hook. I sit on the couch, gazing down at my right knee, which is moving up and down like a restless schoolboy's, and then I raise my head and look at Eric. Sitting across the room, he is engrossed in a yellow notepad, not even bothering to ask who was or was not on the phone, even though his head had jerked up at the first ring.

On a cold day last January, I had huddled behind a pyramid of tomatoes to watch Phillip and a tall blond woman choose an eggplant at the market. After I came home that afternoon, I had gone straight to the telephone, my fingers hanging suspended over the buttons for a few seconds, and then I had dialed Phillip's number, heard one ring, and hung up quickly, incredulous that I was reenacting the pranks of adolescence.

"You slept with her, didn't you," I say.

Eric raises his head, his eyes wide, his brows high, and his mouth slack—the picture of innocence. "What are you talking about? *Who* are you talking about?"

"That Asian woman from your office," I say. "Theresa Chan."

He nods to himself, then, and I find myself astonished at how quickly he has given up his bluff. He must have wanted to confess for a long time. He sighs, his eyes meeting mine. "I slept with her a couple of times before I met you."

"I knew it," I say slowly. I am remembering the way she looked at me when I met her in the office, her head thrown slightly back and her eyes (thin and far darker than my own) cool and reflective as she watched me.

Then I cast my mind eight years further back, recalling what a tall man had said to me about what lies between an Oriental girl's legs, and how I had run from him without offering a word in response.

"And the phone calls?"

Raking his fingers through his hair, Eric tells me how she had wanted to call him at my house one night, how she had demanded my number and how he had refused to give it to her. He says that he had hoped it had all blown over, until one afternoon, weeks later, he answered my phone, and it was her. "I don't know how she got your number, and I don't know what she was thinking. I don't think she knew, herself," he says. For the first time he looks troubled, the lines around his mouth drawn, and his hair, unsettled by his fingers, falling unregarded over one eye. "I knew I should have told you then, but I kept hoping it would just blow over, and she would find someone else. . . . I'm sorry, Kiki."

"Did you sleep with her after you met me, too?" I say, the steadiness of my voice a minor miracle.

"No. Well, yes. Just one night. Remember when you called me last week to make up with me, and I wasn't home? That night," he says, and adds quickly, "But that wasn't all my fault. You've got to take into account how I was feeling—I take you shopping for an engagement ring, and you burst into tears right in the store."

I look at him in disbelief for a few moments, and then I close my eyes, forcing myself to slow my breathing, but when I open them and look again at Eric, my breathing quickens all over again: while he avoids my gaze, his face is not burning red with shame.

I want to throw a shoe at him, something considerably heavier and sharper than a loafer—a boot with high heels and buckles, perhaps. Then, when he goes on to tell me, speaking quickly in prime argumentative mode, that he cannot have an Asian-woman fetish because it was she who first made a move on him, I begin thinking about the satisfying crack of metal against bone. I scout the room for possibilities: the pokers by the fireplace, my cast-iron bookends, and the tall lamp that stands in the corner of the room.

"Besides," he continues, oblivious to the danger he is in, engrossed in the same subject, "I can't have a fetish, because I don't even think she's pretty. Her hair's stringy, her face is plain, and she's way too skinny."

"That's what it means to have a fetish," I say, snapping. "You want to sleep with her, even if you don't think she's attractive, even if—what's far, far worse—she's stalking me over the phone."

We stare at each other, yet I am still the only one who is breathing hard.

"You should have told me about the phone calls as soon as you had an inkling," I tell him. "And how come you didn't tell me you were seeing someone else when we met?"

Eric's words are irritatingly reasonable, and his voice is maddeningly calm. "I just didn't think it was worth mentioning. Why should we get into all that, just after we met, and unnecessarily complicate everything? What I had with Terry had nothing to do with you."

We argue, or is it only talk, in loops, circling and circling back, only sometimes moving a little farther away.

"Were you at least planning to tell me about it at some point?"

"Yes," he says decisively, and then he shakes his head and gives a rueful half-smile, one that would be disarming in any other context. "At some point far-off in the future, anyway. Maybe when we were old and married, with a dog and a mortgage and two children, and we could laugh at it together."

His last phrase hangs in the air between us, and I think back to the first time that we met, the laughter we shared in the darkness a little more than a year ago. His mind must have traveled the same route, because he looks squarely at me and says, "I liked her all right, and who knows? Maybe it would have gone somewhere eventually, but then I met you, Kiki, and it might sound callous but she went clean out of my head." He rubs the back of his neck with his hand, and suddenly asks, "Do you remember the first time we met?"

I shrug. "Sure."

He slips off the sofa to sit on the ground, his legs slightly bent in front of him. "You were late getting back from the intermission, and had to walk by me to get in—"

"Do we have to get into this now?"

"—and you stepped on my foot," he says with fondness. "Do you remember that?"

I shake my head.

"And then your purse got caught on the armrest so you were stuck, wrestling with it and blocking my view completely, for almost a full minute," he continues, inching closer towards me.

"I don't remember that, either."

"Your hair got in my face and made me sneeze."

"Oh," I say. "Well. So much for great beginnings."

"But it was. You sat there shredding your program to bits without even realizing it. You were completely out of it—almost otherworldly, and I thought, if someone doesn't pin that girl down, she's going to float away into the sky, never to be seen by any mortal again." He takes a deep breath and looks down at his knees. "I wanted to take care of you, to protect you—and maybe it sounds awful, but I wanted you to notice me. There was something about you—you were so klutzy and—and fragile, somehow. And beautiful, too, of course," he adds.

"And Terry?"

"I told her about you right away. Honestly, I didn't think she'd care.

We weren't all that serious, and I knew she was seeing other people at the time. But she was terribly upset about it anyway, whether or not she had a right to be."

Eric is sitting beside me on the couch now, his body close though not quite touching.

I try to close my mind off, but the images I have been fighting flash in anyway, in glorious Technicolor and unwanted detail: the two of them entwined and kissing on a leather armchair, half-dressed and writhing on a gray carpet, and naked and straining in his bed. His face transformed with lust, the vein on his forehead enlarged, and those long, rounded calves in flesh-colored stockings, with the run crawling upwards from her heel.

He reaches out a hand and places it on my knee. His touch makes me shiver; I do not know whether from disgust or desire. "I know that what I did was wrong," he tells me, "but you drove me to her."

"I drove you to her," I say slowly. "I drove you to her?"

"You did," he says. "With all that talk about Phillip. The first time I was with her you had just been—"

"The first time?" I ask. "I thought you said it had only happened once?"

"Okay," he says. "You might as well know. I was with her one other time, maybe a month after you and I started sleeping together, but that was it, I swear it."

"You asshole," I say with fervor, and I bend my head down, my hair a curtain for my face.

"Look," he says. "I know I don't have any right to the high moral ground here. And I'm not asking for it. But you haven't been easy to deal with—it actually all started because I was jealous of you."

"Jealous of me," I say, for I have been transformed into an echo. "You were jealous of me."

"Wait. Listen to me first. I did cheat on you, but it was revenge. I couldn't bear it anymore, all that mooning over Phillip."

His palm, resting on my knee, is beginning to feel both heavy and sticky: an unpleasant sensation.

"It was not just about revenge," I say. "Take some responsibility, and stop blaming me for what you did."

"Just listen to me for a second," he says. As I reluctantly nod, he begins explaining: "It happened at a low point in our relationship, when I was starting to think you weren't ever going to get over Phillip, and then my team got sent to Pittsburgh on that case, remember? She went, too, and—"

You lying, cheating bastard, I think. You coward, you conceited fool.

"—I tried to call, but—" He breaks off. "Why are you looking at me like that?"

"I don't know how I'm looking at you."

"I don't know, either. . . . Talk to me," he says, his face growing paler before my eyes. "What are you thinking of when you look at me like that?"

"You're a bastard for having cheated, and a coward for having lied." I sound all right, I think, but when I slap his hand off my knee, I find my hands are shaking, and I sit on them both, hard.

His eyes are a little out of focus when he looks at me, and it takes him a while to answer. "I guess I deserve that."

After due consideration, I have come to the decision that with my aim, throwing a bookend at him is not enough punishment. Nor is it enough contact.

I want to punch him, fist against face, in the same way that my father beat up my mother at night, leaving purple circles around the eyes, swollen lips, bruised cheeks, and traces of blood that have to be scrubbed out of blouses with cold water in the morning.

Minutes pass in silence.

We sit apart from each other on opposite ends of the couch. As hunched over as Phillip ever was, Eric sinks his head into his neck; his legs sprawl open. My knees are curled to my chest, with my arms encircling them so that my body forms a tight ball.

"Are we going to get over this?" he says. His words wobble, and his voice breaks at the end; when I glance over at him, I see that his face is, finally, deeply flushed.

"No matter what, it's going to take a lot of time," I say, warning him. "And I might never get over it completely. But I'll try."

"Thank you," he says.

I nod curtly.

I know about a few of Eric's past lovers in a general way: his college girlfriend, Sylvia, raven-haired, ambitious, and mathematical, addicted to soap operas, the *Wall Street Journal,* and calculus; and voluptuous Elena, a gymnast and law student from Kiev, who could weave her arms around her well-contoured bottom in a way that defied belief— attachments born of a healthy sexual attraction, a trajectory of desire that rose and climaxed and ultimately fell. Those were relationships I could understand. But Theresa Chan is a pull that falls in another category, a threat so immediate I can taste its bitterness on the tip of my tongue.

The thought of her hovers in the background as I uncoil myself from my tight ball and lean towards Eric, who has one hand over his face, hiding his eyes. The run in her stockings is in my mind as I take hold of his wrist and lead him, wide-eyed now, and at first reluctant, to bed. I undress him slowly, and then quickly shed my own clothes. I hold his gaze as I climb on top of him with deliberation, more excited than I ever have been in my life. She is there as I watch his face grow stern, the vein on his forehead swell and, finally, his eyes close.

Grandmother, I will say. *Obaasama.* When you worked as a geisha, did you ever wrap your legs around a man and drain from him pleasure, feeling all the while as if you could kill?

When it is over, Eric closes his eyes again for a long moment. "Jesus," he whispers, drawling out the word: it is a prayer.

Lying flat on my back beside him, the expanse of the bed stretching out between us, I choke back a wave of hysteria, and wish in vain for someone to share the joke: that I had been wrong in doubting Phillip and his love for me; wrong, too, in trusting in Eric and his devotion, but right, all along (in the most minor and bitter of all possible triumphs), in guessing at Eric's fascination with yellow-tinted skin and thin black eyes.

CHAPTER TWENTY-FOUR

As she neared the end of her sixty-seventh year, my grandmother Yukiko found herself slipping into a forgetfulness that was itself both easy and delicious to forget. Names and faces slipped away from her, leaving her bluffing on the sidewalk or stammering over the phone. She misplaced keys, letters, books, half-finished cups of tepid tea, bowls of steaming rice and even, on one occasion, her new car, which she had driven out to the city and then forgotten, taking the subway, a train, and then a cab back, as she was used to doing. Worse still, while deep in search of something precious, on her hands and creaky knees, her head bent as she craned to see under the sofa or the bed, her papers and the furniture around her in disarray, she was apt to realize that she had forgotten what she had lost in the first place.

Yet as her grasp on the life around her crept stealthily away, her memory of the past rose up to embrace and console her as tenderly as a mother. The sights, sounds, and smells of her childhood, even those once believed long lost, returned to her with a clarity that astonished: the calls of her brothers as they played up in the trees, the milky eyes of the lord who owned them, her new breasts turned buoyant in the bath, the smell of grass that heralded the start of the long summers of the north, and the silken sound of her mother's lisping whisper.

She remembered, too, the men whose saké-soaked breath she some-times enjoyed and more often endured, and a flat-footed young man walking through the dust to the geisha house for the first time. She re-membered the baby whose ashes were shut in an urn, and the others who shot up like bamboo, the pressure of her children's bodies as they crouched beside her in the bomb shelter, and the almost-chicken flavor of the grasshoppers they caught in the rice fields. She remembered her lovely, heavy kimonos, their long sleeves billowing as they dried in the wind.

The authority of the past, and the newfound serenity and affection with which she reviewed it, was such that she almost did not care about the changes that had stolen over her body. Her hair, once so thick and full, had thinned and was tinged with gray. The breasts that had once shamed her with their size were sagging heavily now, while her ankles and wrists were thin as sticks, and almost as fragile. On rainy days, her bones ached. The only change that truly grieved her, however, was the thickness of her waist and hips, padding that she could not lose no matter how she tried. Still, she held herself upright as ever, with all of the self-consciousness of beauty intact, the careless bearing and impe-rious eyes of a woman who takes admiration for granted.

It was the most peaceful time of her life, and one rendered sweet by the fact that she shared it with her husband. They spent a lot of time re-minding each other, usually to scant avail, of the numerous pills they had to take, preventive measures for the host of largely nonfatal ills that came hand in hand with their age. Neither of them slept much anymore, his old-age sleeplessness having finally caught up with her perennial insomnia, and they sat far into the night at the dining-room table, he studying the market at one end, she scratching away with her fountain pen in the middle. Their far sight grew keener as their near vision dimmed, so that they held their books and papers increasingly farther away from their eyes as they read. One autumn they made back-to-back appointments and acquired spectacles, thin pieces of steel and half-moon glass that they spent more time searching for than using.

Despite the two years that separated them, Yukiko and Sekiguchi seemed so close in age that it came as a shock to them both when he gave in during the winter of his seventy-third year to a mild, local variety of flu, and emerged a week later looking old. For some years, it was true, he as well as Yukiko had been teetering on the brink of old age, but the suddenness of his plunge, as well as the depth of it, took them by surprise.

Once begun, his decline proceeded rapidly. Although his good eye remained beady and bright, his bad one swelled until it was almost shut, and his left leg often could not bear him up at all. Soon he could no longer sit up on some mornings. The doctors were perplexed. Bowing their apologies, they could only say that it was as if the smallpox that had almost killed him as a boy was now determined to carry him to his death.

Stubbornly Sekiguchi insisted on keeping his job, and Yukiko encouraged him in this. On the days he remained home, sullen and bad-tempered with his pain, she sat by the bed and teased him lightheartedly about being an old bear. When he dropped off to sleep beside her, she never stayed to watch over him, but ran errands or wrote, or took naps in the baths that were her primary indulgence. The wives of his friends whispered of what seemed to be her indifference, and possibly even a desire to speed him to his death. Even the neighborhood women, who had come to tolerate if not accept her, began to say that now that Sekiguchi was reliant on her, she was finally letting her geisha heart show.

In the village where they lived, just a half-hour commute from Tokyo, the people still talk of his death. The medical report stated that Sekiguchi was killed by complications arising from the blow to his head. At least there is that, the thought that he died fast. They had to sift through the ashes to find his body, but while his hair was singed away, only his right elbow was burned, and not even too badly: nothing worse than what an iron could do to you, or a hot stove.

He died on a cool dry night in June, a mere three days short of the monsoon season. A small earthquake, just large enough to set a paper cup rolling, began an electrical fire in their house. At the time there was a brisk breeze blowing, and this fanned the flame into ravenous life. A good fifteen minutes passed before the fire department was notified, and by then the house was already doomed.

It seemed certain that both Sekiguchi and Yukiko were already dead, having suffocated from the smoke in their sleep or, at the worst, been burned alive. The eastern side of the house, which included the master bedroom, was already engulfed in flames. The light timber that made up the house burned well, and even as the firefighters arrived, part of the wall collapsed with a dispersal of sparks that looked like fireworks. All the firefighters could do was make sure that the flames did not spread to the northern side of the house, where Yukiko's study and the bath-house were located, and beyond which lay the servants' quarters, separated from the main house by a few yards. Not all the men were needed to ensure this, and the others joined the neighbors and the handful of old servants, huddling in their kimonos and nightgowns, who were gathered around the fire with their arms folded, and their faces reflecting the flicker of the fire.

It was the youngest maidservant, a mere fifty-seven years old, who heard the singing first. She called out to the others to listen, but her voice was thin and weedy, and only those standing immediately beside her heard. The singing came from her left, and the maidservant guessed that Yukiko had been caught in the bathhouse, which is in fact what had happened. Yukiko never could rest easy after an earthquake.

My grandmother is, of course, a lousy singer. She has a fair sense of rhythm, which had helped her as a dancer, but when she sings, her voice, like mine, strays in and out of tune. Naturally low, her voice was also husky with age by then, and she was surrounded by a raging fire. Yet one by one the crowd fell silent, straining to hear. The song was so faint that the youngest maidservant would have thought she dreamed it, were it not for the others listening around her.

Yukiko sang an old folk love song, and at the end of each verse, she called out Sekiguchi's name. There was always a pause before she began the next verse, and as they listened, the women of the neighborhood, who had whiled away the afternoons gossiping about Yukiko's cold geisha heart, bowed their heads in shame, knowing they had slandered her.

The smoke was so thick that many among the crowd were

coughing. Still the voice continued, tuneless but serene. When almost half of the roof caved in, all knew that the destruction of the bedroom was complete, and they held their breath, waiting, until the voice came through again, weaker now, but still clear. Unconsciously they shuffled forward. The heat warmed the frail bones of the old servants, and reddened their cheeks as if they were young again.

The voice receded slowly, ebbing in and out of reach like the tide. Sometimes the wind, dying now, would float a wisp of song towards the crowd, until at last the voice came so faintly and so infrequently that they knew they had wished it into being. Inwardly they sighed about the growing stillness of the air, as if it were the wind and not the heart of the singer that had failed them.

Almost twenty more minutes passed before all the flames were extinguished. Through the efforts of the fire department, the servants' quarters and Yukiko's study as well as the bathhouse were spared.

They say that for a long time afterwards, the crowd remained at the house, swaying a little as they waited among the embers, their bodies leaning forward as if they still strained to hear.

The fire took Yukiko's kimonos, Sekiguchi's books, their antiques, and their home. Stored in the tea box where she once kept her hair, more than half of the nine volumes of Yukiko's diaries survived. My mother read what was left of them, but she had to guess at the pieces that were missing, and so sew together her mother's life with scraps from her own. It is a job that I have continued. The bedtime stories that my mother told me have become hers and mine as well as Yukiko's, and protected by the tea box that came from her, they are a legacy from my great-grandmother, too.

When the firefighters were finally able to break through to the bathhouse, they found Yukiko lying on the ground with her eyes wide open and alert, and it seemed that the only damage she had sustained were a few minor cuts and bruises on her face and arms. But she was silent when they asked her questions, and they eventually came to the conclu-sion that the trauma had made her mute.

She was laid on a stretcher and carried into a waiting ambulance, and as the number of miles between her and the smoldering remains of her house grew, she began to wonder if her forgetfulness would one day take from her the memory of this night, too. She did not talk for the re-mainder of the night and through all of the next day, and it was not until the following morning, when she lay gazing up at the white ceiling of her hospital room, that she finally let out a cry, for she had suddenly known that her forgetfulness would not erase from her memory that hour that she spent trapped inside the bathhouse, and the slow dying of her hopes for the husband she still longed to hold.

CHAPTER TWENTY-FIVE

ALTHOUGH THE BALLOONS still make my bedroom a riot of colors, while they once were smooth and shiny, they now are shriveled and dull. Littering the floor, they rustle and roll in the dust, and we cannot walk anywhere without kicking at least a few; nudged by our feet, they take off briefly and clumsily before falling and hitting the earth again. Just three days ago, only the ceiling prevented them from floating away to indefinite heights. Now sedately and prudently they refuse to leave the ground; if the floor were removed from beneath them, they would indifferently drift down to the bottom of the earth, dragged to the depths by their own weight. In another three days or so, they will wither away into pieces of colored rubber, just as they were at first, and it seems as if nothing will last forever.

"There are so many of them," I say to Eric as I join him in the living room. He is reading briefs; I am on the last few pages of a Virginia Woolf novel.

"Fifty-two, to be exact," he tells me. "The store was offering a baker's dozen deal, so I got fifty-two for the price of forty-eight. Quite a bargain, don't you think?"

"There are only fifty now. I gave two away to Mrs. Noffz—I hope you don't mind."

"Mrs. Who? Oh, of course, your batty old neighbor." One morning a few months back, when Eric was tiptoeing out of my apartment and quietly easing the door shut behind him so he could leave for work without waking me, Mrs. Noffz scared him half to death by creeping up behind him and commenting loudly on the odds against a snowfall in May. To this day, Eric swears that she made a reference to "an Indian winter," but I tend to think that he made that part up: Mrs. Noffz does not dabble in word play, and her English mistakes are problems of pronunciation rather than vocabulary.

"I wish you wouldn't call her batty," I say. "She's really rather sweet."

"Hold it right there," he says. "Just last week you were making fun of her, too. What makes you so self-righteous all of a sudden?"

"I always liked her. I guess I started feeling guilty about being mean to her behind her back."

"I suppose you're right. We shouldn't make fun of the poor old thing. After all, think how lonely and miserable her life is," he says, shuddering.

He is making a special effort to be agreeable, as he has been for the past five days, ever since we argued about Theresa Chan; our life together has been unwontedly smooth of late. Today, though, I am feeling terribly contradictory. "I don't think her life is so bad," I tell him. "And I don't think she's particularly lonely."

He snorts with laughter. "Kiki, be serious. The woman doesn't do anything. My grandmother might not be running marathons, but she plays bingo at the club and she gets a big kick out of game shows and soap operas, and in three months she's moving to Florida, where the family will go to visit her at least once a year. Didn't you tell me that Mrs. Noffz doesn't even own a television?"

"Her parrot gets nervous around radioactivity," I explain.

"Let me recap here: the woman has no job, no visible family, apparently no friends other than that droopy bird, and nothing but the weather to keep her occupied. According to you, she hardly ever leaves the apartment. What kind of life is that? I would call it a supremely pathetic existence, and that's almost an understatement."

"I don't leave my apartment very much."

"Come on, you two are apples and oranges. Mrs. N. is an old lady who has nothing to do. It just so happens that you like to study and work at home, and you have a brilliant career and years and years of life and happiness still ahead of you, and of course," he says with a self-mocking smirk, "of course you have me. To wit: romance, a love interest, a socially endorsed sexual release and potential source of 2.2 babies in the tried-and-true American fashion. Speaking of which"—he leans forward and grabs my hand—"let's adjourn to your bedroom and commence making some 2.2 right now."

I gently pull my hand away. "I don't think Mrs. Noffz would be any happier if she had a boyfriend or 2.2 babies."

He is beginning to lose patience. "You mean she wouldn't be any less unhappy. Well, you may be right there. But Mrs. N. is a crazy dried-up old woman whose virginity is probably still intact. What do you want to bet that she calls herself 'Mrs.' solely for the sake of status?"

With difficulty I manage to keep my tone light. "Not for the sake of status," I say. "She would never do that. I'll bet you anything you want."

"All right, maybe not. But why is she so damn concerned about the weather when she never goes outside? The whole apartment building has heating, and she does have an air conditioner, doesn't she?"

I hazard a guess. "Because it gives her some contact with the outside world?"

"But that's exactly what I'm trying to tell you. She has no contact with the outside world. If you never go outside, what's the point of worrying about the weather?"

"She has to go out to buy food," I say.

Eric is warming to his subject. "She's so tiny that I'm sure she eats practically nothing at all. Even with her bird to feed, she probably doesn't have to go shopping more than once a week, tops."

"She takes walks." I am feeling defensive.

"In any event, it probably has been years since anybody gave her a present, so it was charitable of you to give her a few balloons. She's almost certainly dying of loneliness. I know I would be, if I were in her situation—God forbid."

"I don't think she's lonely."

He stares. "How can you say that when the woman stalks you just so she can chat to you about the weather?"

"I know," I say. "But at the same time I don't know . . . it seems to me she's being polite more than anything else. I don't think she's actually hungry for human companionship. I'm just one of her daily rituals—she feeds her parrot and she checks out the weather and she chats with her neighbor." I am tired and cross and so I try to instill a note of finality into my next comment. "Oh well, I guess you don't know her as well as I do."

"No," he says, "thank God I don't, but it is sweet of you to care about her so much."

We smile at each other and then we return to our reading. The subject is closed, yet for some time afterwards I continue to think about Mrs. Noffz and the spareness of her life, honed down to the basics over the years: sleeping, eating, feeding her parrot, watching the changes of the seasons through the safety of her window, maybe taking out a tired old memory and hugging it to herself in the comforting quiet of the late afternoon, living with the vagaries of the weather and the humors of Mabel as her sole worries.

I glance over at Eric, studiously flipping through the pages of a brief, and remember once again how Phillip had said that on her mantelpiece Mrs. Noffz keeps a photograph of her and a friend. The two of them wear identical hats; so floppy and wide are the brims that their faces, cast in the shade, are equally hard to tell apart.

When my grandmother Yukiko comes to visit the big city, I will introduce her to Mrs. Noffz on our way out. Down in the lobby I will make sure my grandmother's coat as well as my own is buttoned to the top, and then we will pause for a moment at the door, bracing ourselves for the briskness of the wind, the shrunken but upright figure of Mrs. Noffz still in our thoughts.

Obaasama, I will say (tucking her arm under mine), you know firsthand, don't you, the twisting, downhill paths that lead to such a life.

With Eric striving for harmony in the household, life proceeds in a fashion that I have dubbed contentment, real-life style. While a far cry from the bodice-ripper ups and downs that I knew with Phillip, when I felt as if my very knuckles hummed with life, this existence is not a bad one: the worst that can be said is that I sometimes feel as if I am half-asleep, and that I cannot be bothered to rouse myself. But then again, perhaps this feeling arises because I am living out a dream.

I like to think of this life that Eric and I have arrived at in terms of the ending that Jane Austen's heroines (those lively, slightly untamed girls) finally meet—not their success in romance and the marriage market, but rather the fate that awaits them beyond the margins of the book, after the last page is turned. A pleasant enough existence, no doubt, but hardly the stuff that drives narrative, or pulls in readers, or keeps everyone concerned fully awake.

In this state of sleepy contentment, it seems that Theresa Chan could actually add to our store of riches. For in spite of the occasional moments when I (my father's daughter, after all) snap awake with a desire to bash Eric's head in with an iron, I like the idea, if not the actuality, of dealing with a problem other than Phillip for a change. It was not so long ago that I thought that there would always be the same three people to consider in this relationship, as well as in this apartment.

Besides, Eric has contended with Phillip so patiently that I almost have no option but to try to forgive.

It is Tuesday, eight days since I got back together with Eric. Thinking to give my mother an account of recent events, I tried and tried to call her, but she (strolling the aisles of the Asian foodstore? flipping through the periodicals in the public library? catching a movie at the art cinema?) has not been at home, though I called her four times in three days. I was beginning to worry again, when I finally reached her yesterday. "I've been busy," was all she said in reply to my queries. I must have been irritated by her terseness, for I did not tell her after all how I cried when I went to Tiffany's with Eric, and of how he came back to me anyway.

The third week of August has begun, and Eric is taking a vacation from work. He has been spending it here with me. The apartment has been feeling smaller and smaller: usually I dread going anywhere beyond the familiar environs of the Upper West Side, yet today I am glad to get out, even if it is only for a visit to the gynecologist.

Although I told Eric I am going in for a standard checkup, I made the appointment with the doctor specifically in order to get tested for AIDS. When I once tentatively suggested to Eric that we both get tested, he looked at me incredulously for a second and then laughed as if he thought I was joking, so I decided not to bring up the subject with him again. Besides, at that point it was too late: if he had it, I did, too. This morning I woke up with an urgent need to know whether I was going to die soon because of the virus.

I have gotten tested three times before. The first time was in July, four years ago, one day before my mother had her first arthritis operation (a left shoulder replacement); the second was in September of the following year, two days before I arrived in New York to set up house by myself. I was tested the third time a year and a quarter ago, the day before my oral examinations.

I take a bus across the park to the gynecologist's office. To take the subway I would first have to go all the way downtown to Times Square, and then switch trains and directions, doubling back to climb uptown to the doctor's office. It bothers me that that route is so roundabout, even though it is still almost certainly faster than the bus. Phillip always fretted about the elephantine pace of buses, and the stops they make every couple of blocks, to let passengers on and off.

The gynecologist I go to is not, I think, a very good doctor, and he is quite definitely not a nice person. He is a terribly old man from an unidentified Eastern European country, and he tends to be brusque and even mean as he squints between my legs. Perhaps the only advantage in going to him is that he does not seem to have many other patients, so I can call him in the morning to schedule an appointment in the afternoon, as I did today. My mother consulted him when she was a newly married woman fresh off the plane from Japan, and she has continued seeing him ever since. She says that when she first met him, he was already terribly old, and she does not appreciate his rudeness any more than I do. Regardless, I doubt that she has ever considered looking for a new doctor: old attachments die hard on that side of my family.

The nurse is as indifferent to the ideals of serving humanity as the doctor. She, too, is old, probably nearing seventy. Her face is well lined and her hair iron-gray, and she wears far too much makeup, yet even that cannot disguise the delicacy and refinement of her bones. Her voice, nasal with a broad Brooklyn accent, comes as a disappointment, and so does her name. In the office, at least, she goes by the unlovely title of Nurse Maude, and it fails to do her justice to the extent that whenever I see her, I think of all the possible names her parents could and should have given her: Lilith, Cleopatra, Lolita. I do not like her, but if it turned out I had AIDS, she would make the perfect angel of death.

"How many people have you had sexual intercourse with since you were last tested?"

"Three."

"Did you use condoms?"

"No."

She stops writing. Disdainfully she gazes at me over the rim of her glasses, and then she takes them off.

"You are playing with fire, young lady."

"I like to live dangerously," I reply, or at least that is how I want to reply. Instead I am overwhelmed with guilt and I find myself senselessly apologizing to her.

"Don't apologize to me," she says crisply. "It's your life."

She puts her glasses on and adds a few more lines to my file. When I stand up to go, she does not return my good-bye.

I kiss Eric.

"It's like a real marriage with you coming back and me here, isn't it?" he says.

Trying to figure out what is wrong, I smile absently at him.

Something is different about the apartment. I look around, but all seems as it should—the crimson rug beneath the coffee table, the cushions scattered on the floor, Eric reading documents as he reclines on the sofa, his ankles crossed and his feet up higher than his head.

Yet even though the windows are half open, when I breathe in there is an unfamiliar odor in the air, a funny smell that tickles my nose and makes me feel like sneezing.

I think of reaching for the book by the phone but I am filled with vague feelings of dread, with terrifying presentiments of disaster. When I realize what is missing, I try hard to be casual.

"Eric?"

"What," he says. He does not look up.

"Eric," I say. "Eric, where are the moths?"

From where I stand, I can see that his eyes are not moving across the page. Yet he still does not look up from his document. "I got rid of them for you."

I take a long, deep breath. "You what?"

"I sprayed them with insecticide. Don't worry—I was extra careful about getting a spray that was safe for human beings."

"But—"

"But what?" He puts down the document with an abrupt gesture and gazes levelly into my eyes, challenging me. It seems clear that for now, at least, he is not concerned with trying to make it up to me for Theresa Chan.

I blink, and then I look away. "They were special moths. You know that."

"Kiki, Kiki, Kiki," he says, sighing and sitting up. "They were just common, run-of-the-mill moths."

"No, they weren't." I cannot bear, even, to look at him. "They were purple. I've never seen purple moths before."

He shakes his head and makes a sound that begins as a groan and ends on a laugh. "Christ," he says. "What are you—color-blind or crazy or both? They were just everyday gray moths, Kiki, maybe just a little larger than usual, but otherwise completely ordinary. Take a look again—they're in the trash can."

"I am not crazy," I tell him. "I just want to live in a world more beautiful than yours."

"What bullshit that is. There's only one world. There are different interpretations of it, of course, but there's only one world."

"Okay, fine," I say. "It's just a question of words. I'd rather live in a more beautiful interpretation than yours."

"Kiki, you're being an idiot. We're not going to talk about this anymore. I'm going to watch the news." He gets up and walks away, towards the bedroom. "They were just gray, a-dime-a-dozen moths, really."

"They were violet, and they glowed in the evening," I say, knowing how absurd that sounds but not caring, yet when I look in the trash can into which he has swept up their remains, I find that what he says is true: the moths are gray and ashen as death.

The evening is cool and soft. In silence we walk along Riverside Park to a restaurant, and we talk no more than is strictly necessary during the meal. I am aware of Eric glancing at me from time to time as we eat. After we get home, we read in separate rooms, and at around midnight I take a long bath by myself. I am brushing my wet hair in front of the dresser when he enters the bedroom. Barefoot, he makes little noise, but I see him coming up behind me in the mirror.

We are watching each other as he comes up behind me. His lips curve up in a little smile, and his eyes are humorously pleading. When he places his hands on my shoulders, I stop combing in midstroke, and the brush remains caught in my hair.

"Are you still sore about those moths?" Lightly he massages my shoulders and we look at ourselves, a couple, in the mirror. "Forget about them. You're silly to be so angry when I did it for you. I wanted to save your sweaters and your rugs before it was too late, and besides, I didn't like the way you were so attached to them. I mean, they're parasites, after all. Your attachment was—well, it was a little odd. I never thought you'd be this angry, though." His voice is gentle, and his reflected image is handsome and dignified as he stoops to kiss my neck; I force myself to smile when I see how sour and ungracious my countenance seems in comparison. "I don't really understand why you're making such a big deal about it," he adds.

Then I say what I should have said before, instead of babbling nonsense about special moths. "But it was none of your business." Simple and trite, these are the words I have come up with, repeatedly worked over, and mulled and remulled throughout the whole long evening, and they have the desired effect: Eric's self-assured smile slips, his eyes widen, and he apologizes.

Later, after sex, as we lie panting side by side on the bed, I tell myself that it is really only a problem of language.

Two more days in somnolent mode, and then on Thursday afternoon, a newspaper article on declining mortgage rates gets Eric started on one of his favorite topics.

"Think about it: we could have a cozy home in the suburbs, buy two cars, raise children. . . ."

I know he is only a quarter serious, so I usually tune him out when he talks about our future in the suburbs, but today I attempt to enter the fantasy with him. I envision him and me and the children, smiling with strained smiles in front of a cozy home, safely and neatly closed in by a white picket fence: a snapshot. Then I think of rows and rows of houses, completely the same save for the shade of paint, each with a man, a woman, and 2.2 children (the .2 only a pair of legs, cut off more or less in the center of the thigh) standing in front of it. Of course that is not really the future that Eric wants, even aside from the problem of our poor fraction of a child, but there is something in that image of rows and rows of families and houses, all identical, that cuts to the heart of my life with Eric.

With Phillip no longer a presence to distract me as I lie in Eric's arms, with this one major impediment to our everlasting happiness out of the way for good, I had assumed that life with Eric would be one long song. Yet instead it seems that Phillip (along with the reminder that he carried of the persistence of the past) prevented me not only from being completely with Eric, but also from regarding him with clear sight.

My eyes narrowed against the late-afternoon light, I look across the room at Eric, still rattling off mortgage rates, and I think back on that chance encounter at the concert hall, when I—all but sick from missing Phillip—mistook a handsome stranger's move to sit beside me as the predatory act of an Asian-woman stalker. I recall the walk afterwards through a light summer rain, under his umbrella. My birthday, when he cut his hand on a bottle that he had hid behind a bush in Central Park. Dinners in restaurants, fancy and small; walks through the streets at night; cab rides across town. The unexpected, impromptu proposal, which came with a glimpse at the hole in the heel of his sock. Long nights spent wrestling over sweat-dampened sheets, once with Phillip watching from the window.

I remember, too, Eric's squirming silences on the subject of the prank phone calls, and the neediness in him that drove him back to Theresa Chan, after I had cried when we went shopping for a ring. I recall the moths, and how I loved them; I picture the busy fingers that twine into my hair, ensnaring me so that I cannot escape from Eric's side at night.

I think of the feeling that I have had, that I have been half-asleep for the past ten days.

I had thought that what Eric and I had was a romance that could be preserved in celluloid. During these past thirteen months, when Phillip haunted me still, threatening, as I concluded so wrongly, to pull me deeper into the shadows of my apartment, Eric seemed a knight, always ready with his offer of shelter. He (with his two feet planted firmly in the outside world of offices and mortgage rates and law) was an anchor for me: I hitched a string around him and tied it to my ankle, and that was enough to prevent me, as he himself said, from floating away into the sky, never to be seen by any mortal again.

In this way, edging in sideways, I come to it, the recognition of a truth I had known all along, deep inside, without ever being able to put it into words. Phillip's appearances were never an obstacle to the blissful existence that I was fated to share with Eric. The fact that I missed Phillip, that I pined for him and mourned him so deeply that he returned to me, was, instead, the reason I began going out with Eric in the first place. If I had never met Phillip, then I would not have stayed with Eric for as long as I have.

Fully alert for the first time in days, I sit up. For once, the questions that drift through my mind have nothing to do with my grandmother. Will my mother think I am crazy for what I am about to do? Will she scorn me, or sigh with disappointment at the choice that I have made?

"Eric," I say, interrupting him as gently as possible. "Eric, I need to ask you a question."

Deep in his spiel, which has gone from mortgage rates to the price of fancy cars, Eric looks up, bewildered. The sunlight slants across his face, and makes him blink.

"Yeah? Have I sold you on the house yet?" He taps on the paper in front of him. "It does sound good, doesn't it. . . . Come into the kitchen with me—I want something cold to drink. Christ, it's hot. Even with the air conditioner on, I can't seem to get cool."

Following him to the counter, I sit down on one of the barstools. "Eric—"

"What?" he asks, deftly pulling out two glasses with one hand, and then opening the refrigerator and pulling out the milk carton with the other. "What do you want, iced tea?" I nod and he takes out the bottle while still holding on to everything else; the glasses clink together, but somehow he manages to place everything safely onto the countertop. He opens the freezer and takes out three ice cubes, which he drops smoothly into my glass.

"What is it?"

"I wanted to know whether you still want to marry me. Because I've been thinking we might want to reconsider, or at least hold off on announcing the engagement, and I thought you might be, too," I say, speaking quickly but clearly.

He passes me my tea and pours some milk out for himself. He regards me solemnly over the rim of the glass as he drinks. "Not this again," he says, after he has drained the glass and wiped the milk mustache off his face. "I thought we already took care of your doubts."

"This is different."

"How about we do this?" he asks. "How about we talk about this later, in a few hours or so—by which time you'll have changed your mind all over again."

With a few swift and sure movements, he puts the milk carton and the iced-tea bottle back into the refrigerator, and places his glass in the sink. Then he starts to walk away.

I swivel on my chair and speak to his retreating back. "I'm not going to change my mind."

Without stopping, he tosses a few words to me over his shoulder. "Tomorrow you'll be saying something different."

"No, this time I'm sure." Something in my voice holds him, and he turns slowly.

"We're going to be rational about this." He walks back towards me and sits down on a stool across the counter, so that we face each other. He takes a deep breath. "First of all, what have I done wrong? Or rather, what haven't I done right? Haven't I always been there for you? Haven't I always been patient and supportive?"

The image of a delicate face with arching eyebrows is only the briefest flash in my mind. "You've been great," I tell him.

"Well then," he says, ending the argument. "Just try to be somewhat normal, Kiki. A little rationality is all it takes." He stands up and stretches. "I know you can do it, too."

"We need to reconsider the engagement," I say again, stubbornly. The phrase hangs in the air between us, and I know, suddenly, that it is not only the engagement that will be ending, but our relationship, too.

"Why?" he asks, glaring at me now. "Is this about Phillip again—or rather, still? I knew I should have sent you to a therapist when I first heard about him, but I thought we could deal with it on our own—"

"No, it's not about Phillip. Or Theresa, either," I say slowly, thinking it through.

"Then what the hell is it about?"

I pick up my iced tea, in which the ice cubes have already melted away into slivers, and then I set it down again, untasted.

I want to tell Eric that I (believing that the key to happiness lay hidden in the maze of love stories that make up my family's past) had taken the lessons contained in my mother's and grandmother's lives too much to heart. I want to say that I had latched on to him in part because I had been terrified of turning into my mother, of growing old while mourning a man I could not have.

I would like to say to Eric that when he and I fought or disagreed, it had been too easy to dismiss the differences between us as growing out of the long shadow cast by Phillip's absence. That only now, with Phillip well and truly gone, can I say that Eric and I do not belong in the same story; that the narrative he has scripted and drafted me into is not what I would write.

He will be angry at the implication that I used him to avoid being like my mother; he will mock me, not unjustifiably, for thinking that our lives (those messy, sprawling things) could be compared to the neatly packaged form of a story in a book.

But I want to tender this explanation to him, so I do, albeit in a halting, roundabout way.

"I've been out of control of my life for so long," I say. "It might just be a question of timing, but I think I started going out with you too soon after Phillip died. Everything happened too fast. And now that I'm truly over Phillip—"

"You used me just to get over Phillip, and now that you're over him, you just—"

"That's not true," I say, cutting in. "Or at least I never meant to use you, anyway. But I do think I got together with you for all the wrong reasons."

He gestures grandly for me to continue.

"I got together with you because I didn't want to be like my mother, mourning a lost love forever. And that's not enough of a reason for us to stay together."

"In case you forgot," he says, breaking in with some impatience, "that was over a year ago."

"I know," I tell him unhappily. "But there's also the fact that for pretty much this entire year, whenever we fought, I always figured— and I think you did, too—that the disagreement had something to do with Phillip. And now that we can't blame Phillip anymore for all of our problems, it's a lot harder to ignore that you and I don't really have that much in common."

For a moment there is a look of understanding on his face, and his head inclines in what is an almost imperceptible, perhaps even unconscious nod of acknowledgment.

A rare breeze, probably off the river, bats against the window, then, and makes us both turn. Eric reaches over and opens the window a crack, the muscles in his forearms flexing as he pulls. While warm, the wind is a welcome relief from the stillness of the air. It steals into the room and picks at the sleeves of Eric's T-shirt, and tries to lift the napkins that lie in a heap upon the counter. It winds itself around us like a cat.

247

Refreshing though the breeze is, when Eric turns back from the window, his face is once again stern. He shakes his head vigorously, so that his unruly lock of hair falls loose, and hangs in front of his eyes. His voice, when he begins speaking, is clenched with anger, like a fist. "You've never appreciated me. I've always been there for you, or at least I've tried to be. You never bother to remember how I held you when you were sad about Phillip, how I stayed awake and rocked you until you slept."

"That's not true," I say. My voice cracks, and I will myself not to cry.

"Dammit, tell me the truth," he says, yelling now, "admit it: you forgot about all those times, didn't you?"

"I didn't forget," I say, pleading, hoping, but at the same time doubting that he will believe me. "I will never forget," I add in a whisper: it is a promise, made as much to myself as to him.

A long pause, during which I realize I can no longer hear him breathing. I never did caution him against his habit of holding in his breath.

"We belong in different stories. We want different things in life. It's not right between us—it never has been," I say, and then on a sudden impulse I ask, "You know that just as well as I do, really, don't you?"

He looks up sharply at this question, but does not deny it. "People change," is all he says.

Doused in the glow of the late sun, we face each other across the kitchen counter.

"Once I walk out of here, I will never come back to you again," he warns. When I do not respond, he continues, "You're going to regret this."

"Maybe," I say. "Probably. But I know we'll both regret it more if we go ahead and get married."

As he nods, once again I see it: the acknowledgment of the truth of my words, passing like a ripple over his face.

"That's it, then?"

"That's it," I say, and for once my voice rings loud and clear.

He stands and goes back towards the living room. Stooping to gather together his papers, he walks to his briefcase. He puts his papers away carefully, stacking them into a neat pile, lining up the edges so they will not crease. After closing his briefcase, he, the man with the most agile fingers that I have ever seen, fumbles with the latch on it for a long time, so long that I step forward to help him. But just before I reach him, the latch closes with a snap, and he picks up his briefcase and turns. Only then do I learn the reason for the failure of his fingers, usually so capable and sure: Eric is blinded by his tears.

He drops his briefcase, sinks into the nearest chair, and covers his face. Except in movies I have never seen a grown man cry before, and Eric cries with messy racking sobs and lots of noise, as I do. I remain still, momentarily too shocked to move.

For the second time in the hour, I find myself thinking of my mother. After my father left us, she shut me out of her life for years. So now I know, firsthand, how she came to do so. Mourning Phillip, I placed myself in the center of the universe, and moved forward without bothering to see that others lay in my path.

I walk over to Eric and crouch beside him. When I clasp my arms around him, he does not push me away. Eventually my touch quiets him, as so often his has quieted me.

Soon he is only sniffling, then he is rubbing his eyes dry. His shoulders slump in a defeated way. He takes my hand and spreads it out and examines it as if he has never seen it before, even though it has caressed the secret parts of his body hundreds of nights, thousands of times.

"I hope to God," he says, drawing in a deep, shuddering breath, "I hope to God that you don't end up wasting your whole life."

It takes me a second to realize that he means these words well. I try but I cannot find the words to respond in kind, and so I am silent as he stands and once again picks up his briefcase. Like a little boy he wipes the back of his hand against his runny nose, yet he is every inch a man. He looks into my eyes, but he is looking right through me as if I had stopped existing, and I can tell that he does not want to see me ever again.

He gets up and walks to the front door; he opens it and turns. I am still standing by his empty chair. "I'll be seeing you, Kiki," he says, debonair in his sarcasm.

"I wish you well with your life," I say, finally finding my tongue, but I am speaking to the door, pulled shut so quietly behind him.

....

Obaasama, I will say. Grandmother, dear, is there ever an easy way to say good-bye?

Then I will kneel on the floor at her feet, and I will place my head on her lap. She will place her fingers (so long, says my mother, and so cool) upon my head, and she will rock me and fold me to her as I cry like a child.

CHAPTER TWENTY-SIX

I SPEND ALL my Labor Day weekends with my mother and we celebrate them faithfully, not with visits to the beach or barbecues but in our own way, with one special dinner in the middle of the holiday. This morning, as I showered, dressed, and packed a bag of clothes and books, I felt almost pleasantly adrift in that tinge of melancholy that accompanies these weekends. Even now the mood is still with me, only slightly tarnished by the wait at Penn Station.

Really this day should have brought me nothing but dread, since I have not yet told my mother about Eric, letting her know instead only that he would not, after all, be coming home with me this weekend. I can think of no easy way to break the news to her. Still, as I sit in the train now, watching the view from my window get steadily greener as New York City slips farther and farther away, dread is the last thing I feel.

These Labor Day weekends with my mother are tinged with melancholy not only because they carry with them the earliest hints of an ending, the sense that nature is beginning to shut itself down, that the leaves are beginning to fall, the flowers are turning to seed, and the hours of sunlight are lessening with every passing day; rather they are so because the thought of saying good-bye always rests heavy at least on my mind. Even now, when I no longer spend my summers with my mother, the academic schedule has been a part of my life for so long that I cannot help but think of this first weekend in September as the last time that I will see her for months.

It is odd, perhaps, given how far apart we have grown, given how all our conversations skid lightly across the surface of our lives, that my throat still tightens when I say good-bye to my mother, but she is so very frail, and so very alone in her quiet home filled with beautiful things.

That I have been feeling buoyed today in spite of this sadness is probably due to the fact that I woke today with the comforting sense that I can see, albeit only dimly, the contours of the rest of my life. The job prospects for English Ph.D.'s these days being what they are, I will probably not get a job after finishing my dissertation. Then I will move back home with my mother and my grandmother and we will all live together, three generations of women, under one roof, and these Labor Day weekends will be shaded with melancholy only because they bring with them the first signs of autumn.

Since Eric left, I have been dusting myself off and checking for bruises and broken bones, as after a fall.

Mostly I have been reading to pass the time. Eight days ago, on the evening that he and I parted ways, I reread my favorite parts of *Love in the Time of Cholera*. I did not wake up until the middle of the afternoon on Friday, and then I lay in bed for almost an hour without moving. After I got up I collected all of the balloons into a black garbage bag. It had taken three trips in a packed elevator to bring them up to my apartment, but by Friday the balloons were so shrunken they all fit into the bag with room to spare. I went to the living room and emptied the trash from the wastepaper basket into the space that was remaining. Covering the bright colors of the balloons, the gray moths fell out in a seemingly endless flurry: I had not known how many there were until I saw them dead. Afterwards the bag was full but very light. I took it out into the hall and left it in the pile with the other garbage, and I spent the rest of the day reading T. S. Eliot.

On Saturday I left the apartment building for the first time since Eric's departure. While sitting on a bench in the park, I noticed a few ants crawling inside a potato-chips bag. Almost without thinking I reached out and squeezed two of them to death between my printless index finger and thumb. I regretted my action afterwards, and would have brought them back to life if I could. They had far more of a right to be there than I did.

I spent all of Sunday at the library, working on my dissertation. On my way home I saw Russia looking into the window of the liquor store on West 115th Street. I had not seen her at all throughout the summer, and I had not had a real conversation with her for more than half a year, but I went up to her and stood at her side. "Hi."

She wheeled around, and looked startled when she saw me. "Oh, hi."

"It's good to see you," I said. "It's been such a long time. Where have you been?"

"Oh, I've been around." She laughed a little awkwardly. "You know me, I'm always around, aimlessly flitting through these streets."

"That's funny. I feel like I never see you."

"Yes, well, I see you. I wave and once or twice I even call out to you, but you never notice."

"Oh." I did not know what to say.

"Don't worry," she said. "I don't take it personally. I know how you live in your own little world."

She had said something very close to that on the night I met Phillip. "I'm sorry I didn't return your calls last winter," I blurted out abruptly. "I know it was a long time ago, but I never did apologize—"

"I had an inkling of what you were going through. It's okay." For a while we stood and looked at each other, her hands thrust casually into the back pockets of her jeans, mine hanging on to the straps of my knapsack. Then she turned and looked into the window again. "Hey, I love this cat, don't you?"

Curled among the bottles was a sleeping black cat. "I don't know," I said. "I've never seen him before."

"Really? He's out here all the time, and look—they even have a huge photo of him." She pointed out the photo and I dutifully admired it, and she also showed me how there was a picture of the cat painted on the awning of the shop. We agreed that the store owners must be very special people.

"Kiki," she said suddenly, "are you doing anything on Friday? I'm having some friends over for dinner. Actually," she corrected herself, "*we're* having some friends over. Do you remember Alex from Comp Lit? We started going out in February, and we moved into a place together just last week."

"Oh," I said. "That's great. Congratulations."

She smiled. "Thanks. It's a bit scary, you know, but so far it's been going really well. Anyway, can you come by? I'd love for you and Alex to be friends."

She had a heart of gold and I had always known it. She did not hate me because I took Phillip away and I had always known that, too. It was with something approaching regret that I shook my head. "I can't make Friday," I said. "I'm going home this weekend."

"Oh. That's too bad," she said. "Well, maybe another time."

"I'd like that," I said politely.

"Good. Well, I should be going."

"Me too."

"I'll see you around."

"Bye," I said.

Neither of us moved. For the second time we gazed at each other in silence beneath the spare shade of the shop's awning. There was a moment when I thought she was going to say something, but she did not, and then I reached out and clutched her in my arms.

I had forgotten how much I loved Russia's hugs, which are quick and so hard I can feel all her bones.

When I woke up on Monday, I discovered that I had developed a tic under my right eye. It bothered me as I called up the gynecologist's office and waited to find out the results of my blood test, and then it disappeared. That evening I celebrated my AIDS-free status by ignoring the pain in my tendon and successfully completing a seven-and-a-half-mile run.

Mrs. Noffz and I talk more often than we used to. On Tuesday evening, when I heard her keys clinking in the lock of her door, I went out to the hallway and we shared our thoughts on the possibility of more rain. I found myself smiling without strain when she came out to talk to me on Wednesday, just as I was off to buy some iced tea. For the rest of the day, I periodically caught myself listening for her as I passed my front door.

Last night as I was reading on the sofa, I looked up and saw a lone moth fluttering in the light. For a second I looked up at it with hope, and then I saw that it was just a common gray moth, blind and blundering and stupid. As I read, it luxuriated in the warm glow of the lamp. Finally I put out the light, and after a long time it found its way out the open window and flew away into the night.

Now today, throughout the morning and early afternoon, I had floated on a sure sense that life would finally stop offering me unwelcome surprises. Yet my confidence was misplaced, it seems, for when I am sitting on the porch with my mother, after the flurry at the station and the drive back home, after I dropped my bags off in the room I still have and she brings out the tea, what she says makes the smile on my face freeze, and the pleasant breeziness of the day seem suddenly chill.

"Do you want the good news or the bad news first?"

She has played this trick on me before. The bad news is that she needs another dangerous operation, maybe to replace yet another joint; that they are putting her on yet one more experimental drug with horrifying side effects; or that the troubling cough she had over Christmas was actually pneumonia. The good news is never good news, really: rather just that the operation has a sixty to seventy percent chance of success; that the medication, despite its side effects, is known to have cured some friend of a patient of her doctor's, or even (and I could tell from her face that she knew she was grasping) that the new Japanese restaurant in the neighboring town has been booked up for weeks, but because of her bad cough, the nice woman over the phone took pity on her and gave her a reservation for tonight.

I hate this trick, not only because it inevitably means that I have to endure a sharpening of the worry pangs I always feel when I am around my mother, but also because it means that I have to pretend that I can see the silver lining that she points to so cheerfully, the flip side to the problem that I, no matter how I squint, can only see as dull gray. So it is in a small voice that I answer her. "Oh, the bad news, please."

She regards me quietly over her cup of steaming hot water. She still likes to say that we drink tea together and I keep up with the pretense for her sake, but because her insomnia has worsened as she has grown older, she in fact had to give up caffeine a few years back: just one more of the countless pleasures, both great and small, that she has had to leave by the wayside in the journey of her life.

"It's about your grandmother," she says.

"Well?" I say, setting my cup down with a clatter. "Is she okay? When's she coming?"

"She's fine, but she's not coming. She's decided instead to go back," she says, adding hastily: "Don't worry. You'll still get to meet her, of course. It's just that we'll have to go to Japan—"

"She's decided to go back?" I ask, bewildered. "To—to Hokkaido? To her parents?"

"Well, as you know," says my mother, explaining, "she had a best friend at the geisha house—"

"Kaori," I say. "I remember."

"Kaori's at another geisha house now—a rather famous one in Kyoto. She trains apprentices. She's helped make the arrangements for your grandmother to live at the same house, doing the same kind of work."

Stunned, too startled, even, to feel any disappointment, I only half listen as my mother's voice goes on, explaining how Yukiko has agreed to give up half of her fortune to the geisha house for the privilege of becoming a member of it, and how furious my two Aunt Tomokos are at this decision: in their eyes, naturally, defecting from the status quo is bad, but nothing compared to the fact that it entails depriving their sons of all that is rightfully theirs. My mother recounts how the Tomokos asked her to intercede on behalf of the family, and how she, like her brothers, refused. She tells me how excited Yukiko is at the prospect of this return, more animated and happy than she has been since Sekiguchi died.

"So you see," says my mother, winding down, "she loved being a geisha."

So the rumors were true, then. The neighbors and the wives of Sekiguchi's friends who had guessed at my grandmother's cold geisha heart had been right all along.

Yukiko and Sekiguchi were a love story for the ages, a romance as lush and overblown as any found in the fairy tales that my father told me at bedtime, or in the bodice rippers I later devoured as a teenager—and as false as well. She had not loved her husband. She had married him out of calculation, for his money and his position, and then, having once wed him, she found she had made a grievous mistake. Trapped in a gilded cage, she was a Cinderella who yearned to wallow once again in the dirt of the hearth, in the games, the flirtations, the dirty jokes made at her own expense, and the many, many men, so much so that she was willing to trade back her wealth for this old life of pleasure.

But then I remember the song, sung in that off-key voice, which had transfixed a group of servants at a fire.

"She loved Grandfather," I say, willing it with my words.

My mother's eyebrows arch in surprise. "Of course," she says, scolding, even laughing a little, taken aback at my gift for the obvious. "You know that."

"I know that," I repeat weakly, letting out my pent-up breath all at once, in the unhealthy habit I have caught like a cold from Eric. "Of course."

"She was completely in love with your grandfather," continues my mother more seriously, "from the beginning, all the way until the very end. But she loved being a geisha, too."

"Why? All those men pawing at her, and she having to play all those games, and go through all those stupid rituals—"

"The men aren't the reason she wants to go back. She wants to go back because she's tired of being taken care of. She's proud, you know—she always has been."

I nod, albeit reluctantly, admitting to myself as well as to my mother how glorious it would be for Yukiko to run her own life once again.

"But even more importantly," says my mother, "your grandmother loved being a geisha because of her friends. Because of—well, because of the company of women. In particular, Kaori. Remember how I told you about taking a walk with my mother, and seeing a man who must have been Jun? And how Kaori stood in front of him like—"

"—a traffic cop," I say, nodding, handing her own image back to her.

"I always thought that when my mother cried after that encounter, it was because she was missing Jun," she says. "But it was Kaori she wanted to go back to—it was Kaori she was missing all along."

An image descends upon me, then, with the speed of a camera shutter, a movement that lasts no more than a split second but which leaves a frozen image: a row of girls, lying together in shared futons, whispering and giggling in the dark. It is a memory that has been handled with such care that only its edges, slightly yellowed and curling upwards, give away that it has twice suffered the passage from one generation to the next, a journey of nine thousand miles and sixty years.

"Your grandmother was very happy throughout her marriage," my mother says gently, "but at times she was very lonely, too."

Struggling to make another leap in logic, I cannot attend to her words. "Do you think," I whisper, "that Yukiko and Kaori were lovers?"

She does not flinch. "There are lots of ways a woman can love a woman," she says at last. "But it's possible."

Unexpectedly, perhaps, it is not her admission, tendered with the downbeat of an afterthought, that lingers in my ear. "There are lots of ways a woman can love a woman," I repeat slowly (savoring the phrase), wondering whether there are as many as one hundred and one of them.

"She told me her only regret is that now you won't be able to show her around New York," continues my mother, breaking into my thoughts.

Her voice makes an odd dip at the end of these words, and I glance sharply at her, but she is meditatively peering into her cup of hot water. I look away, rubbing my forehead. My mother is, after all, inured to disappointment only because she has had a lifetime of it; I should not resent her for being the picture of calm wisdom.

"But we'll go see her in Kyoto, maybe even over Christmas," she says. "I know it's not quite the same as her visiting us here, since she will be busy, but Kyoto is a beautiful city, and it's high time we got you to Japan."

I can feel her eyes on me but I keep my own fixed upon my own teacup, the smear of a kiss my lipstick left on it, and the ring of tea staining it beneath its rim.

"She wrote you a letter," she adds, "and sent you a present. Do you want to see them now?"

"Maybe later," I say lightly. Then I stand, mumbling an excuse about work; I push my chair in and run up to my room.

Say that there once lived a Cinderella who had a friend among the soot and ashes, another person to confide in and hold after each day of backbreaking labor, throughout each of the long cold nights. Say, too, that only Cinderella was blessed with a beautiful face and charm and most of all luck, and that when her prince came, she went gladly, but she never forgot her friend, and the warmth they had shared in the dull glow of the dying embers.

Obaasama, I say to myself (self-indulgently—or is that self-mockingly?—knowing these questions will not be an easy habit to break), my seventy-four-year-old grandmother. How could I grudge you this final warmth?

But in spite of myself I do.

CHAPTER TWENTY-SEVEN

I SPEND THE afternoon crying on the bed I slept in for most of my life. I take a nostalgically perverse pleasure in kicking the bedpost as I used to during my old tantrums: my feet were bare, as now, when I did so, but even so the wood is worn from where I kicked against it so many times.

I do not go downstairs until my mother calls me down for supper.

We eat lightly, saving up for the big dinner tomorrow. My mother could not have helped but overhear the sound of my sobbing, nor can she now be unaware of my red-rimmed eyes, for my artfulness with eyeliner is to scant avail after a crying jag of such length. But she allows me to eat in peace, and she fills the silence around my sullenness with chatter about the house, the neighborhood, the town, and even—after my restriction to monosyllables passes the half-hour point—about the world.

It is not until we are carrying the dishes into the kitchen that she brings the conversation back to where it started, five and a half hours ago. "You forgot to ask me about the good news," she says.

"The good news?" I ask, today being my day to repeat everything that she says. Stacking the dishes into the dishwasher now, I find it necessary to concentrate: my hands seem even less efficient than usual, their grasp on the dishes less secure.

"Don't you remember? I asked you if you wanted the good news or the bad news first."

"Oh yes," I say dully, preparing myself for reservations at another popular Japanese restaurant, or more likely plans to go ahead after all with yet another house renovation, for the last had been shelved because of my grandmother's anticipated arrival. Or if I am really lucky, the good luck will be that one of my Aunt Tomokos has decided to pay us a visit—in another four years, maybe, by which time I will have severed all ties with my faithless Japanese relatives. "Shoot," I tell my mother. "I'm listening."

"This is real news," she says, "big news. Or at least it's big news for me."

Had I been that obvious in my indifference? "Okay," I say, suppressing a sigh as I wipe my hands and turn away from the sink and the dishwasher to face my mother. The dirty dishes and pots and pans are still piled high.

She is sitting on the stool we keep in the kitchen. I watch her feet, which are dangling a good three inches off the floor, swing back and forth, bumping against the legs of the stool as they do so. If I were to sit on that same chair, I could not swing my feet.

Then I look up at her face. Something is wrong with her skin and her eyes.

"Mom, you're glowing," I say in bafflement. "Like a—well, like a firecracker."

She begins to smile, but then her forehead wrinkles. "Do firecrackers glow?"

"No," I say. The catching of my throat lasts only for a second. "No, they don't."

"The news is"—she draws out her words, stalling, or is that building up suspense?—"I've invited Ned over for dinner tomorrow; I hope that's okay."

She has spoken those last words so quickly that I cannot be sure I understood. "Ned?" I say (my tendency to repeat her now a confirmed tic). "You've invited Ned over for dinner? Who's Ned?"

"Ned Lewis," she explains patiently, as to a very small child. "Ned Lewis, our neighbor."

"Ne—" I say, starting to repeat her yet again, but stopping myself in time.

"Ned Lewis, who left me the beets and the carrots and the tomatoes on the doorstep. The man I dated last year, for about three weeks?"

I had seen vegetables as a theme running side by side with thwarted passion in the story of my life.

"You do remember him, don't you?" my mother says, laughing at me, teasing just a little, perhaps recalling, as I am, how severely I questioned her about why she let him go.

She had made the overtures necessary for them to begin dating again, showing up at his house one afternoon with a basket filled with neat rolls of sushi and a proposal for a stroll down the street. He did not require much convincing, it seems, or even that much of an explanation for their long separation, although my mother did tender him one of her own will. That he accepted her back with a minimum of fuss, and that she shines with gratitude when she talks about how he did so, are facts that I treasure, for I cannot help thinking that they bode well for their future happiness.

They have been back together, as it turns out, for more than a month, and when she tells me this I know that I have found the reason for all those nights I sat by the phone, worrying as I dialed her number over and over again. On the verge of reproaching her for not telling me earlier, I manage to clamp down on my tongue: it is not as if I am a stranger to the crime of keeping secrets.

She and Ned simply picked up where they left off. They have been attending movies and concerts, going out on bicycle rides and picnics. He has resumed bringing her vegetables; she has been cooking for him again. Lately he has taken up spending nights over here, a confession she makes without blushing.

"It makes up a little," she says at last, concluding, "for the fact that your grandmother's not coming."

I look up, then, startled. Is it something in that phrase, which is, after all, a kind of search yet again for a silver lining? Or is it the tone of her voice, at once melancholy and resigned? Whatever the reason, her words bring it home to me that my grandmother is also her mother.

If I am feeling unfairly cheated of my chance to know the woman whose name, face, and long body I inherited, the woman who reserved a whole wall of her study for photographs of me—if I am reeling with what is almost a child's sense of disappointment and rejection at my grandmother's decision to spend the last years of her life with someone other than me, what my mother must be feeling is infinitely worse. I think then of that first Akiko, who clung to her tall daughter and cried as she said good-bye, and how Yukiko worked through her apprenticeship waiting in vain for her arrival.

I look across the kitchen at my mother, who looks so small sitting high off the ground. This is the woman who despite my resistance held me spellbound with her tales.

"Thank you for telling me all those stories about Grandmother," I say, reaching across the space that separates us to touch her on the arm. "At least I'll always have that."

Reared in a culture in which family members bow rather than hug, my mother is perhaps not surprisingly a woman of reserve, shy even around her daughter. Caught off-balance by the contact, she pulls away from me slightly: a gesture that I, after two beats, mirror.

Yet her physical retreat may not be a rejection of me, even an unconscious one, for there is more than a hint of wistfulness in her next words. "I can listen to stories, too, you know," she says.

"And answer questions?" I interject suddenly, for within this afternoon, the hoard of questions I have been saving for my grandmother has become an almost unbearable weight.

She looks at me strangely: my question was undoubtedly too abrupt. "I can try to answer questions, anyway," she says. "Why, is there something on your mind?"

"Maybe later," I say, echoing myself now, and I wave in the direction of the pile of dirty dishes. I turn on the water and the pots clatter against one another when I pick them up, but even so I can still hear my mother sigh as she stands up behind me.

CHAPTER TWENTY-EIGHT

THE PROBLEM WITH being descended from insomniacs is that it is difficult to find a corner of peace and quiet in the house, even in the earliest hours of the morning. Or so I think when I see my mother hobbling down the stairs, a vision of ghostliness in one of her long white nightgowns, at a little after three.

She yawns, and passes a hand wearily over her eyes. "Why aren't you sleeping?" she asks.

I shrug. "Why aren't you?"

"Want some water?"

"No," I say, shaking my head.

She disappears into the kitchen. Lying down on the sofa, one ear pressed into a cushion, I listen to her move about the kitchen. Presently she emerges, two glasses in her hands.

"I said I don't want water," I say, still in sulky mode.

She sits down at the other end of the couch, her hip brushing against my feet, and reaches over to place one glass on the coffee table in front of me. "Just in case," she says mildly.

A pause during which I try to rouse myself out of my petulant mood, but I cannot come up with anything particularly pleasant to say. "I'm glad about you and Ned," I tell her at last.

"I was lucky," she says. "I was almost too late, you know—I almost lost him." She taps a fingernail lightly against her glass. "I wasted so much time waiting for your father."

Her confession, unusual as it is, does not seem amiss in this place and time. The room is quiet and cool, the hour an odd one; the very darkness closing in around us seems to invite revelations.

"Maybe you did," I say. "But I know how you felt."

"You still miss Phillip, don't you," she says softly.

"Less and less," I say. "But yeah, I do."

"It's been more than a year and a half since he died. You and Phillip—" She breaks off, clears her throat, and drinks some water. Then she asks me a question that Eric, too, has asked more than once. "You and Phillip—you two were never lovers, right?"

I hesitate only briefly, thinking, as I begin to speak, about the convergence of circumstances that makes me want to do so: the strangeness of the hour, most obviously, and the way she found me in spite of it; that both of us are only semiconscious, a mere stone's throw from the borders of sleep; the fact that I am half turned away from her, so that I do not have to see her watch me as I talk. Not least, perhaps, my shame at how I indulged my self-pity all throughout the day.

"The night before he left, we had a fight," I say, reaching for the glass in front of me. "It was silly, really—I was upset because I went to his apartment, and it turned out that he was giving up his lease. . . . I was feeling cross, I guess, because I was worried that he'd never come back. Then he kissed me on the street, and it frightened me, he was so intense— I drew back and he left without saying good-bye."

"And?"

I shake my head slowly, and take a polite sip from the water. "He came back to my apartment later that night. Some time after midnight, even though his flight was for the next morning," I say. "And then— then we spent the night together."

These words (choppy, desultory, stammered) make for a bald and even bleak statement, one that singularly fails to do justice to the light and life of that wintry night, and the sheer wonder of him coming back for me, after the botched good-bye we had had in the street, when the snow was just beginning to fall.

But then again, the details of that night are nothing that my mother needs to hear. So I do not tell her how when I heard the knock, I did not bother to look through the peephole before opening the door. After the way I reacted to our kiss, I had no right to even hope he would show up. Still, I had been pacing restlessly for the past hour, turning sharply at every imagined creak and every phantom footstep outside my door.

As soon as I saw his face (his mouth set in a stern line, his eyes grave, with only a wrinkle between his brows to betray he was not at ease), I threw myself at him. He reeled when the full force of my weight hit him and stepped half a pace back, but caught me squarely.

We moved to the bedroom (kissing, biting, licking, bits of my clothing falling along the way) before the snowflakes covering his shoulders had time to melt under my arms.

After five months during which we saw each other almost every day, after hours and hours of conversation in which I was utterly absorbed, watching and listening as he talked, I knew all the tricks of his speech, the erratic rhythm of his pauses, the angle he tilted his head when he laughed, his impatience with his own constant struggle with the inadequacy of language. Still, a year of observing him, an entire twelve months of wondering what he would be like in bed, would not have prepared me for how he actually was.

He was passionate, even overwhelmingly so, just as I had imagined, but a far cry from the smoothly experienced lover that his innumerable successes with women had led me to expect. There was a rawness to our lovemaking, an edge in his need for me, that I would never have predicted. I had figured him for a bit of a tease, in control, amused, and just a little distant, working me into a fever pitch with delays that I would scarce be able to handle. Yet the reserve that characterized his interactions with the outside world and even, at times, with me, had vanished. Quickly recovering from the force of my attack, he returned my kisses with a ferocity that startled me, and eventually proved contagious. Removing the last articles of clothing from each other, we thrashed about with the awkwardness of overeager teens.

The shyness came later, after that first time, when we lay spent and exhausted, tangled still in each other's bodies. Shaking, shivering, grinning like a fool, I turned to kiss him with gratitude, only to find his face hidden beneath the crook of his elbow.

"Hey," I said.

"Hey," he replied huskily.

"You hiding?" I asked, slowly bringing my face closer, zeroing in on his one visible eye until my nose crashed into his arm.

He shrugged, or what passed for a shrug in the position that he was in.

"'Cause if you are," I volunteered helpfully, "it ain't working."

He remained silent, although he did uncoil a little, enough so that I could see both his eyes. It took me a few moments to place the expression on his face. It was an expression I had seen in the library when I had looked up, weary and dusty, from my own musty books, and gazed with idle curiosity upon the faces of those sitting around me. It was a look I had seen on my mother in her pre-med days, when she spent the evenings poring over chemistry equations. Phillip was studying my face and my body, to learn and remember them.

We stayed up far into the night, as deliriously giddy as children, but we dozed on and off as well. With my back turned towards him and his top arm wrapped around my breasts, I pushed against him in my sleep, clashing against the resistance of his hardness until the sound of my own groans eventually awakened me. All told, we made love perhaps three or four times. My inability to pin down an exact number frustrates me no end, but so often did we drift in and out of sleep during that night that I cannot discount the possibility that I may have dreamed one of those times.

"Damn," he said at one point during the night, rubbing his eyes. "I wish I weren't so tired. Sleep seems such a waste right now."

"We've wasted so much time already," I said, half-wailing and half-laughing. "I can't believe we spent five months being only friends, when we could have been doing this at the same time."

He laughed, too, and wrapping his legs and arms around me, pulled me closer. "We'll make up for it," he said, his words slurring with sleep. "It might take us another thirty, forty, fifty years, but we'll make up for those lost five months in the end."

"Yeah?"

"Yeah," he whispered.

I bent my head down to his chest and rested it there, breathing in the smell of his skin and listening to his heart beat. Lightly I ran my fingers over his collarbone, his shoulder, the angry white streak of the scar on his stomach, the smooth ridges of his ribs.

"I love you," I said, murmuring, my voice barely audible even to my own ears. "I've always loved you. And I'd bet the farm that I always will love you. But you know that, don't you?" I asked, drawing back to look at him with some curiosity.

His eyes were closed, his breathing deep and regular. He was smiling faintly in his sleep.

Throughout this past year I have regretted much about that night. That I did not stay awake to watch and memorize Phillip's face while he slept, or get up to barricade the door and lock him up inside the apartment with me, as I so longed to do. There have even been moments when I felt sorry that I was on the Pill at the time, although the shock of his death would have been far greater if I had been carrying his child.

But the fact that he did not hear me say that I loved him was never something I regretted. For he knew that, of course, just as I always knew, deep down, that he loved me.

All these memories are secrets I fiercely guard, even from my mother. I keep from her, too, how I woke to the gray light of very early morning, and Phillip's head lodged snugly under my chin, my body wrapped around his. It seemed slightly incredible that we had managed to sleep like this, braided so tightly together that it was impossible to tell where I ended and he began.

I was careful to keep my eyes turned away from the window at first, while I wished for snow. If I imagined it hard enough, surely it would have to come true: mountains blanketing the Newark airport, snow of such depth and weight that all the plows in New Jersey would be unable to clear it in time for the 11:35 A.M. flight to Sydney, Australia, where a flight to Kathmandu awaited Phillip. Seventy-foot-long airplanes wedged in tight or, better yet, buried, their outheld wings and dolphin noses transformed into ski slopes fit only for a child. Torrents of white coming down, blindingly hard, so that all the pilots in the area would roll over in bed, take one look at the blizzard raging outside their windows, and snuggle deeper into the covers, knowing already that their flights had been canceled.

When I finally turned, a full ten seconds later, to see only the lightest layer of snow dusting (dancing on, already drifting away from) the windowsill, the disappointment choked my throat and came out in a sound that was horrifyingly close to a sob.

I bit my lip, grateful that Phillip continued to lie still under my chin. Yet I was puzzled as well, wondering what had touched me on the hollow of my throat. It had been a tickle, just barely perceptible, like the tip of an ink brush leaving its mark on my skin.

"You're awake," I said after a while. Phillip did not reply. "It's no use pretending you're not. Your eyelashes gave you away."

What I do tell my mother about is when I wake up yet again, to a light that is still gray, and the sight of Phillip standing naked beside the bed. He held his airplane ticket between his hands, ready to tear it in half.

"What are you doing?" I demanded sharply.

"I can't go," he said, lowering the ticket and turning to look at me. "I won't go. Not after this."

"You're kidding, right?" I asked in disbelief; when I saw that he was not, my toes curled, seemingly of their own volition. I wanted to sing and dance, to cry and laugh. But I trembled, suddenly terrified, when the thought ran through my mind: this is what pure happiness feels like.

"I don't want to go anymore," he said.

"Sure you do. You love to travel. Besides, you have to go," I told him. "You've got an expedition to lead."

I saw it as a pact that I was making with fate. If I let Phillip go now, if

I gave him up for a handful of interminable weeks, then I would have earned him; he would be mine forever.

"But—" he began.

"Will you go, already?" I said in mock exasperation: four words that replayed themselves in my mind without cease for the better part of last year.

He shifted back and forth on his feet, a quickly beating pulse visible above one collarbone. "I'll cut the trip short," he said at last. "Three weeks, and then I'll be back. I swear it: cross my heart and—"

"You can skip the vow," I said, smiling up at him. I held out my arms, and after a pause he bent down and—with an almost bearlike, strangely touching clumsiness—clambered back into them.

"I believe you," I whispered.

There is a small silence when I finish speaking.

"A pretty bleak story, don't you think?" I say, trying to prod my mother into speech.

"No," she replies slowly. "Sad, but not bleak. And it's a relief to me, anyway. I was worried about you, because it seemed you were too deep in mourning for Phillip, after only five months of friendship. It seemed out of proportion. You were depressed for far too long."

"And now?" I ask, summoning a light tone. "Now you're not worried about me, because you know I had a reason to be depressed?"

Even with my head turned away from her, I can feel her nod. "Something like that," she says.

The light from the kitchen juts into the living room in a sharp angle, cutting a triangle of brightness on the floor. Moonlight comes in through the window, as does the dark smell of earth, the chirping of crickets, and the distant baying of a dog. Half-asleep, I lose track of time, and when I find myself jarred back awake by an urgent need to ask a question that I have wondered about for years, the crickets are silent, and the dog's baying sounds even farther away.

"Do you ever regret marrying Father?"

My mother is quiet for so long that I, wondering if she has fallen asleep, turn around to look up at her. Her eyes, clear and bright, show no trace of fatigue; she returns my gaze calmly.

"I regret everything," she says. "I regret all the paths I didn't take, and every step I did, and each of the hundreds of opportunities I passed up." Suddenly she grins, her cheeks rounding into what could almost pass—in this half-light—for something resembling apples, and for a second I see her: the young woman with a keen curiosity about the far-flung corners of the world, as well as an insatiable appetite to experience them.

"But you know what?" she asks. "If I had my life to do over again, I wouldn't change a thing."

I awake with a start to the raw light of morning. Dazed by the sunshine and confused by the unexpected vista of a window framed by brocade curtains, I blink, trying to orient myself. The last night I spent with Phillip is still vivid in my mind.

Not until I hear a rustle and crackle, and the familiar whoosh of air that accompanies the turning of a newspaper page, do I remember where I am. The smell of toast is in the air, and soon I hear the rhythmic sound of munching.

The couch is long but narrow, its cushions far too soft—a terrible place to sleep, as I know full well, having tried in vain to nap there as a teenager. But this morning I roll over, sinking ever more uncomfortably deep into the cushions, and easily slip back into sleep, lulled by the thought that my mother is there, within calling distance, just as she has been through all the past years.

CHAPTER TWENTY-NINE

T HIS MORNING I woke to a premonition that I would see Phillip once again.

I used to think that one day I would answer the door and he would be standing there, fully clothed, more or less nourished, and most of all talking. That Russia was wrong, that the news reports erred, and that the people at the lodge in Nepal that I called lied. That his death was a mistake, or even a joke—a colossal, awful thigh-slapper played upon me by my two closest friends. Then the hours of waiting slipped into days and nights and then into months, yet still I hoped, so that for almost a year every Seventh-Day Adventist who came knocking at my door with pamphlets was met by a woman whose face immediately darkened with disappointment.

My premonition today, almost eighteen months after his death, is ridiculous, running strictly counter to reason and intuition, but then what else is a hunch if not that? Yesterday I had ridden on the certainty that I could guess at the life that lay ahead of me, and I had been proven decidedly wrong; surely my gut instinct could not fail me two days in a row. So I have remained vigilant today, sharply scrutinizing all the dark corners of the house, opening each of the cabinets in the kitchen until my mother, alarmed by all the banging, poked her head in to inquire what I sought.

For of course I am not so foolish as to still hope that he will stroll through my door with his clothes on and his vocal cords intact and functioning. I am not even so greedy as to demand that he return to my apartment to keep me perpetual silent company from inside the fireplace. All I want is for this one premonition to bear fruit: all I want is to see his face once again.

"I'm ready for Grandmother's present now," I say. "And the letter, please."

It is only three but my mother is already hard at work making dinner, and has been so for the past two hours. I offered to help earlier but I was distracted, wheeling around at every sound, and she soon sent me away, muttering that she would not be able to afford it if I broke another glass.

Interrupted in her sushi preparations now, she looks up, a little startled, but merely nods. Wiping her hands on her apron, she walks out to the hall closet. When she reemerges, she is carrying a brown package, dotted with Japanese stamps, maybe the size of a large dictionary.

I take it out to the living room, noting with some relief that it is far too light to be a dictionary, even a small one.

"You have to open the package first," she says, explaining. "The letter's inside."

She leans against the wall and watches as I snip the cord, rip the brown wrapping, open the box, and peel away the layers of bubble wrap and plastic and tissue.

"You know what it is?"

She nods slowly. "But I'm curious to see it again, after all these years."

My hands are shaking just slightly as I push aside the last folds of tissue, for by then I can guess what it is. Lacquered black on the outside and red within, it has a spidery pattern of pine trees along its walls, just as my mother had described. I open it, leaning forward to smell the inside; it conveys nothing other than the not unpleasant mustiness of a long-sealed box. But inside it, as if to make up for its lack of a tea scent, lies a sealed envelope.

"Well? Does it still smell like burning leaves?" asks my mother, watching from her vantage point against the wall. "Will you keep your hair in it?"

"No to both questions," I tell her.

"It's a mystery where she got it," muses my mother, and I nod: she does not need to tell me that she is referring to my great-grandmother Akiko, her namesake. "Those kinds of boxes are worth a lot."

"Even like this?" I say, holding up the top.

She winces as she moves forward to examine the burn, and I know that she is thinking, as I am, of all that was lost in the fire.

I pass her the envelope, then, and she turns it over in her hands, admiring the delicate flowers decorating its edge, but contrary to form she does not sit and open it, holding it back out to me instead.

I look up at her inquiringly.

"It's in *English,*" she says, almost whispering.

I take it back from her. Nothing if not tactful, my mother then murmurs a few words about rice, and a few seconds later I can hear her rattling away with the pots in the kitchen.

My grandmother has written letters to me before, mostly terse cards congratulating me on birthdays, graduations, and other such milestones, but they have always been in Japanese. This is the first time I will be reading her words on my own, without the mediation of my mother.

I tear open the envelope and unfold the letter without haste. The handwriting is sharp and angular, not dissimilar to my mother's, though on a larger scale; it is also unusually clear, as one might expect from a person not at ease with the language.

I think of my grandmother unpacking her fountain pen and pulling out this sheet of rice paper. Her movements are economical as she walks about her daughter-in-law's spacious guest bedroom, but they are slow as well, for the hour is late and she is tired and old. She lays down the pen and the paper on the desk, and she draws up one of the heavy chairs. Two suitcases, one shut and the other three-quarters packed, lie close beside her. As she sets down the date in the upper right-hand corner, she takes pleasure in the old, familiar sound of her fountain pen scratching against the paper.

"Dear Yukiko-san," she writes. "I am very sorry we will not have the opportunity to meet. I looked forward to long conversations with you. I was always sure we are friends. I hope your mother explained about Kaori. Take care. With regards, Yukiko."

I read the letter once, twice, and then again. In itself the letter is what I expected, no more, no less. Built though it is out of stilted phrases dredged from my grandmother's distant memories of traveling abroad, or perhaps even cribbed from a lesson book, I cannot doubt its sincerity: the sentiments expressed in the disappointing clichés mirror too closely what I myself have been feeling about my unknown grandmother, this other Yukiko who lived out another time in another world.

What surprises me about the letter, what draws me to read it again and again, is that the scratching of my grandmother's pen is not my only accompaniment as I sound out its words. Unsought and unexpected, adding to the chorus of sounds, is my mother's voice: her singsong lilt, her measured cadences, and the misplaced pauses when she stops for breath.

While not a tall man, Ned Lewis is built like a block, possessing a bulk that suggests that in spite of the gray in his hair, he can well withstand the harsh winds he sometimes faces when he works in his garden. The vigor of his body stands in marked contrast to the lines of his face, which makes him look slightly older than his fifty-odd years. He moved to our town only recently, but still it is a well-known fact in our small neighborhood that his wife had been a long time dying.

He is soft-spoken and given to few words, but dinner with him is still a far livelier affair than it usually is, his presence spurring my mother on to a new level of animation. He is an appreciative listener, smiling quietly, occasionally laughing, and often nodding, his gray eyes fixed upon her all the while. At the same time he makes sure to draw me out, asking me questions and listening with care to my answers. I am familiar to him from all those times I chatted with him when I visited home; he may also be predisposed to me because my mother told him how often I nudged her to go thank him for the vegetables. Still, even so, even considering that it could only be to his advantage to win me over to his side, I find myself touched by his gentle friendliness.

Not for years, if ever, have I seen my mother so cheerful, but perhaps not surprisingly she sheds most of her glow upon Ned, with just a little of it falling on me. The years of reserve and silence that lie between my mother and me are still there, will possibly always be there. We may never kiss, and we will rarely hug. The warmth of a body rocking and folding me to itself, like the touch of long, cool fingers upon my head, is not something I will seek or expect from my mother.

Once we shared an understanding so absolute it might have started in the womb. So many times have I asked myself why we grew apart that I have long since despaired of answering this question on my own. So now (casting only one wistful glance back at the oracle that was to be my grandmother) I return, as I have so often before, to the far easier question of when we grew apart, and its answer: after my father left us.

Her face flushed from the warmth of the kitchen, my mother stands, turns, and begins to wrestle with the windows. Ned moves quickly to help her, his broad back momentarily obscuring her from my view, and I watch him for a space, wondering whether I am wrong in guessing that someday I might be closer to my mother because of his bulky presence at her side.

Not until it is after nine does dinner begin to draw to a close. The lamps have been turned on long ago; the light from the candles is now a necessity. Outside the night is cool, and the sky is dark and moonless.

Breaking into a short pause, my mother tells me she will wrap the dessert, more than half of which remains, for Eric.

"I have some bad news of my own," I say then, baldly making the announcement I have put off so many times in this revelation-packed weekend. "Eric and I aren't together anymore."

"Oh, I'm sorry," says my mother, a shadow passing over her face, momentarily dimming its brightness. "I liked him, you know."

I smile briefly at Ned, apologizing silently for casting this note of gloom over our first family dinner.

"But I guess you weren't ready for him," continues my mother. "It was too soon after Phillip."

I had known she would be disappointed; I had thought she would be surprised.

"You want to talk about it?" she asks.

"Here?" I say. "Now?"

"Why not?" she asks, countering my questions with one of her own.

Ned smiles. "I can't imagine a better time than now," he says.

"It's an awfully long story," I say, warning them.

"We love long stories," says Ned, "especially after a good meal." He reaches out a hand and clasps my mother's, gently, on the table where it rests. The glow—too peaceful, really, to resemble the light and sparkle of a firecracker—has already returned to her face.

We love long stories? I feel like patting them on their heads, so much do they resemble children playing at marriage and parenthood.

Bending my face low over my plate, I poke for one last time at my pie. A movement catches me out of the corner of my eye, then, and I turn my head quickly but it is only the curtains, swept into life by the night wind; a moment later the candles on the table are straying with it, too. I hold back a sigh, knowing that for the second day in a row my premonitions have played me false.

I turn my attention back to the table. Their hands clasped, my mother and Ned are watching me. Attentive, expectant, my audience of two.

So I lay down my fork and knife, and remove the napkin from my lap.

I will tell them about Eric but I will talk most of all about Phillip, about how I loved him and lost him and grieved for him for more than a year. I will tell them how he returned for a spell, naked and silent and slowly starving, to lurk in the shadows and the corners of my apartment, and how now he is gone.

I will speak of how I watch for him yet, but someday no longer will; I will tell them how I have already let him go, with longing but without bitterness or regret, in thankfulness that I knew him and loved him for as long as I did.

As my mother did with the man she loved, and her mother did before her.

I take a deep breath in, pondering where to begin.

ACKNOWLEDGMENTS

Miranda Sherwin, superb stepsister, brilliant editor, and wonderful friend, a woman who brightens the lives of everyone around her, made this book possible.

Sandy Dijkstra, agent extraordinare, worked tirelessly and wrought miracles; Sandra Zane, whose wise voice kept me going more often than I can say, was both friend and guardian angel.

I was lucky in my publishers. Consistently kind and thoughtful, Irwyn Applebaum and Nita Taublib went out of their way to nurture and develop this, a debut novel. My editors are living proof that, contrary to popular belief, line editing is still vigorously practiced in the publishing industry: Stephanie Kip worked hard on the book, and was graceful and patient in her dealings with its author; Emily Heckman's enthusiasm and unflagging support were a source of great comfort.

My sisters, Yoko and Aiko, are part of me and, as such, inevitably played a large role in the shaping of this work; my father, Shoichi Yoshikawa, taught me the value and wonder of the written word.

Alan Ziegler, in whose class the novel was born, has given me guidance for more than a decade now. Anne Curzan, an insightful reader and a good friend, has helped me on every step of the way.

Simon Gikandi, Suzanne Raitt, Steve Sumida, and Patricia Yaeger inspired me in ways that influenced the novel as well as my dissertation. The English department of the University of Michigan provided the structure that enabled me to pursue both writing and scholarship.

For faith and encouragement during the years it has taken to turn this story into a novel, I am grateful to Sean Baldwin, John Carey, Ioanna Christoforaki, Creighton Don, Victoria Green, Phil Hildebrand, Ken Kurtz, John Merz, Ali Sherwin, Matt Toschlog, and David Wartenweiler.

And last but not least, I owe a special debt to my grandmother, Masako Inoue. Chatty, warm, and almost always cheerful, she could not be further from Kiki's grandmother, but in telling me stories that have done much to cut across the divide of time and space, she is in many ways the presiding spirit of this work.

ABOUT THE AUTHOR

MAKO YOSHIKAWA was born in Princeton, New Jersey, and spent part of her childhood in Tokyo. She has studied literature at Columbia, Oxford, and the University of Michigan, and now lives and writes in New York City.

She is the great-granddaughter of a geisha.